CAPTIVE

A Dark Romance Collection

JULIA SYKES

Copyright © 2021 by Julia Sykes

All rights reserved.

No part of this book may be reproduced in any form or by any electronic or mechanical means, including information storage and retrieval systems, without written permission from the author, except for the use of brief quotations in a book review.

SWEET CAPTIVITY

PROLOGUE

"You don't want to do this," I choked out past the lump of terror that clogged my throat. I kept a wary eye on the wicked hunting knife Cristian Moreno held naturally at his side, as though it were an innocuous extension of his arm rather than a threat to my life. "Let me go."

He threw back his head and laughed, his perfect white teeth flashing as the booming sound assaulted my eardrums. My hands shook violently, causing the ropes that bound my arms behind me to chafe against my wrists. The burn of the rough fibers against my skin and cold bite of the metal chair beneath me were peripheral; my entire focus was centered on Moreno and the way the gleam of the spare overhead light bulb made his dark eyes glint as sharply as the knife in his hand.

"No, Samantha," he corrected me calmly, his light Colombian accent making his deep voice almost lyrical when he spoke my name. "You're never leaving this place. Not alive, at least. If you answer my questions, I might be inclined to mercy.

Otherwise..." He left the unspoken threat hanging in the air, the implication clear. I would experience agony before he finally disposed of me.

No. Don't think like that.

I gasped in several deep breaths so I could manage to speak again.

"My friends will find me," I asserted, knowing Dex wouldn't leave me to die here. My best friend would do whatever it took to rescue me.

"If they do, they won't find more than what's left of your body."

Ice crystallized in my veins. He took a step toward me, raising the knife. I tried to shrink away, but the unyielding metal chair behind my back kept me immobile.

"You can't hurt me," I said desperately, twisting against my restraints. "If you kill me, my friends will hunt you down."

His dazzling smile illuminated his darkly handsome features with cruel amusement.

"I want them to know what I've done. Your death will be a warning. We're going to send a little message to your friends." He gestured behind him, and for the first time, my gaze darted away from the threat before me.

A man loomed a few feet away, the light on his smart phone indicating that he was recording me. A wicked scar puckered his tanned cheek, deepening his fearsome scowl. His black gaze bored into me, his dark glare penetrating my soul. I shuddered and tore my eyes away, unable to bear looking at him.

Moreno laughed again. "What, you don't like my little brother?" He cocked his head at me. "Maybe I'll give you to him to play with, after I'm finished with you. He has... very *unique* tastes." He reached for me, his long fingers trailing down my cheek. I cringed away, my stomach churning. "I think Andrés will like you. Such pale skin. It will mark up nicely." He shook his head slightly, still smiling. "But I'm getting ahead of myself. He can have you when I'm done. I'm going to extract my answers first."

The cool tip of the knife kissed my throat, and I choked on a scream as horror overwhelmed me.

CHAPTER 1
ONE DAY EARLIER

I sat at my computer, my mind completely absorbed in the task before me. The fact that I was staring at the screen didn't register; I'd fallen into my work, as though I was *inside* the code, surrounded by information. I was in my element. I might not be physically kicking ass, but I was powerful in this technological world.

Truthfully, I wasn't all that good at kicking ass. I'd transferred from tech analyst to field agent a few months ago, and I was coming to realize it hadn't been the best life choice. It had been a reactionary thing, a desperate cry for attention. I'd thought that maybe if I put myself in the line of fire, Dex's protective instincts would kick in and he'd finally realize what had been right in front of him for years: me, hopelessly in love with him.

Despite a very small voice in my mind telling me I shouldn't, I diverted from my mission and hacked into the webcam on Dex's computer. He was seated only a few desks away from me in the FBI field office, but I couldn't allow myself to be caught shooting furtive glances in his direction. This was much more discrete.

Some people might classify my activity as *stalking*, but I'd never quite been able to wrap my mind around unspoken social boundaries. Besides, how else was I ever supposed to work up the courage to look the man I loved in the eye?

Dex was frowning at something on his computer screen, deep in thought. With his chiseled features and piercing, pale blue eyes, he was painfully perfect. Not to mention his blond hair that made him appear like a fierce avenging angel when he was intent on protecting those closest to him.

But he'd never seen me as more than a buddy. I wasn't even sure if he saw me as a woman at all.

I really shouldn't have been surprised. With my skinny figure, shockingly orange hair, and decidedly tomboy-ish sense of style, my feminine side was all but invisible. Maybe if I'd put in more effort, he'd have noticed me. But *seductress* wasn't exactly my M.O., and I'd probably trip in high heels.

I sighed. I was certainly the polar opposite of the brunette bombshell Dex had fallen for: perfect, gorgeous, sensual Chloe Martin. No wonder he was smitten with her instead of me.

Cruelly familiar pain knifed through my chest at the thought of them together, perfectly gorgeous and perfectly happy. Grimacing, I closed the connection to his webcam and threw myself back into my work.

"What are you doing?" I recognized the masculine voice, but I still jolted at its proximity.

I whirled in my office chair to face Jason Harper, the agent I'd been working for over the last few weeks.

Working with, I internally corrected myself, even though it didn't feel that way. Jason tended to bark orders, and I tended to comply. We were supposed to be equals, even if he did have seniority as a field agent. But Jason had a commanding presence about him, and when his green eyes flashed, I jumped to obey.

"Sam," he prompted me in that stern tone that made my insides quiver with unease. I snapped to attention, my gaze fixing squarely on him rather than darting around the room in my familiar nervous pattern. "What are you doing?" he asked again, somewhat impatient. He peered behind me at my computer, squinting at the code scrolling across the screen. He'd have an easier time reading it if it were Cyrillic script, and Jason didn't know a word of Russian.

"Nothing," I said quickly, knowing he wouldn't approve of my activities. I mean, he wouldn't like the stalking thing, but he'd be more annoyed at my personal distraction from my work. Jason and I were supposed to be working a case together, off the books. We were tracking the shadowy Division 9-C, a branch of a clandestine organization we knew little about. Well, we knew they were bad guys, and they needed to be taken down. That was enough for me.

Jason was the muscle on the ground, and I was the brains behind the operation. Or the tech goddess. I'd take either title, really.

Jason's dark brows rose up to his neatly-styled black hair. "Nothing," he mimicked me in a reproving monotone. "Do you want to try that again? The truth this time, Sam."

I shifted on my chair and cut my eyes away. My gaze landed on the water cooler, the worn navy carpet, the shiny spot where the fluorescent lights caught on Jason's highly polished leather shoes; anywhere but meeting his steady stare.

"You don't want to know," I mumbled. "Anyway, don't we need to get out and run surveillance on Moreno? I can fill you in on the other thing on the way."

The *other thing* was our Division 9-C investigation. Our official assignment with the FBI was hunting notorious drug lord Cristian Moreno, who had moved his business into Chicago in recent months after withdrawing from New York. He'd been pushing the date rape drug Bliss, and he was using it to start a human trafficking ring.

Division 9-C might be bad guys, but Moreno was his own special brand of evil.

The toe of Jason's shoe tapped against the carpet in a condemning, staccato rhythm, but he decided not to press me. "Fine," he allowed. "Let's go. We can talk in the car."

I blew out a relieved breath. I hated having all that alpha male power focused on me. It was bad enough dealing with men on a normal basis, much less working alongside walking testosterone like Jason. He was nice, but that didn't mean he didn't intimidate the hell out of me.

At least he kept a respectful distance while we walked across the field office and toward the elevator that would take us down to the parking garage. Once we were trapped inside the confines of the tiny metal box, I shifted my body into the corner to keep as much space between us as possible. It was a matter of habit. I wasn't afraid of Jason, but I never allowed anyone into my personal space if I could help it. I didn't do *people*. I much preferred to sit behind my computer screen, where I was a safe distance from everyone on the web, not to mention completely anonymous.

Now that I was a field agent, I had to actually interact with people. Talk to them. Look them in the eye.

Moving into the field had been a stupid idea. Reckless. And my involvement in this secret mission for Jason was even more reckless.

But it was too late to go back now. As the FBI's best tech

analyst, I had a special skill set that Jason needed. I might have transferred to field agent six months ago, but that didn't mean I'd forgotten all my hacking skills. There was no one else who could do this job for Jason, so I'd step up and be the hero. Heroine. Whichever. Was it sexist to apply gender to the term? Probably. I couldn't keep track of social norms.

When the elevator finally came to a stop and the doors opened, Jason gestured for me to exit first. I knew he was trying to be a gentleman, but I'd have preferred to follow him. As it was, I had to scoot past him, my body almost making contact with his.

He didn't seem to notice my discomfort. Or if he did, he was accustomed to it and didn't really think much of what most people would term *Sam's odd behavior*. Well, that was the nice term.

Weirdo. Freak.

The derogatory name-calling didn't faze me. Not one bit.

"Talk," Jason ordered when we were safely in the privacy of the car. I hadn't trusted anyone in the field office. Well, no one but Jason. If we were overheard discussing our secret operation, we could be betrayed.

Dex wouldn't betray us. I knew the truth, but I wasn't willing to pull him into this. For one, I was still struggling with the personal sense of betrayal he'd inflicted when he'd fallen in love with Chloe instead of me. For another, Jason had insisted on keeping our op as under-the-radar as possible. This wasn't an official investigation. That meant limiting our manpower. Womanpower. Person-power.

God, this sexism thing was hard.

"Sam," he said my name sharply, calling my attention back to him. I could tell he was getting impatient with my wayward thoughts.

"Right," I said quickly. "Division 9-C has their own hacker. They set up false identities for Natalie. There's an electronic footprint somewhere. I'm working on tracing it, and that will lead us to more information on the organization they represent. Their hacker is good, but I'm better. I just need a little more time."

"And how do you know you're better?" Jason challenged.

"Because I'm me," I said coolly, utterly confident in my capabilities. "You focus on protecting Natalie, and I'll focus on getting us a new lead."

His hands tightened on the steering wheel, his knuckles going white. No doubt, he was remembering the terrible things that had been done to Natalie, the woman he loved. He might have finally rescued her from the people who had tortured her and twisted her mind, but that didn't mean she was safe. The people who had so ruthlessly used her—the clandestine Division 9-C and the organization they represented—were still out there. There might not be physical leads, but there had to be traces of them buried deep in the web somewhere.

We finished driving to our destination in heavy silence. I wished I knew what to say to alleviate some of Jason's tension, but I didn't really know where to begin. So I twisted my hands in my lap and tried to calm my whirring thoughts. Per usual, they were firing in several directions at once. I had the Division 9-C hacker to consider, Jason's feelings to fret over, and our current investigation into Cristian Moreno.

We pulled up outside a nondescript townhouse, positioning our sedan half a block back from our target. This fieldwork was actually kind of boring a lot of the time. We settled in to wait and watch. I'd so much rather be behind my computer, but at least I wasn't having to interact with anyone but Jason. And he was content to focus on our investigation instead of idle chatter.

We'd gotten a lead that this townhouse was being used by Cristian Moreno in his Bliss trafficking. He seemed to have smaller distribution centers set up all over town. It would have been so much easier to raid a massive warehouse, but Moreno wasn't stupid enough to keep his product all in one place.

Chicago police had arrested a man for dealing Bliss in this neighborhood two days ago, and he'd directed us to this townhouse as the place where he picked up his product. We could have raided the building, but we wanted to monitor the situation for a few days first. Taking out one small distribution center would be a win, but we might be able to find the larger network if we identified Moreno's people coming and going and tracked them from the premises.

Overall, it was a pretty boring day. Watching people and taking notes wasn't all that interesting. By the time Jason dropped me off at my own townhome, I was eager to get back online and do something that was actually mentally stimulating.

I dropped into my ergonomic chair and blew out a long sigh. It felt damn good to be back in front of my personal computer. Away from people.

I was so eager to get back to my coding that I didn't even bother to change out of my work clothes and into comfy sweats before turning on my computer. Unfortunately, a chat box popped up as soon as I logged on.

Dex Scott wants to video chat.

I frowned and hit the *ignore* button. I didn't have time to talk to Dex. I had to find the Division 9-C hacker.

Besides, I didn't want to talk to Dex. I was too fried, too raw to face him. He'd barely paid attention to me since I'd made the reckless decision to become a field agent. Sure, he still contacted me to play an online game from time to time. When he wasn't fucking Chloe. Otherwise, he barely interacted with me at all. Especially not in the office, where he'd made it clear he didn't approve of my choice to transfer into the field.

He was a damn good agent. Far better than I would ever be. I'd longed to train with him when I'd transferred to field agent, to feel his huge body against mine when we sparred.

But he'd refused to help train me.

My cheeks heated and my sex clenched at the thought of him *training* me. After hacking into his internet search history and tracking his sexual predilections for years, I knew my gentle giant of a friend harbored decidedly darker fantasies: domination, bondage, discipline.

I'd never thought I'd be interested in such depraved acts. Truthfully, before I met Dex, I hadn't thought much about sex at all. The girls in my dorm at college had teased me for being an asexual, socially awkward geek. It hadn't bothered me.

Really. Not one bit.

A part of my brain acknowledged the silent lie in my mind.

I'd also tried to lie to myself about Dex for years: that he would come to care for me; that he'd finally realize I was hopelessly in love with him. I craved to be the object of his darker desires.

The beeping emanating from my speakers became incessant.

Dex Scott wants to chat.

I turned off the chat app. Talking to him hurt too much. I needed space to avoid the pain.

Shoving him from my mind, I threw myself back into my work, sinking into the deep web.

I was so absorbed in my task that I didn't hear the lock click back or the soft sound of my front door rubbing across the carpet as it opened. I was jolted out of my work when the back of my neck tingled, an animal response to a lurking threat. A gloved hand clamped over my mouth, muffling my shocked gasp. A sharp sting penetrated my neck as the needle sank in.

The world turned surreal as the drugs instantly cocooned me in soft, dark clouds, and I floated into nothingness.

CHAPTER 2

The safety of my home had been shattered. Someone had drugged me, taken me. My memories of how I'd fallen into Cristian Moreno's clutches were hazy, but there was no denying my terrifying new reality: I was in the hands of the vicious Colombian drug lord, and his knife was at my throat.

Toxic fear engulfed me, freezing the scream that had escaped me for mere seconds. Cristian stepped behind me so his brother's camera could get clearer footage of the horror I was enduring. His big fist tangled in my hair, jerking my head back so I had no choice but to stare up into his cruel black eyes.

The cold tip of the knife scraped upward from the center of my throat, grazing over my skin as it traced a path under my chin. I stopped breathing when the flat of the blade swiped across the line of my lips. A high whimper slipped through them, the resultant vibration threatening to make the knife pierce my skin. As it was, the tightly packed nerve endings on my lips sparked as the cool metal kissed them.

The knife left my mouth, but I didn't have time to suck in a panting breath before the frigid blade returned to my throat.

"You were in my territory today, watching my people. One of my men followed you home. Who are you working for?" he demanded.

"I'm FBI," I said, my voice barely more than a whisper. With the knife at my throat, I could scarcely draw the breath I needed to speak.

He frowned at me. "A sniper made an attempt on my life a few days ago. The feds wouldn't assassinate me. Who are you really working for?" The blade sliced a thin, stinging line across my throat.

"I really am FBI," I said in a rush, the truth spilling from my lips. If he knew I was a federal agent, he wouldn't dare hurt me. "My name is Samantha Browning. I'm a tech analyst. Well, I was. I'm a field agent now. I'm not trying to kill you. We're investigating you. You have to know you're on our radar. Please, I swear I'm FBI." I was aware that I was babbling, but I couldn't stop pleading for my life.

He considered me for a long, terrifying moment, weighing my fate. "You're a tech analyst? That means you have access to all the evidence the feds have on me. If you're telling the truth about who you are."

"I am," I said quickly. "You can't hurt me. If you do, my friends will come after you."

"I think I'll give you to my brother, after all," he mused. "He'll make sure you're telling the truth. I'd rather not mutilate you, if you're going to be useful to me. Andrés has more creative ways of breaking women. And I'll keep our little video to ourselves. If you are who you say you are, I'd rather your friends at the FBI didn't know I have you."

The knifepoint pressed against my cheek, just below my left eye. The pressure increased slightly, and I felt warmth bead on my skin. It slid down my cheek like a crimson tear. My eyes watered, and Cristian's handsome face wavered above me.

"Maybe I'll give you a scar to match my brother's first," he mused.

A deep growl sounded from a few feet in front of me, and I knew it came from Andrés. I couldn't so much as glance in his direction; Cristian's long fingers in my hair kept me immobile.

A sharp grin lit his features with amusement. "Apparently, he wants you mostly intact. Should I give him what he wants?"

The fearsome growl sounded again, a wordless warning. I shuddered, equally as frightened of the prospect of his desire to *have me* as I was of the knife piercing my cheek.

"Not the face, then," Cristian said decisively. "But I think I'll let Andrés see what he's getting to work with."

The knife left my face, but the blade instantly hooked beneath the top button of my shirt. It gave way easily as the sharp steel tore through thread. He continued to move the blade downward, trailing a sickening path between my breasts, over my navel, down to the top of my slacks. The fabric fell open with a flick of the knife, leaving me exposed in my white cotton bra.

A plea for mercy locked in my throat. I couldn't speak, could barely breathe. My mind began to shut down, the adrenaline created by fear clouding my brain.

Cristian's fingers tightened in my hair, giving me a bite of pain. "Stay with us, Samantha," he ordered smoothly.

The world sharpened around me with cruel clarity just before pain sliced into me. The tip of the knife grated a torturously slow line along my right collarbone. The cut was shallow, but blood welled up as the blade scraped bone. The scream that had been trapped inside me burst out as pain seared through me. He hooked the blade beneath the little strip of cotton at the middle of my bra, parting the fabric and exposing me.

My scream choked off on a sob as terror mingled with humiliation.

"What do you think, *hermanito*?" Cristian asked with mild interest. "Is she pretty enough for you? She's not a great beauty, but her nipples stand out nicely against her pale skin."

My skin turned frigid, my flesh pebbling as ice sank into my veins. I vaguely recognized that I was going into shock as my entire body began to shake violently.

"And her eyes are quite lovely," he continued in detached observation. "So much fear there. You like when they're frightened, don't you, Andrés?"

His low grunt in reply rolled around my mind, but my capacity for conscious thought had been ripped to shreds. The knife left my breasts to slice through the ropes that bound my wrists behind me. I slumped forward, my watery muscles incapable of holding me upright.

Strong arms closed around my shoulders, bracing me before I slid to the floor. I was dimly aware of my body being lifted. My head lolled back, and the last thing I saw before my mind short-circuited was Andrés' fearsome, scarred face looming over me.

***

Stinging pain on my chest yanked me back to awareness, and I bolted upright with a gasp. Panic blinded me, but firm hands gripped my upper arms, pressing me back down against something soft that cushioned my body. I was no longer sitting on the unyielding metal chair. I recognized the feel of a mattress beneath me, and my torso was pinned down against it by a strong, masculine hold.

I squirmed and kicked, instinctively trying to fight my way free. I became aware of cool air against my breasts, and I realized I was still exposed. My heart hammered against my ribcage, and I doubled my efforts to fight off the man holding me down, my fingers clawing blindly. His hands easily encircled my wrists, trapping them at either side of my hips.

"Calm down, *cosita*, or I'll have to restrain you." I recognized the soft Colombian accent.

Moreno had me. He'd hurt me, stripped me...

Oh god. He'd given me to his terrifying brother. Andrés.

And now I was half-naked and helpless in his steely hold.

I couldn't stop thrashing, my muscles rippling with effort to break free. My stomach twisted, nausea rising as the full horror of my situation came down on me.

A low sound of disapproval grated against my mind. His grip instantly shifted, tugging my arms over my head. He secured them there with one big hand. Something cool and supple encircled my right wrist. Metal jingled against metal as he buckled the cuff into place.

I twisted my entire body, trying to angle myself so I could kick out at him. Desperation clawed at my insides, and all my training left my head as animal terror took hold. My awkward attempts to resist him made no effect, and he quickly secured my other wrist.

Working in silence, he caught my left ankle, pulling it diagonally toward the bottom corner of the bed. My eyes finally focused and I watched in helpless horror as he bound my legs to either side of the four-poster, spreading me wide. I still wore my slacks, but I felt terribly exposed and vulnerable.

I thrashed against the restraints, but he pressed his big palm against my bare abdomen, pinning me down against the mattress and effectively ending my struggles. All I could do was jerk uselessly against the cuffs. Fear coursed through me.

My fight-or-flight instincts had settled on flight, but there was nowhere for me to go. That didn't stop my body from twisting like a wild thing, panic beating against the inside of my chest.

His dark eyes watched me with calm certainty as he simply waited. I wasn't sure how long it took for my muscles to burn with exertion, and I finally gave up, my limbs trembling where they were stretched above and below me, laying me out before him.

"Are you done?" he asked coolly.

"Fuck you," I seethed, my acid tongue the only weapon left to me.

Keeping me pinned in place with one hand, his other swiftly came down and cracked across the outer swell of my breasts, one after the other in rapid succession. My sensitive flesh instantly began to burn, and I cried out. I couldn't escape the pain; I was trapped in place for the harsh censure.

Tears leaked from the corners of my eyes, and he finally stopped.

"I won't tolerate insults," he said, still unnervingly calm. It almost would have been less disconcerting if he'd shouted. "You will speak to me with respect. Do you understand?"

"No." The refusal came out as a horrified moan.

"You will understand soon," he said, utterly confident. "You're frightened, but you will learn. For now, I'm warning you not to curse at me again. Tell me you'll obey."

The tears came faster, spilling down my temples and falling into my hair.

His face shifted to a forbidding mask. "Tell me."

I couldn't manage more than a fearful whimper, but I nodded shakily. I didn't want him to slap me again, and I recognized that there was nothing I could do to prevent him from doing it if he decided he wanted to.

His countenance softened, his scar easing so it wasn't as

pronounced. "In the future, I will expect a verbal answer. You belong to me now, Samantha. Defiance will lead to punishment. Obedience will be rewarded. You choose whichever you want. I might seem like a harsh Master, but I'm fair. Your behavior has consequences, either painful or pleasurable for you."

"Please," I forced out past the lump in my throat. "I can't... I don't... Don't..." I began to pant out the fragmented words as my breathing turned shallower, until I was gasping but not drawing in air.

His hands bracketed my face, shockingly gentle. "Breathe," he ordered, his accented voice low and soft, as though trying to soothe a frightened animal.

I certainly felt like a panicked, primal thing; trapped and terrified.

His fingers threaded through my hair on either side of my head, massaging gently.

"Breathe with me," he cajoled. He drew in a slow, deep breath and then blew it out on a long exhale. "Again," he commanded, and I vaguely recognized that I'd obeyed and matched his breathing, my lungs too desperate for oxygen to resist. I sucked in another shaky breath, mirroring him. We repeated the process several more times, until I was able to breathe almost normally. I sank down into the mattress as my body went limp, all the fight going out of me as exhaustion sapped my mind.

"Better." He nodded his approval. His gaze finally diverted from my face, and he reached for a damp cloth that he'd placed beside me on the bed. "You're still bleeding," he told me. "I'm going to clean you up. This will sting a little. Stay still."

I couldn't have moved away even if I still possessed any willpower to do so. One of his hands remained bracketed at the side of my face, his thumb hooking beneath my jaw to hold me steady.

The cool cloth gently touched my cheek, and I hissed in pain. Just as he'd warned me, the solution that soaked the cloth stung, and I knew it was more than water.

"Good girl," he said, the warm praise in his tone fucking with my addled mind. I only recognized the comfort in it, unable to process the twisted nature of how he was manipulating me. Anything was preferable to the unrelenting terror that had utterly sapped my will and smothered all thought of resistance.

He continued his gentle ministrations, his dark eyes completely focused on his task as he cleaned the cut on my collarbone. Keening sounds eased up my throat, and he softly shushed me.

When he finished, he sat back and considered me for a long moment, his black eyes searching mine. Instinct urged me to look away, to escape his probing gaze. The intensity with which he watched me made it impossible for me to break eye contact. I shuddered violently, unable to bear his scrutiny.

His grip on my face shifted, and his calloused fingertips smoothed over the furrow in my brow.

"You're hurting," he remarked. "You didn't do anything to deserve this."

He reached for something else on the bed beside me, and I cringed when my gaze fixed on it: a syringe. I didn't want to be unconscious again, helpless and unable to defend myself.

"My brother gave me this in case I needed to subdue you, but it will take away your pain. I told you, I'm a fair Master. I won't hurt you if you don't earn a punishment."

"I don't want it," I managed to whisper.

"I decide what's best for you from now on," he declared calmly.

"Please," I begged uselessly as he carefully slid the needle into my arm.

"Hush now, *cosita*," he murmured. "You'll feel better when you wake up."

"No," I slurred, the drugs making my tongue heavy within seconds.

His long fingers smoothed over my hair, petting me as I fell into darkness.

CHAPTER 3

A pleasant, warm weight pressed against my chest. I snuggled into it, finding comfort in the weighted blanket that helped calm my anxiety. I'd bought it three months ago, and I'd found that it helped soothe my racing thoughts enough so I could actually sleep through the night.

I certainly felt rested, even if my mouth was too dry. Like the time I'd binged on Smirnoff Ice and woken up with a wicked hangover. This time, the headache was mercifully absent.

Although my eyes were still closed, my brow furrowed. I didn't remember drinking last night. What did I...?

My eyes snapped open, and my body jerked bolt upright. Andrés' corded arm fell from my chest, where it had been draped across me. I gasped and scrambled away from him, tumbling over the edge of the mattress to fall on my ass. Terror ripped through me as reality slammed back into place.

I pushed up onto my feet and backed away from the bed, desperate to put distance between us. His dark gaze fixed on me, but he didn't so much as lift his head from the pillow. I expected him to come after me, to attack. But he simply watched me with mild curiosity, as though interested to see what I would do next.

I became very aware of his eyes on me, and I realized cool air kissed every inch of my skin. I instinctively covered my breasts and sex before my mind fully processed the fact that I was completely naked. I remembered the needle sliding beneath my skin while I was bound to his bed, helpless. He'd drugged me, stripped me when I was unconscious.

Then he'd *spooned* me.

And I'd cuddled closer.

Tears burned the corners of my eyes as panic overwhelmed me. I was naked with my captor. He'd touched me while I was drugged and unable to defend myself.

I shuddered at the thought of him *touching* me. He could have done anything to me, and I wouldn't know.

How could I have rested comfortably beside the monster for even a moment?

"I thought you were my blanket," I blurted out, needing to justify my actions to myself but not meaning to speak the words aloud.

One corner of his lips twitched upward. "Excuse me?" he asked, his accented voice colored with amusement. He propped up on one elbow, his gaze sharpening with interest that had become something more than idle curiosity.

I took a hasty step back, clutching my hands tighter against my most vulnerable areas. Fear spiked, instinct driving me to keep as much space between us as possible while trying to cover myself.

"I have a weighted blanket. At home. It helps with anxiety," I babbled, the words spilling out of me as panic addled my mind. "Your arm was heavy. I thought it was my blanket. That's why I... Stop looking at me!" I shouted the last, unable to bear the intensity of his black eyes studying my naked body.

"I like looking at what's mine," he said, his voice deep and even, as though he wasn't saying something abhorrent.

"I'm not yours," I countered, my voice high and thin.

His eyes darkened to flat black as his pupils dilated. He finally stood, the sheets falling from his powerful form. Every inch of him was sculpted, every muscle defined. He wore only sweatpants slung low on his hips, so I got a clear view of just how hulking and strong he was. More than a dozen raised, pale scars crisscrossed his torso and abs, standing out against his tanned skin. They weren't as deep and puckered as the wicked furrow that had been carved into his cheek, but they were no less intimidating. How many times must he have fought and won to bear so many marks of violence on his skin?

I shrank back, feeling small and horribly vulnerable. I might be a field agent, but I wasn't equipped for this. No one had trained me for this terrifying scenario; where I was naked and outmatched by at least a hundred pounds of muscle, facing off against a man who was clearly a ruthless fighter. A man who'd easily wrestled me down and bound me to his bed. A man who had slapped my bare breasts and said I belonged to him.

My flesh tingled with the memory of his harsh rebuke, and a light tremor raced over my skin, making it pebble.

"My brother was right," he said, still studying me intently. "Your eyes are lovely when you're frightened. Wide and blue. Like a pretty doll." He took a step toward me. "Am I so terrifying, *sirenita?*"

I dodged back, and my bare butt hit cool glass. I glanced behind me at the shock of cold, and my stomach instantly dropped at the view. The Chicago skyline stretched out before me, and the people dotting the sidewalk below were far too

27

small. Familiar fear twisted my gut at the sensation of being too high up, adding a fresh layer of terror to my overloaded system. I tried to push away from the floor-to-ceiling window, the only thin barrier between me and a long fall to my death.

I smacked into a wall of warm, hard muscle. Andrés had closed the distance between us swiftly and soundlessly, trapping his prey with ruthless intent. And just like a small, cornered animal, I lashed out at the threat in an attempt to save myself.

My training kicked in without thought, and I swung my fist at his granite jaw. The blow connected, sending pain radiating through my knuckles. He barely flinched. I didn't pause, intent on inflicting as much damage as possible. I brought my knee up, desperate to hit him where he was most vulnerable.

He shifted, his rock-hard thigh blocking my knee before I could make contact. I had a split second to register his disapproving frown before my entire world tilted and spun. His big hands were on my naked body, taking me down to the plush carpet. My hips hit his thighs, and the air rushed from my chest as his palm pressed down between my shoulder blades, pushing my breasts against the floor to the point of pain. My fingernails scrabbled against the carpet, struggling for purchase as my flight response kicked in again.

A high, feral sound left me when his hand left my back, only to catch my wrists. He encircled both with his long fingers, pinning my arms behind me so all I could do was thrash wildly, gasping and kicking my legs at nothing. I was trapped again, unable to fight, unable to flee. My heart fluttered against my ribcage, and I gasped for air as panic clogged my throat.

I heard the *crack* resound against the high ceiling just before the shocking sting bloomed on my upper thigh. I shrieked and writhed, trying to escape the burn of his palm. A twin hit landed on my other leg, and my shocked cry turned to a furious scream. Impotent rage seared through my veins alongside white-hot mortification. He was *spanking* me.

"Don't ever try that again," he admonished in even tones as he delivered another cruel blow, just beneath the lower curve of my ass. "You will not fight me." Another burning hit. "You belong to me. You will accept your place."

"Stop fucking saying that!" I shouted, tears of frustration and pain pricking at the corners of my eyes.

"I get to say what I want. I get to do what I want." Each statement was punctuated by a slap. "You will learn to mind your tongue. You will learn to behave. You're mine, *cosita*. Mine to play with. Mine to punish. Just *mine*."

"No." The refusal came out on a low moan. My flesh was on fire, my mind flooded with fear and humiliation. My naked body was draped over my captor's lap, and he was making it clear that I didn't have a hope of fighting him. I didn't realize that I'd stopped thrashing, but a harsh sob tore from my chest.

The blows stopped, and he smoothed his palm over my heated skin. It prickled with awareness, every nerve ending on fire.

"There," he said, his voice rich with satisfaction. "Isn't that better? Don't try to hurt me again, Samantha."

He continued to stroke my aching ass, and I groaned in relief. The light caress helped soothe away some of the pain.

Fresh shock tore through me when he touched two fingers against the seam of my sex.

"You're wet," he said in a low rumble. "We are going to get along, *sirenita*."

I stiffened in his hold. He was touching me *there*. No one touched me there. Not even me.

Horror washed over me, smothering awareness of what

he'd said. I couldn't focus, couldn't think. Fear clouded everything, seeping into my mind like dense fog.

"Don't," I squeaked out, renewing my struggles. I became very aware of the hard rod pressing into my belly. His erection throbbed and jerked as I twisted on his lap.

He hissed out a breath, and his hand tightened around my wrists, holding me securely in place. "Stop grinding against me," he said tightly. "You want me to touch your little clit, greedy girl?"

You want me to touch your secret place again, don't you, dirty little girl? a long-forgotten, phantom voice whispered across my mind. Terror and shame mingled in a sickening cocktail, making my stomach clench and my head spin. I couldn't think; I couldn't think about the voice. All thought blanked out, overtaken by pure, icy panic. The cold sank into my bones, and I shuddered violently.

Warmth enfolded me. Slowly, the ice ebbed away. I became aware of a low, lilting voice saying words I couldn't comprehend. A few seconds later, I realized they were spoken in Spanish, but I still didn't understand more than a word or two dotted within the comforting litany.

"You're okay. Don't be afraid," he finally said in English as he continued to smooth his big hands over my body, warming my frigid skin. I realized I was cradled in Andrés' strong embrace, but I couldn't bring myself to try to fight my way free anymore. I felt wrung-out, weak. Small and helpless.

Tears streamed down my face, and my brain whirred back to life. I was naked and crying into my tormentor's chest. The voice in my head was gone; wiped away, forgotten. All I knew was that my captor had tried to touch me sexually, and I'd freaked out. I didn't want to be raped.

"Let me go," I whispered brokenly.

"That's not going to happen" he told me in that same sure, calming tone.

"Stop touching me," I begged. I couldn't bear the feel of his hands exploring my naked, vulnerable body, stroking me like he was soothing a frightened animal. Or a favorite pet.

"I will touch you whenever and however I want." He paused and sighed. "We will work on this later," he declared ominously, but he released me.

I shoved up onto my feet, willing my shaking knees to support me as I put several feet of space between us. My eyes flicked to the closed door across from the bed, which I presumed was the way out.

"No," he said sternly, noticing the direction of my gaze. "Don't try it, or I'll spank you again. Go wash away those tears." He gestured at an open door to my right, which led into a bathroom.

I became suddenly, acutely aware that my basic needs hadn't been met for long hours, and I darted into the bathroom without any further thoughts of defiance. As I moved, I noticed the slickness between my thighs.

You're wet. We are going to get along, sirenita.

Mortification burned through me at the memory of Andrés' words. I might not have considered myself a sexual person, but I wasn't completely naïve. I knew that a woman got wet when she was aroused, so her body would be prepared to accept a man. It wasn't the first time I'd gotten wet, either. Watching Dex's BDSM porn had aroused me, even though I hadn't been brave enough to act on my desire. Whenever I'd gotten too turned on, I'd thrown myself into a particularly challenging task, usually involving hacking. Using the analytical side of my brain helped cool my animal physical responses.

My stomach roiled. Had my obsession with becoming the object of Dex's darker needs twisted me so thoroughly? I'd just been spanked by an evil man who claimed to own me, who wanted to rape me. And I'd gotten wet, my body responding to his harsh dominance.

My tears spilled faster as shame heated my cheeks, and I hastily finished my essential business so I could wash my hands and face. I pressed my palms against my flaming cheeks, turning the water colder to help chase away the heat of my humiliation. A few broken sobs heaved from my chest, but I gulped in air and forced myself to calm down.

In the calm, a single imperative took over: *escape.*

I couldn't wait around for my friends to find me, for Dex to come to my rescue.

I'm not the damsel in distress, I told myself. *I'm the hero. Heroine. Whatever. I'm a badass FBI agent/hacker goddess. I can get out of this.*

I couldn't take down Andrés without a weapon—something he had made painfully clear. My bottom still ached and stung from his punishment, but that wasn't enough to deter me. He'd stripped me. He'd touched my sex as though he had every right. I refused to sit around and do nothing to defend myself when he clearly intended to rape me.

So, I'd have to find a weapon. Or make one.

I cast my eyes around the opulent bathroom, searching. There, hanging beneath one of the multiple showerheads: a razor.

I quickly crossed the tiled floor and retrieved it. I glanced at the closed bathroom door, knowing I didn't have long before Andrés would start banging on it. Possibly even breaking it down. I'd locked it behind me, but that wouldn't stop him. He'd already proven how strong he was, how relentless.

Turning my attention back to my task, I tamped down my anxiety and applied pressure to the razor's plastic casing. After a few seconds, it snapped. I gripped the flat of one of the blades between my thumb and forefinger, careful of the wickedly sharp edge. If I bloodied my fingers, I wouldn't be able to hold on to my only weapon.

I went to the bathroom door and turned back the lock, knowing he'd hear the metallic click in the bedroom. I didn't open the door. I needed him to come to me, and then I'd catch him by surprise. He'd seen a broken, frightened woman dart into the bathroom to hide from him. He wouldn't expect me to attack again now.

I'm not broken. And I'm not frightened. Okay, maybe that last part was a lie. My hands trembled, and I focused on steadying the fingers that gripped my blade.

"Samantha?" he asked, his rumbling voice emanating through the closed door. "Come out of there."

I made a little sniffling noise to encourage the illusion that I was crying, weakened. Not a difficult feat, considering my tears still mingled with the water droplets that wet my face.

"Come out here. Now, *cosita.*" There was warning in the last, a clear threat that he'd come in to retrieve me if I didn't comply.

Come on, then, I mentally urged him, my body vibrating with anticipation.

A heavy sigh sounded through the door. "You will regret this," he said. "You must learn to obey me, even if you're scared or upset. I'm giving you one last chance. Come," he commanded firmly, like he was speaking to a particularly difficult puppy he was trying to train.

I straightened my spine. I wasn't going to be trained. I wasn't going to obey. And I certainly wasn't going to walk out into his scary, strong arms and allow him to violate me.

The door swung open, and I launched myself at him. I had the barest moment to register his dark eyes widening with surprise as I slashed, aiming for his throat. I'd never killed a man before, but I had to escape before something terrible happened to me. I tried to find a cold, calm place in my mind, but instead, I attacked with a furious, desperate shriek.

Maybe my roiling emotions made me sloppy. Maybe I just didn't have it in me to tear open a man's throat.

Or maybe Andrés was simply accustomed to people trying to kill him, and his instincts kicked in.

He managed to dodge back, and my blade cut a long, shallow furrow into his chest. I paused, shocked at the sight of his blood welling up.

I'd done that. I'd hurt him.

I didn't feel any sense of heroic triumph. Instead, horror washed over me. Violence might be ingrained in him, but it turned out, killing wasn't in my nature.

In my moment of hesitation, he grabbed my wrist. He barely had to squeeze before the razor slipped from my fingers. I'd lost my only weapon, and now I was faced by a hulking, bleeding madman.

Only, he didn't look mad. He looked... disappointed? What kind of man faces an attempt on his life with such mild emotion? He could have attacked me. He could have killed me and eliminated the threat.

But the laughable truth was, I wasn't a threat.

Keeping his hold on my wrist, he took a slow step toward me. I dodged back as far as I could, watching him warily. I didn't understand his calm response.

"I cut you," I blurted, trying to comprehend why he wasn't responding to my violence in kind.

"You did," he said coolly, completely unconcerned by the little rivulet of blood dripping down over his defined abs. "Are you really so eager for another spanking already? Did you enjoy it so much? I'll have to devise more clever punishments for you." The ghost of a smile flickered over the corners of his lips. "We are going to get along very well."

"Stop saying that," I forced out, my voice trembling. His calm was beyond unnerving. "I don't want you to spank me. I don't want you to touch me."

He moved with lightning speed, and his body suddenly pressed against mine. My back bumped against the wall, and he captured both my wrists in his big hand again, pinning them above my head. He caged me in, his powerful body too close for me to defend myself.

My breath caught in my throat, fear fluttering at the center of my chest.

"Liar," he said smoothly. "I won't tolerate that, either. You enjoyed your spanking." His thigh wedged between mine, forcing my legs apart. He reached between us with his free hand and lightly slapped my sex.

A strange, strangled sound left my chest. It felt... weird, being spanked there. It stung, but the rebuke went deeper than physical discomfort. The punitive touch to my most secret, sensitive area was a causal demonstration of ownership. Something inside me clenched. A shadow of the toxic fear that had overtaken me the last time he'd touched my sex made me shudder.

He stared down into my eyes, his black gaze penetrating my soul. He spanked my sex again. This time, a wet sound accompanied the slap.

I bucked in his hold, struggling to escape. My writhing caused his palm to rub against my bud of sensitive nerve endings. I gasped and shivered, my body alight with sensation that was utterly foreign to me. My toes tingled, and warmth curled low in my belly.

But fear persisted, fogging my brain.

"What are you so afraid of, *cosita*?" he asked, his voice low and silky smooth. "The pain or the pleasure?"

"What?" I managed. *Pleasure?* Nothing about what was happening was pleasurable in any way. My situation was horrifying, disgusting.

He studied me for long, torturous seconds, his hot palm resting against my sex in an obvious proprietary gesture.

"Do you really not understand?" he finally asked. His long fingers played through my sensitive folds, and I felt the slickness of my flesh under his touch.

I pressed my lips together, refusing to contemplate what was happening to me.

Something like a growl rumbled from his chest, and his dark eyes burned into me. "How innocent are you, Samantha?"

"I... I don't like when you touch me there," I whispered the truth.

"*There?*" he repeated. "You mean, your wet little pussy?" He rotated his palm against me, and something strange crackled through my system, making me cry out.

"Stop," I moaned. "I don't like this."

"Liar," he accused again, delivering another stinging slap against my labia. I tried to close my thighs, but he kept me securely pinned in place.

"I don't want you to touch me," I pleaded. Despite the unfamiliar electric current that was coursing through my body, fear still sapped my mind.

Wrong. Dirty.

Dirty little girl.

You want me to touch your secret place again, don't you, dirty little girl? The low, masculine voice whispered across my mind. I stiffened, my horror creeping up my throat to choke off my air supply.

The heat of his hand left my sex, and his palm came up to

cup my cheek, his thumb hooking below my jaw to tilt my face up to his. "Look at me," he ordered in soothing tones.

I blinked, and my eyes focused on his face. His scar was deeply pronounced, drawn downward by the twist of his frown. The sight of his displeasure might have made me flinch with fresh fear, but I detected only concern in his dark eyes. He watched me with such intensity that I was unable to look away.

"You will learn to accept my touch," he said. As though to prove his point, he rubbed his thumb along the line of my lower lip. My sensitive nerve endings crackled and danced, and I sucked in a sharp breath. My body quivered, my skin pebbling. "You will learn to crave it," he continued, imbuing the words with command.

"Please, let me go," I begged, unravelling. All my earlier bravado had been torn away as swiftly and as easily as he'd disarmed me. I was left in a fog of fear and confusion. Trapped by Andrés' powerful body, I had no hope of escape. All I could do was plead with him. I struggled to gather my wits, clinging to the final weapon that remained: my mind.

"You have to let me go," I said, with a little more strength. "You can't... hurt me." I couldn't bring myself to say *rape me*. "My friends will find me. Do you really think the FBI won't do whatever it takes to get one of their own back?"

"My brother isn't so sure of that," he countered, still studying me intently. "It's my job to ensure your honesty. He wants the truth from you, and I will have the truth."

"I'm telling you the truth," I insisted.

He cocked his head at me, then nodded. "Yes, I think you are."

"Then you'll let me go?" I asked, hope swelling in my chest.

His fingers tightened around my wrists, and he scowled, his first true show of anger since Cristian had cut me. "No," he declared. "That's my brother's decision to make. Until he does, I'm keeping you."

I glowered up at him, righteous rage rising. "Dex is going to find me," I warned, an absolute truth. "And if you hurt me before he gets here, he will tear you apart with his bare hands."

"No one will find you," he swore. "You belong to me now."

"You're insane," I flung back at him, twisting against his harsh hold. "I don't belong to you."

He rubbed his fingers over my lips, and I could smell my lingering desire that had coated them. "Your pussy says otherwise," he told me. "You nearly came all over my hand, just from a spanking. Your body knows its Master. Your mind will follow."

I snapped my teeth at his fingers. That was his fucking mistake for putting them so close to my mouth.

I barely managed to nip at him before he pulled back. His hand settled around my throat, applying the barest pressure. My eyes went wide, and my mind blanked. Something primal within me surrendered on instinct, my animal brain recognizing the show of dominance, the subtle threat. I was powerless against him, small and fragile in his grip.

"Good girl," he said with approval. "Don't try to bite me again, or I'll find a better use for your pretty mouth."

I sucked in a small gasp. He couldn't mean... I'd never... I didn't want...

His touch shifted, his hand leaving my throat so he could stroke his fingertips down the column of my neck. "Breathe," he coaxed. "You spook very easily, *cosita*. But you will learn to crave me. All of me. My hand, my mouth, my cock. You will accept me."

"I won't," I forced out on a whisper.

He frowned and opened his mouth to say something else that was probably equally terrifying. But a knock on the bedroom door interrupted whatever he was going to say. A masculine voice penetrated the door, speaking in rapid-fire Spanish. Andrés barked something back that I couldn't understand.

Then his gaze fixed on me again. "I have business to attend to," he told me. "We will work on this later."

Work on this. Not *talk about this.* Whatever Andrés' plan for me entailed, it didn't involve my consent.

CHAPTER 4

He stared down at me, considering. I barely breathed. If I did, I'd inhale his purely masculine, purely intimidating scent. As well as the smell of my own confusing arousal. I didn't understand why my body was reacting to his harsh treatment in this twisted way. Maybe it was a defense mechanism, an instinctive response designed to prevent damage to my sex if he did decide to take me against my will.

But that didn't explain the strange tingling in my flesh, the way the blood pumped faster through my veins as I waited for his next move.

He blew out a sigh. "I need to get dressed," he told me. "Can I trust you not to try to attack me again once my back is turned?"

I scowled at him, lifting my chin in defiance. I'd never stop trying to get away from him, even if I knew that physically besting him was next to impossible. I'd had a slim chance with my puny weapon, and now the delicate razorblade lay useless on the carpet.

But I wasn't about to admit meekly that I'd be a good girl and stop trying to fight my way free.

His full lips twisted in a slight frown, dragging his scar down in a fearsome slash across his face. I dimly noted that he would be handsome, otherwise. Beautiful, even. His stubble-covered square jaw was strong and masculine, his cheekbones high and defined. Heavy dark brows drew together over his onyx eyes, and his black hair curled softly to frame his rugged features.

But the scar that marred his cheek... It was difficult to look at; vicious and violent.

Instinct urged my gaze to flit around the room in its familiar anxious pattern. But his eyes. I couldn't look away. His pupils were dilated, fixed on me. A slender ring of rich chocolate brown surrounded them, nearly swallowed by the darkness of his stare.

A light shiver raced across my skin, but I remained locked in his steady gaze.

His frown eased, one corner of his lips ticking up in a perverse smile. In a shockingly tender gesture, he tucked a stray lock of hair behind my ear. "So frightened, but so defiant. I'm going to have to restrain you, aren't I?"

I jerked against his hold, but his grip remained iron around my wrists. "No."

"So you won't try to attack me as soon as I release you?" he asked, the twist of his smile letting me know the question was purely rhetorical.

I struggled again, and a frustrated noise that sounded a little like a growl slipped between my teeth. He laughed; a low, rumbling chuckle of dark amusement.

"Such an angry *gatita*. Maybe I should keep you in cage. Would that tame you?"

"I don't need to be *tamed*," I shot back, my anger bleeding over fear. "I told you the truth. I'm a federal agent. You said you believe me. If you do, then you know you can't risk hurting me. My friends at the Bureau won't stop looking for me, and if you've..." I couldn't bring myself to say *raped me*. "If you've hurt me when they find me, they won't show you any mercy. You have to let me go."

His frown returned. "That's up to my brother to decide. Until he does, you're mine." His fingers tightened around my wrists as he made the perverse declaration.

"You keep saying that," I hissed out. "You're fucking crazy, you know that, right? You're—"

My next insult didn't make it past my lips. He pressed his hand firmly against my mouth, his frown twisting with disapproval.

"You will learn to mind your language when you're speaking to me," he said coolly. "I need to get dressed, and you need to be quiet and behave while I'm gone. How comfortable you are while I'm out attending to my business is up to you. I can gag you and cage you, or I can leave you free to move around the suite. Make your choice."

My eyes flew wide, finally leaving his face to search the room. *Cage me?* Surely he couldn't be serious.

I sucked in a sharp breath through my nose. I'd been too distressed to notice before. Beneath the enormous four-poster bed were bars. Cushions and a blanket made it look like a second bunk beneath the big bed, but that was just my mind struggling to comprehend what I was truly looking at.

What kind of man had a cage under his bed? One that was clearly waiting to trap a frightened, unwilling woman?

"Choose," he said, his voice gravelly. "Are you going to be a good girl for me, or am I going to have to cage you beneath my bed like a naughty *gatita*?" His cock jerked against my belly, and I shuddered.

I shook my head as best I could, but my movement was restricted by his firm hand on my mouth.

He studied me for a moment longer, then gave a small nod. The weight of his body finally left mine when he took a step back, and my shaky legs nearly collapsed without his support. He maintained his hold on my wrists above my head, keeping me upright until I managed to find my footing. Once I regained my balance, he lowered my arms, but he didn't release them. He kept them trapped in one of his big hands as he moved back toward the bed, pulling me along in his wake.

"Please," I gasped out, my eyes fixing on the cage as panic churned in my gut. "I don't want to go in there."

"I'm not going to put you in the cage," he told me calmly. "You've already been punished for your transgressions. I told you: I might seem harsh, but I'm fair."

"So you're not going to lock me up?" I asked tentatively, my steps faltering as we reached the bed.

He smirked at me. "I didn't say that." He directed me to sit on the mattress and pressed my hands into my lap. "Put your hands on your knees, and keep them there. If you try to fight me again, I think you understand what the consequence will be."

He finally released my wrists, and I slowly directed my trembling hands to my knees, pressing my palms against them and locking my fingers around my kneecaps. He curled two fingers beneath my chin, applying light pressure. I had no choice but to lift my head and straighten my spine.

"Shoulders back," he ordered.

I complied, too intimidated to do otherwise. I'd been hunched over in a last-ditch attempt to protect my most vulnerable areas, but he demanded that I sit upright. In this position, my small breasts were exposed, and his eyes flared as he studied my naked body.

"*Qué bonita*," he murmured. His fingers left my chin, and I started to slump again. He simply clicked his tongue at me and lightly gripped my jaw, returning me to the position he desired.

"Stay," he commanded firmly, using the puppy-training voice again.

The ire that had burned through my veins earlier in response to that tone was utterly absent. Instead, a light shiver raced across my skin. He released my jaw, but I didn't move. He didn't have to touch me in order to restrain me. He'd thoroughly brought me to heel. He might have spanked me, but it was his unnerving calm and gentle but firm touches that were fucking with my mind. If he'd responded to my violence in kind, I might have maintained the determination to fight. As it was, his iron will kept me trapped as effectively as his strong hands.

He stepped back from me, but he didn't take his eyes off me as he crossed the short distance to a chest of drawers set against the wall a few feet away from the bed. He was right to watch me. If he'd taken his steady gaze off me, I would have bolted for the door. As it was, it took nothing more than his dark, stern stare to keep me locked in place where he'd left me.

He opened the top drawer and retrieved a thin strip of black leather, three small silver padlocks, and a length of delicate chain. My breath stuttered as he slowly withdrew the items, allowing me to clearly see what was in store for me.

"I don't want that," I managed breathlessly, my gaze locking on the collar. I'd longed for Dex to give me a collar, to love me and mark me as his own. I knew what it meant in the context of consensual BDSM: commitment, devotion.

With Andrés, it would be a symbol of subjugation. Everything I'd craved would be perverted the moment the leather touched my throat.

A single dark brow rose, and he lifted the collar for me to examine. "Does this scare you? It won't hurt."

"I know it won't," I began to babble. "But I don't want it. Not from you."

He closed the short distance between us. I didn't budge from the position he'd dictated, even though I wanted to shrink away.

He studied me with renewed curiosity, his gaze sharpening on my features. "Not from me? Someone else has collared you before? Maybe you're not so innocent."

"No. He hasn't. I just wanted... I don't want this from you," I finally managed to curtail the words that threatened to spill out of me. Andrés didn't need to know about my heartbreak and secret longings for my best friend. No doubt, he'd find some way to use it against me.

His black eyes narrowed. "You lost the right to make demands when you tried to kill me," he told me. "I can't trust you not to attack as soon as my back is turned. So, I'm going to chain you to my bed, where you'll wait for me like a good girl while I attend to my business."

"I don't want this," I begged, still not daring to make a move against him.

"And I don't want to have to punish you more severely than I already have. Not so soon. This is for your own good, Samantha."

With that ominous declaration, he brought the collar up to my throat. I shuddered as the cool leather encircled my neck, but I remained in position, trapped by the looming threat of further punishment.

The collar tightened slightly as he slid the small padlock through the hasp at my nape, and the soft *click* as he secured it in place made my stomach clench. A single tear rolled down my cheek. This was all wrong. I'd fantasized about accepting a collar for years, and now one was being forced on me. I wasn't willingly ceding my trust and promising my obedience; I was being conquered, rebuked.

He tenderly brushed the wetness from my face with his calloused thumb. "It's not so bad, *cosita*," he cooed, tracing the line of the collar with his free hand. "It's very pretty on you."

I closed my eyes, no longer able to look at him. This violation went somehow deeper than the sting of his hand on my sex. He was taking my most closely-guarded fantasies and twisting them into something dark and abhorrent.

I heard him sigh, and his touch left my face. The chain clanked, and a light weight tugged at my neck. Behind my closed lids, I could envision him locking the chain to the metal ring at the front of the collar. I didn't have to see what he was doing to know what was happening to me.

His heat finally receded, but I could still feel his presence bearing down on me.

"Look at me," he commanded softly.

My wet lashes fluttered open.

"This is what's best for you," he told me with that same calm assurance that so unsettled me. "While you're with me, you're my responsibility. I will take care of you, even if that means protecting you from yourself."

"You're not protecting me," I hissed. "You've violated me. You've stripped me. You've *spanked* me."

His lips thinned, and his scar deepened. "And if you knew what my brother had planned for you instead, you'd be worshipping at my feet right now and begging to be mine. But we'll get to that later. For now, know that I'm the merciful alternative."

"Rape isn't merciful," I flung at him.

He stared at me, his black eyes glinting with fury. Despite the ire in his gaze, he didn't move to strike me or even raise his voice. Instead, it came out low and rough with a strange mix of emotions I couldn't quite identify. "I haven't raped you. I won't rape you. You won't be rewarded with my cock until you beg me to fuck you."

"That will never happen," I asserted, my eyes clashing with his. I'd already told him he was insane, but I didn't bother saying it again. He was clearly too far out of his mind to care if I thought he was crazy.

His head canted to the side, considering. "Your pretty little pussy has already wept for me. Your body craves to be touched. To be marked and owned. I think you are innocent, Samantha. You don't know what I'm capable of. What I can make you feel. Has any man ever made you come?"

My cheeks flamed, and my eyes dropped to the carpet. His words were shameful, and they shook me to my core. Because my body *had* reacted to him. The sensations might have been foreign to me, but I had to acknowledge that they'd been... intense. And not all unpleasant.

What is wrong with me?

"I see," he said, reading the truth in my shamed silence. "Your first real orgasm will belong to me."

I shivered, the air suddenly far too cool against my heated skin.

"Later," he said, and I got the sense he was speaking to himself more than to me. His fingers trailed through my hair, but I cringed away, completely overwhelmed and at a loss for words. He withdrew his touch, and I heard his footsteps whispering across the carpet as he moved away. When I heard the bathroom door shut behind him, I gasped in a sharp breath and finally looked up from the floor.

Just as I'd suspected, he'd locked the length of chain to the front of my collar and affixed the other end to a ringbolt set into the bedpost. I again wondered what kind of man had such tools of depravity in his bedroom, waiting to restrain and punish an unwilling woman.

A dangerous man, I reasoned. *A sadistic man.*

Andrés didn't strike me as sadistic, though. He'd spanked me and humiliated me, but he hadn't truly hurt me. Remembering Cristian's knife slicing into my skin, I glanced down at my injured collarbone. The cut had been cleaned and sealed with a clear, shiny substance. I realized Andrés must have glued the shallow wound closed after he'd drugged me. To spare me further pain.

I didn't understand him at all. The way he touched me was sick, perverted. But he wasn't slashing me to ribbons as his brother had intended. Should I be relieved that I'd been saved from torture and a gruesome death at Cristian's cruel hands?

I shook my head sharply. Of course not. Despite Andrés' claim that he wasn't going to rape me, he'd still locked a collar around my throat and chained my naked body to his bed. There was nothing merciful about his promise of punishments if I didn't *behave.*

Dex will find me, I reasoned desperately. *Or Jason. They'll work together. They'll come for me.* Of course they would. My friends wouldn't rest until I was rescued.

But what would I have to endure before they arrived?

The bathroom door opened again, tearing me from my whirring thoughts.

Andrés stepped back into the bedroom, wearing nothing but a white towel slung low on his hips. His body was even more clearly on display than it had been in his sweatpants. I could see the dark trail of hair leading from his navel down to...

I sucked in a breath and tore my eyes away from the glimpse of his erection, straining against the towel.

"You can look at me," he invited. "There's nothing to be afraid of."

A shrill, maddened giggle bubbled from my throat. "Right. Nothing to be afraid of. Only the huge, scarred, scary man who's chained me to his bed."

"Do my scars bother you so much?" he asked, his voice dropping and becoming rougher. "Am I so terrifying to look at?"

I pressed my lips together, locking in a stream of frightened babbling. Every time I allowed myself to speak in fear, I revealed too much. Better to not say anything at all.

He let out a low, rumbling sound of displeasure. I cringed and kept my eyes trained on the floor, not daring to look at his terrifying arousal.

He didn't speak again. I listened to the soft padding of his feet against the plush carpet as he moved through the room. The whisper of fabric against fabric told me he was getting dressed, but I still didn't glance up in his direction.

After a few minutes, silence stretched between us, and I could feel his eyes on me. It finally ended when he grunted once and started walking again. I glanced through my lowered lashes and watched his shiny black leather shoes retreating across the room. When he opened the door that I'd assumed was the exit, I finally looked up in time to see his suit-clad form filling the threshold. Behind him, I got the brief impression of a lavish sitting room, and I realized there was more to his living quarters than this bedroom. He'd mentioned a *suite*. How many rooms would I have to get through before I reached freedom? What obstacles would stand in my way, once Andrés was gone?

Well, for one, there was the collar around my throat and the chain that locked me to the bed.

My short period of speculation for escape routes abruptly

49

ended when he turned to look at me one last time. One corner of his lips ticked up in a satisfied smirk, and his dark eyes raked over me.

"Good girl," he praised, his tone warm with pleasure and lilting with gentle mockery.

I realized I was still sitting exactly as he'd left me: hands on my knees, back straight, breasts thrust out. My jaw dropped, and he chuckled before closing the door behind him.

Too late, I crossed my arms over my chest and huffed out an angry breath. My show of defiance was wasted; Andrés was no longer there to witness it. And would I have dared to defy him if he were still in the room with me?

With a little exasperated growl, I fisted the chain and jerked at it. My only reward was an aching palm where the metal links bit into my skin. I reached for the padlock that kept the chain tethered to the ringbolt in the bedpost. I pulled down sharply, trying to break it.

I didn't have a hope of snapping the lock on my own. I might have been able to pick it, but I'd need tools for that. I stood and tested my range of movement. I could walk exactly two steps away from the bed before the collar tightened around my throat. Even if I stretched and reached my arm out to the point of discomfort, I couldn't touch the chest of drawers. There was no guarantee that the keys to the locks were kept in there, but it was my best bet.

After a few minutes, I sat back down on the bed, frustrated. I might as well be in the cage, for all the freedom I had.

I shivered and pushed that thought away. My situation was dire, but at least I hadn't been caged like an animal.

Gatita. Andrés had called me a kitten. I might not be familiar with much Spanish, but I knew that word from elementary classes in the language when I was young.

Did he really see me as some sort of unruly little pet he could train into obedience?

The way he'd touched my body made it very clear that he saw me as a woman.

But I fully suspected he still intended to *train* me. He'd claimed that I belonged to him. At least, I would until Cristian decided to let me go.

He *had* to let me go. He'd given me to Andrés to get the truth out of me, and I'd convinced Andrés that I was a federal agent. He'd said he believed me. Surely he'd talk to his brother, and Cristian wouldn't be so reckless as to keep me captive?

I'll get out of this, I thought desperately. I might not currently be able to escape on my own, but my friends would either locate me, or the Moreno brothers would see reason and release me before the full power of the FBI came down on them.

How had it come to this? Before yesterday, I hadn't really stopped to think about how dangerous the Moreno brothers were. I'd been focused on Division 9-C. They were the big, scary bad guys I was targeting.

I hadn't realized how big and scary Andrés was. I hadn't even considered him at all. I'd known Cristian was dangerous, but I'd only been peripherally aware of his little brother.

But I'd been taken from my home, captured. And given to Andrés.

I shuddered at the thought of his scarred face and hulking body, my heartbeat ticking up as panic rose. He'd return at some point soon. I'd need to be prepared, to either route my escape or reason through how I'd convince him to release me.

I took several deep, calming breaths and continued to assess my prison. Turning to my analytical brain was much easier than facing my animal emotions.

The floor-to-ceiling windows that made up one bedroom

wall revealed a stunning view of the Chicago skyline. It was beautiful, but unsettling to be so high up. Even if I somehow got free from the collar, I couldn't escape through a window. No doubt, plenty of Andrés' men stood between the suite and the building's exit. I hadn't been able to fight off the single man who was holding me captive, so the prospect of facing down an unknown number of adversaries didn't exactly sound like a good plan.

That non-plan was pointless, anyway, because I was chained to the fucking bed.

The click of the door latch disengaging made me scramble for cover. I hastily snatched up the tangled bedsheet and barely managed to clutch it to my chest before the bedroom door swung open.

A girl stood at the threshold. No, not a girl. A woman, although barely. The too-thin blonde couldn't be more than twenty, but her dull green eyes belonged to a much older woman. If she gained a few pounds, her body would have been model-perfect, a fact which was made clear by the plunging neckline of her skintight red dress. As it was, her breastbone stood out at the center of her chest, and her cheeks were nearly as hollow as her deadened stare. There was no emotion in her eyes whatsoever. If she'd been afraid, I could have assumed she was a fellow captive here. If she'd been hopeful, maybe she might have been an ally here to rescue me. Even disdain would have indicated something useful; it would have identified her as an enemy.

But there was nothing behind her eyes. They were a lovely, forest green, framed in long, dark lashes. No matter how physically striking she may be, it was difficult to look at her.

"Who are you?" I asked, watching her warily.

"Lauren," she replied, as though her softly-spoken name were all she had to offer in response. She hesitated in the doorway, staring at me. I shifted and pulled the sheet up to my chin.

"What do you want?" I pressed. She wasn't attacking me, but she wasn't helping me, either.

"He told me to bring you breakfast," she said, finally moving. She half-turned and directed a small cart into the bedroom. It looked like fancy room service, only, this wasn't a luxury hotel, and Lauren wasn't dressed for the service industry.

"Who is *he*?" I had a good idea whom she meant, but I needed to know the person responsible for sending the food. I doubted Andrés would poison me. He'd been very clear that he wanted to *keep* me. But I wasn't at all certain of Cristian's intentions.

She finished pushing the cart up to the edge of the bed, but I didn't move toward the food, even though I could smell the delicious scent of bacon.

"Master Andrés," she explained in the same deadpan voice.

My hand shot out, and I gripped her wrist hard. "So you're captive here, too," I said quickly. She must be, if Andrés had broken her and forced her to call him *Master*. Wasn't that exactly what he wanted from me?

"Help me," I urged, tugging at the chain that bound me to the bed. "Do you know where he keeps the keys? They're probably in that drawer." I nodded in the direction of the piece of furniture that held the literal keys to my freedom. "I'm a federal agent. If you get this collar off me, I can get us both out of here."

She blinked at me, then tugged her wrist free from my desperate grip.

"There's no way out," she said flatly.

"Of course there's a way out," I tried to reason with her. "How do we leave this suite? How many men are guarding the building? You know what, scratch that," I said quickly, noting her nonplussed expression. I might have trained as a field agent, but I couldn't get the two of us past multiple guards without a weapon. "If you could just get me a phone, I can call my friends, and they'll come in and get us," I hastened on.

"I can't do that," she said, her refusal devoid of any emotion. "I'll get into trouble. Besides, you don't want to leave this room. You're safest in here."

"What?" I spluttered, beginning to question the woman's sanity. "You see what he's done to me. This isn't safe. I have to get out of here."

"Master Andrés won't let them dose you with Bliss and pass you around," she said, something finally flickering in her haunted eyes. "He doesn't like it."

"He's not your Master," I said vehemently, trying to get through to her. She'd clearly been tormented, warped. If she'd been dosed with Bliss, she would have no control over her body while under the influence. She'd do anything she was told, including begging to be violated. My stomach turned at the knowledge of Andrés' involvement in trafficking the sick drug. He was ultimately responsible for Lauren's fractured state of mind.

"All the girls call him *Master*." She shrugged. "He used to take care of us. But that was before the Bliss. He doesn't like it," she repeated, as though that explained everything.

I reached for her again, but she dodged back.

"Please," I begged. "I can tell he hurt you. But it doesn't have to be this way. Give me a phone. I just need—"

"Master Andrés didn't hurt me," she said with shocking fervor. "He's nice to me. And he will be very angry with me if I help you. He told me to bring you food, and I brought it."

With that, she turned on her heel and stormed out of the bedroom.

"Wait!" I called after her as the door slammed shut.

I threaded my fingers through my hair, tugging at the coppery strands as I struggled to curb my mounting panic.

Master Andrés.

He'd claimed he was my *Master* now. And he'd proven how commanding and relentless he could be. Did he want to twist me into the same broken, fucked-up state as Lauren? She clearly felt some sort of perverted affection for him, even though she'd obviously been victimized.

I pressed my palms against my closed eyes and struggled to breathe normally.

I'll get out of this. I have to.

I couldn't end up like Lauren. I wouldn't.

CHAPTER 5

I wasn't sure how much time passed. Hours, surely. There wasn't a clock in the bedroom, so my only concept of time was the sun intermittently peeking through the overcast clouds.

I'd never been forced to sit without mental stimulation for so long. Usually, if I wasn't on my computer at home, I was at work. Even during my short commute, I passed the time on my smart phone. I rarely even watched TV or movies without also playing a game at the same time. My brain fired in too many different directions at once for me to focus on any one thing for long. Only digging deep into a case for the Bureau or a little side hacking just for shits and giggles could fully occupy my mind.

Now that I was forced to think about it, I doubted I'd gone longer than a waking hour without some sort of contact with technology in years. Possibly not since I was nine and got my first Gameboy.

I'd exhausted all avenues of possible escape from the bedroom within a very short time. Without Lauren's help, I was powerless to free myself from the collar that kept me tethered to the bed. Quite literally, on a short leash.

The breakfast—now stone cold—taunted me from the tray. I hadn't been provided with any utensils, likely because I would have devised some way to fashion them into weapons. Or possibly find a way to break my chains.

As it was, I had freaking bacon and breakfast potatoes. Like that would do me any good.

Well, my rumbling stomach told me I certainly could use the food, but I didn't trust it. While I doubted Andrés would poison me, he'd proven he had no qualms about drugging me. I didn't want to be unconscious and helpless again. Especially considering the fact that it had cost me my clothes the last time he'd drugged me. My only semblance of modesty now was the bedsheet, which I'd managed to wrap around me in an awkward toga. Maybe it would've been neater if I'd ever attended those fraternity parties in college, but I hadn't been invited.

I hadn't been interested in going, anyway.

I blew out a long breath and rubbed my forehead. Why was I thinking about college? Those weren't my best memories, and I much preferred to sink into my work and my online persona rather than remembering those difficult years.

All my years before joining the Bureau and meeting Dex had been difficult, really. When I joined the FBI, I found a community where I was valued and respected. And I'd found a best friend who never judged me or pushed me to talk about personal, unpleasant things. Dex and I shared a special companionship, even though I wanted to be more than his *companion.*

But pursuing that path had been a mistake. My obsession with my friend and his darker sexual predilections had obviously fucked me up. I'd spent too many hours watching his kinky porn. I'd even followed him to a BDSM club on one particularly desperate Valentine's Day, but he hadn't noticed me watching him from the bar. He never noticed me, not the way I wanted him to.

My yearning for Dex was the only explanation for why my body reacted to Andrés' twisted treatment with signs of desire. Fear might still grip my mind when he touched me, but my body didn't seem to care that I was afraid.

I jolted when the bedroom door opened again. So annoying that Andrés hadn't even bothered to lock it, but I couldn't get close to it with this damn collar around my neck. It was like he did it to taunt me. Or to demonstrate his absolute power over me.

If that was his intention, I had to admit to myself that he was doing a pretty good job at it.

I scrambled upright from where I'd been laying dejected, staring up at the pretty crystal chandelier. I braced myself for the sight of Andrés' hulking body and scarred face, but a different man appeared at the threshold. He was nearly as tall as my captor—a few inches over six feet—but his frame was wiry. He appeared to be as young as Lauren, a downy attempt at a dark blond beard only making him seem younger rather than more mature.

Also like Lauren, he behaved oddly. He didn't so much as glance in my direction as he wheeled a cart of cleaning supplies into the room and headed for the bathroom.

"Hello," I said tentatively.

He didn't respond in any way; he just kept going about his business, which I assumed was to tidy the suite while Andrés was out.

"Um, hey." I made an awkward wave to catch his attention.

No response. He disappeared into the bathroom. I heard the sounds of scrubbing, but no words.

Was the man mute? Surely, he wasn't blind.

So why was he completely ignoring me?

"Hey," I called out. "I'm Sam." I felt like an idiot introducing myself when I couldn't even see him from my perch on the bed, but maybe if I made an attempt at normal conversation, he'd pay attention. There was a chance he was frightened, another captive who had been twisted like Lauren. I needed to get through to him.

My efforts were ridiculous and ineffective.

"What's your name?" I asked loudly.

He reappeared in the bedroom, wheeling his cart back toward the exit. He still didn't look at me or respond in any way.

"Wait," I said desperately. "I need your help. Talk to me, please. You don't have to be afraid."

His gray eyes finally riveted on me, narrowed in anger. "Of course I do," he hissed. "Do you know what he'd do to me if I helped you? I have a future to think about. I'm not about to fuck it up by pissing off the boss. Especially not for some whore."

I flinched at the word *whore*, but I plowed on. "I can help you. If he's threatened you, my friends can—"

He barked out a laugh. "You think I'm being threatened into staying here? I'm paying my dues, you stupid bitch. Don't fucking talk to me ever again. And don't you dare tell him I spoke to you, or I'll—"

"You'll what?" Andrés interrupted the man, his voice deadly calm.

My captor had approached far too quietly, appearing in the open doorway out of nowhere. The man paled and swallowed hard before slowly turning to face Andrés.

"She was asking for help," he said quickly, his voice hitching. "I was just saying—"

Andrés took a menacing step toward him. "You were threatening her. You were looking at her. I told you not to look at her. You're lucky she's covered. Do you know what I do to men who look at what's mine?"

The boy shook his head and retreated back into the bedroom, moving toward me. He didn't make it two steps before Andrés' hand closed around his upper arm, vise-like. He jerked the boy's body toward his, getting into his personal space.

"Look at her again, and you'll lose an eye," Andrés said softly. "Threaten her again, and it'll be the last thing you ever do. You're relieved of your duties. Never come into my quarters again."

He nodded, but he couldn't seem to manage to speak. Andrés released him, pushing him away in disgust.

"Leave," he bit out.

The boy hastened to comply, practically tripping over his feet to get to his cart and out of the bedroom. He disappeared further into the suite, Andrés' imposing form blocking my view.

I couldn't have watched him leave, anyway. All my focus was on the terrifying man who'd just threatened to mutilate and murder one of the men who worked for him. Lauren had said Andrés was *nice*. The woman was obviously even more warped than I'd imagined. My captor radiated cold fury, his scarred face twisted in anger.

I shrank back, scooting across the bed until the chain jerked at my collar.

He sucked in a deep breath, and his fierce countenance eased as his eyes focused on my fearful expression. He took a step toward me, and I tried to move farther away. But all I accomplished was pulling at the leather around my neck. There was nowhere to go, no way to escape.

He reached for me, and I flinched. That didn't seem to concern him. He cupped my cheek in his big hand, hooking his thumb beneath my jaw so I couldn't look away.

"Calm, *cosita*," he murmured, stroking my hair with his free hand. "You're safe. He won't hurt you."

"I'm not worried about *him*," I said shrilly. "You're the one who just calmly threatened to cut out someone's eye. And I'm chained to your bed. Naked. I'm freaking afraid of *you*." I brought my hands up to push him away, but he caught my wrists and pinned them behind me at the small of my back. He held them there with one hand and resumed stroking my hair.

"He's lucky I didn't kill him for threatening you," Andrés responded. "I ordered him not to speak to you or look at you. He did both. I can't have a man in my organization who thinks he can disobey me."

"So you murder anyone who defies you?" I asked, my voice shaking. *I'd* defied him. I'd tried to kill him.

"I will never harm you, Samantha," he said in reassuring tones as he continued to pet me. "No matter how defiant you may be." A smile ghosted around his lips.

"But you spanked me," I argued. "You said you want to punish me."

"Only to correct your misbehavior," he said, sounding as though it were the most rational response in the world. "I'd never do anything that would damage you. But yes, I won't hesitate to punish you when you deserve it."

"I don't *deserve* any of this," I countered hotly, struggling uselessly against his grip.

His gaze turned inward, his lips thinning. "Maybe not. But you're mine now, and there's no going back. I'm keeping you, and you're my responsibility."

"I'm not yours," I insisted. "And you're not *keeping* me. You said that's your brother's decision. Did you tell him you believe

I'm FBI? Have you both seen reason and decided to let me go before the Bureau comes for you?"

"I'll let him discuss this with you," he replied.

He released my wrists and wrapped one hand behind my nape, pulling me toward him. I was forced to scramble across the mattress and get to my feet.

"Behave," he ordered, squeezing my neck slightly in warning. Then he called out in Spanish.

Cristian Moreno appeared in the doorway, flanked by two men who were nearly as massive as Andrés.

My stomach dropped, and a horrible memory of Cristian's knife slicing through my flesh flashed across my mind. I took a small step back, not realizing I was positioning myself closer to Andrés.

His grip on my neck eased, his fingers threading through my hair to massage my scalp. It helped ground me in the present, saving me from being thrust back into panic and choking terror.

Cristian's dark eyes—so like his brother's—watched my movements, coldly calculating. It occurred to me that I'd moved away from one tormentor to find shelter with another, and I eased away from Andrés. His fingers tightened in my hair, holding me firmly in place. He waited a few seconds, then released the tension and resumed massaging me once he was certain that I wasn't going to struggle.

"You are Samantha Browning," Cristian announced. "Andrés is convinced, and I had my people look into your story. You're a fed." He sneered the last.

I lifted my chin. "So you'll let me go?"

"No."

"But you have to," I insisted in a rush. "If you keep me here, my friends—"

"They won't find you here," he cut me off with cool

certainty. "One of my shell corporations owns this building. They won't trace it back to me."

"They know I was investigating your organization before you took me," I said. "They'll suspect you're behind my disappearance. They'll follow you until you lead them to me."

"Then it's a good thing I don't come here often. This is my little brother's home."

Home? I thought, baffled. This entire freaking building was Andrés' *home?* How much money did the Moreno family have at their disposal?

"Besides," he continued. "It's not like I'm stupid enough to get out of my car out on the street. And your people don't have surveillance cameras in our private garage for this building. Which, I'll remind you, they have no idea I own. So, Samantha Browning, no one is going to find you."

My heart sank. If anyone could hack into Cristian Moreno's life and trace his financials and properties, it was me. And I was trapped here, isolated from the Bureau and completely cut off from technology.

"You're going to kill me," I surmised, my blood running cold. There was no reason to keep me around anymore. He'd checked into my story, confirmed my identity, and he still didn't care that I was FBI. He wasn't intimidated in the least.

"No," he said again. "You're going to work for me from now on."

"What?" I asked, all the air leaving my lungs.

"You're going to erase all the evidence the FBI has on me. You will protect me and my business from them. If you do, I'll let you live."

A staunch refusal teased at the tip of my tongue, but I held it back. If he wanted me to log into the FBI database, that meant he'd have to give me access to the internet. I could get a message to Dex.

"Okay," I agreed quickly. "I'll need a computer."

Too quickly.

He laughed, a hard, cold sound. "Do you think I'm a fool? You'll contact the feds as soon as you get online. Now, I could just threaten to kill you if you try, but then you'd be useless to me if you're dead. So, I'm going to leave you with my brother for a while longer. I'm sure he'll break you in for me. He's so good at that."

Andrés growled, and his fingers tightened in my hair. He bit out something in Spanish, too fast for me to catch a single word.

Cristian smirked. "All right, *hermanito*," he drawled. "You can keep this one. Just make sure she's useful to me, and we won't have any problems."

"Give me a month," Andrés replied, resuming the calm, assured demeanor that so unnerved me.

"You can have three weeks," Cristian countered. "I don't have time for you to play with your new toy. Break her, or I'll find another way to ensure her cooperation."

Andrés nodded his agreement, as though their discussion of my fate wasn't horrifying enough to make nausea curl in my stomach.

"You can't do this to me," I managed faintly.

Andrés' fingers hooked through the back of the collar, pulling it tight around my throat. I could still breathe, but I was very aware of his control.

"Quiet, *cosita*," he commanded softly. "It's done."

The world blurred with my tears, and I could barely make out Cristian's suit-clad form retreating from the suite, his guards in tow. When they were out of sight, my tormentor pulled me against his hard body, and I sobbed into his chest.

CHAPTER 6

"You haven't eaten, *sirenita*," he murmured as he stroked his big hand up and down my back.

I sniffled against him, collecting my thoughts as my wits returned. I tried to push away from him, but his arms firmed around me, trapping me against his hard body. He allowed me just enough space so I could lift my face to glower up at him.

"I didn't want to be drugged again," I said hotly, a clear accusation.

"I don't need to drug you to keep you compliant." His lips twisted in distaste. "I wouldn't do that."

"You drugged me last night," I reminded him.

He frowned at me. "You were hurting. I was sparing you more pain. Would you have preferred to suffer?"

"Yes," I defied him. "Then I could have at least kept the dignity of my clothing. You stripped me as soon as I was unconscious."

His brows rose. "Do you really think you'd still be wearing

clothes if I didn't want you to? You can't hide from me, Samantha."

His fingers fisted in the sheet at my lower back, and he pulled at the soft fabric until it loosened and slid down my body. I twisted in his hold, struggling to cover myself. But my movements only made the sheet shimmy down my legs, leaving me completely bare against my captor. He still wore his sharply-tailored suit. The dichotomy of power was painfully obvious: he was fully dressed, while I was writhing naked in his arms, a collar still locked around my throat in a sign of his ownership.

"You shouldn't have covered yourself," he reprimanded.

"So you would have paraded me naked in front of everyone? In front of your brother? How fucked up is your family?"

His jaw firmed. "I would have covered you before I invited Cristian in. I don't let other men look at what's mine."

I shoved at his chest, accomplishing nothing. "I'm not your property."

His hand fisted in my hair at my nape, tugging my head back and trapping me beneath his black stare. "You could be," he said smoothly. "I could make you my plaything, my eager little fucktoy. And I think you would be eager, Samantha. Your body aches to be touched."

I squirmed against him, my blood pounding through my veins. "I don't want to be your..." The words died on my tongue. They were so vile and vulgar, I couldn't bear to repeat them. "I don't want you to touch me," I managed.

"You do," he countered coolly. "But you're still afraid. You're so innocent, you're scared for me to touch your little pussy. That ends now. Your innocence is mine. Your pleasure is mine. You will accept my touch."

"I won't," I hissed. "I won't invite you to rape me."

"I will never rape you," he replied calmly. "And I won't fuck you at your invitation. You will beg and weep for my cock before I give you what you want."

I shuddered in his arms, completely overwhelmed. In the space of a day, I'd been stripped of my rights, my dignity. And the way he spoke about breaking me with such calm assurance rocked me to my core. In his mind, my surrender was a foregone conclusion.

Fuck. That. He might spank me, but I could handle it. A little sting on my flesh wasn't going to break me. I glared up at him, defiant.

"Go ahead and *punish* me, then," I challenged. "You can spank me all you want, but I'll never beg you to violate me."

One corner of his lips ticked up with perverse amusement. "I do enjoy a challenge," he purred, his pupils dilating. I felt his cock stiffen against my belly. He leaned down, his lips skimming across my cheek before tickling the shell of my ear. "You enjoyed your spanking, so it's hardly a punishment," he said, the whispered words threading through my mind, reaching deep inside and revealing the truth that I didn't want to acknowledge. "But that's not what I have planned for you. You owe me an orgasm. Your first. I want it. I'm going to make you come hard, so your body has no doubt that I'm your Master. I can give you pleasure. I can give you pain. Obedience is taught through discipline: punishment and reward. It's time you learned exactly what that means."

I trembled, my heart hammering in my chest. I hadn't realized that I'd stopped struggling. He was too strong, too powerful. And his crass words overwhelmed me more effectively than any physical show of force.

His erection pressed against me, thick and hard. "Do you feel what you do to me, *sirenita?*" he asked, his voice rough with lust. "You are so beautiful when you're like this; your little body shuddering in my arms. Are you frightened? Or aroused?"

His teeth nipped at my ear, and I sucked in a sharp breath. "Or both?" His hand slid down the length of my spine, caressed the curve of my bare bottom, and dipped between my thighs. He hummed his approval when I whimpered. "Both," he concluded with dark satisfaction as he found the slickness on my labia.

He pressed a tender kiss against my neck, just below my ear. My nerve endings crackled with awareness, and my skin pebbled.

"Stay," he murmured before finally releasing me.

I remained frozen where he'd left me, my body tingling with fear and something else I didn't want to acknowledge. I watched him with wide eyes as he crossed to the chest of drawers and retrieved a few items. This time, he slipped them into his pocket before I could make out what he'd selected.

When he approached me once again, he held a length of black cloth wrapped around his fist. I took a step back, wariness making the fine hairs on the back of my neck stand on end.

"I like watching your lovely eyes when I'm playing with you, but this will make you more aware of what I'm making you feel," he told me.

"What?" I asked faintly, but I didn't have long to wonder what he meant.

He lifted the cloth to my face and pressed it over my eyes. I closed them automatically, and I felt him knot the material firmly at the back of my head. Panic spiked as soon as the darkness closed around me, and I lifted my hands to rip the blindfold away.

He caught my wrists immediately, guiding them back down to my sides.

"Settle, *cosita*," he cooed. "This isn't going to hurt."

"I'm scared," I admitted on a shaky whisper, the words leaving me without thought.

A low, rumbling sound rolled over my skin. "If I were a good man, I'd tell you not to be frightened. But I'm not a good man." He pulled one of my hands forward, pressing my palm against his bulging erection. "I like having you at my mercy, Samantha. I like when you tremble and whimper for me."

"Please," I whined, trying to tug my hand away from his hard length.

He held me fast. "Just like that," he said with rough approval. "But soon, you'll be begging me to touch you, not to release you."

He finally, mercifully guided my hand away from his terrifying arousal. He released my wrists and gripped my waist, lifting my body as though I weighed nothing. The dark world spun around me as he moved my body and positioned it where he wanted. My back settled onto the soft mattress, and I instantly tried to roll away, disoriented and frightened. I could hear my blood rushing in my ears, and I was very aware of the heat of his hands on my flesh. His masculine scent infused the air I desperately breathed, until I thought I would drown in it.

His steady grip kept me pinned to the bed. He grasped my wrists again, tugging them above my head. Cool metal snapped in place around them, a sensation that wasn't entirely unfamiliar to me; we'd trained with handcuffs at the FBI academy. As soon as his grip left my wrists, I tried to pull my arms down to cover my exposed body. They jerked against the unyielding metal, and his hands returned to my forearms, pressing them down into the mattress.

"Don't struggle," he ordered. "You'll only bruise yourself. I'm interested to see how easily your pretty skin marks up, but not like this."

His words made my fear spike, and I twisted beneath him.

His palm settled over my throat, his long fingers wrapping around my neck.

"*Cosita*," he said, warning imbuing the word. "I gave you an order. Settle down. I'm not going to hurt you."

"But you want to," I whispered tremulously, going utterly still. "You want to break me."

His hand remained at my throat, but his other stroked my hair. "I won't break you. But I am going to tame you."

"I don't want to be tamed. I want to go home." Tears sank into the black cloth that covered my eyes.

"You're scared," he said softly, still petting me while holding my neck in a gentle grip. "That's natural. But it will pass. You have to trust me, Samantha."

"Trust you?" I asked on a maddened laugh. It was impossible, insane.

"You will trust me. You will give me everything. Trust that I will take care of you. I will give you pain, but you don't yet understand the pleasure I can offer. Now, be a good girl and don't pull against the cuffs."

"Fuck you," I hissed, my terror morphing into rage. It was too intense to bear, so my mind redirected the fear into anger.

"Mind your language," he rebuked. His hand tightened around my throat. I could still breathe, but he pressed down just hard enough to restrict the blood flow to my brain. I'd trained in how to choke a man out, so I knew what was happening to me. If he squeezed too hard, I'd slip into unconsciousness. Maybe even die.

Just as panic began to sap my mind, he released the pressure. Blood rushed back to my head, and a strange high I'd never experienced soared through me. I let out a long sigh, and my entire body relaxed as a pleasant buzz quieted my mind. All my fear, my conflicting emotions, melted away, and I floated for a few ecstatic seconds.

"That's better," he praised, his fingertips skimming along the line of my vulnerable artery at my neck. My skin felt electric beneath his touch, *alive*. A low moan left my chest, and I arched my head back, further exposing my throat to him in mindless invitation for more.

"Stay just like that," he commanded. His touch left my throat, his heat receding as the mattress shifted beneath me. I was aware of his hands on my ankles, one after the other. He spread my legs wide, and supple leather cuffs wrapped around my ankles to lock them in place. I didn't tug against the restraints this time. I lay perfectly still and relaxed, relishing the quiet in my mind. This was much preferable to unrelenting terror.

Then he touched my sex, and instinctive fear surged back. My entire body jerked, but the restraints he'd used to secure me kept my body stretched out for him.

He gently shushed me, continuing to lightly caress me despite my struggles. "This part will be over soon," he said, his voice almost tender. There was something slick on his fingers, a thicker substance than my own arousal. He carefully coated my labia, his fingers dipping between them before circling around my clit. I gasped and shuddered as he teased around the tightly-packed little bundle of nerves, pleasure lighting up my system despite my mounting fear. The longer his touch lingered directly on my sex, the more intense my terror grew. My entire body was shaking by the time he finally withdrew his hand, leaving a strange heat behind, as though he'd branded my sensitive flesh with his touch.

It wasn't an unpleasant heat. In fact, it tingled rather than burning. I squirmed and tried to press my legs together to stop the sensation. The cuffs held my ankles fast, and I was left quivering and helpless to stop what was happening to my body.

"What are you doing to me?" I asked on a throaty whisper.

His fingers trailed beneath my breasts, spiraling upward and inward until they reached my peaked nipples. The same slick substance coated the tight buds.

"This is arousal cream," he told me. "Not that you need it to feel pleasure. You've already soaked my hand when I've spanked you. This is to help you get past the fear. Soon, you'll be desperate for me to touch your pretty pussy. You'll beg for me to grant you release. Need will outweigh fear. Then we can move forward with your training."

"I don't want to be trained," I protested on a whine. The same tingling had set in around my nipples, making me squirm as my body instinctively sought stimulation.

He chuckled. "Most wild things don't. And you are a wild thing, aren't you? You're innocent, untouched. But your body hungers to feel pleasure. Once we get past your fears, I suspect you'll be a very greedy girl. You'll crave my touch. You've already responded so well to your spankings. You'll learn to respond to positive reinforcement, as well."

"You make it sound like I'm an animal," I forced out, trying to ignore the heat that flared between my legs. "I'm not."

"No, you're not," he agreed, his hands skimming down my sides, tracing the slight flare of my hips. "You're a woman. But you're *mine*. That means you're whatever I want you to be. My plaything, my pet. Your sole purpose is to please me, to serve me. I'm your Master now, and it's time you understood what that means."

"But I—"

"Shhh." He blew a stream of cool air over my nipples as he shushed me, and my protest ended on a soft cry as the tight peaks lit up with sensation. My back arched, offering my breasts up to him. His approving rumble vibrated against my skin as he pressed his lips against the soft swells, leaving feather-light kisses in a random, scorching pattern across my flesh. A strange, strangled sound left my chest, and rational thought evaporated.

"Has any man ever touched your breasts?" he asked before flicking his hot tongue against my tight, aching nipples.

A rough shout tore from my throat, and I thrust myself toward the delicious heat of his mouth. But my cruel restraints held me in place, and he moved away to blow another torturously cold stream of air over them. I whined and writhed, acting like the wild thing he claimed I was.

"Answer me," he prompted. "Be honest, and I'll kiss your pretty pink nipples."

"No," I said, the confession leaving me in a rapid-fire stream. "Not really. Not like this. I went to a convention once. I dressed up like The Dark Phoenix. From *X-Men*. Cosplay, you know? So this guy was Wolverine. I met him at an after-party. He kissed me and copped a feel. But it was over my costume. So I guess that doesn't really count. Does it? I used to think so. But I—" My lust-addled speech ended on a sharp cry when his lips touched my nipple, his tongue swirling around it before flicking the peak.

Keening, animal sounds left me in a steady stream as he continued to stimulate my breasts, alternating between plucking at my nipples with his fingers and kissing the sting away with his soft lips. My head thrashed against the pillow, and I began to lift my hips up in wanton invitation. My core pulsed to the point of aching, my clit throbbing in time with my heartbeat.

His palm rested on my belly, below my navel and tantalizingly close to my heated sex. His fingers traced little circular patterns just above my clit, teasing.

"And your pretty little pussy," he prompted. "Has any man ever touched you here?"

"No," I whimpered, my mind too far gone to worry over confessing my most embarrassing secrets.

"Poor little virgin," he murmured. "You need to be touched, don't you?"

"I... I want..." I bit my lip, barely holding back.

"Tell your Master what you want," he cajoled. "Tell me how you like to be touched. Do you put your fingers inside your tight pussy? Or do you rub your little clit?"

"I don't. I can't. It's..."

Dirty. Wrong.

Dirty little girl.

Something awful stirred at the edges of my mind. I shied away from it. Instead, I focused on the heat that was consuming me, the tingling in my flesh, the gentle brush of Andrés' fingers against my hypersensitive skin.

"You don't touch yourself?" His deep voice was colored with surprise. "You've never made yourself come?"

"I... No." Shame made my cheeks flame, but the heat in my sex kept me distracted. I couldn't see, couldn't think. All I could do was feel and listen to Andrés' lilting voice as he asked me the most devious questions.

"So you've never had an orgasm at all?"

I shook my head and tried to lift my hips again, but his palm on my belly kept me pinned down.

"Then let me show you what your body is capable of," he said, the words distorted by his hungry growl. "In the future, you will beg me for this."

His hand finally shifted down to where I craved it most. One thick finger parted my wet folds, and my entire body tightened as he slowly slid it inside my channel. He felt huge as my inner muscles gripped him, torn between welcoming him in and pushing him out. Emotion swelled along with sensation, fear and pleasure crackling through my system. A harsh sob tore from my chest, and my tears wet the blindfold.

"Too much," I gasped out, twisting against my restraints. "It's too much. Please—"

"Don't fight it," he commanded, finding a secret spot at the front of my inner walls. He crooked his finger against it. At the same time, he brought his thumb down on my clit and rubbed in a demanding rhythm. "Come for me, *sirenita*."

Pleasure lit up my entire being, tearing through me with the force of a tidal wave. A raw scream echoed through the room as all my muscles tensed and shook. Bliss wracked my body, my mind. The world fell away as unrelenting bliss sang through my veins, sweeping away my lingering fear. All that existed was Andrés: his touch, his scent, his *power*. He'd wrung this unknown ecstasy from my soul, ruthlessly subjugating my being with earth-shattering pleasure.

My sex tingled as he continued stroking me. Little lightning strikes of residual pleasure tormented me, making me tremble. I fully surrendered to sensation and sank back against the mattress, utterly sated and thoroughly conquered.

CHAPTER 7

Andrés pressed tender kisses against my slightly sore wrists when he removed the handcuffs that kept me bound to the bed. I didn't move once I was free, and I didn't stir when he unlocked the collar from around my neck. My eyes remained closed when he unknotted the blindfold; I wasn't ready to face reality yet.

I continued floating in quiet bliss as he unbuckled the cuffs around my ankles and carefully lifted my body up into his strong arms. He cradled me against his chest as he carried me, taking long, sure strides toward an unknown destination. I remained carefully cocooned in warm darkness, clinging to pleasure so I didn't have to face the horror of my defeat.

I noted that his chest was bare against my skin, his dusting of dark hair tickling my cheek. He must have removed his clothes while I lay boneless and mindless in my post-orgasmic haze.

The world tilted, and my eyes fluttered open when my feet touched cool tiles. I watched with detached interest as Andrés reached around me and turned the knob for the shower. Water sprayed from every direction, multiple showerheads raining down. It seemed awfully decadent compared to my low water pressure, single showerhead setup at my shabby townhouse.

My heart squeezed, and I quickly smothered my thoughts before they could start firing again. I didn't want to think about my townhouse. About how far I was from home, even though I was located just across town. I might as well be on another planet.

Andrés gripped my hips and guided me into the glass-fronted shower stall. The water was uncomfortably hot, and my pale skin turned pink almost instantly. He seemed to notice everything about my body, so he immediately turned the temperature to something more bearable.

He stayed positioned behind me, and I was grateful for that. If I didn't have to look at him, I didn't have to process the fact that he was fully naked in the shower with me. I'd felt his erection, and that had been terrifying enough.

He didn't allow me much of a reprieve. His hands closed around my waist, pulling my body back against his so I could feel his hard length pressing into my ass. I tried and failed to swallow a whimper as some of my fear resurfaced, despite my best efforts to remain lost in lingering pleasure.

"You're still afraid of my cock," he surmised, but he didn't move away at the sound of my distress. "But you're not afraid when I touch you anymore, are you?"

To prove his point, he pumped soap into his hand from a dispenser on the wall before returning his touch to my breasts. He massaged them gently, and I moaned as his slick palms grazed my nipples. They were still tender from the arousal cream, and he made sure to tease the tight buds as he washed away the substance that lingered on my skin. My flesh tingled, but not as intensely as it had when he'd first applied the cream.

One hand skimmed down my belly to carefully wash my

sex, his other remaining at my breasts to play with my nipples. I shuddered and leaned back against him for support as pleasure flooded my body again, the tension at my core building.

"You are a greedy girl," he said, his voice heavy with satisfaction. "I knew you'd be like this. But you don't deserve a reward. Not yet."

A humiliating whine slipped through my lips when he stopped touching me intimately. He grasped my shoulders and turned me to face him. My eyes darted around the bathroom, avoiding looking at his imposing body.

He caught my chin between his thumb and forefinger, lifting my face to his. I made the mistake of glancing up, and I found myself trapped in his steady black stare.

"You don't like looking at me," he said, an acknowledgement of fact. "My scars frighten you."

"It's not that," I admitted, the words tumbling out of me in my nervousness. "I mean, you're scary. But your scars aren't why you scare me. Well, kind of, because they mean you're violent. But this is just a tic I have. I don't really like looking at anyone. I have to for work, sometimes. It takes effort. It makes me uncomfortable. I mean..." I finally managed to end my rambling confession. Why was I telling him all this?

Because I babbled when I was nervous, that's why. Especially around alpha males, and especially when they turned their full, potent attention on me to impose their will. I did it with Jason, and I definitely did it with Dex. I could barely look at my best friend under normal circumstances, even when I didn't have a reason to be intimidated. I was always nervous around him, in that butterflies-in-my-stomach kind of way.

Not the way Andrés made me nervous. *Nervous* wasn't an intense enough word to express the enormity of what he made me feel. It was why I couldn't look away once he captured me in his dark gaze. I never maintained eye contact with anyone like I did with him. He didn't give me a choice in the matter.

He considered me for a long, tense moment, his jaw tight. "Would it make you more comfortable if I told you I didn't get these scars in a fight?"

I blinked at him. "What?" That didn't make any sense. "Then how—?"

"That's enough questions," he cut me off. "I am a violent man, but I won't harm you. I'll never let anyone harm you. You're mine, which means you'll be protected. It also means you'll accept my touch and my cock. Look at me." When he said it this time, I knew he wasn't ordering me to look him in the eye. "All of me," he prompted when I hesitated. "Now, *cosita*." The last was dark with warning, and my eyes flicked down his body before I could contemplate further defiance.

Once my gaze landed on his cock, I couldn't look away. I might not have been with a man in real life, but I watched porn. And, despite his scarred body, Andrés could have starred in some of the most depraved videos I'd seen. He was huge, long and thick. His cockhead was purple with arousal, and a feminine part of me marveled that this reaction was for *me*.

"Touch me," he bit out, his control slipping. I gasped when his cock bobbed, straining toward me.

I reached out and tentatively brushed my fingertips along his shaft. His skin was soft and smooth, but he was hard beneath my touch. He hissed in a sharp breath, and I felt him pulse under my fingers. I stared in fascination. I was doing this to him, affecting him the way he'd affected me. A strange sense of heady power teased at the corners of my mind, and I struggled to resist the perverted satisfaction. I shouldn't enjoy my captor's lustful reaction to me.

But it was undeniable that my body instinctively reacted to him, so the knowledge that the balance of power wasn't entirely stacked against me gave me some courage. I wrapped my hand around his length and stroked him from base to head.

"Good girl," he said, his voice more ragged than I'd ever heard it. He was at the edge of his control. I wanted to push him over that edge, to break him the way he'd broken me.

He reached between us with his soap-slicked hand and applied a liberal amount. When I slid my fist back, it glided across his flesh, and he groaned.

"Do you know how hot it is watching you touch me?" he ground out. "Knowing I'm the first man you've touched. The only man you will ever touch. Your first and only, my sweet virgin." A bead of moisture formed on his cockhead, quickly washed away by the cascading warm water.

Emboldened by his words, I used my free hand to cup his balls, gently exploring their shape and weight.

He rasped out something in Spanish that I suspected was a very dirty word. A sly smile tugged at the corners of my lips, and I struggled to smother it. He was coming apart beneath my touch, losing control. The heady sense of power that I'd been resisting finally settled over me, and I handled his shaft with greater confidence.

"Naughty *gatita*," he said hoarsely. His hand fisted in my wet hair, tugging hard enough to make my scalp light up with awareness. "Very naughty." He cursed again, and his grip on my coppery strands increased to the edge of pain. It only served to spur me on.

"Make me come, *sirenita*," he ordered in an obvious effort to take back control with a command.

But the way he pumped his hips toward me to increase my pace let me know who truly held the power in this moment. He came apart on a harsh shout, his hot seed lashing out to coat my stomach, the heat of it lingering on my flesh even as the water washed it away.

His body pressed against mine, backing me up to the tiled wall as he braced his hands against either side of me. He leaned his forehead against mine, breathing hard.

"That's enough," he said with a shudder.

I finally moved my hand away, satisfied at the sight of his undoing.

A sharp grin suddenly lit his features. "Time for your reward, *gatita*."

"What?" I asked, disconcerted by his jovial mood. I'd expected his anger at being broken under my inexperienced hands, maybe even shame.

"Good girls get positive reinforcement." He tenderly stroked my cheek. "Remember, my pet?" He leaned in so his hot breath played across my neck as he whispered in my ear. "Your Master is training you to please him. You did very well. You've earned a reward."

"No," I said, shaken. How had this turned against me? I'd been riding high, triumphant. He twisted my victory into yet another defeat.

"You don't get to refuse, pet."

"I'm not your pet."

"Aren't you? You wanted to act like a naughty *gatita*. You will be tamed, Samantha."

"I won't."

"Your little pussy wouldn't get so wet for me if you didn't want this. You wouldn't have come so hard while you were bound and at my mercy."

"That's so fucked up. You're—"

His hand clamped over my mouth, his long fingers pressing into my cheek almost to the point of pain.

"We're going to have to work on that tongue of yours. I have a pretty gag that I think will suit you well until you can learn to mind your language when you speak to me."

My eyes flew wide, and I tried to shake my head. His hand firmed on my face, stilling the sign of my denial.

"Hush now, *gatita*. It's time for your reward."

I brought my hands up and wrapped them around his forearm, clawing at his flesh with my fingernails in an attempt to free my mouth from his cruel hold.

He growled and released me, but only long enough so he could roughly turn my body to face the wall. His weight pressed against my back, pushing my breasts hard against the cold tiles. I yelped and tried to push back, but my hands slipped uselessly against the slick wall. He wrapped one hand around my throat, squeezing. This time, he applied enough pressure to restrict my airflow. I thrashed on wild instinct, but his weight kept me pinned and powerless.

Please, I tried to beg him to release me, but the word couldn't make it past his hold on my throat, and a strangled sound emerged instead.

"Breathe, *cosita*," he urged, not letting up.

I barely managed to suck in shallow breaths. My head began to spin, and I stopped fighting as the strength seeped out of my body. His free hand dipped between my legs, gathering up the slick arousal that inexplicably coated my inner thighs. He moved his touch farther back, trailing his slick forefinger over a sensitive patch of skin between my sex and asshole, then...

No. My lips formed the word, but I wasn't capable of wasting any air to make a sound of protest.

His finger pressed against my tight ring of muscles. I clenched, resisting. He nipped at my earlobe, and the little jolt of pain sizzled through me, reaching my core and making it throb. As it contracted, his finger slipped inside me. He barely penetrated me, but I felt horribly full and utterly trapped. My knees began to tremble as I continued to struggle for oxygen.

"Are you sorry for scratching me?" he asked calmly, as though he wasn't degrading me in a way I'd never wanted to experience.

I managed a thin whine and nodded slightly.

He kissed the hollow beneath my ear. "Good girl. Don't do it again."

He pressed forward, sealing the rebuke by sliding his long finger all the way inside me. My muscles rippled around him, burning as my body tried to resist the intrusion. Something dark stirred low in my belly, tension coiling at my core.

He finally released my throat, and I gasped in a desperate breath. The rush of oxygen went straight to my head, and the world spun around me. Remaining seated deep inside my most forbidden area, he caught my falling weight with his other strong arm around my waist. I sagged back against him, sucking in air. His hand splayed beneath my bottom, bracing me as a second finger found my wet channel. He eased inside my sex, and I could feel him filling me everywhere.

It was too much to bear, too humiliating. Too stimulating. Rational thought had been obliterated in the wake of the primal imperative to breathe, to survive. My body could only shake and submit to what he was doing to me. All my sensitive nerve endings lit up, and the tension that had been coiling deep inside me released, leaving me on a ragged shout. My muscles clenched around his fingers as I found shameful ecstasy under his ruthless touch. He gently pumped in and out of me, making my nerve endings crackle and dance. Sparks of pleasure raced up my spine to flood my mind, overwhelming all my senses.

The spinning world flickered around me, darkness sliding across my vision. I surrendered to it, closing my eyes as he continued to hold my weakened body upright.

His fingers finally slid out of me, leaving me feeling

strangely empty; hollowed out and utterly defeated. The water stopped falling around us, and he lifted me up in his arms again as though I weighed nothing. He was so strong, so hard and unyielding. A fine tremor raced through my exhausted body, the only movement I was capable of.

He wrapped a warm, fluffy towel around me. I snuggled into it, hiding my face between the soft fabric and his sculpted chest, as though I could simply sink into the warmth and disappear. Anything would be preferable to facing the shame of what he'd just done to me.

I'd thought I'd regained some power over him when I'd made him come, but he'd quickly demonstrated how powerless I truly was. His punitive touch had brought me pleasure, pleasure I hadn't wanted but had been wrought from my body by his masterful hands regardless of my wishes.

He'd claimed he wasn't going to break me, but in that moment, I felt completely shattered.

CHAPTER 8

Andrés carefully dried my body, rubbing the soft towel over every inch of my sensitized skin. My nipples and sex ached, and my bottom burned slightly, a constant, cruel reminder of how he'd subjugated my entire being.

When he was satisfied that I was dry, something tugged at my damp hair. I registered the rhythmic pull of brush bristles through my hair, massaging my scalp. It made my head tingle, a pleasant sensation I tried to deny.

"I'm not a doll," I mumbled, keeping my eyes closed to avoid facing reality. I remained still and compliant where he'd placed me in his lap. I couldn't muster up the will to fight.

"Hmmm," he mused, continuing to run the brush through my hair in methodical strokes. "You're not a pet. You're not a doll. Is there anything you do want to be, *sirenita?*"

"What does that mean?" I asked instead of answering his question. He was teasing me, and I refused to rise to it. If I did, he'd likely devise another devious way to prove to me that I would be whatever he wanted me to be.

"A literal translation would be *little mermaid*," he said.

I finally opened my eyes to study his face. Was he mocking me?

"You mean, like the Disney princess?" I asked.

He chuckled. "It's an endearment. It means I find you beautiful." He traced the line of my lower lip with his thumb. "Sensual."

I blinked at him. No one had ever called me beautiful. And definitely not sensual. I was the awkward geek who was barely worth noticing, unless it was to make fun of me.

"You don't believe me," he said, reading my confusion. "Do you think my cock would get so hard for you if I didn't want you? You are lovely, *sirenita*."

"You're trying to manipulate me," I accused, not quite believing him. Maybe he got turned on by dominating women, and my physical appearance had nothing to do with it. That made much more sense. "It won't work."

"It already is working. I'm not lying when I say I find you beautiful. But everything I do to you is a manipulation, and I won't pretend otherwise. You're being very sweet and well behaved right now. If I'd known how obedient you'd become when I played with your ass, I would have filled it sooner. You came so hard for me. I thought you were going to pass out. I think you enjoy being manipulated, being shaped into my good girl."

I scowled at him. "You're a bastard."

"That might be true. But you will learn to speak to me with respect. There's a consequence coming for that, but right now, you need to eat."

I almost said I wasn't hungry, the urge to defy him automatic. But my stomach was very aware that I hadn't eaten in over twenty-four hours. I still didn't know what time it was, but it was now dark outside. That meant I hadn't eaten since dinner the night before, because I hadn't trusted the breakfast Andrés had sent up for me.

"Okay," I agreed, trying to sound resentful and failing. I was far too hungry.

Now that I'd finally opened my eyes, I noted that Andrés was seated on the edge of the bed, with me perched on his lap. He reached around me and tugged at the small food cart. A silver dome covered the plate, and when he removed it, I realized that my wasted breakfast had been removed and replaced with a mouthwatering steak.

My cheeks heated even as my stomach growled. That meant someone had come into the bedroom while we were in the shower. Had they heard my lustful scream?

I didn't have much time to worry over it, because my basic needs were too insistent. A jug of water sat on the cart beside two empty glasses. I reached for it and filled one, immediately gulping it down.

"You didn't drink anything today, either?" Andrés asked, his voice heavy with disapproval.

"I thought you might drug me again," I reminded him.

"And you believe I won't now?"

I shrugged. "I figured that steak is huge enough for two people. There are two glasses, one water jug. So I'm assuming that you're not going to drug yourself too, you know?" I poured another glass and drank half of it before moving to pick up the utensils. I was so famished, all I could think about was cutting into the steak and getting some food in my system. No wonder I'd been so weak in my attempts to fight my captor.

He caught my hand before I could touch the silverware and guided it back to my lap. He also took the water glass from me and set it down beside the plate.

"Do you really think I'm going to let you handle a fork and knife?" he asked drily.

I glowered at him. "I just want some fucking food. I'm starving."

He frowned, his scar deepening to a disapproving slash. "I will train your tongue later," he warned. "And I'm sure you're hungry, which is more pressing than your punishment. I will always see to your wellbeing, Samantha, but don't continue to test me."

"I wasn't going to use the knife on you," I said honestly. "I just want to eat."

"I'm going to take care of you, *cosita*. Trust me."

I snorted. "You're not really giving me a choice. Is it trust if you don't have a choice? Probably not. No, I don't think it is. Nope. Definitely not."

He studied me for a moment, something like a smile tugging at the corners of his lips. "Do you always speak this way?"

"What way?"

"You talk very fast. Like you're speaking every thought that comes into your head as it comes to you. Are you doing it because you're nervous around me? Is this the same as why you don't like looking at people?"

"I mean, I guess," I admitted. "But I don't talk like this because I'm nervous. Well, I guess it's worse when I'm nervous. I just have a lot of thoughts, and they kind of pop out, like you said. My brain is really busy all the time. Like, my thoughts never slow down. I can't focus on only one thing at a time, unless it's really challenging."

"You focus on me quite intently," he said, grinning with smug satisfaction. "Does that mean you find me *challenging*?"

"It means I find you terrifying," I shot back, but there was less malice in my tone than I'd intended. There was something odd about speaking to him so earnestly. I'd never been able to hold back vocalizing my thoughts when pressed by a domineering male, but this was different. I didn't feel particularly nervous at the moment. I was too concerned with my need to eat, and Andrés' arms were relaxed around me. He wasn't threatening me.

At the moment.

He laughed. "Such a feisty *gatita*. You're not terrified. Not like you should be. Then again, I suppose I haven't shown you what I'm fully capable of yet." His smile somehow seemed to show all of his teeth, and I shrank back a little. That just made him laugh again, a sound of pure, arrogant amusement. "I promised to feed you, and it's getting cold," he effectively ended the disconcerting conversation.

His arms surrounded me on either side as he reached forward and picked up the knife and fork. He cut the steak into several small pieces, then shifted the utensils into one fist. I supposed he was smart not to set them down where I could reach them, but I really was too hungry and weak to try to stab him at the moment.

He picked up a piece of steak between his fingers and lifted it to my lips.

I looked up at him, confused. "What are you doing?"

"Feeding my pet." He was still smiling, but something darker stirred in his black stare. "Aren't you hungry, *gatita*?"

I blew out a sigh. "Fine. But only because I'm hungry, not because I'm your pet."

"Can't you be both?"

"No."

He chuckled, but he didn't argue with me again. "Eat."

Too hungry to continue resisting, I parted my lips and reached for the morsel with my tongue. I probably should have bitten him just for being a bastard, but I really wanted to eat.

Besides, he'd mentioned another punishment and warned me not to test him. Biting him probably counted as worse than *testing*.

As soon as the steak hit my tongue, rich flavors exploded in my mouth, and a soft moan of appreciation left my chest. I loved a good steak, and this one was cooked to perfection. I wrapped my lips around his fingers without thinking, sucking the juices from them as I sought more of the delicious flavor.

"You like *carne asada?*" he asked, his voice rougher than the simple question should have called for.

I pulled back from his fingers, and they left my mouth with a small *pop*.

"I like meat," I said. "All kinds of meat. If it used to *moo*, I'll definitely eat it. This is so good. I want more."

"Greedy and savage," he remarked, his voice lilting with laughter. "You can have as much as you want."

"I'm not savage," I grumbled. "I couldn't even kill you properly."

"No, you couldn't," he said calmly, obviously remembering my pathetic attempt to attack him with his razor. "I don't think you have it in you. That doesn't mean I'll give you access to a knife anytime soon, though."

"I'm a trained field agent," I said, feeling defensive, mostly because I *should* have been capable of fighting him more effectively than I'd managed so far.

"Not a very good one." He said it like a simple observation, not an insult.

And honestly, was it an insult if it was the truth?

"I shouldn't have transferred from tech analyst," I lamented aloud. If I hadn't tried to go into the field, I wouldn't be in this shitty situation.

"Probably not," he agreed. "My brother has his own tech

team. They looked into you. By all accounts, they were very impressed. It's why Cristian let you live."

"Because he wants me to protect him from the FBI," I said glumly. "He wants me to save his miserable life." I tensed, suddenly worried that Andrés might not take kindly to me insulting his brother.

"He does," he responded in a monotone. I couldn't read any particular emotion in it. "And you will. It's my job to make sure you do. You won't do it for Cristian, but for me. I want you to stop thinking about my brother and start thinking about pleasing me. And you can start by finishing your meal."

"You're the one who insists on feeding me one tiny piece at a time," I complained.

"If you'd stop sassing me, this would go faster," he drawled.

I narrowed my eyes at him to communicate my lingering displeasure with the entire weird scenario, but I allowed him to continue feeding me. I ended up eating well over half the steak before he actually used a freaking fork to deliver mouthfuls of the most delicious seasoned rice I'd ever tasted. I might have felt a little guilty that I ate most of the food, but he seemed content for me to have as much as I needed. When I finally turned my face away, he ate what was left.

He finished and lifted me off his lap to place me on the mattress.

"Stay."

He didn't have to restrain me to ensure that I didn't follow as he wheeled the cart out of the bedroom and out into what I now assumed was a sitting room. By the time he shut the door and returned to me, I lay back on the mattress, exhaustion and a pleasant sense of finally being well-fed making me sleepy.

"Go brush your teeth and wash your face," he ordered, grasping my hand and pulling me upright.

I made a little grumbling noise, which morphed to a yelp

when he swatted my ass.

"Go on," he said sternly.

My feet dragged across the carpet as I crossed to the bathroom. Moving seemed much harder than it should, my body aching in places I'd never imagined could feel tired and sore.

I shut the bathroom door behind me and took care of my essential needs. An unopened toothbrush waited for me on the sink, as well as feminine face wash and moisturizer. I wondered when Andrés had gotten these items for me, and I concluded that the boy who'd come in to clean the bathroom must have stocked the place for me.

I glanced at the shower. I hadn't noticed before, but a brand new razor hung from beneath the showerhead, replacing the one I'd broken this morning.

"You got a new razor," I said when I re-entered the bedroom, puzzled as to why he'd let me near a potential weapon again.

He met me with a level stare. "And you didn't break it apart and attempt to cut my throat. I don't need to worry about you trying that again, do I?"

My cheeks heated, and I dropped my gaze from his. I could still see the angry red line of the shallow cut I'd inflicted across his chest. He was covered only in the towel he'd slung around his hips after our shower, his powerful form clearly on display where he lounged on the bed.

"No," I admitted, my voice small with shame. I wouldn't try it again. Not because I didn't want to get spanked, but because I had to acknowledge that I truly didn't have it in me to rip open a man's throat. Besides, it had been a stupid, reckless plan, anyway. Where did I think I was going to go after I took out Andrés? There had to be dozens of men between me and freedom. And I didn't think they'd like it if they found me with their boss' blood on my hands.

"Smart girl," he said with satisfaction. "Come over here."

He stood and pulled back the covers, gesturing for me to get in.

I didn't move toward him.

"What are you doing?" I asked.

"Putting you to bed," he said, as though this was completely normal.

"I'm not a little girl. I don't need you to tuck me in."

A smile flitted around his lips. "Must you be so difficult about everything? You seem to love contradicting me." He patted the mattress. "Do you want a spanking before bed, or are you going to be a good girl for me?"

I huffed out a frustrated breath and closed the distance between us. The sad reality was, I was too tired to keep fighting. I'd managed to get some much-needed calories back in my system, but my mind had been sapped with terror for most of the day. Not to mention the other new, intense experiences he'd forced upon me.

"Only because I'm tired," I said as I slid beneath the sheets.

"If that's what you need to tell yourself," he allowed. "One way or another, you obeyed me, Samantha. That pleases me."

I rolled onto my side, facing away from him, and curled my knees up close to my chest in a protective position. He didn't comment on my small show of resistance. He simply pulled the covers over me and tucked me in like a child. It was weird. Fucked up.

Warm and soft.

And I was so tired.

"Go to sleep, *sirenita*." His long fingers played through my hair, and my eyes slid closed.

Without meaning to, I obeyed yet another of his commands and surrendered to my exhaustion.

CHAPTER 9

The mattress shifted beneath me, rousing me. For a moment, I panicked. I wasn't accustomed to sleeping with anyone else, so the instinctive knowledge that I wasn't alone in my bed startled me.

Then I remembered that I wasn't in my bed. I was in Andrés' bed. The bed where he'd bound me and made me have my first orgasm.

My cheeks colored in the darkness. Shades had been lowered over the huge windows, hiding the Chicago skyline. But no light peeked around them, so I assumed it wasn't morning yet. I hated not having a fucking clock. This room was absolutely devoid of even that level of technology. I'd go mad in here without access to a computer.

I'm going to get out of here, I promised myself. Maybe it wasn't likely that my friends would find me. Maybe there were dozens of men standing between me and freedom. Not to mention my massive, scary captor.

But that wasn't going to stop me from trying. It was nighttime. Most of the building's inhabitants would likely be asleep.

That included Andrés, who was snoring lightly on the other side of the massive bed. I'd awoken when he'd rolled away from me, and his arm no longer weighed me down. If I could slip out without disturbing him, I might be able to make my way out of the suite and get to the exit before he woke up. Once I was in the street, I could shout for help. I could borrow someone's phone.

It occurred to me that I'd have to go out in public naked, but I couldn't risk taking time to rummage through Andrés' drawers for something to cover myself. That would also make noise, and I couldn't afford that, either.

Naked, it is, I told myself, reasoning that I'd attract help faster this way, once I got out into the street.

If I didn't get killed on the way out.

Summoning up my courage, I carefully eased out of the bed, wincing when the mattress shifted ever so slightly beneath me. I paused, barely breathing.

Andrés continued to snore.

I exhaled and began to tiptoe across the plush carpet, making my way toward the door that led out into the rest of the suite. I squeezed my fist open and closed a few times to stop my fingers from trembling, then carefully turned the knob. The softest *snick* sounded as the latch disengaged.

Andrés didn't stir.

I slipped out the door and cracked it behind me, not daring to shut it all the way in case it thudded closed.

City lights flooded the adjoining room, shining through another wall of windows. As I'd suspected, it was set up like a lavish sitting room. Finally, I spotted a clock. Of course, it was an ornate grandfather clock rather than something modern. Analog. Ugh.

Still, at least I now knew it was three thirty-five AM. Hopefully everyone really was asleep at this hour.

My gaze swept over the room, looking for the exit. Another closed door was set into the opposite wall from the windows. I started to make my way toward it when the shifting lights caught on something silver: an elevator. My way out.

I raced toward it on tiptoe, trying to move silently even as I rushed to freedom. I pushed the call button, which was illuminated in blue.

I nearly jumped out of my skin when a loud buzzer sounded. *Fuck!*

I hadn't heard that sound when anyone else had come and gone from the suite. Why now?

Desperate, I punched the button again, knowing I had precious seconds before Andrés' strong arms closed around me. The angry buzz echoed through the suite.

"It won't work for you," he drawled.

I yelped and spun, backing up until my butt hit the cold silver doors behind me. Andrés stood in the doorway to the bedroom, the city lights reflecting stars across his black eyes. He didn't move toward me.

The doors didn't open behind me. Desperate, I hit the call button again.

Buzz.

His teeth flashed white through the darkness. "That elevator is accessed through thumbprint recognition. The only people who can come and go from this suite are those who have my permission. You don't have permission, my curious *gatita.*" He finally began prowling toward me. "Did you want to explore my home?" he asked, the innocuous question made terrifying by the silky smooth tone of his voice. "Were you so eager to see the rest of it? I'm more than happy to show you."

I shook my head wildly. "I didn't... I don't... I just want to go home," I forced out past the lump in my throat. Whatever he was about to show me, I was certain it was terrible. I could read it in the hungry glint of his eyes, the sharpness of his smile. Dark anticipation pulsed around him like a palpable thing. It pressed against me, making me shudder.

"This is your home now," he said when he finally reached me. There was nowhere for me to run, nowhere to hide. All I could do was press my body back against the cold metal doors and tremble.

His hand closed around the back of my neck, his fingers tangling in my hair at my nape as he pulled me against him. He was naked, and his huge cock pressed into my belly.

"You weren't really asleep," I accused, knowing the truth. He was toying with me, testing me.

His grin sharpened. "Clever and curious," he remarked with satisfaction. "No, I wasn't asleep." He leaned in, his cheek whispering against mine as he spoke low in my ear. "You can't escape me, Samantha. There's only one way out of this penthouse, and it's barred to you. I don't have to keep you collared and chained to trap you here. I just like it. I like knowing you're naked in my bed, waiting for me."

"You're sick," I said shakily.

He laughed softly. "You've called me worse already. Do you really think your little insults wound me? I'm going to tame your barbed tongue because I enjoy training you, not because it's capable of hurting me. If you continue to defy me in this, the only time you'll be allowed to use your tongue is when you're worshipping my cock."

My stomach churned, fear clogging my throat. I didn't have any words, anyway. What was there to say in response to such a horrible declaration?

"But you wanted to see the rest of my home," he continued smoothly. "Let me show you."

"I don't want to," I squeaked out. "Please. I'll go back to bed."

He clicked his tongue at me. "The time for being a good girl has passed. You've been a curious *gatita*. You know what happens to curious kittens, don't you?"

Curiosity killed the cat. "You said you wouldn't kill me. Your brother wants me alive."

His hand tightened around my nape. "This is about what *I* want," he growled. "I don't want you dead. I want you crying out and begging for mercy. *My* mercy. Don't talk about my brother. Don't think about him. He's not your concern. I am."

Keeping his grip on my nape, Andrés pulled me along in his wake, moving toward the closed door I'd noticed opposite the wall of windows. Dread settled in my gut, and my feet dragged on the carpet in token resistance. I could have clawed at him, at the very least. But my body remembered the punitive feel of his finger invading my bottom, and I didn't even half-formulate a plan to fight before he'd managed to drag me to the door.

"Please," I begged. "I don't want to go in there."

"You don't even know what you're scared of," he said, his voice colored with amusement.

"Whatever it is, I don't want it. You wouldn't want to take me in there if it were anything good. You're scaring me."

"You should be scared. You've been very naughty, trying to escape from me."

"But you just said I can't escape. I can't use the elevator. You don't have to hurt me to keep me from using it," I babbled on, desperate to stay on this side of that closed door. Even though the words tumbling from my lips made my heart sink as I recognized the truth in them, I had to press on. I didn't want to be punished.

He reached for the knob and pushed. The door swung open into darkness. The city lights shining behind us barely penetrated the blackness, as though refusing to illuminate the ominous space. The light had no place here. The scent of leather and something deeper teased through the air that drifted through the open door.

"Don't," I gasped out as he propelled me forward, into the darkness.

The soft click of a light switch being flipped registered in my ears, just before panic seized my senses.

It was like something out of the scariest corners of the internet. I'd seen some fucked up dungeon porn. Andrés might as well use this room as a set for the most depraved, disturbing videos I'd ever glimpsed before quickly clicking the back button on my browser.

Creepy crimson lights illuminated the space so I could clearly see every object that waited to torment me. It reminded me of the time I'd ventured to the BDSM club Dusk on my particularly misguided Valentine's Day mission to seduce Dex.

"This isn't like Dusk," I told myself softly, not realizing I was speaking the words aloud. "It's not. Dusk is Safe, Sane, Consensual." I knew the tenets of BDSM, even if I'd never practiced it myself. "This isn't. I don't want this. Not like this."

"You've been to a BDSM club?" Andrés' voice penetrated my mounting terror. He kept his grip on my nape, but he stepped in front of me. His angry black eyes filled my vision, botting out the horror that surrounded me. "I thought you were my innocent little virgin. Did you lie to me, Samantha? I wondered when I didn't feel your hymen intact. But those can be broken in other ways, and I thought your surrender was genuine." His scar deepened to a furious slash. "I wasn't the first man to touch you. If you think you've suffered under my hand before, that's nothing compared to what's about to happen to you."

"No!" I half-sobbed. "I wasn't lying. I am a virgin, I swear."

"Then how do you know about Dusk?" he demanded.

"I went there one time," I gasped out. "I was looking for Dex. I followed him there. I wanted to see him. I wanted him to see *me*. But he didn't. He never does. I got drunk and left. I didn't do anything but drink at the bar. I promise, I didn't do anything. I didn't lie to you. Please, don't hurt me."

His eyes softened, his scar easing as the tension left his mouth. He didn't release me, but his grip shifted so his fingers rubbed the back of my neck.

"All right, *sirenita*. I believe you. I don't think you could lie convincingly if you tried. You will explain more about this later. For now, you have a lesson to learn."

"I just want to go back to bed." A tear slid down my cheek, and he wiped it away with his thumb.

"I'll put you to bed when we're finished in here. You must be punished for trying to escape. You need to understand that your behavior has consequences."

I started crying in earnest, harsh sobs wracking my chest as fear seized my system.

"Come here." He pulled me against his hard body, wrapping his arms around me in a firm embrace as he continued to rub the base of my scalp in little circular patterns. "It won't be so bad," he cooed. "I'm not angry with you."

"It will be," I insisted, my voice hitching. "Just because it would be worse if you were angry doesn't mean it won't be bad. This place is... It's not right. I don't want to be in here."

I shuddered against him, and his big hand stroked up and down my back in a reassuring motion.

"You'll get used to it," he said, his voice deep and calm. "We are going to spend a lot of time in here. I think you might even enjoy it, in a way." His soothing tone was so at odds with the horrible things he was saying that my mind couldn't quite process it. I felt comforted, even though my heart hammered against my ribcage.

"Take a deep breath," he said, a softly-spoken order. "Good girl. Another."

I hadn't realized I'd complied, but my addled mind couldn't keep up with what was happening to me. My body obeyed, and my roiling emotions began to subside enough that I was no longer shaking and sobbing against my captor.

"Come with me," he commanded, finally releasing my neck to take my hand in his.

It was a sweet gesture, and he held my fingers so gently that he might have been my caring, kind boyfriend.

A caring, kind boyfriend I'd never had. A caring, kind boyfriend with a scary, scarred body and wicked gleam in his eye. A caring, kind boyfriend who was leading me toward...

I dug in my heels. "No."

"You don't get to say no," he told me, his voice still calm and even. "This is your punishment."

"You said you wouldn't hurt me," I said, trying in vain to jerk my hand out of his suddenly vise-like grip.

"I said I wouldn't harm you," he corrected me. "This won't leave any permanent marks. Although I'm interested to see how easily your pretty skin bruises. I do like seeing my marks on my pet."

I shook my head in wild denial. "Stop it! Stop. I'm not your pet. I don't want be marked or bruised."

"How else will you learn?" he asked, as though the question were completely reasonable.

"I don't need to learn anything. I just need you to let me go."

"You don't know what you need. I know what's best for you."

"You don't know shit," I railed at him, fear morphing to

anger. "You're fucked up. You're so fucking messed up. Fuck you." I continued cursing at him, even as he pulled me inexorably forward. Mostly, I hurled the f-bomb at him. For once, he didn't rebuke me. He didn't say anything at all.

Which scared the shit out of me.

So I cursed at him some more.

He barely looked at me when he gripped my waist and positioned my body over the spanking bench. I knew what it was from years of indulging my perverted curiosity online.

But knowing what it was didn't prepare me for the full blast of terror that slammed into me when he pressed my torso down against the padded surface, forcing me to bend at the waist over the edge so my bottom was thrust up shamefully.

He handled my body with an almost detached air. There were no lingering touches, no reassuring strokes of his fingertips along my skin. He didn't even touch me with violent hands. Even that would have been preferable to the methodical way he captured my wrists and secured them with black leather cuffs.

I tried to push up off the bench, even knowing that I couldn't free my hands. He didn't make a sound as he buckled a thick strap around my waistline, pinning me down against the padded surface. I almost wished he'd click his tongue at me in disapproval. Now, that seemed like almost an affectionate act. This man who so callously arranged my body for torment made my insides quake.

I couldn't stop cussing. I wasn't sure if I was even insulting him directly anymore. A stream of curse words tumbled from my lips in nonsensical, half-formed sentences.

He grasped my legs and guided them apart, securing them with another set of leather cuffs. I was bent over and spread wide, my sex and asshole fully on display and at his mercy.

But I suspected he didn't have any mercy for me.

"Fu—" My final f-bomb was abruptly smothered when something rubbery pressed deep into my mouth, pushing my tongue down as it settled between my lips. He buckled the ball gag closed at the back of my head. I thrashed, as though I could somehow push it out of my mouth.

He gripped my hair, wrapping it around his fist and pulling back sharply. My shocked cry caught against the rubber ball as pain lit up my scalp, commanding my attention.

My head was bowed back, my neck stretched to the point where breathing was difficult. I focused on sucking in air through my nose, my impotent rage and fear finally muffled by the imperative to obtain enough oxygen.

His black eyes stared down into mine, and my mind went oddly blank. I couldn't fight, I couldn't shout obscenities at him. I couldn't do anything but draw in shallow, careful breaths.

"That's better," he said softly, trailing his fingers over my lips, tracing the line of them where they surrounded the red rubber ball that filled my mouth. "Very pretty," he praised.

A fine tremor raced across my skin as a strange sense of relief settled over me. He was looking at me again, touching me. He wasn't treating me like an object. The impersonal way he'd been handling me had scared me more than Cristian's knife cutting into me. The Andrés who held me and promised to protect me in his own messed up way was back, and I was relieved to see him. Fresh tears pooled in my eyes as my toxic fear leaked out of me.

"You're so beautiful when you cry," he murmured, stroking the wetness on my cheeks almost reverently. "Don't you feel better now? You don't have to yell. You don't have to fight. Your Master is in control, and you don't have to pretend otherwise. Not when you're strapped down and spread wide for me to play with. All you have to do is submit. All you *can* do is submit."

Keeping his grip on my hair, he held my face in place as he leaned down and pressed a tender kiss against my forehead.

"Time for your punishment, *gatita*," he said, his soft lips brushing across my skin. "You've more than earned it."

I shivered, but not entirely out of fear. A shadow of it resurfaced, but I couldn't be terrified anymore. There was no point. As he'd said, I wasn't capable of fighting him in my current predicament. Surrendering was so much easier than panicking, especially when panicking was pointless.

He won't harm me, I reminded myself, playing it over and over again in my head like a soothing mantra. *He won't harm me.*

I'd survived his spankings, his violations. Whatever he had planned for me, I'd survive this, too.

He finally released my hair, and my head dropped forward, my cheek resting meekly against the padded bench.

His palm skimmed across my lower back, the heat of his body sinking into mine.

"Good girl. I'll be right back." He said it like the sweetest reassurance, almost as though he was reluctant to leave my side.

Or maybe I was just delusional, and I was hearing what I needed to hear in order to cope with what was happening to me.

He disappeared behind me, his heat receding. I tried to crane my head back to watch him, but he had walked outside my range of sight. Bound as I was, I could only move my head so far.

Giving up, I settled my cheek back against the smooth leather and closed my eyes. The darkness behind my lids was peaceful. Far preferable to examining the torture chamber that surrounded me.

Silence enfolded me. I couldn't hear Andrés moving, but I could practically feel his eyes on me. My skin prickled with awareness, but my body remained limp against the bench. I breathed in deeply through my nose, taking in long draws of oxygen.

I tried not to think, but my brain began firing again, wondering what he was going to do to me. Several horrible possibilities occurred to me at once, terrible images of torment flickering across my mind.

Just as I began to tense with mounting anxiety, something cool and smooth tickled my spine. My shocked yelp was muffled by the gag, and my eyes flew open to assess what was happening to me.

Andrés stood behind me, looming over my helpless form. His black eyes glinted in the eerie crimson light as he studied my reaction. He held a flogger in one hand, allowing its multitude of thin black leather falls to kiss my back.

My eyes widened, and I squirmed in my restraints.

I wasn't entirely trying to get away. I'd been curious to know what it would feel like to be flogged. I'd fantasized about it more than a few times.

But this wasn't the scenario I'd envisioned. For one, Dex had always played the hero in my mind. The man standing behind me was no hero. He was my own personal villain.

And he was staring at me as though I was the most fascinating thing he'd ever seen.

"You know what this is?" he asked, trailing the leather falls down the length of my spine.

A small whimper slipped past the gag as my nerve endings crackled to life. I managed a slight nod in response to his question, never even considering refusing to answer. I couldn't have any secrets from Andrés when I was like this: stripped bare and put on display for him. I couldn't hide from him. He wouldn't allow it.

"But no one has ever flogged you before," he said. It wasn't a question. He already knew how innocent I was.

"Kinky little virgin," he mused. "When I decide to allow you to speak again, you'll tell me every depraved thought you've ever had." He smiled down at me with genuine pleasure. "I knew we'd get along."

He took a step back and swung the flogger down in a slow arc. The falls slapped against my bottom, but it didn't hurt. He was going slow with me, watching me with the careful, focused attention of a predator as he monitored my reactions. The heavy strips of leather slid down over my cheeks. They were cool and smooth against my heated skin.

"This is going to hurt," he warned. "It's supposed to hurt. One day, I'll show you how good it can feel. But not tonight."

I couldn't do anything but shiver and wait for him to begin. The fantasy I'd harbored for so long—Dex lovingly giving me a hit of pain to drive me into a blissful headspace—faded away. This wouldn't bring me to subspace. That was attained through trust and honest surrender. It was something I'd longed for, and it had never been farther from my grasp.

I had to surrender to Andrés, but he wasn't giving me a choice. The restraints around my body weren't part of a kinky game, designed to help me let go of my inhibitions. They were punitive, a means of subjugating me, just as the collar had been. Everything I'd ever secretly longed for was being twisted. As perverted as it was to fantasize about my best friend tying me down and whipping me, that fantasy was sweet and practically vanilla compared to my horrific reality.

I didn't have a safe word. I couldn't do anything to stop this.

When the first hit landed, I shrieked into the gag, my entire body jerking against my restraints in an instinctive effort to move away. The cuffs held fast, and the belt around my waist kept me trapped against the bench.

I stared back at him, silently pleading.

Don't. Not again. I don't like this.

The initial sting of the falls striking my bottom was morphing into a deeper burn, leaving my skin smarting.

"Your eyes are so lovely," he said, studying me with purely masculine appreciation. My wide, shining eyes did nothing to dissuade him. If anything, he was getting turned on. His cock began to stiffen as I shook my head, my pleas muffled by the gag.

A hash cry tore from my throat when he brought the flogger down twice in rapid succession, hitting one cheek and then the other, leaving a scorching path where the thin leather falls raked across my skin.

He paused as I heaved out a sob, but he wasn't looking at my face anymore. He studied my bottom, lightly running his fingertips over my enflamed skin. The contact tingled and stung, and I whined in protest.

"So pretty and red," he observed. He gripped my cheek hard, his fingers digging into my tender flesh. I tried to wriggle away, but there was nowhere to go. "I want to see my fingerprints on your ass tomorrow," he said, as though explaining his actions made them rational. "The bruises from the flogger will remind you of your punishment, but this marks you as mine." He increased the pressure of his cruel hold, and my breath stuttered as tears began to stream down my face.

Finally, he released my cheek. I didn't have time to sag in relief before he brought the flogger down on me again, swift and merciless.

I threw back my head and screamed into the gag, but I

couldn't do anything to stop him. He spread the burn of the stinging falls across my bottom and down my upper thighs, painting my flesh with hot red pain.

My entire body began to quiver as my muscles started to give out. I'd been twisting and tugging against my restraints on animal instinct, but I couldn't keep up even that much resistance. I went limp against the bench, trembling.

"Good girl," he said, his voice deeper than I'd ever heard it. "Accept your punishment. You know you've earned it."

My tears came faster. I didn't deserve it. I didn't deserve anything that was happening to me.

But the gag kept my protest locked inside. I couldn't do anything but surrender.

I drew in a shuddering breath, submitting to the pain. As soon as I did, my mind entered a quiet, resigned space. Each blow still stung, but I noticed the heavy thud permeating deeper into my flesh. It was rhythmic. Hypnotic. My breathing began to even out as I focused solely on the sensation of harsh leather hitting my burning skin, the *whoosh* and *smack* of the flogger moving through the air before making contact. Everything else faded: thought, worry, emotion.

I barely registered when the blows stopped. I'd retreated to a protective place in some deep corner of my mind I'd never found before. My rapid-fire thoughts and volatile emotions couldn't touch me here.

I was dimly aware of Andrés' deep voice murmuring a soothing litany in Spanish as his calloused hands traced the contours of my motionless body.

The gag slipped from my mouth and the restraints fell away, but I didn't try to get up. I couldn't have moved a muscle, even if I wanted to. And resistance didn't even occur to me. That defiant line of thinking had been thoroughly obliterated.

He lifted me up and tucked me against his chest. My tears wet his skin as he carried me away from the bench where I'd been bound and whipped.

I was too exhausted and wrung-out to even register relief. I passed out in his arms before we made it back to the bed.

CHAPTER 10

I rolled onto my back and jolted awake with a gasp when my bottom throbbed. Wincing, I immediately positioned myself on my side. Something tugged at my neck as I moved. I reached up and touched my throat, finding smooth leather beneath my fingertips. Andrés had collared me again. I must have been totally passed out not to have woken up when he was locking around my neck.

I don't have to keep you collared and chained to trap you here. I just like it. I like knowing you're naked in my bed, waiting for me.

His sick words played through my mind as I remembered our terrifying encounter in the middle of the night. I closed my eyes as the full shame and horror of everything he'd done to me washed over me. He'd toyed with me, allowing me to try to escape just so he could punish me for it. He'd taken me to that awful room, strapped me down, gagged me; he'd rendered me completely powerless and flogged my helpless body.

Gingerly, I touched my bottom and winced again as pain flared. I twisted my head back so I could look down at myself. My breath caught at the sight of mottled purple bruises marring my pale skin. Five smaller marks formed a rough circular pattern on my left cheek.

I want to see my fingerprints on your ass tomorrow, he'd said. *The bruises from the flogger will remind you of your punishment, but this marks you as mine.*

I cringed and tore my eyes away from the brand he'd left behind. I didn't need the physical reminder of the pain for the punishment to be burned into my mind.

I wouldn't try to use the elevator again.

It would be stupid and pointless, anyway. If I had access to a computer, I could hack into the building's security system and override the thumbprint recognition, no problem. But without technology, I was powerless. Andrés had made it painfully clear that I wasn't cut out to be a field agent. Months of training in hand-to-hand combat hadn't helped me at all when it came to facing him.

He hadn't needed to collar me and chain me to his bed to keep me from trying to access the elevator. Even though I was alone in the bedroom, I wouldn't have tried to escape that way in his absence. The security system probably logged failed attempts to press the call button. He'd know if I touched it without him here to witness my transgression. I didn't want to risk another punishment for nothing.

My stomach rumbled, rousing me from my dejected state.

Survive, my body reminded me.

I had to keep going, keep fit. I'd never get out of here if I let myself waste away into weakness. I needed to keep my calorie count up and stay hydrated in case an opportunity to escape did present itself.

I sat up in bed and hissed when my weight settled on my bruises. Even the soft mattress was almost too hard to bear.

Grimacing, I glanced around the room. As I'd hoped, the

food cart was waiting for me, the fancy platter covered to keep my meal warm.

I wasn't sure how long I'd been alone, but when I removed the cover, the bacon beneath was still warm, at least. I glanced out the windows and noted that the sun was up pretty high. Was that like, ten AM?

I wasn't sure. I wasn't exactly a nature girl, and surviving in the wild with the sun as my only clock wasn't a skill I'd ever had to acquire.

Even the nearly obsolete grandfather clock in the sitting room would have been preferable, but the bedroom door was closed again. Hell, I'd settle for a freaking sundial at this point.

Sighing, I bit into a particularly crispy piece of bacon. I nearly moaned at the rich, salty flavor.

Andrés might be a sadistic madman, but he was a sadistic madman with a great chef.

I tore my way through five strips of bacon before moving on to the most delicious spicy sausage I'd ever tasted. The breakfast was protein-heavy, and I wondered if Andrés had remembered what I'd said about being a meat lover.

Or maybe he was just trying to keep me slow and sleepy with all this heavy, salty food, because by the time I'd devoured everything and downed a jug of water, I lay back on the bed and closed my eyes.

I was so tired, my brain weirdly fuzzy and slow. My thoughts were still firing, but not in as many directions as usual. My emotions—which should have been spinning in response to my dire predicament—were oddly subdued.

Idly, I wondered if Andrés had decided to drug the food, but I didn't believe he'd do that. No, he much preferred physically demonstrating my helplessness. As he'd said, he didn't need to use drugs to keep me compliant.

I wasn't sure how long I lay there, stray thoughts gliding

across my mind from time to time as I settled into a state on the edge of sleep.

The click of the bedroom door opening roused me, and I sat bolt upright. I let out a little yelp at the sudden weight on my bottom, and I scrambled to cover my body with the sheet when I saw Lauren standing at the threshold.

"I just had breakfast," I said when I saw the cart she was pushing into the room. "I'm not hungry."

"I'm not here to bring you food," she said, her voice a hollow monotone. She was looking right at me, but her deep green eyes didn't spark with any emotion whatsoever. I might as well have been a statue she was talking to rather than another woman. She wasn't here to help me, even if she was a victim. She worked for my captor, regardless of whether or not she'd been brutalized and broken.

"Then what's that?" I asked warily, eyeing the items on the cart. There was a small silver pot and a stack of cloth strips, as well as what looked like cleansing wipes. I had no idea what I was looking at.

"Wax," she replied.

"Wax?" I repeated, still not following. Why would she have wax?

Something sparked in her eyes for the briefest moment. My stomach twisted when I registered it as pity.

"For your pussy," she replied bluntly.

I pulled the sheet all the way up to my chin and squeezed my thighs together, ignoring the flare of pain as I shifted my weight.

"No," I refused, sharp and immediate.

"I'm really good at it," she said, something like kindness softening her tone. "It will barely hurt. I do it all the time."

"Nope. Uh-uh. Not happening. You can leave now."

Her brow furrowed. "I can't do that."

"You totally can. Because I'm not getting my... I'm not getting waxed down there."

"You mean your pussy," she said, eyeing me strangely.

"I mean my lady parts, yes," I replied, my voice higher than usual. "They're not getting waxed. So you can go now, and take that shit with you." I gestured at the cart.

"Master Andrés doesn't like cussing," she said, setting the cart next to the bed.

"I know," I said bitterly, shifting my weight off my aching bottom. Something awful occurred to me. If Lauren wasn't my ally, was she my enemy? "You won't tell him, will you?" I asked desperately. I didn't want him to take me back into that scary room and hurt me again.

"No," she promised, her gaze softening with sympathy. "Just don't do it again, please."

I nodded, knowing she would probably get into trouble if he ever discovered she was keeping my transgression a secret. He was cruel, insane. What would he do to her if he found out she was showing me the smallest kindness? After my punishment last night, I was beginning to understand why Lauren was so compliant.

"Does he hurt you?" I asked quietly. "I don't want him to hurt you because of me."

She blinked at me, surprised. "Master Andrés is nice," she asserted for the second time.

"Okay," I said slowly, trying to wrap my mind around her warped headspace. "But does he hurt you? You can tell me. He hurt me, too."

"I wish Master Andrés would take care of me like he's taking care of you. You're lucky."

"Are you listening to me?" I demanded, my patience slipping. "I said he hurt me. He's not taking care of me."

She glared at me. "Do you want to be downstairs with the

rest of us? Where they dose you with Bliss and make you beg them to rape you? Master Andrés is honest. He's fair. He's kind."

I bit my tongue to hold in a frustrated tirade. Lauren had obviously been driven mad. Through my frustration, guilt and pity twisted my gut. Piecing together what she'd revealed, Lauren was being regularly drugged and violated, but not by Andrés. I knew from my investigation that Cristian Moreno was involved in trafficking Bliss and using the sick drug to capture and sell women.

My stomach roiled. Andrés had claimed I'd beg him to fuck me, but at least he wasn't drugging me. We were locked in a battle of wills, and even though he'd won every round so far, I still had my wits about me to keep fighting. He might have forced me to surrender to punishment and wrung pleasure from my untried body, but I still had my mind.

"I'll help you get out of here, Lauren," I swore. "I'm going to get you out."

She stiffened. "I'm not going to help you escape."

"I didn't expect you to," I replied sadly. She was obviously too far gone to defy Andrés. She'd been broken a long time ago. "But that doesn't mean I'm not going to help you. We'll get out of here."

She started at me, nonplussed. "I have a job to do," she announced after a few seconds of silence, as though I hadn't just made a passionate oath to set her free. "Lie on your back, please."

I blew out a long breath and complied. I could physically resist Lauren, but I didn't know what Andrés would do to her if I prevented her from following his orders. I remembered how he'd frightened the young man who'd defied him yesterday. Andrés had threatened to cut out his eye for looking at me.

I didn't want him to hurt Lauren because of my defiant choices. I'd choose another battle to fight with him, one that only involved the two of us and didn't risk collateral damage.

I stared up at the ceiling as she slid the sheet off my body, leaving me bare. I did my best not to squirm with discomfort at being stripped. I'd always been painfully modest, even around other women. I hadn't grown up with sisters or even female cousins, so I wasn't accustomed to anyone seeing me naked.

My cheeks heated, and I resolutely fisted my fingers into the sheet beneath me, preventing myself from slapping Lauren's hands away as she began to work.

The wax was almost painfully hot, but she was as practiced as she'd claimed. Every time she pulled a wax-covered cloth free, she'd apply pressure to my enflamed skin to alleviate the horrible sting that followed. There was nothing sexual about the way she touched me. She was almost clinical in the way she handled my most secret area, her eyes assessing her work rather than studying my sex.

"Done," she announced after a few uncomfortable minutes. She pulled away from me and started tidying everything on the cart.

"Thanks," I said automatically. "I mean. No, thanks. I mean, I didn't mean to thank you. That was totally fucked up. I mean, fuck. I didn't mean to cuss. Damn it. I just—" I stopped rambling before my social awkwardness could get me into more trouble.

Her hand settled over mine, squeezing gently. "I won't tell," she promised. "But you need to be good for Master Andrés."

"Why?" I challenged. "Because he'll beat me if I'm not?"

"Because he needs it."

I gaped at her. "He needs me to be good for him," I said flatly. "I don't know what kind of psycho world you've been living in, and whatever's happened to you, I really am sorry. And I am going to help you get out of here. But I'm not going to roll over and give up just because you told me to. I'm not going to behave for my sadistic captor who gets off on torturing women, no matter what you say."

She shook her head, her shining blond hair waving around her delicate face. "You don't understand him. You don't know him."

"And you do? Just how well do you know *Master* Andrés? What did he do to you, exactly?" Ugly emotions clawed at my insides: anger, bitterness, fear.

She lifted her chin. "He's nice," she insisted, as though that was the only way she was capable of thinking of Andrés.

Ice crystallized in my veins. What had he done to her to warp her so thoroughly?

"Thank you, Lauren," his accented voice rolled through the room. "You can go now."

I jolted and grabbed the sheet, jerking the fabric over my body. Andrés smirked at me as he stepped into the bedroom.

"You know you're not allowed to cover yourself, *cosita*," he said, more amused than stern. "Show me your pretty pussy. I want to see it."

Lauren hurried out of the room, but I couldn't focus on her retreating form. All my attention was riveted on the threat posed by Andrés. My body became very aware of his proximity, remembering the pain he'd inflicted the night before. My heartbeat picked up, my pulse racing. I wanted to pull the sheet all the way up over my head and hide like a child seeking protection from a monster.

But my bottom throbbed, a cruel reminder of what he was capable of if I disobeyed him. I'd already been naked around him pretty much since I'd gotten here. Why risk another punishment just to cover myself now? He'd look at me, one way or another.

Slowly, I curled my fingers into the sheet and forced myself to drag it off my body. His eyes went straight to my bare sex, and they darkened with hunger.

"Very pretty." He made a little rolling motion with his forefinger. "Turn over. I want to see my marks on you."

I glared at him.

He met me with a steady stare, waiting.

I huffed out an angry breath and rolled onto my front. It felt nice not having my weight on the bruises, anyway.

"On your hands and knees," he commanded. "Spread your thighs. I want to see my marks and my pussy."

My eyes narrowed farther, and I didn't move to comply. That was too much. He couldn't honestly expect me to present myself to him so wantonly. Not without putting up a fight.

Only, I didn't have time to fight. His arm snaked beneath my hips, pulling me up onto my knees.

"Hey!" I cried, indignant.

His hand cracked across my bruised thigh, and I shrieked.

"You will learn to obey me," he said calmly. "Spread your legs. Now," he added, the word imbued with warning.

My cheeks burning hotter than my thigh, I slowly eased my knees apart while he kept me in place with his arm braced beneath my stomach.

"Beautiful," he remarked, his voice a low rumble. He touched his fingers to my labia, stroking over my bare skin. My sensitive flesh danced and quivered. It was strange to feel so smooth down there, his touch gliding over my sex in a gentle caress. His fingertips grazed over my clit as he stroked me, and I couldn't quite manage to smother a small gasp as pleasure crackled through the little bundle of nerves.

He chuckled. "I think my kitten likes when I pet her pretty pink pussy."

"Stop," I begged, not daring to say I didn't like it. That would be a lie. I couldn't deny that it felt good when he touched me like this. But that didn't mean I had to admit it aloud. I didn't want to like his touch, but my body betrayed me.

"But I like petting your pussy, *gatita*," he said, not stopping his tender exploration of my bare flesh. It still stung slightly from the waxing, but my core fluttered as he continued to stroke me. "You were very well behaved for Lauren, weren't you? I think you've earned another reward."

"Is this what you did to her?" I hurled at him, my fury rising at the mention of the broken woman. "Beat her and manipulated her until her mind warped? Did she used to hate you before she started worshipping the ground you walk on? Did you—?"

My tirade ended when he abruptly flipped me over and settled his hand around the front of my throat. He didn't apply any pressure this time, but the warning was clear.

"I've never harmed Lauren," he said, his voice rough with his own anger.

A maddened laugh bubbled from my throat. "You've never *harmed* her? Just like you didn't harm me when you strapped me down and whipped me after mindfucking me into thinking I had a chance to escape? How crazy are you?"

Something cold and scary settled over him, his features shifting to a blank mask. "I never claimed to be sane. Do you think a normal man wants to take an innocent woman and turn her into his plaything? Do you think a good man wants to bend her will and shape her into his obedient little fucktoy?"

"So you..." I swallowed down the lump of horror in my throat. "You did do this to Lauren."

"No," he said, still frigid. "The Bliss broke Lauren, not me."

Tears burned at the corners of my eyes. "So you do want to break me," I whispered.

A frown tugged at the corners of his lips, and some of the ice melted from his gaze. "I told you, I'm going to tame you. I'm going to make you mine and teach you to obey. I don't want to see you broken."

"You told your brother you'd break me for him," I countered, fear pooling in my gut.

His frown deepened to a scowl. "My brother likes to break things. He likes to take things that aren't his and shatter them. If I left you with him, he'd torture you until he discovered what you love most in the world. Then he'd make you watch while he destroyed it. Is that what you'd prefer? That I hand you back over to him?"

Dex. Dex was the only person left that I cared about. My parents had died in a car crash when I was twenty-three. They'd been the only family I had, until I'd met my best friend.

"No," I said faintly, a vision of Cristian's knife slicing into Dex's throat flashing across my mind. I couldn't let that happen, no matter what it cost me.

Andrés wiped away the horrified tears that had spilled down my cheeks.

"I'm not going to let him break you," he promised. "He'll never touch you again. You're mine now. I will be harsh with you. I will hurt you sometimes. And I will enjoy your pain. But I will never cause you harm, not to your body and not to your heart. Do you understand?"

I closed my eyes and turned my face away from his touch. He was basically telling me that I had to sacrifice myself to save Dex. It was a sacrifice I'd make without a second thought, but that didn't mean despair didn't swallow me up as I chose to do so.

"I can see that you don't understand," he said with a sigh. "But you will. It won't be so bad, *cosita*. I'm not so bad." He murmured the last so softly, I barely heard it.

The mattress shifted, and I listened to him moving away from me. I waited until the door closed behind him before I started crying in earnest. I'd do anything to spare Dex pain, but this? Whoring myself out to a man who admitted he enjoyed hurting me? I wasn't sure my mind wouldn't break in the process, no matter what Andrés said.

I can do this, I told myself. *I can be the hero. Heroine. I can keep Dex safe.*

I'd find a way out of here somehow. If I got to safety, Cristian couldn't hurt me. He couldn't threaten Dex. I'd save myself and my best friend. I just had to survive whatever Andrés had in store for me until I was able to devise a way to escape. I had to avoid being turned over to Cristian at all costs. Dex's life depended on it.

CHAPTER 11

"You're sad," Andrés observed, tucking my hair behind my ear in a perversion of affection.

"I'm not sad," I countered. "I'm pissed."

"You're not angry." He cupped my cheek so he could study my expression more carefully. "My angry *gatita* is cute and fierce. You're sad."

I huffed out a breath. "I'm bored," I admitted. I'd spent the entire day alone, with nothing to do but mull over my desperate situation. It hadn't exactly been good for my headspace. Lauren had returned briefly to bring my lunch, but other than that short visit, I'd been on my own. It had been dark outside for ages before Andrés had finally returned.

"You keep me chained up. I can't even use the freaking bathroom. Do you know how fu—" I caught myself before the curse word left my lips "—messed up that is?" I finished.

One corner of his lips tilted in a crooked smile. "There's my angry *gatita*," he said with satisfaction, ignoring my accusations. "I was worried about you."

"If you were worried about me, you wouldn't leave me

alone for hours with nothing to do. I'm going crazy here. Solitary confinement drives people crazy, you know that, right? Especially people like me."

He frowned slightly. "What do you mean, *people like you?* The purpose of leaving you like this is so you'll wait for me. You'll depend on me for everything. It helps you feel my control, even when I can't be here with you."

I shoved at his chest, but of course I couldn't push him away. It was more a token show of anger than anything else. I'd already given up on physically besting him.

"Do you know how many thoughts I have? Like, all at one time? If I don't have something to focus on, they overwhelm me. I can't live like this."

"It's only been two days," he pointed out. "You'll adjust."

"I won't," I asserted. "You don't know me at all. I'll go nuts if you keep leaving me like this."

His frown deepened. "If you're trying to manipulate me into letting you walk freely around the suite, it's not going to work. That's a privilege you have to earn."

"I'm not trying to manipulate you," I asserted, although now that he said it, I realized it would have been a good try. "That's what you do, right? Manipulate people. Mindfuck them. Well, I'm not like you. I'm telling you the truth. I can't handle this." I tugged at the collar for emphasis. I was no longer chained to the bed, but he'd left the collar locked around my throat while he held me in his lap for this maddening conversation.

He studied me for a long moment, then his frown finally eased. "No. You're not like me. I'll take this into consideration." He brushed a feather-light kiss across my forehead. "I think I have a way to calm that busy brain of yours. You were so good accepting your punishment last night and behaving for Lauren today. I never did give you your reward."

"I don't want it. Having you touch me is not a reward."

"You're still upset," he noted. "This will help you calm down. And before you keep arguing with me, I'll promise that I won't make you come, unless you ask me to. Does that make you feel better?"

I eyed him warily, not trusting him for a second. "What are you going to do to me? I don't want to go back into that torture room."

"It's not a torture room," he said calmly. "But no, we won't go in there. I want you to relax, not get more worked up. No more questions," he announced before I could come up with another rebuttal. "Come with me."

It wasn't like I really had a choice, because he simply picked me up and carried me. He kept doing that, like I weighed nothing more than a doll. I was a toy he could pick up when he wanted to play with me.

I crossed my arms over my chest and scowled up at him.

The bastard laughed. "You really are cute when you're angry."

"You think I'm cute when I'm angry. You think I'm pretty when I cry. You're messed up, you know that, right?"

"Yes, so you've told me," he said, still amused rather than disturbed by my barbed comments. "I'd like to see you smile, too, but I don't think that will happen for a while yet."

I gaped at him. "You think I'm going to *smile* for you?"

"I think you'll settle down and find a way to be happy with me. Once you adjust and accept your place here."

"*Accept my place?*" I demanded, slapping his chest in a burst of anger.

He clicked his tongue at me. "That wasn't very nice. But you're not trying very hard, either. You're upset, and I'm going to make you feel better."

"Short of releasing me, that's not going to happen," I

informed him. "Do you really think I'm going to *feel better* about being trapped with a sadistic psycho?"

"Mind your tongue," he said sharply. "I've indulged you too much. You will speak to me with respect."

"Right," I said, unable to bite back the sarcasm. "You've been so indulgent with me. Beating me, violating me, chaining me up. You're so *nice*," I finished spitefully, using Lauren's description of him.

He set me on my feet and stared down at me, his dark eyes curious rather than reproving. "You really can't stop yourself, can you? You're not capable of holding in your thoughts, even knowing they could get you into trouble. I think a little discipline will be good for you. You can learn some self-control over these tics of yours."

I instantly clapped my hands over my bottom. "I don't want you to punish me again."

He smoothed his hand over my hair, reassuring. "Discipline doesn't necessarily mean punishment. Now, try your best to be quiet and stay right here."

He stepped away from me, and I finally was able to assess where he'd placed me. We were in the sitting room, and he'd positioned me in the farthest corner from the door to the torture room. Relief washed through me, strong enough to make my fingers tremble. I hadn't realized just how much fear was building in my chest until it finally released. He really wasn't going to take me in there.

But what was he going to do to me? He still hadn't said, and I knew he wouldn't. I'd just have to watch and wait and hope it wouldn't be too painful.

He was a few feet away from me, drumming his fingers on the highly polished mahogany desk. On the desk was...

I lunged for the laptop without thinking. I caught sight of his sharp grin just before he caught me around the waist and manhandled me down onto the carpet. He placed one hand between my shoulders, easily pinning me down on my front while he opened one of the desk drawers. I thrashed and cursed, but he quickly secured my arms behind me by locking handcuffs around my wrists.

"Do you just have kinky shit stashed everywhere?" I demanded on a growl. I'd thought I was safe from his perversions in this room, but I'd been wrong.

"Of course," he replied coolly. "Settle down. This won't hurt."

"You think I'm going to *settle down* when you basically just taunted me with a laptop? Do you know how starved I am for the internet? For technology? You don't even have a real clock, for god's sake, and you've been hiding a *laptop* from me?"

His hand curled around my nape, pressing my cheek down against the carpet and stilling my shaking head.

"I need my laptop for work," he said calmly. "I'm going to take care of some business, and you're going to be quiet and look pretty for me while I do."

"Work," I said scornfully. "You mean drug trafficking and selling women."

His fingers tightened around my neck. "Be very careful what you say next, Samantha," he warned. "I know you struggle to control your tongue, but I'm warning you to try very hard. I don't want to punish you now, but I will."

"But it's what you do," I said, truly unable to stop myself. "You and your brother. That's your *business*."

"I take care of a lot of things for my brother," he said, his voice still rough with anger, but his grip on my neck didn't tighten. "I do all the things he'd rather not bother with; I deal with the boring details. I keep things running. And yes, what you've accused me of is part of it."

"But you don't like the Bliss." The words popped out of me

as I remembered what Lauren had told me. Now that I thought about it, Andrés had seemed almost regretful when he'd told me Bliss had broken Lauren. And he'd expressed distaste for drugging me to make me more cooperative.

He was silent for a moment, his hands unmoving on my body.

"What I like or don't like about my business isn't your concern," he finally said. "I need to work, and you need to be quiet. Your runaway mouth is very distracting."

"But—" My rebuttal was smothered when the now-familiar rubbery taste of the ball gag hit my tongue. I tried to twist my face away, but that only pressed it deeper into my mouth as he buckled it in place.

His hand settled against the side of my head, pressing my cheek back against the carpet as his fingers massaged by scalp.

"This isn't to punish you," he said gently, as though it made a difference. I was still rendered silent and helpless, no matter what his intentions. "You can't control your tongue, so I'll control it for you. You'll be much calmer now."

I tried to tell him there was nothing calming about being gagged, but my words were nothing but a garbled growl.

"There's no need to keep arguing with me," he said in a reassuring tone, running his fingers over my hair. "There's no point trying to fight. Surrender. You'll feel much better. We'll calm that busy brain of yours."

I wiggled beneath him, but with my arms bound, there was little I could do to escape.

His touch left me, and he retrieved something else from the desk: a huge coil of rope. "I think you'll like this, my kinky virgin."

He grasped my right thigh and lifted it off the floor, wrapping the rope around it. I tried to kick out at him, but he grabbed my flailing ankle and forced me to bend my knee. He wound more rope around my calf and connected it to the bindings around my thigh, pulling tight so my heel touched my bottom.

When one leg was fully restrained, he grasped my shoulders and pulled me into a kneeling position. I would have tried to push to my feet, but with my leg bound securely beneath me, that was impossible. He continued to bind me, drawing the rope around my waist and looping it between my thighs, framing my sex. I shuddered as he teased around my bare flesh, trying to ignore the growing wetness on my labia.

He tied off his work and moved up my body. More rope wound around me, passing beneath my breasts, wrapping behind my back, and coming back over my chest. He looped it over my neck and back through the lengths that framed my breasts. He pulled it taut, and the rope tightened around my sensitive flesh, squeezing my breasts lightly and making them stand out from my body on lewd display.

They rose and fell rapidly as I began to draw in panting breaths. My skin tingled everywhere the slightly rough fibers trailed across my flesh, and my nipples tightened to hard buds as the pressure of the rope made my breasts feel heavy and full.

He lightly brushed his fingertips across the soft swells, and electricity danced across my skin. I groaned, and my head dropped back as I mindlessly arched into him, pressing toward his touch.

I found myself caught his black stare. He loomed over me, a darkly amused smirk tilting his lips.

"You like being bound, don't you, kinky virgin? Has anyone ever tied you up before? Of course not," he continued before I could even shake my head in response. He traced the line of my lower lip with his thumb, and I shivered as my sensitive nerve endings jumped to attention. "So innocent," he rumbled. "And so beautiful in my ropes."

I blinked hard, struggling to maintain my wits when my entire body was singing with awareness. I should be struggling, at the very least. Not leaning into his hands. I should...

Oh!

He fully cupped my breasts and caught my tight nipples between his fingers, gently pinching them. My eyes practically rolled back in my head, and I moaned as pleasure washed through me.

"That's better," he praised. "You don't have to fight me. You don't have to worry or think."

I shook my head, trying to clear it. Of course I had to worry. My captor had me bound and at his mercy again. If he chose to hurt me, there would be nothing I could do to stop him.

But he wasn't hurting me.

God, his hands on my breasts felt so *good*...

I was barely aware that he'd unlocked the handcuffs with one hand while continuing to play with my nipples with the other. The cuffs fell away, and he directed me to bend my arms behind me, so I grasped my elbows. He tied my hands in place, somehow threading the rope around my arms through the chest harness so it drew even tighter around my breasts.

My breathing stuttered, and my clit began to throb in time with my heartbeat.

His hands closed around my shoulders, and I realized I'd been swaying. I felt dizzy and warm, disoriented. It should have been disconcerting, but I was having trouble focusing on anything but the feel of the braided ropes caressing my skin, manipulating my blood flow to the most sensitive parts of my body.

He placed one hand on the top of my head, lightly gripping my hair to steady me. With the other, he pressed a button that was set beneath the desk. A soft whirring sound caught my attention, and I looked up, past Andrés.

A large metal ring slowly lowered from the ceiling, dangling from a thick cable. I put two and two together from my time spent on the darker corners of the internet and recognized it for what it was.

Of course he has a retractable suspension point built into his penthouse. Why wouldn't he? The thought skittered across my mind, and I giggled. I was feeling lightheaded, and everything seemed a little surreal and silly.

"That's a lovely sound," he said, touching my lips again. "I'm almost sorry I gagged you so I can't see that pretty smile." His grin sharpened. "Almost. You're very sweet when you can't do more than moan and whimper."

My brow furrowed. I should be mad. The most I could summon up was frustration, and even that wasn't as strong as it should be. I didn't understand this weird detachment from my thoughts and emotions, but I couldn't muster up enough concern to fully examine it.

He tapped my nose with his forefinger in light reprimand. "Stay just like you are," he ordered. "Focus on me."

What else could I do? I was completely under his power, bound and gagged. Only, where the same sensations had brought me misery while he whipped me, now they felt pleasurable. There was no pain this time. Just the soft, sure touches of his masterful hands and the slightly rough caress of the rope. My core ached, and slickness coated my inner thighs. My breasts were growing heavier, my nipples tingling with awareness.

The metal ring came to a stop, dangling a few feet above my head. Andrés picked out another coil of rope and began looping it through the harnesses he'd created around my chest and hips, focusing on the right side of my body. He then fed the ends through the ring and pulled. He braced one arm beneath me as my body tilted and lifted. A strangled cry left me as the ropes shifted and pressed into me. Andrés had arranged them so they held my weight evenly, cocooning my body as he pulled me higher. When I was fully horizontal, he tied off the rope to secure me in place. He wrapped one final length around my left ankle, causing my knee to bend. Gravity kept that leg dangling beneath me, while the restrictive tie around my right leg kept it lifted. My thighs were spread wide, and cool air teased along my exposed, swollen sex.

I drew in shallow breaths as my entire body pulsed with awareness, my world narrowing to focus on the man who'd so thoroughly bound me. His soft smile was at odds with his hungry eyes. I stared into them, fascinated by the black striations that darkened the chocolate brown of his irises.

His hand cupped my cheek, supporting the weight of my head. I realized it was taking effort to hold it upright in this position. My hair dangled toward the floor, weighing me down.

"I'm going to take care of a few things now," he murmured. "You look very pretty, *sirenita*. I think I'll keep you like this more often."

He finally withdrew his touch and sat at the desk. I was positioned at his side, so I could watch him in profile. My heart gave a little twinge when he opened the laptop, and a high whine slipped past the gag as longing tugged at me. I couldn't formulate concrete ideas about escape, but I knew I wanted to get to that computer.

"Hush now," he commanded, not looking in my direction. "The sooner I finish, the sooner I can play with your wet little pussy."

Lust surged through me, redirecting my longing to other, darker things. I did want him to touch me. My sex pulsed and fluttered, desperate for him to stroke me. I whined again, but he ignored me.

His long, elegant fingers began flying over the keyboard. The light, rapid tapping sounds were comforting, familiar. The room started to go hazy, and my body melted into the ropes that held me aloft. I was floating, euphoria settling over me. The world started fading around the edges. I vaguely realized that my head was lolling forward, my eyes drooping closed. But it was so hard to hold upright, so hard to keep my eyes open. After a while, I surrendered to the velvety darkness, sinking into it. I sighed, relishing the comfort of the pitter-patter of his fingers on the keyboard. I was one of my favorite sounds in the world, and it filled my consciousness, lulling me into a quiet, peaceful headspace.

"Is my pet sleepy?" His low, accented voice rolled over me. "Or horny?" I could feel the heat of his words on my exposed neck as he leaned in.

A pitiful, needy keening reached my ears, but I didn't register that I was the one making the sound.

"I have a few questions for you, kinky virgin," he said, his warm breath teasing across my sensitized skin. "If you're honest with me, I'll let you come."

The tension of the gag eased, and the rubber ball slipped from my mouth. I swallowed several times, my tongue feeling thick and unwieldy.

"I'm the first man to touch you, is that true?" he asked.

"Yes," I answered softly, still cocooned in warm darkness. I could feel his heat pulsing against my body, and I ached for him to touch me. If I answered his questions, he'd grant me the release I so desperately needed.

"But you know about BDSM. You've been to a club. You knew what the flogger was when I used it on you, even though no one has disciplined you before, correct?"

"Yes," I confirmed again.

"I want you to tell me how you know these things."

"Porn," I responded. "I watched Dex's porn."

"And who is Dex? You've mentioned him a few times."

"He's my..." I fumbled to find the right words. "My best friend."

"Why did you watch your friend's porn?"

"I wanted to know what he liked. So I hacked into his browser history."

"Why would you care what kind of porn your friend watches?"

"I love him," I slurred, the words leaving me without thought.

Hard fingers gripped my jaw, lifting my face almost violently. "Look at me," he snarled.

My eyes snapped open, instantly focusing on his burning black glare. Fear stirred in the back of my mind, and I tried to scramble away. The ropes around my body twisted and tugged, and a fresh hit of bliss washed through my system. I moaned softly, and my eyelashes fluttered closed.

His fingers tightened on my face. "No," he said, the command low and rough. "Look at me."

I focused on him again, my entire world centered on his dark gaze.

"You're *mine*," he growled. "From now on, you don't think about other men. You exist to please *me*." He reached between my legs and grabbed my sex, thrusting two fingers into my wet channel and cupping his palm over my clit in a possessive hold. I cried out at the sudden, rough intrusion, but his fingertips curled against the sensitive spot at the front of my inner walls, and his palm ground against my clit. "You're mine," he said, the words almost savage. "Your body, your mind. All of you. Your pain, your pleasure, they belong to me." He twisted my nipple, and I cried out, even as my core contracted around his fingers.

"Come for me," he demanded. "Come for your Master."

He continued to pinch and pull at my nipples as he pumped his fingers in and out of my pussy and rotated his palm against my clit. Pain and pleasure entwined, tormenting me with the cruelest bliss. Tears spilled down my cheeks, and I screamed as my orgasm claimed me.

My scream was abruptly muffled when he crushed his lips against mine in a brutal kiss. His teeth sank into my lower lip, and his fierce growl vibrated into my mouth as his tongue surged inside. I whimpered and opened for him, completely overwhelmed and stripped down to my most basic, animal self. Rational thought was long gone. All I could do was feel the pain of his fingers torturing my breasts, the pleasure of his hand wringing ecstasy from my pussy, the mind-blowing intensity of his mouth subjugating mine. The kiss was raw, primal; an act of force and dominance. I couldn't do anything but submit to the sensations he inflicted upon me, submit to his power over me.

My orgasm went on and on, ecstasy lashing through me. My body jerked and writhed, making the ropes shift around me. It only increased my pleasure, heightened my sense of helplessness. He continued pumping his fingers in and out of my pussy even as my orgasm began to subside. I became overly sensitive, his touch too much to bear.

I whined into his mouth, and he finally showed mercy. He withdrew his hands from my sex and my breasts, but his lips lingered on mine, the kiss slowing to a deep, thorough claiming of my mouth.

When he finally released me, I gasped for air, my head dropping toward the floor. I didn't have any strength left in my body. The world was surreal, and I was still floating; blissed out and buzzing.

I watched with detached interest as he retrieved a pair of shears from the desk. He braced my body with one strong arm while he used the shears to cut away the ropes that bound me. I sagged against him, boneless. He dropped to his knees and cradled me in his arms, holding me close. I closed my eyes and snuggled into him as he stroked me and murmured in Spanish. I couldn't understand the words, but the lilting cadence and low rumble of his voice were comforting.

Without realizing what I was doing, I pressed my lips against my captor's neck, tasting the salt of my own tears on his skin.

CHAPTER 12

The next morning, I awoke to the feel of leather being wrapped around my throat. I sighed and opened my eyes as Andrés locked the collar in place.

"Do you have to do that?" I complained.

He chuckled. "The fact that you still take that tone with me means yes, I definitely have to." He took my hand and pulled me upright. "Go brush your teeth and come back here."

"And then you won't chain me to the bed?" I asked with asperity.

"With that attitude, of course I will," he laughed. He seemed to be in a very good mood this morning. After he'd cut me down from suspension last night, he'd bathed me and fed me before putting me to bed. I'd been too strung out to think about complaining or resisting, but now my spirit was back in full force after a night of the deepest sleep I'd ever had.

I grumbled under my breath about being kept like an animal, but I went into the bathroom to take care of my daily needs. As I splashed warm water on my face, my mind began piecing together my hazy memories of the night before.

He kissed me.

My captor had actually kissed me. That was a surprise. He'd touched my most intimate areas with propriety, but a kiss was... unexpected. It certainly hadn't been tender and loving. But it hadn't been sloppy and awkward like my few other experiences with men.

From now on, you don't think about other men. You exist to please me.

I gasped and braced my hands on the sink.

I'd told Andrés about my feelings for Dex. That put him at risk. I'd made him a target for the Moreno brothers. They would go after him to make me cooperate. I couldn't let them hurt him.

I stormed back into the bedroom, going straight for Andrés. His brows rose in surprise, but my unexpected ire didn't slow his reaction time when I launched myself at him.

He dodged to one side, catching my fist where it had flown past his face. His other hand caught me in the center of my chest, knocking the air from my lungs as he shoved me away. I fell, my back hitting the mattress. His weight settled over me as he straddled my hips and pinned my arms above my head with one hand. My legs kicked out uselessly as he locked the chain to the front of my collar, tethering me to the bed again.

He gripped my jaw, stilling my wild thrashing. "What's this about?" he demanded.

"You leave Dex alone," I shouted at him, jerking desperately against his hold. "I'll kill you if you do anything to him. I swear, I'll kill you."

His fingers tightened around my face to the point of pain, and he snarled down at me. "I have no interest in this man. And from now on, neither do you."

"But you said Cristian would kill him if he found out," I

said, panic seizing my senses. Oh god, I'd betrayed Dex for an orgasm. How could I do that?

"I am *not* my brother," he growled, the words so garbled I could barely discern them. "I won't torture you or threaten the people you care about to get what I want out of you." He leaned in close, so I could feel the heat of his anger slapping against me. "I don't need to torture you to get what I want."

"And what do you call tying me down and whipping me until I scream? Is that not torture?"

"If you knew what torture really was, you wouldn't have to ask," he said roughly.

"And how would you know?" I challenged. "It's not like you'd ever let anyone whip you until you cried."

"You think I don't cry when I'm hurt? You think I don't bleed when I'm cut? You think I don't scream just like any other man in pain? I might not be sane, but I'm still human, Samantha. Don't talk about things you don't understand."

I stared up at him, wide-eyed. "Is that how your face..." I trailed off when he bared his teeth at me in feral rage, his scar twisting into something terrifying.

"Don't talk about things you don't understand," he repeated, enunciating every word. "And don't say your friend's name ever again. I don't want you to even think about him. I'm the only man you should be concerned with, the only one you should think about. Your purpose is to serve me, to please me. No one else."

"Please," I forced out, my eyes watering. "You're hurting me." His fingers were digging into my face, hard enough that I thought I might bruise.

He instantly released me and rolled off me with a curse. He didn't look at me as he stiffly crossed the bedroom to his wardrobe and started getting dressed.

"Andrés?" I asked timidly.

He didn't respond.

I decided I believed him when he said he wouldn't go after Dex. He seemed furious that I'd even think he'd hurt someone I loved in order to hurt me.

I will never cause you harm, not your body and not your heart. I remembered the promise he'd made me. Maybe he did hurt me when he flogged me. And maybe he did enjoy my pain. But he'd never lied about what kind of monster he was.

Guilt nipped at me. Someone had hurt him. That should have been obvious from the very beginning, given his scars. But I'd been so focused on how scary they were that I hadn't stopped to think about the pain he must have endured when he got them. Not to mention the reminder of it when people cringed away from looking at his ruined face. I hadn't been able to bear looking at him when I'd first seen him. What must it be like to have people flinch at the sight of you?

"I'm sorry," I said quietly.

He stiffened further, and he stopped in his tracks. After a few tense seconds, he spoke, but he still didn't turn to look at me.

"I got something for you," he said. "It's on the tray next to your breakfast."

I glanced at the food cart that must have arrived while I was still sleeping. A large, gift-wrapped box sat beside the covered tray.

"What—?"

"I'll see you tonight," he cut me off and strode out of the room.

Curiosity spiking, I went straight for the gift rather than the bacon. I tore off the iridescent white paper and pretty blue bow to find a plain cardboard box. When I opened it, my jaw dropped.

"Wow," I whispered, running reverent fingers over the

laminated, first edition X-Men #101 comic book. The first one featuring The Dark Phoenix. It must have cost a fortune. Not to mention acquiring it so quickly. I'd confessed my geeky cosplay kissing session to Andrés like, two days ago. And only yesterday I'd appealed to him about my boredom. How had he managed to get this for me?

He managed with all his drug money, I reasoned. But that didn't stop me from picking up the comic.

Another first edition of the following book lay beneath it.

And another beneath that.

I carefully, lovingly removed each one and laid them out on the bed beside me so I could stare at them in awe. In all, there were twenty collectable comic books that told the entire Dark Phoenix story arc. It was any nerd's wet dream, including mine.

Okay, maybe I wasn't actually wet from looking at them, but the knowledge that Andrés had been paying such close attention to the little things I'd told him touched me somewhere deep inside. He might be a sadistic psycho, but he could be thoughtful. Kind.

God, I'm going to turn into Lauren, I rebuked myself.

Still, there was no denying that giving me the comics was a small act of mercy. Apparently, Andrés didn't want me to go completely insane from being left alone with nothing but my own racing thoughts.

Even though I was almost hesitant to touch them, I was desperate enough for reading material that I eventually opened them. I knew the stories already, but being able to handle these precious editions in person rather than reading reproductions of them on my computer screen was an entirely new experience.

I barely paused to talk to Lauren when she brought me lunch. She didn't seem keen on talking, anyway. And after hearing her disturbing take on Andrés—how *nice* she thought he was—I didn't really want to discuss it with her any more.

Despite taking my time with them, I'd been finished with the final book for quite a while before Andrés returned for the evening. I'd actually started re-reading #101 and was almost done for the second time when he came into the bedroom.

I beamed at him, high on nerd-endorphins. "Thanks," I said, genuinely grateful.

He blinked at me, momentarily stunned. Then he grinned. "You are even more beautiful when you smile than I imagined."

My smile faded at the reminder of our real relationship dynamic. He wasn't some nice boyfriend who'd bought me a cool gift. He was my captor.

"You're manipulating me again," I accused.

"So you don't want the comic books?"

"No," I said quickly, clutching #101 to my chest. "I mean, I want them. I um, actually already read all of them. But I'll read them again," I babbled on, not wanting him to take them away if I sounded ungrateful.

His brows rose. "You read all of them today?"

"I tried to go slow, but they're so good," I said. "And I process things really fast. I usually do more than one thing at a time to stay occupied. But this was good," I hurried on. "Way better than staring at the ceiling."

"I'll have to get you more, then," he said, smiling again.

"You don't have to get first editions," I replied. "I like newer stuff, too. Graphic novels are awesome. Works by Frank Miller and Alan Moore are great."

"I'll get those for you, then," he said. "And more first editions."

"But I just said you don't have to. I've read most of them online, anyway."

"But they made you smile. So you're getting more. Don't argue with me, Samantha," he said sternly before I could protest further. "I'll put in an order tonight, and they'll be here in the morning."

"How did you get them so fast?" I asked. "These had to be really hard to find."

"There was a store in New York that had them in stock. I sent someone to go get them."

"But I just told you I was bored last night."

He shrugged. "It's not a long flight."

I gaped at him. "You flew someone from Chicago to New York and back again overnight to get me some comic books?"

"Yes, and it made you smile. So the fifteen minutes it took me to set it all up was more than worth it."

The full power of what his dirty money could get him came down on me like a hammer, deflating the last of my joy.

"What's wrong?" He sounded a little strained.

"I don't want anything you bought with your Bliss money," I said quietly.

His jaw firmed. "You'll get the books, anyway."

"I won't read them."

"That's your choice. You'll still have them."

I glared at him. "You're trying to manipulate me again. You know I'll go out of my mind and end up reading them if they're in here."

A small smile tugged at the corners of his lips. "If you already know this, then why bother fighting me on it?"

"Because you're a smug bastard, that's why."

He shook his head at me, but his smile didn't waver. "I'm going to find a better use for that dirty mouth."

He crossed to the bed and unlocked the chain from the bedpost. He kept the length of it attached to my collar.

"Come," he commanded, coiling the chain around his fist

and tugging gently. The pressure on my neck forced me to scramble to my feet.

"Where are we going?" I asked, having no choice but to follow him as he walked out of the bedroom.

"What was it you so charmingly called it?" he mused. "Oh, yes." He shot a wicked smirk at me. "My *torture room*."

I tried to stop in my tracks, but he kept walking. The chain pulled taut, and I stumbled forward. I fisted the metal links in both hands and yanked. His arm barely tugged back toward me, but he stopped and turned to face me.

My chest rose and fell rapidly, my breaths coming too fast as my heart raced.

"I don't want to go in there," I said, my voice higher than usual. "I won't cuss at you again. I won't."

He shook his head, but the tilt of his lips was almost indulgent. "You will. You can't seem to help yourself."

"I'll try really hard," I promised. "Just don't take me in there. Please."

He took a step toward me. I flinched back. He frowned and pulled on the chain, forcing my body to tumble against his. I clutched at his shoulders for balance, but his hands had already closed around my waist to prevent me from falling.

"This is part of your training," he said calmly. "It will feel good. Not everything in that room is meant to cause you pain."

"It scares me," I admitted on a shaky whisper, remembering my helplessness when he'd flogged me.

Shock obliterated my growing fear when he leaned in and softly pressed his lips against mine. I tried to jerk away from him, but his hand curved around the back of my head, holding me in place while he continued the kiss. It was gentle, coaxing. My lips began to shape to his, and he increased the pressure of his mouth on mine, turning more demanding. My body softened against him, even as my fingernails curved into his shoulders, clinging on tight.

He growled and nipped at my lower lip. I opened for him on a gasp, and his tongue invaded my mouth, sweeping in to claim me hard and deep.

This kiss was different than our first. That one had been punishing, branding. This one wasn't tender, but it was more careful. A slow, thorough seduction.

He didn't stop until I was desperate to draw breath, and when he finally pulled away, I gasped for air, my knees going weak as oxygen hit my system. He held me tightly against him, supporting my sagging weight with one strong arm around my lower back. His erection pressed into my hip, straining against his slacks. He still wore his suit, and I was still naked. The power dynamic should have been disconcerting, but my head was spinning from his scorching kiss.

"Are you still scared?" he asked, running his fingers through my hair.

I leaned into his touch without thought. "No," I said, my voice strangely husky.

"I promise this isn't going to hurt," he swore. "Only pleasure today."

"But I cussed at you." I didn't understand. "I called you a bastard."

"I heard you the first time," he said drily. "We're going to train your mouth. From now on, every time you curse at me, you're going to make it up to me by using your tongue another way."

I trembled against him, knowing exactly what he meant. "I don't... I haven't ever..."

He continued to stroke my hair. "I know you haven't," he said, his tone low and soothing. "I'm going to teach you. And

I'll make it feel good for you, so you associate my cock in your mouth with pleasure."

"You're trying to condition me again." My accusation came out more shakily than I'd intended. "I don't like when you do that."

"You'll like this." His arm slipped from my lower back, his hand skimming over my bottom before dipping between my legs. He cupped my sex, his fingers playing through my soft folds. Pleasure began to pulse at my core. I couldn't help but respond to his touch.

"Did you know your body is capable of having multiple orgasms?" he asked as he played with me. "I wonder how many you'll have before you can't take any more."

"Please..." I wanted him to stop, before I couldn't stop myself. Heat coiled in my belly, and my lower lips grew slick with my arousal.

"Please make you come?" he asked, lightly mocking. He sensed my internal struggle, and it seemed to amuse him. "Not yet, *sirenita*. You have to come into my playroom first."

"It's a torture room," I countered breathily.

"It's where I play with my fucktoy. That makes it my playroom."

"I'm not your fucktoy."

"It's not an insult, so there's no need to look so spiteful," he said, still amused. "You're my toy, my plaything, my pet. And you love when I play with you and pet you. See? You're creaming all over my hand."

"Just because my body feels one way about it doesn't mean I like it."

"Don't lie, *cosita*. You wouldn't have watched all that kinky porn if you didn't like it. If you didn't long for it."

"I longed for—" I cut myself off before I said Dex's name. I wouldn't risk that again. "I don't want this with you."

"Then why am I the only man who's ever touched you? You were so skittish at first. Do you really think you would have found pleasure with someone else? They wouldn't have understood how to handle you. Not like I do. You need a firm hand."

"I don't," I protested weakly. I really was getting embarrassingly wet as he spoke, responding to all the twisted, crass things he was saying about me.

He brushed a kiss over my lips. My head tipped back in response.

"No more lies," he murmured against my mouth. "You don't have permission to speak. I'm not going to gag you, but know that there will be other consequences if you defy me. The next time you use your mouth, it will be to suck my cock. Once I come down your throat, you'll be allowed to talk again."

I gaped at him, and he traced the *O* of my lips with his fingertips.

"Just like that," he said with satisfaction. "I'm not going to force your mouth, but you will accept me before we leave the playroom."

I shook my head in denial, not daring to utter another word when I knew he was about to take me into the torture room, whether I wanted it or not. But no way was I going to take his cock in my mouth of my own volition. Just the idea was dirty.

Dirty. Wrong.
Dirty little girl.

"*Cosita*," he said firmly, his fingers threading through my hair. The light pull against my scalp grounded me. "Don't be afraid." It was an order. "This is new for you, but I'll guide you through it. You're safe with me."

Safe.

I felt myself nodding, even though that didn't make any

sense. All I knew was the fear that had been creeping at the edges of my mind had subsided, and I was grateful for Andrés' commanding touch.

Inexplicably, I felt secure in his firm arms. When he finally released me and began to walk toward the playroom, I followed him without further protest.

CHAPTER 13

A shudder rolled through me when Andrés flipped on the crimson lights. My gaze went straight to the spanking bench, and I took a small step back toward the sitting room.

"No, *cosita*," he said soothingly, wrapping his arm around my waist and guiding me forward. It might have been a sweet gesture, but the way his fingers curled around my hip communicated his control. "We're not using the bench today," he promised, leading me past it. "Do you know what this is? You have my permission to speak."

I blinked and looked down where he pointed. I recognized the black device that curved up in a half-sphere, the flat side resting on the floor. It was built to be straddled. If I went down on my knees, the curve would fit between my thighs as I lowered my weight onto it.

"A Sybian," I answered breathily, knowing exactly what it was.

"Such a clever, kinky virgin," he said with pleasure.

"But I can't... There's not a dildo attached." In all the porn

I'd seen, women rode huge dildos as they bounced up and down on the vibrating machine.

"My fingers and my cock will stretch your tight little pussy before I put anything else inside you." His hand tightened possessively on my hip. "The vibrations will be strong enough that you'll feel it everywhere. Your clit, your pussy, your ass. I don't need to fill you with a fake cock to make you scream in pleasure."

"That... That sounds... intense," I said, fumbling over my words. It certainly didn't sound painful. Quite the opposite. But it also sounded like I'd come unraveled if the pleasure was as intense as he claimed. I'd confessed my deepest secrets to him in exchange for orgasms already. What would I do when subjected to this?

Suck his cock.

That was what he wanted from me.

I glanced at the bulge of his erection, which stood out clearly against his slacks. The knowledge that he wanted me made something warm unfurl in my chest; a pure, feminine satisfaction.

The rational part of my mind noted his size, and I remembered how big he'd felt in my hand when I'd touched him in the shower for the first time.

"I won't be able to fit... It won't fit," I mumbled, my cheeks flaming. I couldn't say *your cock won't fit in my mouth* aloud. It was far too shameful.

"We'll go slow," he promised. "You can take me. You will learn."

He was talking about it like my surrender was already a foregone conclusion.

"And if I say no?" I asked quietly.

"Are you saying no?"

"I... I'm nervous. I mean, you're so big. And I've never... I don't know..." I was babbling, my sentences unfinished and incoherent.

He leaned in and captured my lips with his, taking my mouth slow and deep, until my mind quieted. The anxiety that had started churning in my stomach subsided, giving way to warmth that spread down between my legs.

"You don't have to talk anymore," he murmured, pressing a sweet kiss against my cheek. "It's okay to be nervous. I'll be right here to tell you what to do."

I nodded, almost grateful that he'd forestalled the words that had started spilling out of me. I didn't like when my mouth ran away with me out of nervousness. It felt... comforting, knowing I didn't have to say anything else. That I wasn't allowed to say anything else. His command for my silence freed me from my nervous tic, and it was kind of nice. Liberating.

His grip shifted to my upper arms, and he applied pressure to guide me down. "On your knees."

I sank down far more gracefully than I ever could have managed on my own. When he moved my body, I didn't have to worry about being awkward or ungainly.

"So beautiful," he praised when I fully lowered myself onto the Sybian, my wet pussy coming to rest against the hard, cool surface.

He leaned down and moved my left ankle closer to the device. Supple leather closed around it, and he buckled the cuff closed to secure me in place.

Why? The word teased at the tip of my tongue, but I swallowed it back. I wasn't supposed to talk. It was so much easier than questioning him, anyway.

He cuffed my right ankle on the other side. Testing my range of movement, I tried to push up on my knees, but I couldn't rise up off the Sybian with my legs bound beneath me.

He wasn't done restraining me. He grasped my wrists and directed them above my head. Another set of cuffs dangled from a chain that hung from the ceiling. I didn't resist as he buckled them around my wrists. There was no point. I was already bound to the Sybian, and fighting would have only earned me a punishment.

I didn't want another one of those, especially not with the reminder of the spanking bench looming in front of me.

He's not going to hurt me, I told myself. *He's not going to—*

"Oh!" I cried out as the machine began to vibrate beneath me. My fingers and toes curled as ecstasy rolled through my entire body in a shockwave.

Andrés smirked down at me and fully removed the small black remote control from his pocket.

"You like your new toy, *gatita*?"

I moaned and nodded, not even thinking about forming a verbal response.

He stroked my cheek, communicating his pleasure with me. "Greedy girl. I want you to keep count of how many orgasms you have. Can you do that for me?"

I swallowed another moan and nodded again. The vibrations rumbled through me, just as he'd promised. I should have been ashamed at the pleasure I was finding in the stimulation, but all I could focus on was how good it felt. I started to roll my hips in wanton abandon. As I did, the vibrations concentrated on my clit, then my pussy, then my ass. I really should have felt ashamed of the particular pleasure I found in that, but I couldn't stop myself once I started.

"You're going to be so beautiful when you're riding my cock like that," he said, his voice rough with need. He traced the line of my lower lip with his thumb before pushing inside. I opened for him, and he rubbed his calloused fingertip over my tongue. The sensation of his rough skin against my sensitive nerve endings was wickedly decadent. I groaned and pressed my tongue against him, licking and exploring the slightly salty taste of his skin. He started to gently pump his thumb in and out, pushing a little farther in each time, until he neared the back of my throat. I had to focus on breathing and suppressing my gag reflex. It felt so good, and I didn't want to ruin it.

"Good girl," he ground out, his own desire riding him hard.

My sense of feminine satisfaction intensified, and my eyes went to his erection. I started rocking faster on the Sybian, moving on instinct as I sought more pleasure. The chains that held my arms above my head clanked as I undulated my body. Even though I was bound, I felt powerful, beautiful, blissful. The need in Andrés' voice and the evidence of his hard cock sent me flying high. He wanted me. And I wanted...

With his free hand, he reached down and pinched my nipple, rolling and pulling it gently. "Come for me," he commanded.

The little bite of pain sent me over the edge. Heat shot straight from my tormented nipple to my clit, and I ground against the Sybian, rotating my hips as I screamed around his thumb. He continued stroking my tongue as I came undone, and I started licking his finger like it was my favorite candy. I couldn't get enough of the sensation of his firm touch inside my mouth. It made me tingle everywhere: my mouth, my pussy, my ass. Dark ecstasy raced through me, and I shuddered in my chains as my orgasm claimed me.

His thumb popped out of my mouth, and I whimpered at the loss.

"Don't forget to count for me," he said as he turned off the machine, his crooked smile filling my chest with warmth. The expression tugged at his scar, but it didn't scare me anymore. He looked... powerful where he loomed above me in his sharply-tailored suit. Dark and definitely dangerous, but utterly masculine and confident. He wanted me, but he found pleasure in giving me pleasure. It was evident in the hungry way he watched me, the way his cock strained toward me.

He chuckled and touched two fingers beneath my chin, redirecting my gaze to his face. "You were supposed to count your orgasms," he reminded me.

"What? Oh. One," I said faintly.

He tilted his head at me. "That's not nearly enough for my greedy *gatita*, is it? I want more, too."

For a moment, I thought he meant he wanted to come himself, but he turned the Sybian on again, obviously intent on giving me more pleasure.

My gaze riveted back on his erection, and I couldn't help imagining what it would be like to feel his cock with my tongue instead of licking his thumb. My surrender was inevitable. Why fight it? Especially now that I knew how good it felt to have something filling my mouth. I'd never have imagined that it could feel so deliciously sensual.

"You want to see me?" he asked huskily, noting the direction of my gaze.

I nodded and started rolling my hips against the Sybian again, moving without thought. Pleasure was already building at my core, my entire body tingling as little sparks crackled through my system.

A low, feral sound slipped through his teeth, and he quickly freed himself from his slacks.

My eyes widened, and trepidation made my stomach clench. I already knew he was huge, but seeing him from this perspective was much more intimidating. I shrank back slightly, my sensual haze beginning to clear in the face of reality. His thumb had felt good in my mouth. This was something entirely different.

He fisted the base in his hand, squeezing slightly. "You're going to make me lose control," he growled. "Do you have any idea how delicious you are? So innocent and nervous about pleasing me." His fingers touched my chin again, lifting my face so I was captured in his dark gaze. "You do please me, Samantha. Very much."

Something warm buzzed through my veins, something more than physical pleasure. He trailed his fingers over my heated cheek.

"You're perfect. So pretty with your body bound and shaking for me. Do you want to come again?"

"Yes," I gasped out, rolling my hips against the machine.

"You can come when you kiss my cock. Show me how much you want to come. Show me how much you want me." He ground out the words, and a bead of moisture formed at his cockhead.

He shifted his hips toward me, and I pressed my lips against him in a soft kiss. The salty flavor of his pre-cum hit my tongue, and I whimpered against him as my need began to crest.

"Come," he ordered, pinching my nipples, alternating between them with one hand as he continued to fist his cock in the other.

I shrieked as my second orgasm claimed me, and he rubbed his cockhead around my parted lips, spreading his pre-cum on them. I started to come down, panting against his shaft, but he didn't turn off the machine beneath me.

"Please," I begged, my legs beginning to tremble. "It's too much."

"Count," he reminded me.

"Two," I whined, trying to push away from the torturous vibrations.

His fingers left my nipples to twine in my hair. "You're

going to have another one. You're going to cry out in pleasure while your mouth is full of my cock. I want to feel you scream."

A small whimper eased up my throat, but my discomfort eased. My core contracted with fresh need, and the vibrations began to stimulate me again rather than torment.

"Taste me," he commanded. "You can come as many times as you want."

I flicked out my tongue, barely touching the underside of his purple head. He hissed out a breath through clenched teeth.

"More," he demanded.

I obeyed, craving more of his unique flavor. His skin was soft, so different from his thumb. It felt velvety smooth as I glided my tongue down his length, traced the underside, and swirled around his cockhead.

"Very good. Just like that." He was breathing hard, his accent thicker than I'd ever heard it.

I pressed my tongue flat beneath his shaft and cried out as another orgasm wracked my system. It started deep inside me, building until the pressure was impossible to bear. I started licking him in earnest, tasting every inch of him as I reveled in the decadent feel of his hard cock under my sensitive tongue. He bit out a curse, and I moaned in satisfaction. Knowing I had such an effect on him was heady. This powerful man who craved control was struggling to hold back his lust for me. I wanted him to come undone, to feel the same wild abandon that had completely overtaken me.

"How many?" he asked roughly as my orgasm finally started to subside.

"Hmmm?" I hummed against his shaft, and his fingers tightened in my hair.

"You know, *gatita*. Don't toy with me. How many?"

"Three," I sighed, rubbing my cheek against him.

"That's it," he encouraged. "Worship my cock. Just like that."

The vibrations continued to torment me, but I didn't bother begging for him to turn off the machine. I knew he wouldn't, and truthfully, I didn't want him to. I was as greedy as he'd claimed I'd be. I wanted more: more pleasure, more power, more *Andrés*.

"Suck me," he ordered, on the edge of his control.

I opened my mouth and invited him in, stroking him with my tongue as he slid inside. He stopped me with his fist on my hair when I tried to take him all the way to the back of my throat.

"Slowly, *sirenita*," he corrected me, his accent so heavy it took me a moment to discern what he'd said.

Using his grip on my hair, he eased my face back so only his cockhead remained inside my mouth. I rolled my tongue around it and stared up at him. His nostrils flared and his eyes turned flat black. He bared his teeth in an expression that was almost vicious. It made my pussy flutter, and another orgasm shuddered through my body. I screamed around his cock—just as he'd ordered me to do.

He thrust forward, hitting the back of my throat. I gagged, and he immediately pulled back so I could gasp in a breath.

"Relax," he growled, but there was no menace in the word, only desire. "I'm going to come down your throat."

I moaned, the only sound I was capable of with him filling my mouth. He pressed farther back, testing me. I breathed through my nose and focused on suppressing my gag reflex.

"Good girl." His hold eased on my hair, and he massaged my scalp as he pushed into my throat. He threw his head back with a roar and finally released, his cum lashing into me. He pulled back so it coated my tongue, filling my mouth.

"Swallow," he snarled. "Take everything I give you."

As I did so, pleasure claimed me again, the vibrations of the machine beneath me relentless. My entire body twisted against the restraints, mindless with ecstasy. He finally pulled free of my lips, but I continued to lick him, cleaning off the last of his desire.

He started murmuring in Spanish, running his fingers through my hair as he praised me.

Finally, he turned off the Sybian, and I collapsed in exhaustion as all my muscles melted. He freed my wrists from the cuffs and bent to catch me before I could fall. He went down on one knee and captured my lips with his.

Surprise sparked through me that he'd kiss me after coming in my mouth, but he didn't seem to care. If anything, he seemed hungrier for me than ever.

When he finally pulled away, he freed my ankles and lifted my sated body up in his arms.

"How many times did you come?" he murmured as he carried me out of the playroom.

"Oh. Um... Like, five? Maybe?" I was too sleepy to really think about it. I pressed my face against his hard chest, enjoying the way it rumbled as he laughed.

If that was what giving a blowjob was like, I wasn't sure why I'd waited so long.

Because I needed Andrés, I realized, recognizing the truth in what he'd said to me earlier. I'd needed him to push past my fears and my weird tics and show me what my body was capable of.

I should be upset at the realization that I needed my scary captor in order to experience intimacy with a man, but he wasn't all that scary, really. His scars might look mean, but he hadn't forced me to suck his cock. He could have beaten me until I broke down and did anything he wanted, but he'd ensured that I enjoyed the experience, possibly even more than he did. He'd come once. I'd come... How many times?

I decided I was too tired to worry about it. Sighing in post-orgasmic contentment, I snuggled against Andrés' chest and drifted in warm bliss.

CHAPTER 14

Somehow, everything started feeling routine. Andrés fed me, bathed me, teased me, and gave me the most mind-blowing orgasms. With the occasional spanking if I got too sassy. He still kept me chained to his bed while he was gone, but the stacks of comics he brought me every morning helped me pass the time.

It had been a week since he'd taken me into his playroom and taught me how to give him a blowjob. I'd had to suck him off several times since due to my penchant for cursing, but I didn't hate the experience, so it wasn't much of a deterrent, really.

For long stretches of time in the evenings, he'd tie me in various positions from the suspension point next to his desk. He claimed that he liked having something pretty to look at while he worked.

Pretty. I'd never thought of myself that way. Despite my fucked up situation, Andrés made me feel beautiful, desirable. And that made me feel powerful in a way I'd never known before. I'd always been confident in my hacking abilities, in the sharpness of my mind. But physically, I'd always felt out of place. Awkward and weird.

I didn't have to worry about being awkward with Andrés. He simply moved my body where he wished, and with his guidance and instruction, I didn't trip all over myself. I couldn't get stuck in my own head and in my own insecurities when he handled me. His strong arms and dark eyes grounded me, keeping me focused on him rather than getting swept up in my racing thoughts.

But I wasn't a fool, and no matter how much Andrés tried to condition me to want to be his pet, I wouldn't cave. Maybe I did like the way he touched me, but that didn't mean I wasn't still intent on escaping him. I had a life to get back to, and I refused to spend my days as the plaything for an evil drug lord.

Evil. I often had to remind myself of what Andrés did for his *business.* He petted me and doted on me, and it would have been much easier on my psyche if I'd just allowed myself to fall into a fantasy of being his cossetted, kinky girlfriend.

But I couldn't forget that all the expensive nerdy gifts he brought me had been purchased with drug money. Money that came from trafficking Bliss and selling innocent women like Lauren.

Not to mention that all of it was a manipulation to *tame* me. To make me docile and obedient so I'd work for his brother without trying to get a message back to my friends at the Bureau the second I had access to a computer.

I'd certainly become docile, despite my best efforts. He kept me drunk on pleasure, and if I did start getting too bold, a sound spanking or his cock in my mouth would subdue me.

For a few days, I'd internally railed at myself that I should have been stronger than this. But beating myself up about enjoying Andrés' kinky games wasn't going to help me escape. I needed my full wits about me, and self-loathing was a distraction I couldn't afford. I could give him my body, as long as I kept my mind. Submitting kept me safe from being punished again. It was the smart thing to do, not weakness.

I didn't bother to look up from reading *Watchmen* when the door opened. Most days, I tried my best not to look at Lauren directly. Her eyes were so disturbing, and the only time anything sparked in them, it was resentment. She clearly would have preferred to be *Master* Andrés' pet to being drugged and whored out to dozens of men.

After facing the reality of captivity with Andrés, I suspected I'd prefer my situation, too.

And that realization was so disturbing, I'd rather ignore Lauren than face it head-on.

I gasped when strong fingers fisted around the collar at my nape, pulling me up off the pillows.

"Andrés," I forced out, struggling to speak with the collar tight around my throat. "What are you doing here?"

Lauren hadn't brought me lunch yet, so it couldn't be past midday. He never returned this early.

I looked up at him, alarmed at the almost violent way he was handling me. His dark eyes were fixed on his task: unlocking the chain from my collar. As soon as it fell away, he lifted me up and tossed me over his shoulder, knocking the air from my chest.

"Put me down!" I demanded, twisting in his hold as panic spiked.

He hadn't spoken to me, he wouldn't look at me. Anger was evident in the stiff way he held me, the too-sharp smack of his hand against my upper thigh.

Fear fluttered in my chest, my heartbeat picking up speed. This wasn't my indulgent captor who cradled me against his chest and kissed me. This man who held me so dispassionately scared the shit out of me. It reminded me of his cold detachment the night he'd strapped me to the spanking bench and flogged me.

"I didn't do anything wrong," I protested, squirming against him as we entered the playroom.

No. *Torture room.*

Because we were headed straight for the spanking bench.

I beat my fists against his lower back, thrashing like a wild thing. "No! Please."

He ignored me, handling me roughly as he pinned my body down on the bench and strapped me in place. Tears dropped down my cheeks as the false image of him I'd built in my mind shattered. He wasn't doting. He wasn't nice.

He was unstable, insane.

And every small kindness he'd shown me had been a lie, a manipulation.

"What did I do wrong?" I heaved out on a sob as terror took hold of my mind. He'd been harsh with me, but he'd always been fair, in his own way. "I didn't do anything. I didn't. Please."

Once I was fully bound beneath him, he paused and finally looked down into my eyes. His face was drawn, his scar puckered and twisted as he clenched his jaw tightly. He stared down at me for several agonizing seconds, then he drew in a deep, shuddering breath. He trailed his fingers over the leather restraints that held my body at his mercy, and his fierce expression eased. He reached out and brushed at the wetness on my cheeks. I tried to cringe away, but there was nowhere to go.

"Please," I whispered brokenly. "I promise I didn't do anything wrong. Don't hurt me."

"I'm not going to hurt you," he promised, his accent thick. "Much," he amended. "Hush now," he said in his usual soothing tones as he stroked my trembling body. "This isn't a punishment."

"But you're angry," I said tremulously. "You're going to hurt me."

"I'm not angry with you," he replied, calm settling over him as he continued to pet me. "My brother..." His fingers firmed on my skin, pressing too hard. He drew another deep breath and resumed stroking me, concentrating his attentions around the leather straps that held me down, as though seeing me helpless and at his mercy comforted him in some perverted way. "I need to accelerate your training," he said. "My brother is not a patient man."

I tensed. Andrés continued stroking me, his focus shifting to my hair.

"I'll protect you," he promised. "But I've been too indulgent with you. You must learn your place."

"So you're going to beat me," I said in soft accusation.

"I'm going to train you," he countered. "You will experience a little pain, but you will enjoy it. I know you will. You like your spankings. You'll like this, too."

"I don't want you to flog me again," I whispered.

"I don't want you to be scared of me, *cosita*," he said instead of responding directly.

"I thought you like it when I'm frightened," I said bitterly, remembering all the fucked up things he'd said about my lovely eyes when I was crying from fear.

His lips firmed, and he cut his gaze away from mine. "That doesn't mean I want you to fear *me*. But yes, a part of me likes your fear."

"Please let me up," I begged. "You don't have to do this."

His gaze snapped back to mine, hard with determination. "Yes, I do. It's for your own good."

I didn't dare say how crazy that statement was. I was too intimidated, and he held all the power. He could do anything he wanted to me, and there would be nothing I could do to stop him.

He placed his hand on the back of my neck, lightly squeezing. In his messed-up world, this was a comforting gesture. At least, it seemed to comfort him. It was a demonstration of control, of ownership.

"You'll like this," he said. "You'll see. You have to trust me."

I bit back the retort that I'd never trust him. He might be calmer, but his mood was precarious, violence lurking just under his skin. No matter what he said about me enjoying whatever he was about to do, he needed to hurt me. I could see it in his eyes; I could see the all dark things that stirred in their black depths: desire, anger, pain.

Something about what had happened with his brother had triggered him, and he needed me to soothe him. If he were a normal man and we were in a normal relationship, I'd hold him and kiss him and tell him everything was okay.

But this wasn't normal. He was my captor, and right now, he was on the edge of sanity. There was only one way the madness inside him would be soothed: my complete subjugation. Already, just having me bound and crying beneath him seemed to have quieted his more volatile emotions. Next, he'd extract pleasure from my screams.

I shuddered, my teeth chattering as cold terror settled into my bones.

He dropped to his knees beside me, his face leveling with mine. Through my watery vision, I saw his brow furrow with concern.

"Samantha," he said my name almost hoarsely. "You're okay. You're safe with me."

"I'm not," I said, my voice hitching. "I'm scared. You're scaring me. And you like it."

"I don't. Not like this. Please. Don't be afraid."

Please. I'd never heard him utter the word.

"I don't want to be in here," I whispered.

"All right, *cosita*. It's all right. You're safe." He started murmuring to me in a stream of soothing Spanish, running his fingers along my chilled skin as he released me from the cuffs that trapped me against the spanking bench.

A relieved sob heaved from my chest when he lifted me in his arms and cuddled me close. My hand fisted in his shirt, and I turned my face against him as I wept and shook.

He carried me back into the bedroom and settled me on his lap when he sat on the edge of the bed. He held me while I cried, all the fear and pain that lingered inside me from the night he'd flogged me spilling out to soak his chest with my tears.

"*Lo siento.*" I caught the words several times as he continued to speak to me in low, calming tones.

I'm sorry. I knew what it meant.

That helped bring me back to my senses more than anything. My big, scary captor was apologizing. Blinking up at him, I studied his taut features. He seemed truly distressed, and when my sobs finally quieted, he pressed a tender kiss against my forehead.

"I was worried about you," he rumbled, his arms tightening around me to pull me closer to his warmth. "I didn't mean to upset you."

"You did," I countered quietly. "You wanted to see me cry. You wanted to hear me scream."

His eyes flicked away from mine, and he tensed beneath me. "I do want those things from you, Samantha," he admitted, his voice strained. "But not like this. I won't break you. I won't." He still wasn't looking at me, and he seemed to be speaking to himself as much as he was reassuring me.

"I don't want this," I said, my voice small. "I don't want to be here. I don't want to be tamed. I don't want to work for your brother."

"You don't have a choice in that. Neither of us do."

"What do you mean?" I didn't understand. Of course Andrés had a choice. He could hurt me, he could beat me, he could savor my pain. He could choose to do anything he wanted with me.

But he chose to cuddle me close and run his hands over my cool skin, imbuing my body with his steady warmth.

He didn't answer my question. Instead, he suddenly crushed his lips to mine in a fierce, hungry kiss. Every stroke of his tongue dominated my own, his mouth caressing mine hard enough to leave my lips swollen and tingling. I finally softened against him as my body warmed, the last of the chill of terror leaving my system as I found comfort in my captor's desperate kiss.

CHAPTER 15

Andrés stayed with me for the rest of the day, holding me until Lauren brought lunch. She seemed surprised to see us together, and she had to come back a second time with more food for him. I wondered what had happened with Cristian to drive Andrés back to me in such a black mood, but I didn't dare press him on the subject. I didn't want the scary, violent man to resurface. I much preferred the sweet, caring man who petted me and draped my body across his chest while he leaned back against the headboard and read *Watchmen* with me.

I went back to the beginning of the story since Andrés had never read it before, and I found a strange joy in sharing it with him, almost as though I were able to experience it again for the first time myself. Only better than that, because he wasn't jaded by years of warring fandoms. There was a weird innocence in watching him begin to enjoy the story, his lips curving with satisfaction as he turned the pages faster and faster.

He glanced down and noticed me watching him.

"Am I more interesting than your superheroes?" he asked, ruffling my hair.

"Anti-heroes," I corrected him. "Well, some of them, anyway. That's what makes them interesting."

"Then why are you looking at me?"

I shrugged. "I already read it. I know the story."

He set the book aside. "Then I'll get you a different one. I don't want you to be bored."

"I'm not," I answered honestly. "You can keep reading it."

His smile twisted. "I don't want to read right now. Not when you're watching me like that, my curious *gatita*." He took my hand and pressed it against his growing erection. His suit was rumpled from laying on the bed with me for hours, but he still looked powerful. Magnetic. The feel of his desire for me through his slacks made power pulse through my veins. This was for *me*. I wasn't scared of him when he was like this, even though a part of my brain acknowledged the fact that my captor's arousal should definitely terrify me.

But he'd never used me against my will. He'd never forced me to take his cock. He might have conditioned me to like it, but the knowledge that I'd been conditioned didn't make his training any less effective.

My core fluttered and heated, my lower lips growing slick with my own arousal.

His hands closed around my waist, and he shifted my body off his. "On your hands and knees," he ordered, his voice dropping deeper with desire.

I got into position without argument. After the intense fear and vulnerability of our scene in the playroom that morning, I was feeling particularly clingy. I wanted to be close to him, for him to touch me and tell me I was safe. Even though he had been the one to scare me in the first place. It was fucked up, but I ached to please him, to make him laugh and look at me with pleasure in his dark eyes.

I told myself that my weird feelings were a survival imperative; if my captor was happy with me, he wouldn't hurt me.

But I'd seen the pain that lurked alongside the rage when he'd strapped me down to the spanking bench. I'd seen the calm that came over him once he had me bound, unable to escape him. He needed this from me.

"You are so beautiful," he murmured as he traced the line of my spine. "Stay."

He left me briefly to retrieve a few items from the chest of drawers where he seemed to stash a multitude of kinky toys. I waited, trying to remain calm without his touch to ground me. It was unnerving, this... *need*. I craved physical contact with Andrés, and even in those few seconds of separation, a hollow sensation began gnawing at my gut.

Subdrop. I'd read about it online. Submissives could go into a depressive state after an intense BDSM scene, and they needed to be cuddled by their Doms until the feeling passed.

Only, Andrés wasn't some dreamy Dominant partner I'd willingly gifted with my submission.

My animal brain warred with my rational mind.

Rational mind: *resist, fight, escape.*

Animal brain: *pet me, hold me, kiss me.*

"Settle, *cosita*," he ordered, smoothing a hand down my back when he returned to my side. He'd read the mounting tension in my body, and it was soothed away as soon as he touched me.

My animal brain won. With Andrés so close, it was impossible to cling to rationality. I was too fragile from my breakdown a few hours ago, and neediness obliterated my brittle willpower to maintain emotional distance from him.

"I'm not going to restrain you, so you're going to have to be very good for me," he said, continuing to pet me. I sighed and relaxed under his hand, enjoying the sensation of his skin on mine. "Just like that," he approved. My heart squeezed at the pleasure evident in his twisted smile.

"I want you to trust me," he said. "So I'm going to trust you, too. I'm going to trust you to stay in position for me. I wanted to tie you down so you wouldn't be able to move away from me. It's safer for you if you stay still. That way, I won't inflict pain unintentionally." He shushed me before I could question him about *inflicting pain*. "You'll like this," he continued. "I'll make sure you do, I promise. But you have to trust me. Can you do that for me?"

Fine lines of strain appeared around his eyes. He was asking for my trust, not demanding it. He was leaving me free to resist, to fight. It was my choice to submit or not.

And the fact that he gave me a choice made the decision for me.

"Yes," I said softly. "I can trust you."

His grin dazzled me, knocking the air from my lungs. There was no dark satisfaction in it, no triumph at my defeat; only pure joy at my willing surrender.

His touch eased down my back, over the curve of my bottom, before tracing the line of my soft folds. I moaned and pushed back into him, welcoming him to press inside me. Two fingers entered me, slowly penetrating my tight channel. I'd adjusted to taking him like this, so there was no pain as he stretched me, sliding his fingers in and out as I rocked my body in a rhythm to match.

I stilled with a soft whine when something hard and wet touched my asshole. I craned my head back to find him watching me carefully. He captured me in his warm gaze.

"Trust me," he urged. "This will feel good."

His fingers withdrew from my sheath to play with my clit,

and he increased the pressure of the small red anal plug against my tight ring of muscles. It glistened with lubricant, and I knew he was going slowly so he wouldn't hurt me. As his calloused fingertips traced teasing circles around my clit, my muscles relaxed. The tip of the plug slipped inside me, reminding me of how he'd penetrated my ass with his finger for the first time in the shower. That seemed so long ago now. It had been scary, and he'd done it to demonstrate his complete ownership of my body.

This was different. It wasn't a power play, even though the power dynamic was definitely shifting between us. The farther he pressed the plug in, the more I submitted. He made it pleasurable for me, taking care to ensure that I enjoyed every deliciously deviant second of my virgin hole being stretched. I surrendered to the pleasure, surrendered to *him*. Dark bliss sizzled through forbidden places, lighting up my body in ways I'd never imagined I'd accept. Anal play had always seemed too taboo, too humiliating to contemplate.

With Andrés staring down at me with such intensity, I certainly didn't feel humiliated. I felt precious. Revered. His hands might be masterful, knowing exactly how to make my body flower open for him, but there was also something worshipful in his touch.

A light burning sensation threatened to erode my pleasure, but he rubbed my clit more firmly, giving me a hit of ecstasy to mitigate the discomfort.

"Almost there," he assured me. "You're doing so well. You're going to love taking my cock in your ass, once you're properly prepared."

The widest part of the plug sank past my tight ring, and my muscles closed around the slender base as it settled deep inside me. I drew in short, panting breaths, struggling to adjust to the sensation of being filled.

His thumb stayed at my clit, and his forefinger returned to my sheath, sliding inside with aching care. I cried out, and my fingers clawed at the sheets beneath me as twisted pleasure washed over me. I could feel him stroking along the length of the plug through the thin barrier inside me. Although I'd learned to accommodate two fingers inside me, I felt almost unbearably full with the added pressure of the toy in my bottom.

"Come for me," he urged, increasing the pressure on my clit as his forefinger found my g-spot. At the same time, he gently tugged on the plug. All my pleasure centers lit up at once, and I screamed as my orgasm claimed me. I felt my body clamping down on his finger and on the plug, and the sensations of my inner walls undulating around them heightened my release. I couldn't push him out, could only submit to being penetrated and played with as he wrung the final drops of bliss from my shuddering system.

I gasped against the sheets, breathing hard. He finally pulled his hand away, but he didn't remove the plug.

"Stay just like that," he ordered, his voice thick with his own desire. "Don't move."

Before I could turn my head to see what he had planned, a small *pop* reached my ears and fresh sensation assailed me. A light sting bloomed on my bottom, and my inner muscles tightened and danced around the plug. I looked back at him as I cried out at the shock of pleasure.

I groaned at the sight of Andrés towering over me, dressed in his suit, a crop in his big hand. It was like something out of one of my dirtiest dreams. I'd never before envisioned a man like him—dark and unquestionably dangerous—but desire flooded my entire being as he smirked down at me.

He touched the tongue of the crop beneath my chin, letting me feel the buttery soft leather as he lifted my face. "I like when you look at me like this," he said, his accented voice lilting with his own pleasure. "My kinky virgin."

He slid the crop up to my lips, and the rich, slightly salty scent of leather intoxicated me. Without thinking, I kissed it, the same way I'd worship his cock.

A low growl left his chest, the sound rumbling through me to heat my core.

"You please me, Samantha. Very much."

I hummed in response and licked at the length of the crop, words escaping me. My rational mind had utterly receded, leaving my base instincts to rule me.

"You like the crop?" he asked, the question light with arrogant amusement. "You're not scared of it? You're not scared of me?"

"No," I moaned, lifting my ass in wanton invitation. "Please."

"All right, greedy *gatita*," he chuckled. "Don't move."

He tapped my bottom with the crop. My flesh jiggled slightly, making my asshole contract around the plug. More sparks of pleasure crackled inside me, heating my empty pussy. I let out a long sigh, and my head dropped forward as I submitted fully, waiting for more.

He struck me again on the opposite cheek, a little harder. The sting of the leather hitting my flesh made my skin heat with pleasant warmth. When I didn't protest or move away, he increased the intensity of the next blow, then then next. I groaned as my entire body relaxed. Everything tingled, and I started to float. It felt like he'd suspended me, but no ropes held me aloft. The harder the crop landed, the higher I flew. The world was beautiful and dark and warm, and all that existed were the sensations being inflicted upon my body and the man who was inflicting them.

"Andrés," I moaned his name, needing... more.

The hits stopped, and his heat washed over me. "I could fuck you right now, couldn't I, kinky virgin?" he asked, his silky voice threading through my mind. "Your tight little pussy would welcome my cock."

"Andrés, please..." I wasn't sure what I was begging for. Just... *more*. More pleasure; more connection; more of his power washing over me, taking me high and setting me free.

"You shouldn't say my name like that, *sirenita*. You really shouldn't." He sounded breathless, hoarse.

He bit out a curse. "Open your mouth."

My lips parted, and my eyes fluttered open just in time to watch his cock surge between them. I whimpered around him as he slid all the way to the back of my throat, but I accepted all of him. His fingers tightened in my hair, and he held himself deep for a few seconds before easing almost all the way out.

"I'm going to fuck your mouth," he told me roughly, surging forward again. "The way I want to fuck your little pussy. But not today. Not when you're like this."

I didn't understand what he meant, and I was too high to care, anyway. I didn't have to think when he was in control. I didn't have to worry.

He held my face and worked his cock in and out of my mouth as I sucked and swirled my tongue around him, lost in a sensual haze. All I wanted was to connect with him, to bring him the same bliss he'd given me.

He kept one hand in my hair and picked up the crop from the bed beside me. He tapped it against the plug in my ass, sending vibrations rumbling through my core. I came apart, my scream of release muffled around his thick cock. He followed me, throwing his head back on a rough shout as his cum coated my mouth. I swallowed it all down, just as he'd trained me to do.

He withdrew, and he caught me as my trembling limbs gave

out, no longer able to support my weight. The mattress dipped as he collapsed beside me. He pulled my body tightly against his, kissing the top of my head as his hands roved over my sweat-slicked skin.

I remained cocooned in warm darkness, reveling in the blissful headspace I'd found in finally, fully submitting to Andrés.

CHAPTER 16

Andrés stayed with me late into the following morning. The sun was already high when I finally awoke. The last few nights, I'd been getting the deepest, most peaceful sleep of my life with Andrés' corded arm draped over me, his hard body shaped around mine. I wasn't accustomed to sleeping so many hours, or to feeling so well rested. It helped calm my buzzing brain.

Trapped in my captor's strong arms was probably the last place in the world I should get a good night's sleep. That definitely would have been my attitude when he'd first captured me. He'd been huge and scarred and scary, and his claims that I belonged to him had terrified me.

I was still being kept here against my will, but I was coming to understand Andrés a little better. He might be violent and mercurial, but he'd always been completely honest with me. He planned to train me to accept his touch and even come to crave it—something he'd managed with almost laughable ease.

But he'd also promised never to harm me, and I was

coming to truly believe that. I was starting to trust him, despite everything. He might be harsh, but he had his own code. There were lines he wouldn't cross, and he'd proven that to me when he'd freed me from the spanking bench and taken me into the safe haven of his arms, holding me and apologizing for scaring me.

He'd wanted to hurt me. He'd needed it. I'd seen it in the wildness of his eyes.

But he'd held himself back. He'd put my needs before his own. And considering he could do absolutely anything he wanted to me as his helpless captive, that meant more to me than was probably healthy.

I mulled all this over while I went through my morning routine, separated from my captor by the flimsy barrier of the bathroom door. Since he was still in the suite with me, I was allowed to leave the bed and see to my needs.

Andrés hadn't yet collared me for the day, and I found myself touching my fingers to my bare throat. It was a little weird, not feeling the soft leather there. I was becoming accustomed to it, and its absence made me feel...

I shook my head sharply, deciding to stop contemplating it. I should definitely resent the collar, even if I couldn't bring myself to hate Andrés the way I should. He'd taken my freedom from me. And no matter how kind and caring he might seem at times, he still wanted to keep me as his pet, his plaything. He didn't respect me as a woman, as a fully-functioning human being with a mind of her own.

"*Sirenita*," he called out, his stern voice emanating through the bathroom door. "Your breakfast is getting cold. Come."

I blew out a long breath and tried to quiet my whirring thoughts. Like a puppy being called to heel, I had to go back into the bedroom. If I didn't, he'd just come in here and retrieve me. And then he'd probably punish me for defying him.

I was feeling particularly brittle after the intensity what had passed between us last night, and I didn't think I could handle his rebuke at the moment. Even though part of me got turned on by his discipline, I much preferred when he praised me and cuddled me. My nightmare scenario of being held captive was so much easier to bear when he was being nice.

Nice.

God, I am turning into Lauren, I thought bitterly, but I made my way back into the bedroom without complaint.

Andrés was seated on the edge of the bed, fully dressed. That meant he was going to leave soon. A pang shot through my chest, and the irrational reaction only darkened my mood further.

"What's wrong?" he asked as I walked toward the bed, going to him without thought of resistance.

"Nothing." I waved him off, not willing to further examine my conflicted feelings, especially not with my captor.

His brows drew together. "Don't lie to me," he warned

He reached for me, grasping my waist and positioning my body so I was seated in his lap, the way we usually shared meals. He didn't bother trying to keep the cutlery from me anymore. I eyed the knife and fork where they sat on the tray beside my huge plate of bacon. I could just grab the knife and...

My stomach turned before I could even begin to visualize Andrés' blood spilling onto my hand.

"*Cosita?*" he prompted, waiting for my honest response.

I tore my eyes from the knife and focused my gaze on him. "I am a little upset this morning," I admitted. "But I don't want to talk about it."

He cupped my cheek in his big hand, his dark eyes studying mine intently, as though he could see straight into my soul.

"You don't have any secrets from me," he said, but his tone held a note of strain. He wanted me to share with him, even though he was trying to command me to open myself up and give him everything.

I was starting to understand him, but it seemed he might be coming to some revelations of his own. He was beginning to realize he couldn't force my devotion, even if he could condition my obedience.

"Please," I whispered. "I don't want to think about it right now."

That was the truth. When I saw pain stir in his eyes, an illogical yearning to erase it rose up within me. Laying all my tangled emotions bare for both of us to see would only cause more hurt and confusion.

"You do have a very busy brain," he said, pressing a tender kiss against my forehead. "If your thoughts bother you, let me put them at ease."

I knew Andrés was capable of making my mind go quiet. I'd found peace in his ropes, under his masterful hands.

And that power he held over me scared me, even as his touch aroused me.

He leaned in to capture my lips with his.

I turned my face away. "Wait."

He frowned and lightly gripped my jaw to hold me in place. "No. I know what's best for you. You're upset. I'm going to make you feel better."

"You can't just kiss me and make everything okay," I told him, even as my head tipped back slightly, my body already surrendering despite my protest.

"I can. But I don't have to. I can distract you from your thoughts in other ways, if you don't want me to kiss you."

He shifted my body in his lap, turning me so my back pressed against his chest. He hooked my ankles around his calves and spread his legs, opening my thighs wide. One hand tangled in my hair and tugged to the side, exposing my neck. His teeth sank into my sensitive flesh, the flare of pain making my sex clench. He held me trapped in his harsh bite as his free hand skimmed over my breasts, his palm teasing my peaked nipples.

I cried out as sensation assailed me, my entire body lighting up with awareness. He growled his approval against me, and the sound rumbled over my skin, making it pebble and dance.

He finally released me from his bite, running his hot tongue over the little indentations his teeth had left in my skin. I moaned and tipped my head farther to the side, offering him better access to my neck. He pressed feather-light kisses along my throat, up to my ear before nipping at my lobe. His hand left my hair to trail down my waist, over my hip, moving down between my legs. He suddenly slapped my exposed pussy.

I shrieked at the sting that bloomed on my flesh, and I tried to close my legs. He bit down on my neck again and kept me spread wide, his legs keeping mine splayed apart.

I writhed, my ass grinding against his thick erection. He spanked my pussy a second time, and I whimpered, accepting that I couldn't fight him.

His bite eased, and he resumed kissing my neck sweetly, even as his harsh hand smacked my tender labia. I groaned as dark pleasure settled over me, my thoughts floating away as I became lost to sensation. I was powerless to escape him, and bliss began to pulse through me as I slipped into submission.

"Are you still upset?" he murmured, his lips teasing the shell of my ear.

"What?" I struggled to gather my wits and focus on forming a coherent response. "No. I'm not upset. I'm..." I trailed off on a low moan when he traced around my clit in a little circular pattern.

"Horny?" he finished for me. "Does your wet little pussy want to be filled after being spanked?"

"Yes," I begged on a ragged whisper. "Please."

Suddenly, the world spun as his strong hands maneuvered my body. When everything settled into place, I found myself lying back on the mattress, staring up at him. The sight of him towering over me in his suit made lust pulse through my system. I remembered how alluring he'd been when he'd stood over me last night, wielding a crop.

He grinned down at me with savage pleasure. "I do like when you look at me like that, *sirenita*." He reached for his zipper and freed himself from his slacks. I licked my lips, and he growled in satisfaction. "Are you as hungry for my cock as you were last night?"

I nodded, my mouth watering for him.

"But what about your pussy?" he asked, his voice dropping deeper, rougher. "I could have fucked you last night. But you weren't aware enough to know what you would be agreeing to. You weren't capable of knowing what you were begging for." He began to stroke his shaft. "*This* is what you're begging for. I'm going to fuck you, Samantha."

Some of my euphoria ebbed, trepidation burning into my bliss. My body might be aching for him, but I wasn't ready for this.

Was I?

"You have to beg me," he said, his black eyes boring into mine as he imposed his will. "Beg me to fuck you."

"Andrés..."

Please teased at the tip of my tongue, but I swallowed it

back. I didn't want to lose my virginity like this: begging my captor to fuck me. It was twisted and wrong, and it felt like defeat. My arousal soured as I was reminded of the early days of my captivity, when he'd told me how he'd subjugate me.

"I can't," I said, my voice small. "I don't want to. Not like this."

He stared down at me, his jaw working. His dark eyes shuttered, and he abruptly tucked himself back into his slacks. I could still see his cock straining against the expensive material, but he turned sharply and started walking away from me.

"Wait," I called out. "I didn't mean..."

I wasn't sure what to say. I hadn't meant it when I said *no*? That wasn't right. I'd definitely meant to refuse.

What I hadn't meant was to hurt him.

"I'm sorry," I whispered, my eyes burning.

My mind registered that it was fucked up that I was apologizing to my captor for preventing him from taking advantage of me. But that didn't make my sense of guilt abate.

He stopped in his tracks and stiffly turned back to me. For a moment, my heart leapt. I thought he was coming to kiss me, to hold me and tell me he'd never ask me to debase myself for him again.

Instead, he picked up my collar where it already lay on the mattress, chained to the bed and waiting for me. Without a word, he locked it around my neck.

He turned to leave, but I caught his wrist in the strongest grip I could manage.

"Wait," I asked again. "Don't leave like this. I didn't want to upset you. I just... I can't give you what you want."

He turned back to face me, his face carefully blank. "I won't force myself on you," he said, his voice rough.

"Thank you," I whispered. I pulled his hand toward me and pressed my lips against it, softly communicating everything I didn't know how to put into words. I wasn't sure how to express what I was feeling, but I knew I didn't want to hurt him.

He blew out a shuddering breath, and the tension melted from his powerful body. He leaned down and brushed a kiss across my lips, a silent apology.

"I'll see you tonight," he promised.

He pulled his wrist free from my grip and walked out of the bedroom, leaving my body and my heart aching for him.

CHAPTER 17

"A board game?" I asked, nonplussed. "You want to play a game that involves an actual board?"

Andrés' dark brows rose as he set the chess pieces out between us, white for me, black for him. "Is there some other kind?"

"You're kidding, right? How about *World of Warcraft*? You know, something with multi-layered storytelling, cool effects, and kick-ass heroes?" I gestured at the board. "Who's the hero in this game? What's the story? There isn't one. It's just us, staring at some funny pieces that don't have any special abilities at all."

"Chess is a battle of wits. It's just you, against me. But you can be the hero in this scenario, if you want." One corner of his lips tipped up in an indulgent smile.

I considered making a quip about him being the perfect real-life villain, but I held it back. Mostly because it hit too close to home, and I didn't want to hurt him. He might be my captor, but I was coming to see him as more than that. Andrés wasn't an evil

184

man, even if he was holding me against my will. He put my needs first, in his own weird way. Even when he was obviously desperate to fuck me, he held back. After I'd refused to give him my virginity a few days ago, he hadn't pressed me for it again. Instead, we split our time between reading comic books and playing kinky games.

Tonight, he had a much more vanilla, much more boring game in mind.

Chess. Ugh. So analog.

"You don't have to look so disdainful," he said, still smiling. "I'll teach you how to play. If you really hate it after a few games, we can stop. I'll warn you now, I will win. So don't let that deter you from enjoying the game."

"You're a little cocky," I remarked drily, reaching for my queen to examine the exquisitely-carved pieces. They were worn from age and use, but the quality of craftsmanship was still discernable.

"I've been playing for years, and it's an impossibility for a new player to beat someone with my kind of experience."

"Who says I don't know how to play? They do have online chess, you know. I've dabbled. I know the rules, even if I do find it boring."

He grinned. "Knowing the rules won't prepare you for playing against me, but it will certainly make these first few games more interesting. How advanced are you? Who taught you how to play?"

"An online tutorial taught me how to play. I get the rules and know some trickier strategies. I pick things up quickly."

He shook his head. "A tutorial isn't going to prepare you for playing against me, but show me what you know, and we'll go from there."

I was starting to get irritated. Didn't he value my intellect at all?

"Why bother playing chess with someone when you think they won't be able to beat you?"

"Because I believe you will be able to challenge me, just not in the first few games. Or even the first dozen."

I eyed him, considering. His response allayed my irritation. Just a little. I still wasn't sure if I wanted to play a game that Andrés would certainly win. He already won all of our kinkier games.

Didn't he?

If attaining multiple orgasms is me losing, I guess I don't mind.

I shook it off, focusing in on the current challenge.

"How long have you been playing?" He'd assessed my skill level. It was only fair that I do the same.

He picked up one of his knights, stroking the edges of the piece. It was a familiar touch, something he seemed to be doing without realizing. "This was my first chess set. I got it for my tenth birthday. That's when *Abuela* taught me how to play."

"*Abuela?*"

The ghost of a smile flickered around his lips before giving way to something harder. "My grandmother."

"Oh." I could tell from his suddenly tense demeanor that she'd passed away. I hadn't meant to pry into painful topics.

He placed the knight back on the board, and his dark gaze focused on me again. "White goes first," he prompted me.

"I know." He'd given me the slight advantage, presumably because he thought he'd defeat me so easily.

Well, too bad for him, I'd picked up some pretty sweet strategies, even in my dabbling. I wasn't being overly-proud when I said I was a quick study. It was just the way my brain worked. A little bit of internet research had told me some of the strongest opening moves.

Since he'd made the mistake of letting me play white, I'd

checkmate him in six moves.

I moved my pawn from E2 to E4.

Andrés studied the board, then made his countermove. It didn't affect my strategy at all.

Okay, maybe this was going to be fun, after all. He'd been so cocky with all that talk about how I didn't have a chance at beating him. I was really looking forward to seeing his crestfallen expression when I made him my bitch.

This felt almost as good as winning a battle in *World of Warcraft*. Maybe even better, because this was *Andrés* I was defeating, not some anonymous person online.

I took a minute to pretend to consider my next move, even though I was about to win. It would be even more satisfying to take him by surprise.

I moved slowly as I placed my bishop on C4, trying to make it look like I was hesitant about my choice.

Andrés' face remained impassive. He sat for a full two minutes of silence before making his next move.

Usually, I would have found such a long wait boring, but anticipation sizzled through me.

I didn't bother to hold back when I maneuvered my queen to attack his pawn. I clicked it down on the board decisively.

Andrés grinned, and my heart did a funny flip. That sharp, arrogant smile made something flutter low in my belly.

He knew.

"Scholar's Mate," he observed. "I'm impressed. You did study properly, *cosita*."

He moved his knight to F6, blocking me.

His black eyes glinted as he captured me in his steady stare. "Now, we can play."

"When did you realize my strategy?" I asked.

"I suspected on your first move. I knew by the second."

"But you didn't try to stop me."

"You were so cute, trying to fool me. I thought I'd let it play out for a few moves. You're not capable of lying to me, Samantha. You can't play dumb with me, either. I know you better than that."

I flushed with pleasure. Did Andrés really respect my intellect? He'd proven he cherished me in his own way, but I'd never thought he might care about my mind. So far, he'd seemed more interested in my body. Even though he'd expressed that he wanted me to be happy, that wasn't the same as respecting me.

"Who do you play with?" I wondered who usually was capable of challenging him.

"Believe it or not, I do play online mostly. There's not anyone here I'm interested in playing against. It doesn't compare to sitting across from your opponent, though. Studying you is part of the game."

"You play online? I thought you only got on your laptop to work. There's like, no technology in this penthouse. I never even see you with a phone."

"I don't like to be easily reached once I come home. This is my space. And if you're worrying that I'm wasting my time playing chess while you're tied up, don't. I'd much rather play games with you. I really am taking care of my business in the evenings. This is the first time I've played a game in weeks."

My mind chose to skip over the topic of his *business*. Instead, I focused in on the fact that he'd chosen to play chess with *me*. He could just tie me up and toy with me. He could fuck my mouth and take his pleasure from my body, even without taking my virginity.

But he was choosing to play chess with me instead. What had seemed ridiculous and boring at first now made my chest warm.

Andrés valued me as more than his plaything.

"Don't be too disappointed when I win this game," he continued. "I really am impressed with your knowledge of chess. But I've known Scholar's Mate for years. Valentina beat me with it half a dozen times before I caught on."

"Who's Valentina?" Something ugly stirred in my gut at the thought of him playing with another woman.

His face hardened again, the same way it had when he'd mentioned his grandmother. "My sister."

I'd managed to pry into some secret pain again. "I'm sorry." Guilt nipped at me, even though I wasn't sure exactly what I was apologizing for. "You lost her?" I asked quietly.

"Yes," he bit out. "I lost her."

"How—"

"It's your move," he said tersely, a clear warning not to press him on this topic.

I nodded and moved a pawn, not really focusing on my choice. I was so caught up worrying over the fact that I'd upset him that he managed to beat me in five more moves.

He barely took the time to say "checkmate" before putting the board away.

"Can we play again?" I asked timidly.

He blinked and focused on me for the first time since I'd asked about Valentina's fate. "You want to?"

"Yes. I'll do better next time. I know I can beat you."

A half-smile tilted his lips, and my heart squeezed. "Tomorrow," he promised. "I have another game I want to play with my clever *gatita*."

He hurt me that night. He made sure I enjoyed the experience, but he still left marks on my skin. My tears seemed to calm the dark mood that had settled over him.

I gave him my tears willingly, hoping that by shedding them for him, I could ease some of the pain that he kept locked inside.

CHAPTER 18

Andrés kept beating me at chess. But I persevered, if for no other reason than the fact that I liked watching his brow furrow in intense concentration when I actually managed to outmaneuver him. He was clearly a master strategist, which shouldn't have surprised me, given the way he'd handled me over the last few weeks. He seemed to anticipate my every move—in chess and in the kinkier games we played.

I should have been scared at how complacent I'd become, but I couldn't help finding moments of joy when we were together. I'd never shared this kind of intimacy with anyone, and it felt good to be so connected. It made me ache for more, and sometimes I almost broke down and begged him to fuck me.

I couldn't quite bring myself to do it. I didn't want to beg him for it. That reminded me of our first few days together, when he'd been demanding and scary. I enjoyed the fantasy of our relationship too much to face the reality that he was still demanding. And even if I no longer found him scary, he could definitely be intimidating. He touched me however he wanted, whenever he wanted. Just because I liked it didn't mean my consent was necessary.

Was it? He still hadn't taken me against my will. He held himself back, even though I could tell it caused him almost physical pain to deny himself what he wanted: me.

He wants me to beg, I often reminded myself. *I won't beg.*

I might beg him to touch me on a daily basis, but I wouldn't beg him to take my virginity. It was my last shred of dignity, of control over my own body and my own life. I couldn't surrender it. No matter how badly my body ached for him to fill me, to connect with him in the most intimate way possible.

After years of fear and isolation, his touch was like a drug. I doubted even Bliss would have been more effective at keeping me wet and needy for him as soon as he walked into the bedroom in the evening. He'd been right from the very beginning: he didn't need drugs to make me compliant.

At times, dark thoughts plagued me. Despite our chess games, it occurred to me that perhaps I was nothing more than his plaything, his pet. That made my chest ache, a sensation I didn't fully want to contemplate.

So I'd ignore it and concentrate on potential opportunities to escape. Even if that made the ache persist.

But it wasn't like he ever afforded me an opportunity to escape. He still kept me collared and chained to the bed in his absence, and I was completely reliant on him to see to all my needs. It should have made me resentful. I should have hated him.

But the way he held me so tenderly when he cared for me made me feel cherished. Even the pain he gave me was a form of caretaking; he brought me transcendent bliss with his deviant toys. I wasn't scared of the playroom anymore. I wasn't even scared of the flogger. He'd shown me how good it could feel when applied with my pleasure in mind rather than wielding it to punish.

When I did think about escape, it was to plan for the day when Andrés would give me access to a computer. The day he decided I was ready to work for his brother. It was the only opportunity I could see available to me.

And it was coming soon. Some of my days were hazy, but I thought my assessment of three weeks in captivity was about accurate. That was the deadline Cristian had given Andrés. I'd been so well behaved, surely my captor would think I was ready to be trusted with access to the internet.

Then I could finally get away from him and make my way back to the Bureau. Back to my friends. Back to Dex.

I rubbed at the dull throb in the center of my chest and turned my attention back to my comic book.

I'd only been reading for a few minutes when the bedroom door banged open and Andrés stormed in. It was the middle of the afternoon. He shouldn't be back yet. And the fire in his eyes and furious twist of his scar mirrored his expression on the day he'd dragged me to the spanking bench and threatened to hurt me while he was angry.

I scooted back on the bed and held up my hands to stall him.

"Wait!" I gasped out. "Andrés, wait. Please."

He stiffened and stopped in his tracks, only three steps away from grabbing me.

"You're upset," I said quickly. "I don't like it when you're like this. You scare me. Please, don't... Don't hurt me." My heart twisted as the words left my lips. He might give me pain sometimes, but never more than I could handle. He was always fully in control, carefully administering how much pain he was inflicting. But he wasn't in control right now. I hadn't begged him not to hurt me in... How long?

Long enough that I'd forgotten how terrifying he could be when he was in a truly black mood.

A low, feral sound rumbled from his chest, and his fists clenched at his sides.

"Please. Talk to me. Tell me what's wrong. What happened. Is it your brother? Did he—?"

"Of course it's my brother!" he shouted, and I cringed away as his rage slammed into me. He closed the distance between us and grabbed my upper arms, pulling my body up against his. I struggled, but he snarled down at me. "He wants to see you. He expects you to be ready by now. But you're not. I've been too soft with you."

"You haven't," I insisted, desperate. "You don't have to hurt me."

"I don't want to hurt you," he bellowed. "He does. Why can't you understand that? I'm not the one who wants to break you. I want to save you. I want to protect you. I can't do that if you continue to defy me."

"I haven't defied you," I gasped out, my fear rising. "I've done everything you've asked."

"No," he railed, shaking me. "I've given you everything *you've* asked. I've tried to make you happy here with me. I've indulged you and played with you when I was supposed to be training you. And now he wants to see you, and you're not ready."

"I am," I squeaked out, needing him to believe he could trust me with a computer. Terror rode me hard, and in that moment, I wanted to escape him more desperately than I had since the day I'd first been captured.

"Don't lie to me, Samantha," he warned on a growl. "You think you can manipulate me with your pretty tears? You think

I'll do anything you ask if you smile for me? I won't allow you to play games with me. I'm in control. You belong to *me*."

His eyes took on a feverish light as he spoke.

"You're not in control," I said, trying to blink back the tears that burned at the corners of my eyes. "You're scaring me. You're hurting me." His fingers were digging into my arms hard enough to bruise, but that ache was nothing compared to the horrible sinking sensation in my chest.

Fighting him would get me nowhere. He wasn't rational at the moment. He was in pain. I could see it in the wildness of his black eyes, the deep furrow of his twisted scar. With trembling fingers, I reached up and tentatively touched his cheek. He flinched away. I tried again, pressing my palm against his scar.

"Talk to me," I begged. "Tell me what happened."

"What happened is my brother takes everything from me," he said on a harsh whisper. "*Abuela*, Valentina. Now he wants to take you." He pulled me impossibly closer. "He can't have you. You're mine."

"Yes," I agreed, trying to soothe him. "I'm yours. I'm not going anywhere. You won't let Cristian take me away. I... I trust you." Despite his bruising grip on me, I knew the truth deep in my soul. Andrés would do anything to protect me from his sadistic brother.

I traced the line of his scar with my fingertips. I'd never touched it before. I'd never touched his face with tenderness. We came together in carnal need, but I never initiated intimate contact.

He shuddered, but he leaned into my hand. His hold on my arms eased, and he embraced me, cradling my body carefully against his.

"*Sirenita*," he said, his voice strained. "*Lo siento*." He turned his face into my palm, kissing my hand.

"What happened to them?" I asked softly. "The people your brother took from you. Your grandmother and sister." I didn't really want to hear the horror of it, but Andrés needed to purge some of the pain from his soul. It was eating at him, driving him to the edge of sanity. I'd known he'd lost them, but it wasn't until just now that he'd revealed Cristian's role in that loss.

He grimaced, but he kissed my palm again, and his arms didn't tense around me with renewed aggression. He was so big, and I felt tiny in his embrace. But he held me carefully, as though I was something precious and fragile.

"Valentina..." His voice hitched on her name. "My sister. Half-sister. Cristian and I share the same father as Valentina. Our father kept her mother as his mistress after our mother passed away, but she died giving birth to Valentina. Father let Valentina's grandmother live on our estate, so she could care for her. Valentina was my best friend. Her grandmother became *mi abuela*. I spent more time in their home than my own. Cristian was always jealous of our friendship, our little family. As the oldest, father was harder on him. He had more responsibilities, a legacy resting on his shoulders."

He paused, his eyes sliding out of focus as he fell into memory.

"Your father dealt in cocaine," I prompted, knowing their family's criminal history. "He wanted Cristian to take over the business?"

"Yes. But then father died when I was sixteen. Heart attack."

"I'm sorry," I said softly.

His jaw firmed. "He was not a nice man. But I had a home with *Abuela* and Valentina. Until Cristian took over father's organization. He resented us, our family. Maybe if I hadn't left him alone with father, things would have been different. But he always had a sadistic streak, even as a child. I wanted nothing to do with him. He scared me, so I stayed away."

"What did he do?" I asked, softly prodding. This was the most personal information Andrés had ever shared with me, and I was beginning to understand his warped relationship with his brother. Andrés was bigger than Cristian. Scarier. Smarter. It didn't make sense that he worked for him when he so obviously hated him. Unless the emotional scars went deeper than the ones carved into his flesh.

"He sold Valentina," he whispered, his gaze dark with pain. "She was fourteen. He traded her for money, for bribes to secure his place as father's successor. Well, he said it was for money. He did it to punish me. To punish both of us for our happy childhood. One that had been denied him."

My stomach churned, and my heart ached for the innocent, teenage Andrés who'd lost his sister and best friend in such a horrible way.

"*Abuela* died nine months later," he said bitterly. "Breast cancer. She didn't even try to fight to survive it. Not after losing Valentina. She left me alone. With Cristian."

I suddenly understood Andrés' fierce desire to *keep* me. He didn't want to lock me in a cage like an animal, to keep me as a pet. He just wanted someone who was his, someone to care for and protect. Like he hadn't been able to protect his grandmother and sister.

Lauren had been right when she'd said Andrés needed me to be good for him. He needed my submission, my willing surrender to his control. He needed to see me restrained, because it reassured him that I couldn't leave him. He needed to see me cry, because he couldn't shed the tears himself. He wanted to care for me, but more than that, he craved my devotion in return.

Cupping his scarred cheek in my hand, I leaned up into

him and lightly pressed my lips to his. For a moment, his mouth was tense beneath mine; a hard, anguished slash. Then he groaned, a long sound of pained release, and he opened for me. His fingers threaded in my hair, pulling me closer as his tongue swept into my mouth, devouring me like a starving man.

Hunger rose within me, more than physical need. I craved his closeness, skin-to-skin. He'd just dropped so many barriers between us, letting me see into his tormented soul. I wanted to offer him something in return, something I'd never offered to anyone.

But I didn't want to beg. I didn't want to prostrate myself before him and cheapen our connection to nothing more than his victory and my subjugation. I wanted *him*. All of him, good and bad, ugly and beautiful. And I'd give myself to him, willingly, eagerly.

My hands went to his shirt, tearing at the buttons in my haste to feel his hard chest, the thick ridges of the scars that were physical marks of his inner pain. I wanted to touch them, to explore every lash that had been inflicted on his soul and heal them.

He growled against my mouth, kissing me harder as he shrugged out of his shirt and helped me remove the rest of his clothes. When we were both naked, he gripped my waist and guided me down onto the bed, his weight settling over me. His hard cock pressed against my inner thigh, straining toward my virgin channel.

"I want you, Andrés," I gasped when he broke our kiss so we could both draw in much-needed air. "Don't make me beg. I want to give this to you. I want to give myself to you."

He pressed his forehead to mine, so we exchanged each ragged breath. "You don't have to beg, *sirenita*. You just have to say *yes*. I need to know that you want me. Let me in."

The tears that spilled from my eyes welled up from a place deep inside as emotion flooded free. "Yes," I whispered. "Please, Andrés."

I begged because I chose to. Because he didn't demand my surrender. I gave it willingly.

"Samantha," he groaned my name and lined up with my slick opening. I was wet and ready for him, my core throbbing with need. "Do you feel what you do to me? You are so perfect."

His swollen cockhead pressed at my entrance, parting my pussy lips as he eased inside. I whimpered at the burning stretch of him pushing in, but he didn't stop at the sound of my discomfort. He stroked my cheek with one hand and reached between us with the other, playing with my nipples, giving me the little bites of pain that always drove me wild. My whimper turned to a high whine, and my inner muscles relaxed as my arousal grew, easing his progress as he penetrated me slowly.

Once he was fully seated inside me, he paused. My core contracted, struggling between pushing him out and welcoming him in. His jaw was clenched, his scar drawn deep and fierce. But the sight didn't scare me. I touched the mark again, tracing the furrow across his handsome face. He closed his eyes, a shiver running through his entire body as his cock jerked inside me.

He withdrew slowly, using aching care with my untried body. His cockhead dragged across my g-spot, and pleasure lit up my system, burning away the discomfort. My core heated and relaxed, opening for him. I wrapped my legs around his hips and dug my heels into his sculpted ass, pulling him back inside me.

A rumbling shout left his lips at my bold movement, and he grasped my wrists, pinning them over my head with one hand while his other played with my breasts more harshly. He pinched and pulled at my nipples. Each little hit of pain went straight to my pussy, making it flutter around him.

He began to move, pumping his hips faster and harder as he clung to his control by a thread. I knew he was holding back so he wouldn't hurt me, but I didn't want that. I didn't care if it hurt. I welcomed the burn of his huge cock filling and stretching me. It made me hyperaware of our intense connection, bound together by pleasure and pain. This was how it was meant to be between us: our bond so tight that it was nearly too much to bear.

"More," I begged, rocking my hips up to meet his thrusts. "Please, Andrés…"

My pleading triggered him. With a snarl, his control snapped, and he started fucking me in harsh, possessive strokes. His hand tightened around my wrists, and his weight pressed me deeper into the mattress, pinning me down so there was no escape from his onslaught.

I cried out, welcoming more. I didn't want to escape. I wanted to stay right here, in Andrés' brutal hold.

He hit my g-spot over and over again, making pleasure build deep inside. My entire body tensed, my toes curling and my legs shaking around him.

"Come for me, *sirenita*," he ground out, the order barely intelligible.

My body conditioned to come on his command, I let go. My orgasm claimed me with shocking force, ripping through my system in a vicious rush of ecstasy. My scream mingled with his wild roar, and his scorching seed pumped into my pussy, branding me with heat.

He drove deep one last time, holding himself inside me as he emptied his cum into me. Primal chemicals mingled in my body, easing my harsh rush of pleasure to something softer, cocooning me in tingly bliss.

Our shaking and spent bodies remained locked together as his lips crashed down on mine in a soul-searing kiss, marking me as his.

CHAPTER 19

Andrés was gone when I awoke the next morning. The warm glow that filled my chest dimmed as soon as I opened my eyes to find myself alone in his bed. My fingers searched the cool sheets, as though I could summon up his warmth somehow.

He'd held me all night after our mind-blowing first time together. He'd petted me and told me how beautiful and perfect I was. It had felt real. I'd felt... whole.

I didn't like waking up without him beside me. I needed his touch, needed to be cuddled close after the intensity of what had passed between us.

I sat up and crossed my arms over my chest to ward off the sudden chill that clung to my skin.

Something was different. When I moved, the familiar sound of metallic clanking didn't reach my ears. I lifted my fingers to my throat. The collar wasn't there. I wasn't chained to the bed.

Tears pooled in my eyes as an irrational sense of loss knifed through my chest.

Why hadn't he put it back on this morning? Didn't he want me to bear the mark of his ownership? The symbol of my devotion to him?

I took several deep breaths, telling myself that I was being unreasonable. My emotions were raw and exposed, and I didn't like not having Andrés' strong arms to cling to when I was feeling so vulnerable.

The bedroom door opened. My heart leapt, then sank to my stomach.

It was only Lauren, bringing my breakfast.

"Where's Andrés?" I asked.

She shrugged. "Master Andrés doesn't tell me about his business."

Something ugly stirred in my gut when she called him *Master* Andrés. I'd never liked it, but this time it stung. I tried my best to ignore it and act rational.

"He instructed me to give you this." She held out a large white pill and offered me a glass of water.

"What is it?"

"The morning after pill."

A block of ice formed in my stomach. "Oh." The sound left my chest along with all the air from my lungs, as though someone had punched me.

"He wants me to give you a birth control shot, too." She gestured at the waiting syringe on the cart.

My fingers went numb, and the glass of water dropped from my hands, soaking the carpet.

Lauren was saying something in a harsh tone, but I couldn't listen. I couldn't focus on her. All I could do was feel the pain my heart ripping open. I gasped for breath, pressing a hand against my aching chest.

I had unprotected sex with my captor. I could have gotten pregnant. And I begged for it.

A maddened laugh bubbled from my throat. Of course I couldn't have gotten pregnant. Andrés had made provisions to ensure his fucktoy didn't inconvenience him with a pregnancy. He'd sent his mindless slave to give me the morning after pill and a birth control shot.

Stupid. So fucking stupid.

I'd Stockholm-Syndromed the shit out of myself. I'd been scared of him in the beginning of my captivity. How could I have forgotten that was exactly what I was: his captive?

He'd told me so many times that I was his fucktoy, his pet. But my brain had reasoned its way around that horrible reality and presented me with a pretty fantasy that he actually had secret feelings for me.

He'd never lied about the fact that he was a master manipulator. And I'd fallen for it. I'd let him shape me into his willing, eager plaything.

I had to get out, before I lost my mind completely.

My training kicked in, and Lauren wasn't at all prepared for the half-crazy FBI field agent who launched herself at her. I tackled her to the floor, pinning her on her front. I wrapped my arm around her throat and squeezed, putting pressure on her artery.

"I'm sorry," I whispered, tears almost blinding me as she went limp beneath me, slipping into unconsciousness. I released her immediately, not wanting to cause her any lasting damage. Lauren might be loyal to Andrés, but she was still a victim.

I pushed up off her still form and raced to Andrés' wardrobe. I slipped on one of his huge dress shirts, only taking the time to secure three buttons with shaking fingers, just enough to cover myself.

Lauren groaned, and I hurried back to her. I braced my arm around her waist and dragged her upright. She stumbled along beside me, somewhere partway to consciousness. I pulled her through the bedroom, into the sitting room, and straight to the elevator. I pressed her thumb against the call button.

The door slid open without a sound. No angry buzz. Nothing to alert anyone that I was escaping.

I shoved Lauren back into the sitting room and jammed the button for the door to close before she could come back to her senses. She was still blinking up at me from where she was sprawled on the floor when the silver doors slid closed. I pressed the button for the ground floor, praying no one else had access to this elevator except for those Andrés trusted. I couldn't afford to be stopped on my way down.

Adrenaline coursed through my system, my body preparing for a fight. If I did meet anyone, I'd remember my training for once.

I have to get out. I have to.

The elevator glided all the way down to the ground floor without stopping. When the doors opened, I found myself at the end of a long corridor. I could see light at the end of it, streaming through a glass door.

I started moving before I fully thought it through, my feet racing toward freedom. If I could just get outside—

A hulking body blocked the light in front of me, blotting it out as he ran straight for me.

"Hey!" he shouted. "Stop right there."

I didn't stop. I launched myself at the man, my fist connecting with his jaw. He reeled back, and I darted past him. His fingers tangled in my hair, and a defiant shriek left my lips as he dragged me back, away from the light. Using his leverage on my hair, he jerked me toward him so he could grab my upper arms. Before I could get my hands up, he slammed me back against the wall. My head cracked against it, pain lancing through my skull. The world flickered around me, and I lost control of my limbs.

"How did you get out?" he asked, his voice rough with anger. "I saw you running down here on the security feed. You whores are supposed to be locked up on the third floor."

Blinking hard, I willed the world to stop spinning. As soon as his furious, red face came into focus, I slammed my forehead into his nose.

He dropped me with a curse, and I stumbled forward. My head ached, and my vision swam.

I struggled to right myself, to run. I made it two fumbling steps before his weight barreled into me, taking me down to the hard marble floor.

"Bitch," he snarled. "You almost broke my fucking nose. You'll pay for that, dirty little whore."

I felt something hard pressing against my ass where Andrés' shirt had ridden up, leaving me exposed. I screamed and scrambled against the marble, my hands slipping uselessly against the smooth surface.

Dirty little whore.

Dirty little girl.

You want me to touch your secret place again, don't you, dirty little girl?

Dirty. Wrong.

Pure, icy terror seized my lungs as I heard his zipper lowering, heard the dreaded sound of his fist pumping his shaft.

I didn't want this. I didn't. It was dirty and wrong. It felt good for a little while when he touched my secret place, but then it hurt.

I beat my fists against the marble as I thrashed and screamed. All my training left my head as my mind receded to a long-forgotten, long-buried place.

I don't want this.

I don't want this, Uncle Robert. Please...

I couldn't breathe. I gasped for air, but nothing filled my lungs. He was on top of me, his breath hot on my neck as he pinned my tiny body down...

His weight was lifted off me, and a furious roar reverberated through my skull. I curled my knees up to my chest and hugged them tight, trying to protect myself in the only way I knew how. I heard a horrible, wet sound; a man screaming; bone crunching; silence.

"Samantha." Red-painted hands reached for me, and I flinched away, curling more tightly into myself.

"*Cosita*, it's okay. You're safe now."

"Andrés?" My voice was soft and strangely high, like a child. Past and present mingled, toxic fear clouding my brain. "I don't want him to touch my... I don't want this. I don't... I don't..." I started hyperventilating, my chest convulsing as hysteria overwhelmed me.

Strong arms closed around me, but they didn't frighten me. They were warm, powerful enough to protect me.

I turned my face into his chest and sobbed, my fingers fisting in his shirt as I struggled to get closer. A soothing stream of Spanish rumbled over me. Even though I couldn't understand the words, I focused on the lilting cadence, allowing it to fill my mind and blot out all the awful things.

But now that the memories had finally been unearthed, I couldn't bury them again. They played out in my head in horrible, vivid detail. Every muffled cry, every shameful gasp. The wrenching pain between my legs as Uncle Robert violated my small body.

Big hands stroked my back, my hair, my cheeks. They were warm. Familiar. I leaned into them, seeking more heat. I was so cold, frigid down to my bones. My entire body shook, except for my fingers, which were fisted so tightly in his shirt that my knuckles were white.

I didn't want to remember. I didn't want...

"Where is your uncle now?" he asked in English. His soothing voice roughened, and his arms were tight around me.

"What?" I asked, struggling to move from memory to reality.

"You said..." He trailed off on a growl. "You mentioned *Uncle Robert*. Where can I find him?"

I shuddered at his name. "Why?"

"I'm going to kill him for you, Samantha," he swore, his hand firming on my head where he'd been stroking my hair. I realized I wasn't the only one shaking. Andrés' strong body practically vibrated with barely-restrained violence.

"He's dead," I said hollowly, remembering the day I'd watched his casket being lowered into the ground. I'd been fifteen then, when his alcoholism had sent him to an early grave. Six years after my parents had left me alone with him so they could go on a week-long vacation. They hadn't known about his drinking at the time. They hadn't known about *him*. About what he wanted to do to me.

"I cried at his funeral," I whispered, anguished. "I didn't know why I was so upset. I fucking cried over him."

"How old were you?" Andrés asked. "How old were you when he—?" His teeth snapped closed, as though he couldn't let the words leave his tongue.

"Nine," I said softly. "But I forgot. How could I forget?"

Everything made so much sense now: my nervous tics, why I was so uncomfortable around men. I'd always been awkward and shy, even as a child. Before. But I'd had friends at school. People I wanted to play with.

After, I stopped going to my classmates' birthday parties.

The idea of a slumber party, especially, gave me crippling anxiety. I didn't want to leave my parents.

So I'd stayed at home. I'd found solace in my computer games. I hid behind a screen, isolated from everyone. No one could touch me.

Until Andrés. He hadn't let me hide from him. He'd pushed past my barriers and demanded that I let him in. It might have been fucked up, but he'd been right: I never would have found intimacy with another man like what I shared with him. Not even Dex. My gentle giant of a friend might be a Dominant, but he was far too sweet to have given me what I truly needed.

I needed ruthlessness. I needed darkness. I needed Andrés.

"I'm sorry," I choked out. "I'm sorry I tried to leave. I thought you didn't care about me. I thought—"

"You thought I didn't care?" he demanded, his muscles tensing and rippling around me. "Do you know what it did to me, seeing another man hurting you, touching you? Seeing you broken and crying when you remembered what—?" He cut himself off again before he fully verbalized what Uncle Robert did to me.

His black eyes bored into me. They sparked with fury, but lines of anxiety tightened around them. "Did I hurt you?" he asked, his voice strangely thick. "Last night. Did I hurt you?"

He thought he'd hurt me during sex?

"No," I reassured him, touching my fingertips to his cheek, tracing the line of his scar just as I'd done when he'd been buried deep inside me.

"Then why? Why would you leave me?"

Shame heated my cheeks at the hurt in his voice. "I woke up, and you were gone," I said, my voice small. "I didn't have my collar. Then Lauren brought me the pill and the shot, and I thought I must have imagined... I thought you didn't care."

His face shifted to a carefully blank mask, but something stirred in his dark eyes. "Do you want to get pregnant?"

"I... No. Not... Not right now."

The thought of having a child with Andrés—of having a family again after losing my parents—made something tug in my chest.

He started petting me again. "That's for the best," he said, sounding as though he was talking to himself as much as to me. "You need to take the pill."

"I... okay." It was the rational thing to do.

But then why were my eyes stinging?

"You were upset because I was gone?" he asked, cuddling me close. "Then I'll stay. Do you want your collar back on? I thought you resented it."

"I, um, I got used to it. I like it," I amended truthfully. "It makes me feel safe. Like you're with me, even when you're not here. But I'd rather not be chained to the bed," I added. It would be nice to be able to take care of myself during the day, instead of relying on Lauren for everything. In a weird way, part of me would miss it, knowing Andrés was thinking about me waiting in his bed. It seemed I'd developed a kink to match his.

He traced the line of my jaw, rubbed his thumb along my lower lip. "You can have your collar, but I'm not going anywhere. I left this morning to see my brother. I was convincing him to give me more time with you."

"Oh. Thank you." I'd thought he'd been playing me this whole time, but he'd been honest with me from the beginning. Yes, his kinky games were meant to train me in how to please him, but everything he did was ultimately meant to protect me. He wanted me to cooperate for his brother so Cristian wouldn't hurt me.

"I still don't want to work for him," I said quietly. "It goes against everything I believe in."

"I know. I've read enough about your superheroes to see that."

"Then what are we going to do?"

He sighed, his eyes clouding with anxiety. "I don't know yet. I'll figure something out."

"*We'll* figure something out," I told him. I was no longer willing to sit around and wait for rescue. Cristian was the one threatening me, not Andrés. He wasn't my captor, he was my protector.

He stared at me with something like awe, cupping my cheeks in his hands before pressing his lips to mine.

Despite the horrible memories that had just resurfaced, I didn't flinch away from his masculine touch. I leaned into him and parted my lips, offering myself to him. I wanted him to claim me. I wanted to be his.

CHAPTER 20

Andrés held the final bite of bacon to my lips, and I playfully nipped at his fingers as I took it. His lips curved up in a doting smile. There was no sharp warning in his eyes, no rebuke. Just pleasure.

He'd held me all day after my ordeal and cuddled me close through two nightmares involving my uncle. It had been a difficult night, but he'd comforted me and kissed me back to sleep.

This morning, he was staying late again. I worried about our timeline with Cristian, but Andrés didn't seem to want to leave me.

That suited me just fine, because I didn't want him to leave, either. Until we figured out how to deal with Cristian, I didn't want him to face his cruel older brother.

"Yesterday, you said you wanted your collar," Andrés murmured, trailing his fingers along my bare neck. "Do you still want it?"

"Yes," I said immediately, leaning into his touch.

He beamed at me. "Then you'll have it."

He lifted me off his lap where we'd been cuddled on the bed and went to the chest of drawers. When he turned back to me, he held the thin strip of black leather in both hands, touching it with careful reverence.

"Kneel for me." It was an order, but there was a hint of trepidation in his tone that made it clear that I could refuse. He wanted me to choose to obey. He wanted me to choose *him*.

I got up off the bed and sank to my knees before him, moving more gracefully than I ever would have imagined I was capable of. He'd never asked me to kneel for him before, but I knew how to present myself from what I'd seen online. I spread my thighs so my pussy was open to him, and I pulled my arms behind my back, placing my hands on the opposite elbows. The position made my back arch, offering my small breasts to him. Keeping my spine straight, I bowed my head and waited to feel the leather kiss my throat.

He was silent for a long moment. Then his fingers brushed over the top of my head, trailing down through my hair before exploring the line of my jaw. His forefinger curled beneath my chin, and he lifted my face so I looked up into his dark gaze. The light flashed against his eyes, making them shine brighter than I'd ever seen.

"You are so beautiful," he said hoarsely. "So perfect. *Mi sirenita*."

I flushed with pleasure. "So are you."

I still saw his scars clearly, but they weren't repulsive. They were physical reminders of his vulnerability. They were slices in his armor, and he'd allowed me to open them up and look inside to the man underneath the monster.

He stared down at me in awe. "You're not scared of me? I don't frighten you?"

"No," I promised. "I'm not scared of you, Andrés."

His lips parted, as though he was about to speak. Then he closed them and swallowed hard. His eyes shone with a worshipful light as he brought the collar up to my throat and wrapped the leather around my neck.

I heaved out a sigh of relief at the familiar, reassuring feel of it encircling my throat, a physical reminder of our connection.

"Mine," he said, tracing the line of the collar.

"Yours," I replied with fervor.

He bent down and gripped my waist, lifting me up and guiding me back down onto the bed.

"Are you ready for me?" he asked, his voice strained with need.

He was asking my permission. He didn't want to push me after the dark memories that had risen up to torment me.

But those memories couldn't destroy my desire for Andrés. He'd taken me in his harsh hands and ripped down all my barriers, helping me conquer my fears, even when I didn't understand them.

"Always," I promised, taking his hand and moving it between my legs so he could feel my desire for him. "I want you."

He groaned and grasped my ankles, pulling my ass to the edge of the bed before resting my calves against his shoulders. Still standing while I lay on my back, he gripped my hips and entered me in one hard thrust.

I cried out as he stretched me, my lingering soreness from our first time making me hyperaware of his size.

He paused, his brow furrowing. His dark eyes studied me, tight with concern.

I placed my hands atop his, curling his fingers deeper into my hips. "Please, Andrés..."

A low sound of longing left his chest, and he withdrew

from me before slowly pushing all the way back in. He claimed me in long, careful strokes, playing with my clit and lighting my body up with pleasure.

He fucked me until I saw stars, and we both came undone.

No. Deep in my soul, I knew that wasn't right. He didn't fuck me.

We made love.

※

LOVE.

I was still contemplating my feelings hours later, as Andrés and I lay tangled in the sheets. He'd dozed off for a while after we'd had sex, but I'd been wide awake, my brain buzzing.

I had feelings for him. On a rational level, I had to acknowledge that they'd been building within me for weeks.

But *love*?

It was insane. He was a dangerous drug lord. How could I share a life with a man like him?

I hadn't thought about a future with him before. I'd just been living day to day, vaguely planning my escape with waning enthusiasm.

I didn't see how I could be with him in any real way.

And that made my heart twist in my chest.

There was one obvious way out of this that I could see, but it put him at risk: I could pretend to work for Cristian, and I'd get a message back to my friends at the Bureau. They'd come in to rescue me, and they'd arrest Cristian for abducting me.

They'd also want to arrest Andrés.

I couldn't let that happen. I might be able to arrange immunity for him if he turned on his brother, but that wasn't a guarantee.

I could also try convincing Andrés to give me access to a

phone, so I could call my friends. That way, I wouldn't have to face Cristian at all.

It still wouldn't guarantee his safety, though. I couldn't see how to get back to my life without betraying Andrés.

But the idea of going back to my life without him in it made my chest ache. I wasn't ready for my time with him to end, even if I didn't want to stay locked in this penthouse forever.

"What are you thinking about?" he asked, his fingertips brushing over the furrow in my brow.

I blinked and propped up from where I'd been resting against his chest.

"I thought you were asleep," I said instead of answering.

"I was, but I could hear you thinking." He gave me a languorous smile and stroked my hair back from my cheek. "You do have a very busy mind."

"Let me guess. You're going to help me make it go all quiet and blissful?" I was only half-teasing. That sounded kind of nice right now. It would free me from my inner turmoil.

"I can, if that's what you need," he said. "But I like your clever brain."

"You do?" He'd never openly expressed admiration for my intellect before. After our games of chess, I'd come to suspect it, but he'd never said it outright. It made my heart do a funny flip. I'd worried so many times that he saw me as nothing more than a pet, but actually respected me as an intelligent woman.

"Of course," he replied. "You challenge me. I find you fascinating. Did you not know?"

"I..." I swallowed down the lump in my throat. "No. I guess I didn't know that. Not for sure."

"I should tell you more often, then."

He was being so sweet. I just wanted to melt into him, to

feel his weight settle over me as he drove deep inside me, connecting us intimately.

His fingers curled beneath my chin, lifting my face so he could study my expression. "Did I make you sad?"

"No," I said, my voice catching. "That... means a lot to me."

"Then why are you crying?"

"Because I don't want to leave," I whispered. "I don't want to leave you, but I should."

His jaw firmed, his eyes flaring. "You're still thinking about how to escape?"

"No," I said quickly. "I mean, yes. I mean, I want to get out of working for Cristian. I don't want to spend my days locked in this penthouse, fearing the day your brother comes for me. And if you really value my mind like you say you do, you won't want that for me, either."

He scowled. "This is the safest place for you. You should fear Cristian. This is the only way I know how to protect you."

"This isn't the life I want," I said, desperate. "I can't stay trapped in a cage forever. I need to do something meaningful. I need to help people."

"You've been reading too many comic books. You can't be a superhero, Samantha. You're far too breakable, and I won't put you at risk."

"I can be a hero," I informed him, anger rising. "I used to do it every day, before you took me. I had a life. I had purpose."

He wrapped his arms around me and rolled, settling his heavy weight on me so I was pinned beneath him. "Your life is with me now," he said, his voice rough. "And my purpose is to protect you."

"You won't be able to keep me from Cristian forever," I tried to reason with him. "Let me call my friends at the

Bureau. If you go into hiding before they come for Cristian, I can cover your tracks. They won't find you. You'll be safe."

"And what about you?" His black eyes burned into me. "Where will you be while I'm in hiding? Will you go back to your friends? To your Dex?"

"I... I don't know," I whispered, torn. I didn't want to go back to my life without Andrés.

"You're *mine*," he snarled. His cock was hard against me, pressing at the entrance to my sex. "And you're not going anywhere. Not back to your Dex. And not to my brother. You belong to me."

"I'm yours," I agreed. "But I can't—"

He crushed his lips to mine, silencing me on a warning growl. My body heated for him, and I softened under his onslaught. My pussy grew slick with arousal. As soon as I moaned against his mouth, he thrust into me in one brutal, possessive stroke.

He fucked me hard, claiming me in deep, merciless thrusts. My body welcomed his ferocity. Because I didn't want him to let me go. I didn't want to return to my old life and have Andrés disappear forever.

I couldn't yet see a clear path to a future with him, but I knew I didn't want to lose him. I wrapped my legs around him and pulled him impossibly deeper, welcoming his harsh claim over me.

CHAPTER 21

Andrés woke me early the next morning with a soft kiss against my neck. I turned my head, offering him better access. He rumbled his approval, the sound humming against my sensitive skin as he nipped at me. I pressed my ass back against his erection in wanton invitation, my body awakening for him before my mind was fully aware.

"It's time for your punishment," he murmured against my neck.

"Punishment?" I asked sleepily, not at all alarmed by the threat. "Why?"

"You tried to escape," he reminded me, but he sounded more aroused than upset. "That was very naughty, *gatita*. I've owed you a punishment for days."

"Oh. Okay," I agreed, knowing he needed this from me. After almost losing me, he needed to see me bound and begging for him. And I needed it, too. I felt guilty and foolish for thinking he didn't care about me, especially after our last few days of intense intimacy. A little pain and his forgiveness would absolve me.

He kissed the tender spot he'd bitten. "Good girl."

He gave me a few minutes for my morning routine, and I emerged from the bathroom with my teeth brushed and face freshly washed. He was waiting for me, his powerful body on full display where he stood at the threshold to the sitting room. He held out his hand, beckoning me toward him.

"Come."

I crossed the bedroom and placed my hand in his, allowing him to lead me to the playroom. I knew pain was coming, but my body heated at the prospect. He'd conditioned me to enjoy a little pain. Or maybe I'd always been built this way. I'd gotten aroused when he'd spanked me the first time, on the day I woke up in his bed after my capture, scared and confused.

I wasn't scared anymore. Not of the pain, and not of Andrés.

I followed where he led, trusting him implicitly even as we entered the room that had once terrified me. We came to a stop at the far wall, where he kept a multitude of implements designed for my torment hanging in neat, orderly rows.

He selected a length of crimson rope, and I shivered in anticipation. I'd come to love rope: the slightly earthy smell of hemp, the rough fibers that stimulated my sensitive skin. I felt secure when he bound me so thoroughly. He often used leather cuffs to strap me down, but rope was more intimate, methodical. Almost artistic. I was his to mold and shape, to bend and stretch into whatever position he desired, making me into something beautiful to be admired.

I took a deep breath and released it on a long, shuddering sigh as he began to wind the rope around me, forming a familiar harness around my chest. He took extra time and care to create a pretty lattice pattern above my breasts, turning my body into his work of art.

When he was finished tightening the rope around my

chest, he drew my arms behind my back, binding them together from shoulder to wrist, until my back arched and my breasts stood out proudly, my nipples peaked and throbbing for his attention.

He tied off his work and took another length of rope, feeding it through the large metal ring bolted into the thick wooden beam above my head. He then looped it through the bindings on my arms, pulling them up behind me so I was forced to bend at the waist. My breaths came faster, shallower as carnal need began to take hold of all my senses. I spread my legs without him having to issue a command, wantonly offering my wet pussy to him.

Satisfied with my helpless state, he knotted the ropes in place and stepped back. He took a long minute to admire me, but he didn't touch me. I whined for his attention, but he returned to the wall to select the next item for my punishment.

He held up the shiny set of rubber-tipped nipple clamps so I could see them clearly. A chain dangled between them, decorated with little red gemstones. It was pretty and perverted and perfect. I wanted the pinch of the clamps, the pull of the swaying chain as he toyed with it. I wanted him to take full control of my body; my pain, my pleasure.

He came back to me and lightly cupped my breasts, his calloused fingertips barely skimming my flesh as his palms kissed my tight, aching nipples. I tried to lean into him, but the ropes kept me trapped. The sense of helplessness I had once feared now sent me soaring, granting me the sweetest release. I put myself fully in Andrés' domineering hands. I was his to play with, his to punish, his to cherish.

He began to roll my nipples between his fingers, preparing me for the harsher bite of the clamps. When I whimpered and wiggled, torn between wanting relief and craving more, he caught my tight peaks in the clamps. I cried out as he turned the screws on the sides, slowly increasing the pressure to ensure they'd stay firmly in place when he tugged on the chain that connected them. I hissed out a breath and struggled to adjust to the pinch.

As I settled into acceptance, euphoria flooded my mind. He flicked the gems that dangled from the chain, and it swayed beneath me, tormenting me sweetly. I moaned, and my eyes slid closed as my head dropped forward, my weight sagging into the ropes that held me so securely. They shifted around me, tightening and caressing, embracing me.

I felt his heat recede, but my eyes remained closed as I drew in short, panting breaths. As my chest rose and fell, the chain tugged at my nipples. Every little hit of pain sizzled through me, sending scorching lines of pleasure straight to my clit. My inner thighs grew slick with my arousal, and my core contracted, eager for him to fill me.

I sighed in bliss when I felt the snap of the crop against my ass. He started slow, peppering my flesh with little sharp slaps, the smooth leather tongue leaving bright patches of heat everywhere it landed. My skin warmed and tingled. Little sparks danced over my flesh, crackling up my spine to flood my mind with bliss.

Suddenly, he cracked the crop hard against my upper thigh, a harsh, punitive stroke. I cried out at the rush of pain, but I didn't try to move away. I welcomed it, craving the absolution he offered.

"Never leave me again," he said, his voice rough with emotion.

Another blow cracked across my thigh, stinging and burning.

"You don't get to leave me. Never leave me." There was

something desperate in his harsh tone, yearning mingling with command.

"I won't," I promised, tears of release spilling down my cheeks. "I won't leave you. I love you."

The blows stopped, and the crop clattered to the ground. Both of his big hands curled into my ass, spreading my cheeks wide.

"Say it again," he ground out.

"I love you." The soul-deep truth left me on a sob. "Please, Andrés."

He snarled and slammed into me, his cock thrusting deep into my wet channel. "Tell me," he demanded, driving into me with ruthless, branding strokes. "Tell me again. Don't stop."

"I love you!" I cried out as he thrust into me mercilessly. "I love you, I love you..." The words left me in a litany, over and over again as his cock dragged across my g-spot, driving me higher. He reached beneath me and pinched my clit.

"Andrés!" I screamed out his name as I shattered. His raw shout echoed around us, and his cum filled me, marking me as his. He kept pounding into me, riding out the last of our pleasure with brutal force. I welcomed his claim over me.

Finally, he stopped, completely spent. He withdrew from me and carefully removed the clamps from my nipples. I whimpered when blood rushed back to the abused buds, but he soothed the sting away with gentle fingers, morphing the pain into pleasure.

He cut me down, severing the ropes that bound me. He supported my limp body and eased us down to the cool tiled floor, holding me tight.

"Mine," he murmured, tracing the contours of my body as though seeking to memorize every inch of me. "All mine."

I kissed his neck, tasting my tears on his skin. The salt mingling with his unique flavor was intoxicating. Better than any drug. I licked at it, craving more. A low, rumbling sound left his chest, vibrating against me. The sensation rolled through my body, making its way to my core. Despite the rough way he'd fucked me, my pussy wept for him, wanting him again.

I shifted in his hold, straddling him. He stiffened for me, needing me as desperately as I needed him. I boldly lowered myself onto him and captured his lips, welcoming him to claim my mouth the way he'd claimed my pussy. I moved against him, slowly sliding up and down on his shaft. His hands captured my waist, guiding me to take him faster, deeper. We found our bliss together, our sweat-slicked bodies entwined as closely as possible.

I screamed out his name, my fingernails scoring his back. I gave him everything, but at the same time, I claimed him as well, marking him.

I loved Andrés, and he was all mine.

CHAPTER 22

Andrés left me with a promise to return in a few hours. He was going to see Cristian to convince him to give me more time. Despite my devotion to Andrés, I couldn't bring myself to help with his business. And he wouldn't ask me to. In the beginning, he'd been determined to make me cooperate in order to protect me, but we were past that now. He promised he wouldn't force me to do anything that went against who I was.

Because he cared. He cared about *me*, not some version of me that did exactly as he said. I wasn't his doll. I wasn't his pet. I wasn't his fucktoy.

He might not have told me he loved me, but I could feel it in the reverent way he held me, the way he called me *his*. I knew he'd lost the people he loved in the past. He wasn't ready to say the words aloud, because he was afraid he'd lose me, too. I was still targeted in Cristian's crosshairs, and I didn't expect Andrés to admit his feelings for me until I was safe. Until he was certain his sadistic brother wouldn't take me away like he'd taken Andrés' beloved sister and grandmother.

So for now, I was content with his branding kiss, with his harsh claiming of my body. His possessive touch communicated all the things he wasn't ready to say to me.

I still didn't understand how we could have a future together, but I resolved to come up with a solution. I needed to push aside my worry and focus on formulating my plan.

Not worrying was difficult when I knew Andrés was facing his brother right now, defying him in an effort to protect me. I didn't particularly enjoy feeling like a damsel locked in a tower for safekeeping while my dark knight fought my battles. But without a computer, I really wouldn't have been much help in a fight.

I resolved to ask Andrés about that when he returned. Now that there was trust between us, he might allow me access to his laptop. I could take down Cristian's organization piece by piece, destroying his financials and leaving him utterly ruined.

But it was Andrés' livelihood, too. And although I knew he didn't approve of the Bliss and human trafficking, that didn't mean his hands were clean. I'd become convinced that he had a good heart, but he'd never known anything but a life of violence and crime. Circumstance had twisted him into a cruel monster on the surface, but I'd seen the damaged man at his core, the boy who had lost everything. His scars ran deep, and although he wouldn't like to admit it, he feared his brother. He was as much a captive in his dark life as I was in this suite.

I just had to convince him that I could help set him free, if he'd let me. He might not be able to take on Cristian, but I could do it for both of us. A few clever keystrokes would bring his entire empire crashing down.

I was only idly turning the pages of my comic book out of habit as my mind was absorbed in plotting Cristian's downfall.

I wasn't sure how long I'd been skimming through the story without reading when Lauren arrived with my lunch.

I sat up in bed, covering myself with the sheet. I still wasn't comfortable with anyone but Andrés seeing me naked, even though Lauren had seen everything already.

She didn't even look me in the eye today. I suspected her jealousy of my relationship with *Master* Andrés might be growing into resentment. Not to mention the fact that I'd recently attacked her.

Without a word, she handed me the morning after pill and a glass of orange juice. I'd taken the birth control shot a few days ago, but it wasn't guaranteed to be effective immediately, and Andrés hadn't been using condoms with me. I didn't want him to, anyway, so I'd accept the slight nausea that came along with the pill. I really wasn't ready to get pregnant.

I drained the glass of juice and handed it back to Lauren. She finally looked me in the eye. Her lovely face was drawn with anguish.

"I'm sorry," she whispered.

I blinked at her. "Why? Because of Andrés? I know you care about him. That's okay." I didn't begrudge the woman her admiration of my captor any longer. I understood everything she'd claimed about him. He *was* kind. He was a good man, deep in his soul.

"No," she said softly. "Master Andrés is going to be so angry with me."

"What are you talking about?" I asked, more sharply. Fear for Andrés flooded my chest, pressing against my heart.

"Cristian made me," she said, wringing her hands. "You have to come with me now."

I shook my head. It felt lighter than it should, but I couldn't focus on that. "I'm not going anywhere without Andrés."

"You will in a minute." Her eyes filled with tears. "He's going to hate me."

My body heated with anger. Or was it just hot? No. I was very aware of the cool air caressing my skin, making it pebble. I shivered, feeling as though Andrés was running his fingers down my spine. My core warmed and pulsed, need blossoming low in my belly.

"What did you do?" I asked, even as a pleasant, floaty sensation settled over me. It felt almost as good as being suspended in Andrés' ropes.

"Cristian made me put Bliss in your drink. He wants you to be with the other girls, since you won't work for him. You have to come with me."

"I don't..." The refusal died on my tongue, and a soft moan left my chest as my clit began to pulse.

"I'll try to keep the worst ones away from you," Lauren sniffled. "Come on. We have to go."

I got to my feet, shuddering as the sheet slid down my sensitized body. My rational mind receded as desire swelled. My feet followed where Lauren led, with no thought of resistance. There was no thought at all. Just need.

I needed to be touched, to be kissed, to be fucked.

I needed Andrés.

We arrived at the elevator, and the silver doors opened for Lauren. She took my hand, and I gasped as my fingers tingled with awareness. She started to cry as she pulled me into the elevator with her, but I didn't understand why. How could she be sad when everything felt so *good*?

I was warm. So warm. I leaned back against the cold mirrored wall, and a whine eased up my throat. My eyes slid closed as my inner walls began to contract, aching for Andrés to fill me.

"Andrés," I groaned his name.

"You'll see him later," Lauren promised, her voice hitching. "After."

The elevator stopped, and the doors slid open. Lauren was still holding my hand, and she tugged me out into the long corridor. I followed without question, without concern. All I could focus on was the lust coursing through my system, the need building deep inside me.

She led me a few steps down the hall and stopped at a closed door. She retrieved a key from her dress pocket and turned the lock before ushering me inside. The door closed behind me with a sharp *click*, but I barely registered it.

The room was huge, yellow lights filling the decadent space. Everything was red velvet and gold gilding. It was warm, soft, sensual. Couches lined the walls, and a massive circular bed dominated the center of the room. People lounged on the couches in varying states of undress. One particularly voluptuous woman was dancing to a heavy, hypnotic beat, her naked body undulating around a silver pole. A musky scent filled the space. It made my pussy clench and my blood race.

Several sets of eyes turned on me, male and female. I heard deep, masculine voices rumbling beneath the music, a harsh laugh punctuating the sensuous beat.

A man approached me slowly. I recognized him. It was the boy who'd come to clean Andrés' suite, the one who'd threatened me. His eyes flicked past me to focus on Lauren.

"What's she doing here?" he asked. "She's supposed to be upstairs. Do you know what Andrés will do to us if he finds her in here?"

"Cristian wants her down here," Lauren said, her voice still trembling with tears. "He said he'd deal with Master Andrés."

Something stirred at the edges of my mind.

Andrés. He was with Cristian. And he...

God, I needed him. My body was on fire, my pussy throbbing to the point of discomfort. I needed relief, release.

Not caring that I was naked in front of a room full of strangers, I closed my eyes and cupped my breasts, squeezing them to make the tingling in my nipples abate. My firm touch only made my desire grow, and my wet arousal slipped down my thighs.

"If you're sure..." I heard the boy's voice getting closer, but I didn't care about him.

I cared about getting back to Andrés, so he could help me ease this craving that was gnawing at my insides.

Long, masculine fingers closed around my wrists, directing my hands to my sides. Warm flesh touched mine, and I cried out at the shock of sensation as he caressed my breasts. My nipples were hard peaks against his soft palms.

Soft. Not calloused.

This was wrong. It felt wrong. But *so good...*

A loud *bang* sounded behind me, accompanied by the *snap* of splintering wood. My eyes flew open when the hands were jerked away from my breasts. Andrés' savage snarl filled my senses, and a pleasurable shudder ran through my body at the sight of his scarred face. It was twisted with maddened fury. He held the boy's face in both hands and twisted sharply. Bone cracked, and the boy's body fell to the floor, his neck at an odd angle.

Andrés positioned his body in front of mine, his fists curled tight at his sides.

"Who else touched her?" he roared. "Who?"

"N-no one." Lauren's voice was a high squeak. "I'm sorry, Master Andrés. I'm so sorry."

"Do not speak to me." He bit out each word. "You're lucky I don't snap your neck, too."

I heard her heave out a despairing sob, heard her soft footsteps whispering across the carpet as she fled.

"*Master* Andrés," I said. "I don't like that she calls you *Master*."

He turned to me, his black eyes burning with rage. Despite his fury, he handled me as though I were a fragile doll as he lifted me up in his strong arms and carried me out into the hallway. I moaned and rubbed my face against him, like the needy kitten he'd always claimed I was.

"You're not hers," I murmured, snuggling into his heat, loving the feel of his corded muscles rippling beneath me. "You're mine. My Master." I giggled. "Isn't that funny? I always wanted a Master. And you're mine."

The elevator took us up to his penthouse, and he carried me to the bed. He tried to set me down and pull away, but I locked my arms around his neck, keeping him close.

"Touch me, Master," I breathed. "Please. I need you."

My pussy ached, and my desire for him coated my thighs.

He grasped my arms and pried them away from him. His hands slid up to my wrists, and he pressed them into the pillows above my head. I whimpered and arched my back, lust pulsing through me as he dominated my body.

"I can't," he rasped. His lips were twisted downward, pulling his scar to a deep slash. "I can't be with you like this."

Holding my wrists in place with one hand, he brushed my hair back from my face with the other. I hummed my pleasure and nuzzled into him.

"My Master," I sighed. "Mine."

"You don't know what you're saying," he said tightly. "I'm sorry," he continued, his voice breaking in a way I didn't understand. "I'm so sorry. I wasn't here. I didn't know. When Cristian told me..." He gnashed his teeth. "I should have killed him. I should have fucking killed him."

I wasn't used to hearing Andrés curse in English.

"You're upset," I observed. "Don't be upset. Make love to me, Master."

"Don't call me that," he growled, his eyes tightening with anguish.

"But you are," I said. "I love you, my Master. My Andrés."

He cupped my cheek in his hand. "Please, don't say that. Don't."

I wasn't used to hearing him beg, either.

"Don't be sad," I said, dimly noting the wetness pooling at the corners of his black eyes.

He blinked hard, and some of the wetness fell to splash against my cheek.

"Make love to me," I urged again, arching my back, lifting my tingling breasts in wanton invitation. My entire body was *alive*, my nerve endings crackling and popping. Heat was building inside me. I was going to burn up if he didn't touch me where I craved it most. "I need you."

He pressed a tender kiss against my forehead. "All right, *cosita*," he murmured. "I'll help you. I know you must be aching."

"I am. My pussy hurts."

"I'll kiss it better," he promised.

"Thank you," I sighed in relief. He was going to touch me. He was going to kiss me. I lifted my face to his, but he turned away.

"Not your lips," he said, still sounding oddly pained. "I can't when you're like this."

"But you said you'd kiss me," I whined. "You said— Oh!"

Ecstasy lashed through me when he lowered his mouth to my tight nipple, flicking the tip with his tongue before sucking the peak into his mouth. He didn't use his teeth, and I was grateful. Just the heat of his mouth was intense enough to bring tears to my eyes.

"Please," I begged, lifting my hips. I needed him to touch my pussy. It was starting to throb to the point of pain.

He shushed me gently, pressing his palm against my stomach to pin me down. He moved onto the bed with me, but his body didn't settle atop mine. I wanted his comforting weight holding me down, but he positioned himself between my quivering thighs.

I watched in rapt fascination as he lowered his head to my pussy and touched my wet folds with his tongue. His hungry groan mingled with my harsh cry. He'd never kissed me there before. And it felt...

"So good," I panted, my fingers spearing in his thick hair as I pulled him closer. "More."

He traced the line of my opening, teasing the little patch of skin between my pussy and my asshole before licking all the way up to my pulsing clit. I thrashed as stars burst across my vision, bliss singing through my veins. He growled against me, and his hands locked around my thighs, forcing me wide open. His tongue circled my clit, applying firm, hot pressure. My inner walls contracted and clenched, yearning to be filled. He licked and sucked at my pussy lips, tormenting me with ruthless pleasure.

It wasn't enough. I needed him inside me, needed him to mark me with his cum.

Tears leaked from the corners of my eyes as pleasure turned to a deep, knifing pain between my legs. The building pressure had to release, or it would destroy me.

"Please," I choked on a sob. "I need you inside me. It hurts. Please, Master..."

He pressed one final kiss against my clit before his body

covered mine. He freed his hard cock from his slacks and lined up with my soaked pussy.

His eyes searched mine, dark with hunger and yearning. "You shouldn't call me that," he ground out, hesitating at my opening. "You shouldn't."

I wrapped my legs around him and drew him into me. "My Master," I moaned in relief when he filled me to the hilt.

A deep, pained sound slipped between his clenched teeth. He braced his arms on either side of my head and started to move within me, thrusting hard and deep. His forehead dropped to rest on mine, and he stared down into my eyes, his face drawn tight in an expression I didn't understand.

"Forgive me," he whispered. "Forgive me, *sirenita*."

I didn't know what he was talking about, and I couldn't focus on his words. All I could think about was how good his big cock felt stretching my tight sheath, how perfectly we fit together. The ruthless pleasure that had been building inside me crested, and I shattered on a scream.

My fingers fisted in his hair again, and I pulled his face down to mine so I could revel in his exquisite taste while my orgasm rolled through me. I caught his rough shout on my tongue, felt more wetness on my cheeks as his hot cum lashed into me, soothing the need that had consumed me. I shuddered beneath him as bliss flooded my body, making me light and tingly. My numb fingers fell from his hair, finally releasing him as all my muscles turned to jelly.

I closed my eyes and slipped into velvety darkness, his softly-spoken words following me down into sleep: "Forgive me."

CHAPTER 23

I stirred, slowly coming back to awareness. My body felt strangely heavy, and I was sore between my legs. I opened my eyes to find the shades drawn, with only the soft glow of city lights peeking around the edges. Night had fallen, but I was just waking up. Everything started to come back to me in pieces: Lauren, dosing me with Bliss; the red and gold room; the boy touching me; and Andrés, coming to my rescue like some dark avenging angel.

I sat up, searching for him. He sat on the edge of the bed, watching me with bloodshot eyes. His posture was stiff, his face a blank mask. He was fully dressed in his sharp suit, but his hair was wet, as though he'd just taken a shower.

"Thank you," I murmured, reaching for him.

He shifted away, grimacing. "Don't thank me. I fucked you while you were high out of your mind. I violated you."

"No," I said fiercely, grabbing his hand before he could retreat farther. "I begged you to." Even though I hadn't been able to control myself while under the influence, I remembered everything clearly now. "I needed you to. I was hurting. You helped me."

He turned his face away from me, but he didn't pull his hand from my grip. "You shouldn't have called me Master," he said hollowly. "You shouldn't have done that. I couldn't—" He pressed his lips to a thin slash, holding in whatever he was going to say. "I'm not blaming you. You didn't know what you were saying. It's not your fault. None of this is your fault. You didn't ask to be trapped with me. You didn't ask to be beaten and raped."

"You didn't rape me. Don't you dare call it that. Don't you dare." Angry tears made my vision swim, and I swiped them away from my cheeks. "You were helping me. I trusted you to help me. I love you, Andrés. And I meant what I said. You're my Master."

He rounded on me, his eyes blazing. "Don't call me that," he barked, his hand tightening around mine in a vise-like grip.

I moved toward him, scooting across the bed so I could get in his face. "You did nothing wrong," I said, imbuing the words with as much fervor as I possessed. "You saved me. You've been saving me this whole time. You've been protecting me from Cristian. He would have—"

"He would have what?" he shouted over me. "Ordered Lauren to slip you Bliss and whore you out? That's what he wanted, Samantha. He wanted you to scream in pleasure while they violated you. He wanted them to send you back to me, broken and used. He wanted to punish me for my failure. I should have killed him," he hissed, his gaze turning feverish. "But I didn't. I ran back to you as soon as he told me. He fucking laughed while I ran away from him."

"You got back to me in time." I cupped his face in my hands, trying to get him to focus on me. "You saved me. You protected me."

He grabbed my wrists, squeezing to the point of pain. But he didn't move my hands away from his face.

"I can't protect you," he rasped. "I'm a coward. You deserve better than me."

"I don't, and you're not," I asserted. "I want to be with you, Andrés. You're not a coward."

"I'm afraid of him," he admitted on a bitter whisper.

"I know," I said softly. "And I understand."

"You don't. My face..." He trailed off with a shudder and cut his eyes away.

I touched his scar, applying enough pressure to guide his face back to mine. "Tell me what he did to you." It was a steady command. Andrés needed to purge this from his soul. It was the only way he'd be able to free himself from the power his brother held over him.

"It was three years ago," he began, the words bleeding out of him. "Cristian made a deal with some Russians. He started dealing in Bliss. I'd never dared to challenge him, but I hated it. It was too far, too much. He was selling women, just like he sold my sister. So I decided to stage a coup and take over the organization myself. I'd always been the one to keep the business running. I could do it without him. My life would be better without him."

He paused, his eyes sliding out of focus as he fell into memory.

"He found out," I surmised, quietly urging him to continue.

His jaw tightened beneath my hands. "One of my men betrayed me. Cristian came for me before I made a move against him. He strung me up in front of all of our people—the ones he hadn't killed for following me. He cut me. He made me scream. He humiliated me. Then he stitched me up himself to make sure the marks lasted."

My stomach churned, nausea rising in my throat.

"Andrés..." I said his name shakily, struggling to get my tears under control. I wanted to weep for him, but that wasn't what he needed from me. He needed me to be strong. He needed me to show him that his scars only made him more beautiful in my eyes. They were marks of his defiance, of his goodness. He bore them because he'd tried to put a stop to his brother's evil.

I leaned in and brushed my lips across the deep furrow in his cheek. "I love you," I said with the weight of an oath. "We're going to get away from your brother. Together."

His brows drew together, his face twisting in lines of anguish. "I have something for you," he said instead of responding to my fervent declaration. I didn't like that he was avoiding what I'd said, but he pulled me into his lap, cuddling me close.

I sighed and pressed my cheek into the crook of his neck, relief washing through me at the feel of his strong arms around me.

He shifted slightly, reaching for something on the cart beside the bed. Confusion threaded through me as he uncapped the syringe.

"Lauren already gave me the birth control shot," I told him.

One corded arm wrapped around me, pinning me against his hard body as he carefully slid the needle into my upper arm.

"It's not birth control. I should have sent you away hours ago, but I had to see your lovely eyes one last time."

"What are you...?" My tongue grew heavy in my mouth, and lethargy rolled over me as my eyes drooped closed.

"I can't protect you," he said, pressing a kiss against my motionless lips. "Goodbye, *sirenita. Te amo.*"

I knew what it meant. *I love you.*

CHAPTER 24

I awoke to the sound of someone's fist pounding on wood. Forcing open my sandpaper eyelids, I struggled to assess my surroundings. In my gut, I knew something was wrong. The bed beneath me, the too-rough sheets that covered me, the slacks I wore.

Wrong.

I could still smell Andrés' unique, masculine scent. But that was because I was covered by one of his huge shirts.

The pounding increased in volume, escalating to banging. The sound reverberated in my skull, and I winced, my aching brain working overtime to process everything.

"Sam!" A familiar voice bellowed. I glanced toward the locked hotel room door that separated me from my friend.

"Dex?" I rasped, my throat too dry.

Wood splintered, and the door burst open. My best friend rushed toward me.

"No," I breathed.

Dex couldn't be here. That meant...

"No!" Anguish wrapped around my heart.

Andrés had sent me back to my friends, back to safety. And he'd left himself at his brother's mercy. Cristian would punish him for letting me go.

"It's okay, Sam. It's me." Dex stopped a few feet away from me, keeping the same careful, respectful distance he always did.

"Are you hurt?" Jason asked. He stood even farther away, barely inside the broken doorway. Tension gripped his body, and his dark green eyes studied me intently. His lips twisted in disgust when his gaze fell on Andrés' shirt covering me. It obviously belonged to a man; it nearly swallowed my much smaller frame. "Who did this to you?" he ground out, clearly putting two and two together. He saw my state of dress and assumed I'd been violated by my captors.

"Where is he?" I asked thickly, struggling to control my tongue. The drugs lingered in my system, sapping my strength and dulling my mind. All I knew was I had to get back to Andrés before Cristian hurt him.

"Who?" Dex asked, kneeling beside the bed so he could study my face. "Who were you with? We got an anonymous call saying you'd be here. Are you..." He eyed Andrés' shirt, his pale blue gaze igniting with rage. His jaw clenched, and he took a deep breath. "Are you hurt?"

"I'm fine." I slurred. "I have to go."

"Go? Sam, you've been missing for almost a month. You're not going anywhere."

I tried to sit up, but the world wavered around me, and I dropped back onto the pillows.

"I have a bus on the way," Jason said.

I didn't want an ambulance. I didn't want to go to the hospital. I wanted to get back to Andrés before something terrible happened to him.

But I couldn't seem to move. I could barely think. I heard

Dex talking, but I couldn't quite focus on what he was saying. The room kept sliding into darkness. Every time the world disappeared, I tried to force my eyes back open.

I was fighting a losing battle. Everything dissolved around me, until all I had left was fear for Andrés.

WHEN I FINALLY CAME BACK TO FULL AWARENESS, I FOUND myself in a hospital bed. Dex was standing at the threshold to the room, his massive body blocked by a short nurse who was clearly struggling to hold her ground.

I heard her murmur the words *rape kit* as she tried to shoo Dex away, and my stomach dropped.

I couldn't let them run a rape kit. I'd had sex with Andrés a few hours ago while under the influence of Bliss, and he'd come inside me. I doubted his DNA was on file anywhere, but I couldn't allow them to collect that kind of evidence against him.

"I want to talk to Dex," I said loudly, alerting them both to the fact that I was awake.

His blue eyes blazed when they focused on me, his tanned face oddly pale. He evidently hadn't liked the words *rape kit*, either. Although, he was disturbed for entirely different reasons. He thought I'd been used against my will, violated.

"I need to talk to you," I said, more softly. "Please."

My mind whirred to life. I had to figure out a way to save Andrés before Cristian realized I was missing. I'd start by questioning Dex. I needed to know what the FBI suspected about my abduction and what was being done to try to find the people who'd taken me.

The nurse finally stepped aside and allowed Dex to enter. He approached me carefully, moving slowly so he wouldn't spook me. He reached for me, almost touching my shoulder. Then his hand clenched to a fist, and he pulled away. He never had been willing to push past my barriers and touch me. We were buddies, and he respected my personal space issues.

Once, I'd longed for him to look at me with desire, with love. Now, he was watching me with concern.

And all I wanted was for him to get out of my way so I could get back to the man I loved before something terrible happened to him. I knew where Andrés' building was located. I'd spent enough time staring down at the cross streets below his penthouse windows to know exactly how to find my way back to him.

Andrés obviously thought I'd accept the sanctuary offered by the Bureau. He thought he could send my friends to retrieve me, and I'd quietly go back to my life with the FBI, kept safe by my fellow agents.

He was wrong. I was going straight back to him.

Te amo.

He loved me. He loved me, so he'd let me go. He didn't believe he was strong enough to fight his brother.

But he hadn't counted on having me by his side. He'd only seen me in my weak attempts to fight as a field agent. He'd never seen me in hacker-geek-goddess mode. If I could get back to him, I could show him how easy it would be for the two of us to take Cristian down.

I just needed his laptop, and I'd be able to destroy Cristian financially, backing him into a corner before sending the full power of the FBI after him. I'd send all the incriminating evidence straight to Jason and Dex, and they'd handle the arrest.

Especially if they knew Cristian was the one responsible for my abduction.

"It was Cristian Moreno," I said quietly, looking straight into Dex's eyes. "He kidnapped me."

His jaw clenched. He knew about the Bliss and human trafficking. He'd seen me in Andrés' shirt, and he was clearly coming to some dark conclusions.

"Jason thought Division 9-C had you. We looked into Moreno, but there was no evidence. We didn't think you were on his radar. We were looking in the wrong place. Fuck, I'm sorry. I'm so sorry, Sam. Did he... Were you hurt?"

I cut my eyes away from his, even though I didn't feel any particular compulsion to do so. My nervous tic seemed to have been eradicated, but I didn't want him to see the truth in my eyes. I hadn't been hurt. Not really.

But it was to my advantage if Dex thought I had been. I needed him to think I was weak, shaken. Not fully mentally sharp and calculating the best way to get Andrés away from both his brother and the FBI.

"Where's Jason?" I asked instead of answering him.

"He's out looking for the people who did this to you. I'll call him and tell him it was Moreno."

"What about you?" I pressed quietly. "Will you go after Cristian?"

"No. I'm staying right here with you."

Crap.

I needed him to leave. I had to get back to Andrés, especially while the FBI was distracted with tracking Cristian. I'd been running through all the potential ways to save Andrés, and one had become clear to me: I had to get him and his laptop from his penthouse and go into hiding.

I didn't know how to get in touch with Andrés directly. I'd never seen him with a phone, and while I knew he must have one, I didn't know how often he kept it on him. Certainly not when he was in his penthouse. That was a mostly technology-free zone, except for his laptop. Even if I was able to find his number somehow—and I'd need access to a computer for that—it would take too long to track down.

I wasn't sure how long I'd been out of it, but Cristian could find out I was missing at any time and decide to hurt Andrés for letting me go.

So the time factor ruled out trying to communicate with Andrés remotely. That meant I'd need to go to him in person. Which was an impossibility as long as Dex was hovering over me. He'd follow me. Or worse, prevent me from leaving the hospital.

I couldn't risk telling him about Andrés, because then the Bureau would know exactly where to find the man who'd been holding me captive. They wouldn't treat him gently if they knew his role in my abduction, no matter what I said to defend him.

Once I got away from Dex and back to Andrés, we'd leave Chicago. I wasn't sure what kind of private transportation Andrés had at his disposal, but I was fairly certain he'd have something we could use to leave the city. A car would do. A jet would be awesome.

I'd never cared for his drug money, but in that moment, I hoped to hell Andrés had a private jet. If he didn't, I'd have to get us fake passports, and that would be a snag I wasn't quite ready to deal with. Maybe he'd have a connection somewhere that could help. What good was being in love with a master criminal if he didn't have some useful seedy connections?

Somehow, we'd get out of the country. I'd move all his money to an offshore account—at least, as much as we needed to survive. And then we'd ride off into the sunset together.

Now that I was faced with the prospect of being returned to my old life, I realized I didn't want it. I'd spent years hiding behind my computer. I was ready to live my life, and I wanted to share it with Andrés. I didn't care where we went, as long as we were together and he was safe from Cristian.

But I had to get past Dex first. My eyes searched the room. He'd left his keys and phone on the table in the corner, beside a chair where he must have been sitting while I slept.

I needed those keys.

Not the phone, because that could be tracked. I didn't know how to call Andrés, anyway. Access to the internet from the smart phone would have been nice, but I didn't have time to do any hacking, especially not from a phone. I could do much more significant damage to Cristian once I had access to the raw data on Andrés' laptop.

"Um, can you do something for me?" I asked, still not meeting Dex's eye. He wouldn't think anything of it; I rarely looked directly at him.

"Anything," he said hoarsely.

"Can you get me some real clothes?" I wore a hospital gown, which wasn't ideal for escape.

"I got Chloe to bring you some," he said, gesturing at a pile of neatly-folded clothes on the table beside my hospital bed.

"Oh. Thanks. Could you, um, get me something else?"

My mind raced, trying to think of some errand I could send him on to make him leave me alone for a few minutes.

"Coffee," I said quickly. "I haven't had coffee in weeks."

It was true, but I hadn't needed it, so I hadn't really missed it. I'd slept so soundly with Andrés that I hadn't required my usual two cups a day.

"I don't want to leave you," Dex said. "I can wait until another agent comes to relieve me, and then I'll get you anything you want."

"Please," I begged, letting my real desperation shine in my eyes as I finally looked up at him. "I miss it. Coffee is normal.

And I haven't... I couldn't..." I trailed off, letting Dex read whatever dark things he wanted into my unfinished sentences.

His jaw worked as he ground his teeth together, and he nodded tightly. "Okay, Sam. I'll get you coffee."

"Is there a Starbucks here? You know what I like. Quad venti iced Americano with two pumps of mocha syrup. Please," I added again when he looked hesitant.

"That's all the way downstairs," he said gently. "It will take a few minutes. I don't want to leave you here by yourself."

"I'll be fine," I said, feigning a yawn. "I'm still so tired. I'll nap while you're gone."

"Okay," he said reluctantly. "There's a CPD officer just outside the door. She'll keep you safe while I'm gone. You don't have anything to worry about."

"Thank you," I forced myself to say.

Shit. Now, I had to talk my way past a police officer, too.

I set about formulating another plan as I watched Dex leave my hospital room. A small pang speared my heart as he walked away. This would be the last time I saw him. In person, anyway. I fully intended to keep in touch online, if he was willing.

As soon as the door closed behind Dex, I got out of bed and quickly pulled on the clothes Chloe had brought for me: a pair of yoga pants made for a woman with a much more toned butt than me, and a soft black t-shirt. It felt weird wearing clothes after spending so much time naked in Andrés' bed, but they were comfortable enough.

I picked up Dex's car keys and made my way to the door, opening it with purpose.

"Excuse me," the officer said as soon as I stepped into the hall. "Where are you going?"

"I need to find a nurse," I said. "My call button isn't working, and I need some painkillers."

The woman eyed me, assessing. "You don't look injured to me."

I dropped my eyes again to hide my lie, hoping it made me appear frail and damaged. "Um, you can't really see where I'm hurting."

"Oh. I'm... I'm sorry. I'll go find someone for you."

"Thank you," I murmured. I watched her walk down the hall through lowered lashes. As soon as she rounded a corner, I took off in the opposite direction. I wasn't familiar with the hospital's layout, but it wasn't difficult to find my way to the elevators and ride down to the parking garage. Once I was there, I hit the panic button on Dex's keys so I could locate his car.

I raced across the garage, sprinting toward the sound of shrill beeping. As soon as I got to his black sedan, I turned off the panic signal and got into the driver's seat. I was careful to leave the garage at a normal speed, even though I wanted to tear across town to get to Andrés. I couldn't get a cop tailing me for speeding right now.

I was only a few blocks away from the hospital when a phone started ringing in the glove compartment. Sighing, I retrieved Dex's personal phone and noted his work phone number on the caller ID. I also noted that he had a spare SIG stashed in there.

Good. I could use a weapon, just in case.

"Don't be mad," I requested as I answered the call.

"Where are you?" he growled. "You took my keys. The officer said you were wearing Chloe's clothes. Do you know what I thought when I came back and you were gone? I thought he'd come back for you. I thought—"

"I'm fine," I promised, cutting off his tirade.

"Why?" he demanded. "Why would you leave? And where the hell are you going?"

"Back to him," I said truthfully. "I have to save him, Dex."

"You're going back to Moreno? Are you crazy?"

Dex probably thought I was unhinged, warped by my time in captivity.

I hadn't been warped, but I had been changed. Maybe I was a little darker than I had been, a little less pure. Maybe some of my light had spilled into Andrés, just as some of his darkness had seeped into me.

I had to get back to him, to grab him and his laptop and get the hell out of Chicago before Cristian realized I'd been freed. Once we were off the map, we could take Cristian down. I wasn't exactly sure where we'd go, but I'd make sure to set enough of Andrés' money aside in an offshore account to establish a safety net for the two of us. The rest could be donated to various charities, to start to set right some of the evil Cristian had brought into the world. Evil that Andrés had facilitated, even if he hadn't wanted to do it.

I'd help him atone.

I'd have some atoning of my own to do. After all, I was stealing Dex's car and going on the run with a notorious criminal.

I grinned to myself. Maybe I was a bit of an anti-hero.

Cool.

"Sam, come back to the hospital. Please."

"I can't. Sorry, Dex."

"Do you know what it did to me when you went missing? I can't lose you again. Come back to me."

I didn't like the anguish in his voice. I didn't want to hurt my best friend. I owed him an explanation.

"I'm going back to Andrés," I told Dex. "I love him."

"Andrés Moreno? No, you don't. You're confused."

"I'm not confused," I said calmly. "Not anymore. I used to think I was in love with you. Did you know that?"

"What?" His breathless tone let me know he'd had no idea.

"It's okay. I'm supposed to be with Andrés. Just like you're supposed to be with Chloe. If she were in danger, you'd do anything to save her, wouldn't you?"

"Of course, but—"

"That's what I'm doing right now. I'm saving the man I love. I'll send you all the dirt you'll need to arrest Cristian in a few hours. Call Jason and tell him to start getting ready to move in on Cristian. I need you to find him fast, Dex. I'll do what I can to drive him out into the open."

"Don't do this, Sam," Dex pleaded. "Let me help you. I know I failed you, but let me help. I can't make it right, but—"

"I made my own choices," I said firmly. "And I'm making my own choices right now. You didn't do anything wrong, Dex. I'm happier than I've ever been in my life. Well, I will be," I amended.

I just had to go save my man.

"Don't try to look for me," I warned. "I'll see you online, if you're ever up for a game."

"I'm going to find you, Sam," he promised. "Whatever's happened to you, I'm going to help you."

"I don't need your help. You need mine. I'm going to keep tracking Division 9-C for Jason. I'm going to make sure Natalie is safe for good. I'll email him. But don't bother trying to trace it, because you'll just be wasting the tech analysts' time. I mean, I know you'll make them try, but don't be too mean to them when they fail."

I was in full-on hero mode, and it felt damn good. I was armed with a weapon and my wits, more powerful than I'd been in weeks. Possibly ever. Now, I just needed to get back to Andrés, log on to his laptop, and proceed to destroy his sadistic brother for good.

"Sam. Come back. Please."

"I really do hope I'll see you online," I said, softening. "Don't shut me out. You're my best friend."

"I'll see you in person," he said firmly.

"Webcams have been around for like, a quarter of a century, Dex. And I'm going to have a really great internet connection, so you'll be able to see me crystal-clear. Tell Chloe she'd better take good care of you. I'll be checking in."

I ended the call and dumped the phone out the car window so Dex couldn't use it to track me. I'd leave his car in the garage for Andrés' building. By the time he traced it there on traffic cams, we'd be long gone.

It took me precisely twelve minutes to get to Andrés' building. I relished knowing exactly how long it had taken me down to the minute. I really had missed everyday conveniences like digital clocks. Wherever Andrés and I ended up, we would have one in every room. I'd insist.

I diverted myself from my little fantasy of our home together and pulled into the garage. Well, I tried to pull in. The barrier didn't open for me.

Fuck.

I put the car in park and hurried out of it, grabbing up Dex's SIG on my way. I'd have to go in through the front. Which was a shitty non-plan, but I couldn't linger here, either. If someone noticed Dex's unauthorized sedan blocking the entrance to the garage, I'd be a sitting duck.

I needed to get up to the penthouse, get Andrés and his laptop, and get out.

Mustering up all the new-found confidence as I possessed, I strode through the glass front doors. The atrium was surprisingly bland, like any nondescript office building. But I supposed it wasn't in Andrés' best interests to be ostentatious about where he lived.

A man in a security uniform looked up from a row of

computer screens as soon as I stepped through the door. He stood quickly, pushing out of his chair where he'd been lounging behind the front desk.

I pointed my weapon at him and shook my head before he could reach for his own gun.

"Don't even think about it," I warned. "I'm taking the elevator up to the penthouse. Do you have access?"

"No," he said quickly, shaking his head and holding his hands up high to prove he wasn't a threat.

"Okay, then. I'm going to the third floor. Is there another elevator?"

"Yeah. That way." He pointed toward a darkened corner, and I saw little glowing circles that indicated call buttons for a set of elevators.

"You're coming with me," I told him, gesturing for him to come out from behind the desk. "Keep your hands where I can see them."

He moved where I'd instructed, and I closed the distance between us to take his gun from its holster.

"Let's go." I ordered, and he began walking toward the elevators, his hands still held high.

I just needed to get to the third floor and find Lauren. She had access to the penthouse. Well, she did as of yesterday. I hoped Andrés hadn't had time to revoke her clearance.

I shook my mounting worry from my mind. If she couldn't take me upstairs, she'd know how to contact Andrés. I'd never seen him with a phone, but he must have one he used when he left his suite. I considered asking the guard if he was able to call Andrés, but I had to guarantee that he'd bring his laptop down with him. His most likely reaction to finding out I'd returned to his building would be to storm downstairs and try to make me leave. He'd be too enraged to think to bring his laptop, even if I asked.

No, I needed to personally get up there and get both my man and the computer. The guard and I were only three yards away from the elevators when something sharp pierced my lower back. Pain lanced through me as electricity jolted my system. I lost control of my limbs, and I dropped to the hard marble floor, my guns slipping from my hands as I went down.

Fuck!

I knew what a Taser felt like. I also knew I wouldn't be able to move for another minute or so.

The guard I'd taken as my hostage bent down and scooped up my weapons, training one on my heart.

"Wait," a new, unfamiliar voice said. "We need to call this in and see what the boss wants us to do with her."

A second man appeared over me, holding the Taser that had taken me down.

Yes, I wanted to say. *Call Andrés.*

The words were an unintelligible groan.

"Took you long enough to get here," the guard complained. "She could have fucking shot me."

"You're lucky I came back from my break early, then," the second man said coolly. "Cuff her," he advised.

The guard nodded and grabbed the handcuffs attached to his belt. He quickly secured my wrists at the small of my back while the second man pulled out his phone and placed a call. He spoke into the receiver in rapid-fire Spanish that I couldn't follow.

I'd been disarmed and restrained in a matter of seconds.

I really sucked at being a field agent. As soon as Andrés got me out of this mess, I promised myself I'd never fight crime in person again. I could work far more effectively from the comfort of my ergonomic chair behind my computer screen.

"Moreno wants to see her," the second man said, ending his call. "Get her downstairs."

Downstairs? Not up?

The two men gripped my upper arms and wrenched me to my feet. I couldn't support my own weight, so they started dragging me the short distance to the elevators. Once we were inside and the guard had pressed the button for the basement, I started to regain some control over my muscles.

I'd only just managed to get my legs to support me when the doors slid open, and my knees gave out.

Andrés wasn't waiting for me. Cristian was.

CHAPTER 25

"Samantha," his accented voice caressed my name. "I thought you were gone." His sharp smile flashed in the dim light of the spare bulb overhead. I recognized this as the same room where he'd brought me when he'd initially captured me. The day he'd given me to Andrés.

I didn't respond. What was I going to say? The phantom chill of his knife on my skin made me tremble as fear pulsed inside me.

Andrés will come, I told myself. *He'll find me.* He always did. He'd come charging in and kill everyone who threatened me.

Wouldn't he?

Did that vicious protective streak extend to his brother? I wasn't certain Andrés would be able to challenge him.

He will. For me, he will.

I hoped I wasn't lying to myself. My own fear of Cristian was enough to blow all the wits right out of my mind. I couldn't imagine the clawing, instinctive panic Andrés must lock inside every time he faced his brother.

The men holding me upright dragged me forward. I tried

to dig in my heels, but my feet stumbled uselessly as they closed the distance between me and Cristian. His black eyes—so like Andrés'—studied my face, searching.

"You came back," he said, his head canting to the side as his eyes narrowed at me. "Why? My men say you were armed. Were you going to kill Andrés?"

"No!" The word popped out before I could hold it back.

"Then why return, when my brother set you free?"

"I..." I swallowed hard and braced myself for the lie, drawing on a defiant mask. "I came to kill *you*. I was trying to find you. I was going to deal with him after." I couldn't tell him about my feelings for Andrés. If I did, he might hurt him again.

Andrés had warned me about Cristian, even in our early days together. The sadistic bastard liked to force you to watch while he hurt the person you loved most. When Andrés had first told me about his brother's sick proclivities, I'd feared for Dex's safety. Now, I feared for Andrés. I had to make Cristian believe I saw Andrés as my cruel captor, and that I was coming for revenge on the Moreno brothers.

Cristian laughed, the sound rich with genuine delight. "You do want to kill him? He'll be so devastated. He does tend to get a soft spot for his pets. You, especially. I thought he was actually going to try to attack me when I told him I'd ordered Lauren to dose you with Bliss. He didn't like the idea of other men fucking you."

I remained silent, willing my brain to start figuring a way out of this.

"How about we make a deal?" Cristian continued before I could gather my thoughts. "I can't let you kill Andrés. He's the only family I have left, and he's very good at running my business. But I'll let you cut him up a little. I was about to do the same, myself. He really shouldn't have let you go back to the feds. That puts my entire organization at risk."

My stomach turned. I couldn't hurt Andrés. But if Cristian was offering to hand me a knife...

No. That would be suicidal. There were still two armed guards in the room with us. If I tried to stab their boss, they'd shoot me.

"Take off the cuffs," he ordered his men, but he didn't take his eyes off me. "I'm going to need to make this look right to keep Andrés in line. I'm sure you understand."

The handcuffs fell from my wrists, but I didn't have a chance to think about defending myself. Cristian's fist slammed into my jaw. Pain cracked through my skull, and I tasted blood in my mouth as my cheek cut against my teeth. The basement flickered out of existence.

When I started to come back around, I became aware of the familiar feel of leather cuffs around my wrists. My arms were being pulled above my head, and my weight started to fall on my wrists. I scrambled to get my feet under me, but the tension on my arms increased, forcing me up onto my toes.

I blinked hard, fear helping clear away the throbbing pain in my skull. It receded to a dull ache as adrenaline kicked in.

Cristian came into focus, his handsome face filling my vision. He touched his long fingers to my injured jaw, and I hissed as pain spiked.

"This will do," he said, studying me as though I were an object instead of a person. Worse than that: a tool he was going to use to hurt Andrés. "I had this set up for my little brother," he explained, gesturing at the restraints that stretched my body taut. "He screamed so much the last time I did this to him. I didn't think he'd ever want to repeat the experience, but then he let you go. Imagine how upset he'll be when he sees you here instead, after he tried to save you from me." He grinned. "He'll be absolutely destroyed once you start to work on him. Don't worry. I'll let you down so you can get your revenge, once I have him where I want him. Then, the offer to work for me still stands." He gabbed my jaw hard, making me cry out. "If you refuse, I'll find another use for you. Did you enjoy your time in my brothel?"

"I'll work for you," I forced out, struggling to speak when pain lanced through my jaw. I'd say anything to buy some time.

I'll get us out of this, I promised myself. *I will.*

"Good." He released my jaw, and I sagged forward, my weight falling onto my wrists before I caught myself on my tiptoes. "My brother might be obsessed with you, but you're too skinny to earn me much as a whore. No matter how pretty your skin is. I knew Andrés would enjoy marking it up."

He reached around me, and his fingertips trailed over my bare thigh, tracing the line of one of the faint bruises Andrés' crop had left when he was punishing me for trying to escape. I gasped and tried to move away from his hand, but there was nowhere for me to go. His touch on my exposed skin made me look down to assess my body. I'd been stripped again. But in this horrible place, it didn't feel normal to be completely bare. Cold air teased across my skin, making me very aware of how vulnerable I was.

"*Mi hermanito* is on his way down," he told me. "Should we put on a little show for him?"

He reached for his belt, where he kept the wicked hunting knife close to his side.

"Don't," I begged, remembering the grating agony of the blade scraping across my collarbone.

"I need to make a point," he told me, waving off my plea as though it was nothing to be concerned about.

He stepped behind me and touched the knife to my throat, the cold steel barely kissing my skin. My breath stuttered. I knew how easily it could part my skin, carving me up the way he'd tortured Andrés.

The soft *thump* of the elevator arriving sounded just before the doors slid open. I had a moment to register Andrés' face fixed in a carefully blank mask before his features twisted with rage.

"Samantha," he snarled out my name and launched himself out of the elevator.

"Stay right there," Cristian commanded.

The knife sliced a stinging line into my throat, and Andrés stopped in his tracks, his entire body vibrating with barely-suppressed violence.

"Be a good boy and have a seat, or I'll cut her open right now. Do you want your pet returned to you scarred or dead?"

"Let her go," Andrés ground out. "I know I'm the one you want to punish. Just let her go."

"And send her back to the feds, like you did? I don't think so. Samantha has agreed to work for me, once we're finished here. Sit down, *hermanito*. Or I'll slit her open and let you watch her pretty insides spill all over the floor."

I gagged, my body's nauseated reaction to the horrific mental image.

Andrés' dark eyes were drawn tight with anguish, his scar twisting deep into his cheek. A growl slipped between his clenched teeth, but he began to move stiffly toward the spare metal chair that had been positioned a few feet in front of me. The two guards flanked him, pushing his shoulders down so he dropped onto the chair before securing his wrists behind him with a length of rope. Once his arms were bound, they trained their guns on the back of his skull.

"That's better," Cristian said with satisfaction.

The knife left my throat, and I heaved in a gasping breath.

"How should we punish my little brother for his transgressions?" he mused, as though he didn't already have his twisted plan in place. He suddenly cupped my breast with his free hand, squeezing hard. I bit back a whimper, but my eyes began to burn. He tutted at me and twisted my nipple. I cried out at the bite of pain, and wetness slipped down my cheeks.

Andrés' nostrils flared, his eyes blazing. He tried to push up onto his feet, but the guards held him down with a firm grip on his shoulders.

"He doesn't like that," Cristian observed. "I thought you enjoyed when she cried, Andrés. Or are you the only one who's allowed to enjoy her tears?" He leaned around me, so his chest pressed against my back as he brought his face close to mine. His hot tongue touched my face, tasting my tears.

I shuddered and flinched away.

"I should fuck her raw while you watch," he continued, his tone conversational.

"You said..." I gasped for breath, desperate to get away, to save Andrés before Cristian could use me to destroy him. "You said this was for show," I managed on a ragged whisper. "You promised I could hurt him if I worked for you."

I had to get down and get my hands on that knife. It no longer mattered to me if I got shot. It was the only opening I'd get, and I had to take the risk.

Cristian laughed, running his hand along the curve of my hip.

"She's a vicious little thing," he said. "No wonder you couldn't manage to break her. Is that why you're so obsessed with her? All of your other pets were very obedient by the time you handed them over to me."

My gut churned at this horrible revelation. Andrés had trained other women before me. Of course he had. I'd always known, even if I didn't want to dwell on it. Why else would he have kinky toys stashed all over his penthouse, with a built-in playroom?

But the knowledge that Cristian had taken them for himself once they were trained made nausea creep up my throat. No wonder Andrés had been so possessive of me from the very beginning. I remembered Cristian promising that he'd be allowed to keep me. I was the only woman his brother had ever allowed him to keep, and now, he was trying to take me away from Andrés, too.

I wouldn't allow him to take anything else from Andrés. He'd taken his family, his innocence, his pride. He'd stripped him of everything and everyone he cared about, leaving him scarred and cold.

"Let me down," I demanded with as much vindictive fervor as I could manage. I drew on my hatred of Cristian to channel righteous rage into my features. He had to believe I'd hurt Andrés for him. "Give me what I want, and I'll give you what you want."

"Savage," Cristian remarked with approval. "Your little pet is going to cut you up for me," he told Andrés. "You risked your life to set her free, and she came back here to kill you. But don't worry. I won't let her take things that far. You'll survive this, and I'll patch you up again after. I'll always take care of my baby brother."

Andrés had gone pale, and his body shook with something other than rage. He stared at me, his eyes wide with disbelief. Then his jaw firmed, and he nodded.

More tears flowed down my cheeks. I wasn't sure if he thought he deserved for me to hurt him, or if he was trying to tell me it was okay to do what I had to in order to survive. Either way, his response was unacceptable. I wanted to scream at him that I loved him and I'd never hurt him.

But I had to get the knife first.

Cristian reached up and finally unbuckled the cuffs around my wrists. My body dropped, and I barely caught my hands on the concrete floor before my face smashed into it.

"Get up," Cristian said coldly. "You have work to do."

I pushed up onto my feet and turned to face him. He held out the knife, offering it to me hilt-first.

I drew a deep breath and then sprang into action. I grabbed the knife at the same time as I jammed my forefingers into his throat. He clutched at his neck, dropping to his knees. Gunshots rang out. Pain seared through my right hip, but adrenaline coursed through me, keeping my body going. I ducked behind Cristian for cover and pressed the knife to his carotid artery while my other hand fisted in his thick hair, yanking his head back to expose his throat.

I could have killed him in that moment. I would have killed him for everything he'd done to the man I loved, but the guards were still armed, and Andrés was still bound and at risk of being shot.

"Drop your weapons," I ordered. "Do it, or I'll kill your boss."

The guards slowly lowered their guns to the ground, their eyes fixed on the knife I held to Cristian's throat. He was still making horrible choking sounds as he struggled to draw in air.

"Untie Andrés," I barked the command.

They hesitated, so I increased the pressure of the knife just enough to make a drop of blood bead on Cristian's skin.

They hastened to comply, sealing their fates.

As soon as Andrés was free, he attacked. He was breathtaking in fluid, violent motion. My dark avenging angel. I watched with detached interest as he snapped their necks. The world was going hazy, surreal, but I kept my hold on Cristian as he continued choking beneath the knife.

Andrés turned to me as the second guard's lifeless body hit

the floor. He closed the distance between us and went down on one knee so he was eye level with me.

"Hand me the knife, *cosita*," he ordered, his voice oddly smooth and calm.

My fingers were going numb around the hilt, anyway, so he easily plucked it from my hand.

His gaze left me to focus on his brother. A vicious snarl twisted his scar deep into his perfect face, and he lashed out. Cristian screamed as the blade sliced through his cheek, deep enough that I caught a flash of teeth and bone. Andrés closed his eyes and took a deep breath, savoring the sound. Then his gaze found Cristian again, piercing him with a wickedly sharp black stare.

He drew the knife back and slammed it into the center of his brother's chest. He growled as he twisted the blade. Cristian's entire body shuddered, then sagged back against me where I was still crouched behind him.

His dead weight fell on me, and I couldn't seem to get my hands up to push him away. The room was growing darker, the spare lightbulb dimming.

Andrés heaved his brother's body off me, his expression twisted with some emotion I didn't understand.

"*Sirenita*," he said, strained. "Stay with me."

"I came back for you. I'll never leave you," I promised, my voice strangely faint. I tried to reach up to touch his face, but my arms wouldn't work. "I love you."

He scooped me up against his chest, and agony lanced through my hip. A strangled cry ripped its way up my throat as he rushed me to the elevator. As it slowly ascended, Andrés started murmuring to me in Spanish in the soothing way I loved so much. I sighed and pressed my face into his chest, the pain receding as I slipped into warm darkness.

CHAPTER 26

ONE MONTH LATER

"Seriously, Dex, I'm fine," I told him for the thousandth time. My webcam specs and internet connection were flash enough that I could see the little furrows in his brow where his face filled my laptop screen. "Are we going to play a game, or what?"

"Where are you?" he asked. "Come home. Please."

I shook my head and lounged back against my headboard, glancing down to make sure Andrés' shirt wasn't gaping open. I didn't want to accidentally flash my best friend. I'd only covered myself with the shirt so I could video chat with him. Otherwise, I wasn't really allowed clothes these days.

I didn't mind at all. I liked being naked here. It was warm and humid on our little private island, far too hot to bother with clothes.

"I *am* home," I told him firmly. "Andrés and I are perfectly happy and settled here."

He scowled. "You shouldn't be with him. He's a criminal."

"Not anymore," I told him, repeating something I'd said another thousand times. "I'm starting to regret telling you we're together. I want to share things with you. I don't want to lose you as a friend. But if you keep interrogating me every time we talk, I can't keep doing this. You already know you won't find me. I've made sure of that. If I worked so hard to cover my tracks, do you really think I'm just going to tell you if you pester me often enough?"

He blew out a long sigh. "No, I don't expect you to tell me. Even though I wish you would. I worry about you."

"Don't," I insisted. "I've never been happier. Really. Now, if we're not going to play a game, fill me in on what's going on. Did you get all the dirt I sent you on Cristian Moreno? I want to make sure all his people get rounded up and the people they've hurt are saved." I thought about Lauren, my heart squeezing. Dex had told me they'd recovered her and the other girls from Andrés' building weeks ago. I hoped she was okay and able to get the help she needed to heal.

"Yes," Dex confirmed, his lips still thin with disapproval. "Although there seems to be a key player missing in everything you've sent us. You know, the man who was actually running the organization."

I waved him off. "Andrés was acting under duress. He's squeaky clean now. And he'll never hurt anyone else."

Well, he might still whip me occasionally, but that was just for fun. And Dex definitely didn't need to know about it.

"Tell Jason I haven't given up on helping him, either," I shifted topics. "I'm still trying to track Division 9-C for him. We'll find them and trace them back to whatever organization they represent."

I was in full-on hero mode these days, kicking ass and taking names. From behind the safety of my screen, of course. I was working on ensuring all Cristian's people were arrested, tracking Division 9-C for Jason, and—although I hadn't told Andrés—looking for any whispers that Valentina was still alive.

I didn't want to open up old wounds, only to let him down if I found something horrible about his sister's fate.

"I'll tell Jason," Dex promised. "But I wish you weren't going all vigilante on me. I can't keep you safe if I don't know where you are."

"That's not your job," I told him. "Andrés is here to protect me. Trust me, he's way scarier than you. He'll keep me safe."

"Always," he swore, his accented voice rumbling over me. Even after spending nearly every waking moment with him for a month, I still got all shivery and blissed out in his presence. I didn't think that would ever fade.

He crossed our bedroom, closing the distance between us. He took a moment to glance at my screen, shooting a warning glare at Dex before he tangled his fingers in my hair and crushed his lips to mine. It was an obvious display of ownership. He still wasn't entirely happy that I'd maintained contact with Dex, even though I'd managed to convince him I only saw Dex as a friend.

He deepened the kiss, claiming my mouth in firm, dominant strokes of his tongue against mine. I moaned and brought my hands up to capture his face, pulling him closer.

Dex cleared his throat pointedly.

Refusing to break our kiss, Andrés reached out with his free hand and snapped the laptop closed. I giggled against him, giddy at his possessive instincts when it came to me. He loved me fiercely, to the point of obsession.

I was equally obsessed, so I didn't mind at all. I couldn't get enough of him, and I never would.

His hands fisted in the shirt that covered me, and the buttons popped free with a powerful jerk of his arms. He wore only a towel, his hair still wet from a shower. I tugged the soft fabric from his hips, revealing his hard desire for me.

His weight settled over me, pinning me down against the

massive bed we shared. Andrés had spared no expense in selecting a home for us and furnishing it with all his favorite kinky gear. Other than three members of staff, we lived alone on our private little slice of paradise. No one was around to complain about my screams of tormented ecstasy that floated through the humid air.

I felt a little guilty at the extravagance, but after looking at Andrés' financials, I decided we could keep a small piece for ourselves to ensure our safety and comfort. No one would find us here. I'd donated the rest of the money from his drug empire to various charities, mostly organizations that supported women who'd suffered abuse. Andrés had approved, wanting to do what he could to atone for Cristian's Bliss trafficking.

He was so good at his core, so kind and caring. He'd carry guilt for what he'd helped his brother do for the rest of his life, but I'd be here to help purge him of the dark moods that claimed him.

He wasn't in a particularly dark mood at the moment, just possessive. Hungry.

He kissed his way down my neck, between my breasts, pausing to press his lips against the raised pink scar on my hip where the bullet had ripped through me. He'd managed to get his private physician to arrive at his penthouse in time to stop me from bleeding out. One of my ovaries had been damaged, but the doctor said I'd still be able to have children. My birth control shot would be effective for another three months, but I didn't think Andrés was going to provide me with another one when it wore off.

I didn't want him to, anyway. I wanted a child with him. Our lives would be unconventional, but we'd be a family.

He finished lavishing attention on the mark I'd gotten when I'd saved us, my wet pussy distracting him. He gripped my thighs with harsh hands and pinned them down, spreading me wide for him. My eyes closed on a groan when he licked me, his clever tongue knowing just how to caress and play to drive me wild. My fingers speared into his hair, pulling him closer. He growled against me and nipped at my clit. I shrieked as my pleasure spiked in response.

"Please, Master," I panted, loving the feel of his title on my tongue. "Please fuck me."

As much as I reveled in his hot mouth on my pussy, it couldn't compare to the feel of him filling me, marking me.

He pressed one last kiss on my clit before pulling away. Shifting his grip from my thighs to my hips, he flipped me over onto my front.

A delighted laugh bubbled up my throat as giddiness soared through me. The strong, assured way he so easily handled my body send bliss pulsing through my veins. When he was in control, I could let go and relax. I didn't have to worry about being a hero or think about the weight of everyone who was counting on me to save them. I could just be *me*. I could be vulnerable with him, because I knew in my heart I could trust him to take care of me. I hadn't withered in his captivity; I'd become stronger than ever. He'd torn me down to my basest self and built me back up again, making me whole for the first time in years.

He made me whole. And I'd made him whole, in return. He still bore the marks of his brother's torment, but they didn't go deeper than his skin anymore. He'd escaped. We'd both escaped. In so many ways, we'd freed each other.

"I need you," I moaned as he pulled me up onto my knees, positioning my pussy where he wanted it. "I need you inside me." I needed to feel him penetrating me deep, for him to complete me.

He entered me in one hard thrust, stretching me ruthlessly.

"Mine," he snarled, driving into me in harsh, fast strokes. This wasn't slow seduction, but it was our own particularly dark brand of lovemaking. My pleasure crested as his cockhead dragged across my g-spot, delicious tension coiling low in my belly. His hand fisted in my hair at my nape, pulling my head back sharply so I was forced to arch into him. At the same time, he pinched my clit.

I screamed and shattered, my inner walls fluttering around him as he roared out his own release. His cum branded me with the heat I loved so much.

He held me in place as he emptied his seed deep inside me, keeping our bodies locked together as we both rode out the last of our ecstasy.

When he finally pulled out, he collapsed onto the bed and draped me over his chest so he could cuddle me and pet me. He needed to touch me as badly as I needed to be touched.

We lay there for several minutes, catching our breath while our fingers explored the lines of each other's bodies. After a while, I trailed my hand down his abs, making my way to his cock. It jerked beneath my soft touch, his desire for me rising to meet my own craving for him.

He sat up, propping his back against the pillows as I straddled his hips and guided him inside me once again. He hissed out a long breath as I slowly lowered myself onto him.

"*Te amo, mí sirenita,*" he said on a rough whisper. "*Te amo.*"

"I love you, my Master. My Andrés."

I leaned into him and captured his lips, claiming him as he'd claimed me. Andrés was mine, and I would never let him go.

CLAIMING MY SWEET CAPTIVE

Andrés P.O.V.

PROLOGUE

There was nothing particularly remarkable about the woman bound to the chair before me, except for her flame red hair. I studied her with detached interest as she blinked and shook her head in an attempt to come back to full consciousness. I'd sent my men to pick her up. They'd drugged her and brought her here, to me.

Me. Not my sadistic brother. But I'd made the mistake of informing Cristian that the young woman had been caught spying on our people, and he had insisted on being the one to interrogate her.

I swallowed hard and tore my eyes away from the gleam of the wicked hunting knife he held at his side. I knew what it felt like to be carved up, tortured. The scars on my chest and face wouldn't allow me to forget it.

Sweat beaded on the back of my neck, but I kept my expression carefully blank. I couldn't show any sign of weakness around my brother.

The woman's eyes finally focused on Cristian and the knife he held. I caught a flash of lovely sky blue as her pale lashes fluttered and then flew wide on a gasp. She twisted against the ropes that bound her arms behind the metal chair. I couldn't help but note how her struggles made her small breasts strain against her blouse. Her little fearful whimper made something dark stir inside my chest.

I took a breath and pushed down my more perverted instincts. This woman wasn't mine to train. She was facing a horrific death at the hands of my brother. One that I would have to watch and pretend it didn't bother me to see her ruby blood splatter all over the concrete basement floor.

"You don't want to do this," she choked out, her voice high and thin. "Let me go."

An interesting response. She was certainly fearful, but her first instinct wasn't to beg for her life. She was warning Cristian not to hurt her. Despite her situation, the woman—Samantha—was brave.

My stomach churned. I was going to have to watch my brother break her of that bravery before he finally killed her.

"No, Samantha," he said, his tone chillingly calm. "You're never leaving this place. Not alive, at least. If you answer my questions, I might be inclined to mercy. Otherwise..."

He let the unspoken threat hang in the air. My brother knew just how to extract the most toxic fear from his victims.

We have to do this, I reasoned. *She's nothing to me. Nothing but a threat that needs to be dealt with.*

I'd killed plenty of men—more than I could remember. But I hated watching Cristian tear people apart, especially women. I might have my own sadistic streak when it came to women, but I never truly harmed them.

That made me less of a monster, didn't it?

Samantha gasped in several deep breaths, visibly mastering her fear. "My friends will find me," she flung out, defiant.

"If they do, they won't find more than what's left of your

body."

I remained silent, allowing Cristian to terrorize her while I recorded the horrific events on my smart phone. I wanted no part of this, and although watching her death would make me sick, it was almost a relief that I didn't have to question her like this myself. I could let my brother get his hands dirty.

Samantha redoubled her efforts to twist out of the ropes that bound her. "You can't hurt me," she said desperately. "If you kill me, my friends will hunt you down."

Cristian grinned, baring his perfect white teeth. "I want them to know what I've done. Your death will be a warning. We're going to send a little message to your friends."

He gestured toward me, and Samantha looked directly at me. First, her eyes caught on the phone that was recording her torture. Then her gaze lifted slightly, finding my face. Her eyes met mine for a split second before she saw the scar that twisted my face. She shuddered and tore her gaze away.

Something ugly stirred in my gut. Cristian laughed, delighted at her reaction. "What, you don't like my little brother?" he taunted. "Maybe I'll give you to him to play with, after I'm finished with you. He has...very *unique* tastes."

I bit back the demand that he give her to me *now*. If he wanted me to get answers out of her, I could do that without mutilating her.

But I didn't make demands of my brother. I'd learned that lesson a long time ago.

He touched her freckled cheek, and she cringed away. "I think Andrés will like you. Such pale skin. It will mark up nicely."

I hated that his words rang true. I'd so much rather see the marks of my whip leaving their angry red brand on her skin than see him cutting into her flesh.

Cristian shook his head slightly, still smiling. "But I'm

getting ahead of myself. He can have you when I'm done. I'm going to extract my answers first."

He touched the tip of the knife to her throat, and her breath stuttered. A foolish urge to surge forward and tear him away from her rushed through me, but I quickly mastered it. I might be bigger than my brother, but he was far more powerful in so many ways.

All I could do was hope that Samantha gave him the answers he wanted before he hurt her too badly. I wasn't sure if he was threatening to give her to me in order to scare her or if he was taunting us both. He knew I'd rather have her for myself than witness the gory scene he intended for her. He was teasing me, testing me. Tormenting me just as he was terrorizing her.

Cristian stepped behind her so my camera could get a clearer view. He intended to send this footage to whoever she was working for as a warning.

His fist tangled in her copper hair, and he tugged her head back sharply, further baring her throat to his knife. She stared up at him, her breaths turning shallow as she focused solely on the threat he posed.

He scratched the knifepoint upward from her throat, grazing under her chin. Her skin turned pink beneath the blade, but he didn't cut into her. Not yet.

He pressed the flat of the blade against her full lips, and I tensed. It would be a shame to ruin such a pretty mouth. There were so many other ways I'd like to use it.

She whimpered again, the sound going straight to my cock. I might not want Cristian to torture her, but seeing her bound and frightened called to my darker urges. I wished I were the one towering over her, feeling her silken hair wrapped around my fist as I commanded her full attention.

Cristian decided to show a shred of mercy, and he lifted the knife from her lips. She gasped in a quick breath before the blade returned to her throat.

"You were in my territory today, watching my people," he drawled. "One of my men followed you home. Who are you working for?" The last held a harsh ring of command.

"I'm FBI," she whispered.

Fuck. We'd abducted a fed? If she was telling the truth, we'd just made a grave mistake. It was one thing to protect our product from rivals. Provoking the feds was stupid and reckless.

Cristian frowned. "A sniper made an attempt on my life a few days ago. The feds wouldn't assassinate me. Who are you really working for?"

He increased the pressure of the knife, and a drop of crimson beaded on her throat.

"I really am FBI," she said in a rush. "My name is Samantha Browning. I'm a tech analyst. Well, I was. I'm a field agent now. I'm not trying to kill you. We're investigating you. You have to know you're on our radar. Please, I swear I'm FBI." She was babbling, fear making the truth spill from her lips.

She might be a very accomplished liar, but I doubted it. I could practically feel the terror pulsing off her, could see the fine tremors that wracked her slender body.

Cristian studied her for a moment, considering. "You're a tech analyst?" he said slowly, mulling over the information. "That means you have access to all the evidence the feds have on me. If you're telling the truth about who you are."

"I am," she said quickly. "You can't hurt me. If you do, my friends will come after you."

She was right. If we cut her up and dumped her body, there would be hell to pay. Sending the video I'd been recording was out of the question. I turned off my camera and slipped my phone into my pocket. I'd delete the footage later.

"I think I'll give you to my brother, after all," Cristian mused. "He'll make sure you're telling the truth. I'd rather not mutilate you if you're going to be useful to me. Andrés has more creative ways of breaking women. And I'll keep our little video to ourselves. If you are who you say you are, I'd rather your friends at the FBI don't know I have you."

I didn't have time to draw a relieved breath before he touched the tip of the knife below her left eye. Another drop of blood beaded on her pale skin.

"Maybe I'll give you a scar to match my brother's first," he said. I knew he was taunting me now, but I couldn't hold back a growl. If he truly did intend to give her to me, I wouldn't allow him to carve her up.

A sharp, amused grin lit Cristian's features. "Apparently, he wants you mostly intact. Should I give him what he wants?"

I growled again, a wordless warning. Now that she was mine, I couldn't bear to watch him touching her, tormenting her. I'd barely been able to remain detached when he'd first threatened her with his knife. Now that he was dangling her in front of me like a toy he could take away, it was all I could do to keep myself from attacking him.

But that would only make things worse for her and for me.

"Not the face, then," Cristian declared. "But I think I'll let Andrés see what he's getting to work with."

The knife left her cheek, and he hooked the blade beneath the top button of her shirt. I clenched my teeth and swallowed a snarl. He was going to bare her. And while I wanted to look at her, I hated watching him strip her for me.

Tears finally spilled down her cheeks, but she stopped struggling. Her eyes clouded over, her lashes fluttering. She was barely breathing, and I knew she was on the verge of passing out.

Cristian's fingers tightened in her hair, denying her the

release of unconsciousness. "Stay with us, Samantha," he chided.

Her eyes focused on him again, and more tears glistened on her cheeks.

Cristian finally cut her. He grazed a crimson line across her collarbone, the cut shallow but painful as the metal grated against bone. Her scream ripped into me.

I wanted her screams for myself. I wanted her tears.

But not like this. Not with blood. And not with Cristian.

He hooked the blade through the little strip of cotton that connected the cups of her innocent white bra, parting the fabric and exposing her.

Her scream choked off on a sob. She was terrified, humiliated.

"What do you think, *hermanito*?" he asked me. "Is she pretty enough for you? She's not a great beauty, but her nipples stand out nicely against her pale skin."

My gaze locked on her dusky pink nipples. They were peaked from the coolness of the knife on her flesh. Just as Cristian said, they were pretty and perfect against her alabaster skin.

She began to shake violently, the cold of the blade sinking deep into her bones as she started going into shock.

"And her eyes are quite lovely," Cristian continued in detached observation. "So much fear there. You like when they're frightened, don't you, Andrés?"

My only answer was a low grunt. I didn't want to admit it aloud. I didn't want him to hear the eager rasp in my voice. He really was going to give her to me. He had hurt her, but I'd patch her up and take care of her. She probably wouldn't see it that way, but she'd come around, once I trained her.

Cristian's knife finally left her skin to slice through the ropes that bound her wrists. She slumped forward, and I immediately closed the distance between us to catch her before she slid to the floor. Out of the corner of my eye, I saw Cristian's smirk. He knew he'd just given me a gift, and he also knew he could take it away at any time.

I did my best to school my features to a blank mask, so he couldn't see how badly I wanted to get her away from him. No one should see her bare body but me from now on. He might not find her beautiful, but that didn't mean he wouldn't touch her just to taunt me.

I lifted her slight frame up and cradled her against my chest, holding her fragile body with care. For a moment, her sky-blue eyes caught mine. Then they rolled back in her head, and she went limp in my arms as her terror finally overwhelmed her.

My gut clenched. She was as frightened of me as she was of Cristian's knife.

"You're welcome," Cristian drawled. "It's been a while since you had a plaything, hasn't it? If you'd just make use of our whores, you wouldn't be so needy."

I ground my teeth together, saying nothing. Those women were kept drugged to make them compliant. It made me sick. I might have my own deviant perversions, but I'd never raped a woman. I wouldn't.

Cristian sighed, disappointed that I hadn't risen to his bait. "Make sure she's telling the truth about being a fed," he ordered. "Then I'll decide what to do with her. Until then, she's yours."

Mine. I pulled her tighter against my chest. Cristian smirked again. I turned sharply and strode toward the elevator that would take me up to my penthouse, carrying my precious prize with me.

CHAPTER 1

I laid her slim body down on my bed and placed the necessary items to tend her on the mattress beside her: damp cloth, surgical glue, sedative. The last was in case she turned out to be a more formidable opponent than I suspected. She claimed she was a trained FBI field agent. She might be small, but that didn't mean she couldn't be fierce. Once she woke up, I'd have the drugs nearby as a precaution. I wasn't too concerned about her ability to overpower me, but I wasn't stupid enough to underestimate her, either.

For now, I needed to clean the bloody cut on her collarbone and glue the wound closed. As soon as I touched the antiseptic-soaked cloth to her torn skin, she hissed and bolted upright.

I gripped her upper arms and pushed her back down. She squirmed and kicked out in blind panic, her fingers curling and clawing ineffectively.

Not so formidable, after all.

If Samantha was a field agent, she was either not very well trained or she'd never been in a high-stress scenario before.

Her physical defensive reaction should be far more methodical, precise, and ingrained.

I grasped her wrists to save my skin from her raking fingernails, pinning them against the mattress at either side of her hips. She whined and writhed, and blood oozed from the cut on her collarbone.

"Calm down, *cosita*, or I'll have to restrain you," I warned.

I grumbled my disapproval of her continued flailing. She was giving way to panic, and she was only preventing me from treating her injury.

I lifted her arms above her head and quickly secured her wrists in place with the cuffs I kept attached to my bed. Her struggles only increased, and she twisted her body in an effort to kick out at me. She might not be very skilled, but she was still a fighter at heart. She was terrified, and her instinct was to try to escape. She could have just trembled and cried and surrendered to her fate, but she wouldn't give in so easily.

I'd enjoy the challenge she posed.

I moved down the bed and caught her ankles, cuffing them to the bedposts. She was stretched out before me, and I finally allowed myself to really look at her for the first time. Despite her bonds, she hadn't stopped struggling. I admired the way her small breasts bounced slightly as she twisted and turned. She was still exposed where Cristian had cut away her shirt and bra, but I hadn't allowed myself to truly appreciate her lithe body in his presence. The darker part of me very much enjoyed seeing her bound beneath me, helpless and trapped.

She wasn't going anywhere.

Her crystalline blue eyes finally focused on me, and they widened, like a frightened doe.

I pressed my hand against her bare stomach, pinning her down against the mattress like a delicate butterfly. I simply watched and waited for her to exhaust herself. She wasn't giving up easily, but eventually, she'd surrender to her predicament. Then, I'd be able to close her wound and begin to learn her body.

Finally, she stilled beneath me, but her limbs still quivered, practically vibrating with the desire to escape.

"Are you done?" I asked calmly.

"Fuck you," she flung at me.

I couldn't allow that kind of language. It seemed her training would have to begin a little sooner than I'd intended. She needed to understand her place with me.

Keeping her pinned in place with one hand, I brought the other down on her breasts, slapping the outer swells just hard enough to leave a fierce sting. Her shrill cry made my cock stiffen. But it was too soon for that. No matter how alluring I found her, I wouldn't take her before she was ready to accept me without fear.

That didn't mean I wouldn't handle her body as I wished. I didn't stop slapping her breasts until her eyes began to shine with tears.

"I won't tolerate insults," I informed her. I wasn't angry. This was discipline. She simply had to learn how to behave properly. "You will speak to me with respect. Do you understand?"

"No," she moaned, but the word was more horrified than venomous.

"You will understand soon," I promised her, deciding she didn't require further punitive correction. "You're frightened, but you will learn. For now, I'm warning you not to curse at me again. Tell me you'll obey."

Her tears spilled over, glistening on her lovely skin before falling into her flame-red hair.

She didn't answer immediately, so I fixed her with my most forbidding stare. "Tell me."

That little whimper that had already tempted me slipped through her lips, and she managed a shaky nod. Her capitulation sent dark satisfaction coursing through me. I softened toward her, pleased with her surrender.

"In the future, I will expect a verbal answer," I told her. "You belong to me now, Samantha. Defiance will lead to punishment. Obedience will be rewarded. You choose whichever you want. I might seem like a harsh Master, but I'm fair. Your behavior has consequences, either painful or pleasurable for you."

"Please," she choked out. "I can't... I don't... Don't..." Her breaths turned sharp and shallow as her panic began to take hold of her again. She wasn't drawing in enough air, and I didn't want her to faint again.

I cupped her face with both hands, bracketing her cheeks. "Breathe," I ordered, lightly stroking her smooth skin, both to soothe her and to satisfy my own curiosity. She was even softer than she appeared, delicate. I could break her with my bear hands.

But that would be a waste. I had so many more deviant ways I wanted to touch her.

She still wasn't calming, so I allowed myself to explore further, threading my fingers through her silken hair and lightly massaging her scalp.

"Breathe with me," I ordered gently. I drew in a slow, deep breath, and she mirrored me. "Again." She continued to comply, and after a while, her breathing returned to a more natural rhythm. She went limp against the mattress, all the fight finally leaving her. Her eyes glazed over slightly as exhaustion claimed her.

I wanted to keep touching, exploring. But I was mindful of her injury. I needed to take care of her immediate needs before I could satisfy my own desires.

"Better," I nodded my approval and returned my attention to my task. I picked up the cloth I'd been using to clean the cut before she'd roused. "You're still bleeding. I'm going to clean you up. This will sting a little. Stay still."

I kept one hand against her cheek, hooking my thumb beneath her jaw to lock her in place. Dried blood was smeared on her porcelain cheek where Cristian's knife had pierced her skin when he threatened to give her a scar to match my own.

I smothered my fury and shoved the memory down. Samantha was mine now, and I wouldn't allow him to harm her again.

I touched the cloth to the tiny cut, and she hissed in pain. But she didn't move away.

"Good girl," I praised, pleased that she wasn't fighting me anymore. It seemed she would respond to a firm but fair hand. That would make things easier for her in the coming days.

I moved my attention to the cut on her collarbone. This one was more painful for her, and she made little keening noises through clenched teeth as I worked. I shushed her, the soft sound meant to comfort rather than rebuke.

When I was satisfied that the cut wouldn't become infected, I drew back and considered her for a long moment. Her lovely eyes were still wide and frightened, but pain lingered in the fine lines around them. She shuddered, her terror still riding her hard.

I frowned and smoothed away the crease in her brow with my fingertips.

"You're hurting," I observed. "You didn't do anything to deserve this."

I wouldn't put her through any more of the pain that Cristian had inflicted. I reached for the sedative. She cringed away from the syringe.

"My brother gave me this in case I needed to subdue you,

but it will take away your pain. I told you, I'm a fair Master. I won't hurt you if you don't earn a punishment."

"I don't want it," she said on a tight whisper.

"I decide what's best for you from now on."

"Please," she begged, her body tensing again.

Unconcerned with her pleas, I carefully slid the needle into her arm. "Hush now, *cosita*. You'll feel better when you wake up."

She made a slurred sound of soft defiance, but her tension eased. I stroked her hair back from her forehead, soothing her as she slipped into unconsciousness.

When I was certain that she wouldn't feel any pain, I closed the wound before freeing her from the cuffs. Then, I removed her ruined shirt and bra. I worked methodically as I stripped her, careful not to touch her sexually. I had no desire to explore her body when she was drugged. I wanted her fully aware when I began demonstrating my claim over her, my control.

I tucked her beneath the sheets. I should return to my work. She wasn't going anywhere and couldn't try to escape while drugged.

But I decided I'd rather stay near her, just in case. I got ready for bed and stripped off my own clothes, deciding to wear sweatpants at the last minute rather than sleeping naked beside her. I didn't want to frighten her too badly when she awoke. I didn't want her to think I'd violated her in the night when she couldn't resist me.

The very thought made me sick.

I told myself I wouldn't touch her again until she was conscious, but my body shaped itself around hers in the night.

CHAPTER 2

I didn't move away from her when I awoke the next morning. Instead, I studied the way the light streaming from the floor-to-ceiling windows played through her hair, the way it illuminated her ivory skin, making her dusting of freckles stand out. She was cute when she was like this: soft and sleepy in my arms.

Although, I found myself wanting to see her wide blue eyes again. They were remarkable, shining from within like aquamarine gemstones.

She stirred beside me and snuggled closer. A strange sensation tugged at my scar, and I realized I was smiling. It felt odd, unfamiliar.

Her brow furrowed, her eyes remaining closed for a few seconds longer as she came back to awareness.

Then her eyes snapped open, and she jerked upright. I allowed my arm to fall away from her chest, although I could have easily kept her pinned beside me. I was curious to see what she would do next. She'd proven feisty thus far, brave and defiant. But reasonable and compliant when she realized she couldn't fight me.

Would that same fire persist this morning? Or would she tremble and cry?

I wasn't sure which outcome I'd prefer. I found her especially alluring with pretty tears glistening on her cheeks.

She gasped and scrambled away from me, tumbling off the bed to fall on her ass. I smothered a laugh as she pushed up onto her feet and began to back away. Her eyes were wide and wary when they locked on mine.

Beautiful.

Her chest rose and fell rapidly, and her nipples pebbled. I wasn't sure if it was in response to cool air or the weight of my gaze on her. She clapped her hands over her breasts and pussy, trying to hide herself from me.

She really was cute.

Her eyes began to shine, tears pooling at the corners. Something dark stirred inside my chest; a deep, perverse satisfaction.

"I thought you were my blanket," she blurted out.

My smile widened, stretching my scar strangely. I certainly hadn't expected her to say anything like that. I propped up on one elbow and studied her more intently, fascinated. No woman had ever reacted like this when realizing she was trapped with a monster.

"Excuse me?"

She took a hasty step back, clutching her hands tighter against herself. "I have a weighted blanket. At home. It helps with anxiety. Your arm was heavy. I thought it was my blanket. That's why I... Stop looking at me!" she shouted.

I smothered the laughter that threatened to bubble up. "I like looking at what's mine," I told her truthfully.

"I'm not yours," she defied me, although her tone was high and thin rather than acidic.

I couldn't allow that kind of defiance of my claim over her. I finally got out of bed and prowled toward her.

Her remarkable eyes flicked down my body. I wished her eyes were widening in response to my physique, but I knew she was only seeing the raised scars that marred my chest and abdomen.

But I was too intrigued by her to get caught up in my dark memories.

She shrank back, trembling.

"My brother was right," I said. "Your eyes are lovely when you're frightened. Wide and blue. Like a pretty doll." I took another step toward her. "Am I so terrifying, *sirenita?*" The Colombian endearment slipped off my tongue without a thought.

She dodged away, but there was nowhere for her to go. Her back hit the window, and she glanced behind her at the Chicago skyline. She yelped and tried to push away from the dizzying view, but I closed the distance between us. She smacked into my chest, and I didn't give her the opportunity to evade me.

Her fighting spirit returned. I saw it in the flash of her eyes just before she attacked. Her fist swung wildly, and I didn't bother to evade it. She lightly connected with my jaw, but I barely felt the impact. Then she brought her knee up. I wasn't willing to allow that particular blow to land. I shifted so my thigh blocked her before she could knee me in the balls.

I frowned down at her in disapproval. I couldn't let that slide. I might find her efforts to fight me intriguing, but she needed to learn that I wouldn't permit her to truly harm me.

I handled her carefully but firmly as I gripped her waist

and turned her away from me. I dropped to my knees, taking her down with me and positioning her over my thighs so her pert little ass was raised for my discipline.

She continued to struggle, trying to push up onto her hands and knees. I caught her wrists and secured them at the small of her back with one hand. Without her hands to support her, she folded over my lap, her cheek coming to rest on the plush carpet.

She made a fierce little sound, like an angry kitten. I allowed myself a moment to savor it before bringing my hand down on her ass, administering her first spanking. She shrieked and writhed, kicking out as she tried to avoid the sting of my palm.

But she wasn't going anywhere. She would feel the heat of my discipline and learn her lesson. "Don't ever try that again," I admonished. "You will not fight me." I struck her upper thigh, and she howled out her rage. "You belong to me. You will accept your place."

"Stop fucking saying that!" she shouted.

I increased the intensity of my next blow, ensuring she felt the sting of my rebuke. "I get to say what I want. I get to do what I want. You will learn to mind your tongue. You will learn to behave. You're mine, *cosita*. Mine to play with. Mine to punish. *Mine*."

A strange kind of fever overtook me as I spoke the words, and my cock began to stiffen against her belly.

"No," she tried to refuse, but the word came out on a low moan. I became aware of the musky scent of feminine arousal.

Perfect. Samantha responded to a little carnal pain. She might not realize it, but she liked being dominated. It wasn't an uncommon reaction, but I was pleased by it.

Finally, she stilled her struggles, and a harsh sob left her chest. I immediately stopped spanking her and smoothed my palm over her burning flesh. It was meant to soothe her, but I enjoyed the heat emanating from her reddened ass. I did love seeing the glow of my discipline on her pale skin. It was every bit as lovely as I'd imagined.

"There," I praised. "Isn't that better? Don't try to hurt me again, Samantha."

I continued stroking her, and she let out a throaty groan. I was sure she didn't realize what she was doing, but her thighs parted slightly, inviting me to touch her needy pussy. Taking advantage of the silent invitation, I touched two fingers against her soaked lower lips, exploring the silky wetness that coated them.

"You're wet," I confirmed. "We are going to get along, *sirenita*."

"Don't," she squeaked, twisting against me as she renewed her struggles.

Her movements stimulated my hard cock, tormenting me. I hissed out a breath and tightened my grip on her. "Stop grinding against me," I ordered. She was rubbing herself on me, seeking more stimulation even as she begged me to stop. "You want me touch your little clit, greedy girl?" I asked roughly, barely able to contain my desire.

She stiffened, her entire body going rigid. Despite her instinctive lustful reaction to my discipline, I'd spooked her. Her skin pebbled, and she began to shake violently.

This wasn't the response I'd wanted at all. My desire cooled, and I turned her body so I could cradle her against my chest. I stroked her chilled skin, murmuring to her in Spanish. She might not understand the words, but I slipped into my native tongue without thinking about it.

She drew in a shuddering breath, and her shaking lessened to a light tremble.

"You're okay," I assured her in English. "Don't be afraid."

She blinked, the terror clearing from her eyes to be replaced with hollow defeat. Her tears no longer pleased me. Not like this.

"Let me go," she whispered brokenly.

"That's not going to happen." I spoke to her calmly, trying to soften the fear I knew my words would inflict.

"Stop touching me," she begged.

That wasn't what she needed. And it wasn't what I wanted. I wanted to hold her, to soothe her. "I will touch you whenever and however I want." I studied her frightened eyes for a moment longer. Then I sighed, and I finally released her. "We will work on this later," I promised.

She shoved up onto her feet and took several steps back from me, watching me like a wary, cornered animal. Her gaze flicked toward the closed bedroom door.

"No," I told her sternly. "Don't try it, or I'll spank you again. Go wash away those tears." I gestured in the direction of the bathroom. She needed a little space from me, and I'd allow it. For now.

She darted into the bathroom and slammed the door, locking it behind her as though that could keep me out if I wanted to get to her.

I heard water running for a few minutes. Then silence. The lock finally slid back, but she didn't emerge. I allowed her some time to collect herself, but she stayed too long. She was testing me, and I couldn't allow that.

"Samantha?" I prompted. "Come out of there."

A little sniffling noise sounded through the door. She was crying, trying to hide from me.

"Come out here. Now, *cosita*." I imbued the last with warning. She needed to understand that I wouldn't hesitate to come in and retrieve her. Nothing she did could keep me from getting to her, from holding her and touching her if I wanted to.

She didn't respond in any way. I sighed, resigning myself to go in if she didn't come out in the next ten seconds. "You will regret this. You must learn to obey me, even if you're scared or upset. I'm giving you one last chance. Come."

She didn't respond. She didn't obey.

I opened the door, expecting to find her huddled and weeping. Instead, she launched herself at me with a maddened shriek. Something sharp and silver glinted in her hand, and I dodged back just in time to prevent the razorblade from nicking my throat. Her aim had been off, and she wouldn't have done any real damage. As it was, the blade grazed a thin, shallow line down my chest.

She paused, her eyes fixing on the blood that welled up from the tiny cut. She froze in shock. Maybe she had intended to cut my throat, but it seemed she didn't have it in her. She might have just been sloppy, but her reaction to drawing my blood let me know she'd never truly hurt anyone before.

In her moment of hesitation, I grabbed her wrist. I barely had to squeeze before the razorblade dropped from her fingers to fall harmlessly on the carpet.

She might have expected my ire at her half-hearted attempt on my life, but all I felt was mild disappointment that she'd done something so foolish. If anything, her bravery and resultant shock at harming me intrigued me more than ever. She didn't strike me as a liar, but she couldn't possibly be an FBI field agent if she couldn't stomach hurting a man.

Keeping my hold on her wrist, I took a step toward her. She stepped back.

"I cut you," she blurted, her eyes clouding with confusion.

"You did," I responded calmly. She'd have to be punished for her little transgression, no matter how remorseful she appeared. "Are you really so eager for another spanking already? Did you enjoy it so much? I'll have to devise more clever punishments for you." Another strange smile tugged at my scar. "We are going to get along well."

"Stop saying that," she demanded, her voice hitching. "I don't want you to spank me. I don't want you to touch me."

She might think those things, but they were outright lies.

I stepped forward, closing the distance between us. Her back hit the wall, and I captured both of her wrists in one hand, pinning them above her head. Her little body was trapped by mine, caged in by my much larger frame. I liked how small she felt in my hold, how helpless. I liked how she stared up at me with wide eyes as she drew in panting breaths.

"Liar," I informed her smoothly. "I won't tolerate that, either. You enjoyed your spanking." I wedged my thigh between hers, forcing her legs apart. I reached between us with my free hand and lightly slapped her pussy.

She let out a strangled cry. Her eyes remained wide with disbelief, but on the second slap, they clouded over with confusion. Her lower lips would be burning and tingling. If her reaction was anything like it had been when I'd spanked her before, she'd become aroused by the punitive touch.

I stared down at her, watching her reactions closely. I scented her wetness again.

She bucked in my hold, her body torn between a desire for escape and a yearning to seek more of the burning heat of my hand. Her writhing into me caused my palm to rub against her clit, and I pressed forward, allowing her to stimulate herself.

She gasped and shivered. Her eyes darkened with lust, but her brow furrowed with distress.

"What are you so afraid of, *cosita*? The pain or the pleasure?"

"What?" she asked faintly. She stopped grinding against

me, but I kept my palm pressed firmly against her pussy in a demonstration of ownership.

"Do you really not understand?" I asked. Surely, she knew the pleasure of a man's touch, even if she didn't know why her body was reacting this way to punishment.

She pressed her lips together, and her cheeks turned scarlet.

A low, hungry growl rumbled from my chest. If she truly didn't understand, she was more innocent than I would have suspected for such a lovely woman. That innocence got me hard. I wanted to brand her with my touch, to claim her for myself and no one else.

"How innocent are you, Samantha?"

"I... I don't like when you touch me there," she whispered.

My desire spiked. "*There?* You mean, your wet little pussy?" I rotated my palm against her clit, and she cried out. Her wetness coated my hand, making satisfaction course through me.

"Stop," she moaned. "I don't like this."

"Liar," I accused again, slapping her labia in rebuke. She tried to close her thighs, but she couldn't resist my superior strength.

"I don't want you to touch me," she pleaded.

Her eyes tightened with fear, and her pulse jumped at her throat. She gasped in a sharp breath, her panic claiming her again.

I removed my touch from her immediately, my hand coming up to cup her cheek instead. "Look at me," I commanded.

She blinked and focused on me again.

"You will learn to accept my touch." To prove my point, I rubbed my thumb along her pouty lower lip. She shivered, and her nipples pebbled against my chest. "You will learn to crave it."

"Please, let me go. You have to let me go." Some of her defiant strength returned. "You can't...hurt me. My friends will find me. Do you really think the FBI won't do whatever it takes to get one of their own back?"

"My brother isn't so sure of that," I said, studying her intently. "It's my job to ensure your honesty. He wants the truth from you, and I will have the truth."

"I'm telling you the truth," she said desperately, her eyes clear and beseeching.

"Yes," I said after a moment. "I think you are." Despite her awkward attempts to fight me, she seemed sincere. She'd said she used to be a tech analyst before recently transferring to field agent. She must be very green to be such an inexperienced fighter in a high-pressure situation.

"Then you'll let me go?" she asked, hopeful.

"No." I scowled at the very idea of releasing her. "That's my brother's decision to make. Until he does, I'm keeping you."

She glowered up at me, righteous rage surfacing. She was a fierce little thing, no matter how innocent she was. "Dex is going to find me," she warned. "And if you hurt me before he gets here, he will tear you apart with his bare hands."

Something ugly stirred in my gut at the sound of another man's name on her lips.

"No one will find you," I swore. "You belong to me now."

"You're insane," she flung back at me. "I don't belong to you."

I rubbed my fingers over her lips, forcing her to taste the wet desire that lingered on them. "Your pussy says otherwise," I reminded her. "You nearly came all over my hand, just from a spanking. Your body knows its Master. Your mind will follow."

She snapped at my fingers, but I pulled away before she

could bite. She really was adorable, but I couldn't allow such behavior. I settled my hand around her throat, applying just enough pressure so she was aware of my control. Her eyes went wide, and she stilled, softening on instinct as she realized she was powerless against me.

"Good girl," I approved. "Don't try to bite me again, or I'll find a better use for your pretty mouth."

Her lips parted in shock, and she trembled as her fear rose again.

I released her throat so I could stroke my fingertips down the column of her slender neck. "Breathe. You spook very easily, *cosita*. But you will learn to crave me. All of me. My hand, my mouth, my cock. You will accept me."

"I won't."

I opened my mouth to correct her, but I was interrupted by a sharp knock on my bedroom door. I scowled. My people should know better than to interrupt me in my penthouse.

Then the man called out in Spanish, letting me know Cristian wanted to see me.

That was the only reason anyone would dare disturb me. I didn't keep my phone on me when I was in the privacy of my own suite, because this was my time for myself. But if my brother wanted to meet with me, nothing would stop him from invading my privacy.

I barked back that I would be there shortly before returning my attention to Samantha. "I have business to attend to," I informed her. "We will work on this later." I stared down at her, considering what to do with her. "I need to get dressed. Can I trust you not to try to attack me again once my back is turned?"

She frowned at me and lifted her chin in defiance.

I frowned back at her. I didn't like her challenging posture.

Then she shivered and softened, and my frown melted into

a pleased smile. Despite my displeasure with her attitude, I found her fascinating. I tucked a stray lock of copper hair behind her ear. "So frightened, but so defiant," I observed. "I'm going to have to restrain you, aren't I?" Dark desire stirred within me at the prospect. I remembered her writhing in my cuffs, and my cock began to stiffen again.

She jerked against my hold, but my fingers remained firm around her wrists. "No," she defied me.

"So, you won't try to attack me as soon as I release you?"

She continued to struggle, and a cute little growl slipped between her bared teeth. I laughed, the sound feeling strange in my throat.

"Such an angry *gatita*. Maybe I should keep you in a cage. Would that tame you?"

"I don't need to be *tamed*," she shot back. "I told you the truth. I'm a federal agent. You said you believe me. If you do, then you know you can't risk hurting me. My friends at the Bureau won't stop looking for me, and if you've...if you've hurt me when they find me, they won't show you any mercy. You have to let me go."

Some of my anger returned, but it wasn't directed at her. My lips twisted in distaste around my next words. "That's up to my brother to decide." I hated that the decision rested with him. I'd do anything within my power to keep Samantha. "Until he does, you're mine."

"You keep saying that," she hissed. "You're fucking crazy, you know that, right? You're—"

I pressed my palm firmly against her lips, my frown deepening to something more forbidding. "You will learn to mind your language when you're speaking to me. I need to get dressed, and you need to be quiet and behave while I'm gone. How comfortable you are while I'm out attending to my business is up to you. I can gag you and cage you, or I can leave you free to move around the suite. Make your choice."

Her eyes finally left mine to search the room, as though she didn't quite believe me. She needed to see it for herself, so she could understand. I knew the moment she saw the iron bars beneath my bed when she sucked in a sharp breath. Her eyes widened with fear as she processed the fact that it truly was a cage, and I wouldn't hesitate to keep her in there if she continued to defy me.

"Choose," I demanded, my voice roughening with arousal at the thought of her caged beneath my bed, waiting for me to return and resume her training. "Are you going to be a good girl for me, or am I going to have to cage you beneath my bed like a naughty *gatita?*"

My cock pressed into her belly, and she tried to shake her head as best she could with my hand pressed against her mouth.

I studied her for a moment longer. As much as I liked the idea, I wouldn't cage her if she agreed to behave. I had to be consistent, so she knew her behavior had consequences.

Finally, I nodded and stepped back, freeing her body from mine. I kept hold of her wrists and began tugging her toward the bed.

"Please," she gasped. "I don't want to go in there."

"I'm not going to put you in the cage," I reassured her. "You've already been punished for your transgressions. I told you: I might seem harsh, but I'm fair."

"So you're not going to lock me up?"

I glanced back at her, smirking. "I didn't say that."

I directed her to sit on the bed and pressed her hands into her lap. "Put your hands on your knees, and keep them there. If you try to fight me again, I think you understand what the consequence will be."

I finally released her, and she slowly directed her trembling hands to her knees, pressing her palms against them and locking her fingers around her kneecaps. I curled two fingers beneath her chin, applying light pressure. She had no choice but to lift her head and straighten her spine.

"Shoulders back," I ordered.

She complied, thrusting her small breasts out so I could admire them.

"*Qué bonita,*" I murmured, studying her creamy skin and slim frame. She was so fragile, like a porcelain doll.

I released her chin, and she started to slump again. I clicked my tongue at her and lightly gripped her jaw, redirecting her to the proper position. "Stay."

She shivered in response to my firm tone, and she remained in place when I released her.

Perfect.

I stepped away, but I didn't take my eyes off her. I didn't trust her enough for that yet. She remained locked in place, staring at me as I crossed to the chest of drawers where I kept all my favorite kinky toys. I retrieved the items I needed: a length of chain, three small silver padlocks, and a thin black leather collar. I held them in open hands so she could see them clearly.

"I don't want that," she said breathlessly.

I paused, considering her. "Does this scare you? It won't hurt." I didn't want to leave her alone and frightened all day. I simply wanted her to feel my control while I was gone. And I needed to keep her restrained so she wouldn't try to attack me again.

"I know it won't," she said quickly, words spilling from her pretty lips. "But I don't want it. Not from you."

I closed the distance between us. She remained in place, but she stiffened.

"Not from me? Someone else has collared you before? Maybe you're not so innocent." My stomach sank at the prospect. I much preferred to think of Samantha as untouched by anyone but me.

"No. He hasn't. I just wanted... I don't want this from you."

My ire spiked. She didn't want this *from me*?

So, she did know what the collar was, what it meant. And she'd wanted it from someone else.

"You lost the right to make demands when you tried to kill me," I told her coldly. "I can't trust you not to attack as soon as my back is turned. So, I'm going to chain you to my bed, where you'll wait for me like a good girl while I attend to my business."

"I don't want this," she pleaded.

"And I don't want to punish you more severely than I already have. Not so soon." She wasn't ready for my harsher methods of training yet. "This is for your own good, Samantha."

I finally wrapped the collar around her throat, securing it at her nape with one of the padlocks. I then locked the chain through the ring at the front of the collar before securing the other end of the chain through an eyebolt embedded in the bedpost.

A single tear slid down her cheek, shining in the morning light. I gently wiped it away with my thumb. "It's not so bad, *cosita*." I traced the line of the collar. "It's very pretty on you."

She closed her eyes, as though she couldn't bear to look at me. I sighed, deciding it was time to leave her. She needed time to process her new situation, and I had to go.

I pulled away, but I couldn't leave her when she was trying to shut me out.

"Look at me," I commanded softly.

Her wet lashes fluttered open.

"This is what's best for you," It told her. "While you're with me, you're my responsibility. I will take care of you, even if that means protecting you from yourself."

"You're not protecting me," she hissed, her ire rising once again. "You've violated me. You've stripped me. You've *spanked* me."

I pressed my lips together, not caring for the picture she painted of me. "And if you knew what my brother had planned for you instead, you'd be worshipping at my feet right now and begging to be mine. But we'll get to that later. For now, know that I'm the merciful alternative."

"Rape isn't merciful."

Fury rose within me, and I struggled to swallow it down. "I haven't raped you. I won't rape you. You won't be rewarded with my cock until you beg me to fuck you."

"That will never happen," she said, her tone harsh with spite.

My rage melted, and I considered her for a moment. "Your pretty little pussy has already wept for me. Your body craves to be touched. To be marked and owned. I think you are innocent, Samantha. You don't know what I'm capable of. What I can make you feel. Has any man ever made you come?"

Her cheeks flushed crimson, and her gaze dropped to the carpet. I knew the truth.

"I see. Your first real orgasm will belong to me."

A light tremor raced across her skin, and it took all my careful control to stop myself from touching her again.

"Later," I murmured, speaking to myself more than to her. I allowed my fingers to trail through her hair, the only contact I could allow myself. If I explored her further, I'd never leave.

She cringed away, helping me find the resolve to withdraw from her. She didn't look up at me again, so I stepped away and went about getting ready for my day. Leaving her chained to the bed, I went into the bathroom to take a quick shower. My cock was rock hard when I stripped off my sweatpants, but I didn't have time to see to my needs. My brother was waiting, and I wouldn't risk drawing his attention to Samantha by being tardy.

I was still hard when I slung a towel around my hips and returned to the bedroom. She blinked, and her gaze focused on me. Her eyes dropped from my face, trailing down my chest and abs before coming to rest on the bulge of my erection against the towel.

"You can look at me," I invited. "There's nothing to be afraid of."

She giggled, a shrill, maddened sound. "Right. Nothing to be afraid of. Only the huge, scarred, scary man who's chained me to his bed."

My gut clenched, all my pleasure turning sour. When I'd been toying with her lovely body, I'd almost forgotten about my disfigurement.

"Do my scars bother you so much?" I asked roughly. "Am I so terrifying to look at?"

She pressed her lips together and shuddered, refusing to look at me any longer. I growled my frustration as my lust finally cooled. I moved with swift, jerky movements as I dried off and pulled on my suit. She didn't so much as glance in my direction.

I didn't look at her, either. It made something ache in my chest to see her disgust. But when I reached the bedroom door, I couldn't help turning back for one last look.

She sat exactly as I'd left her: back straight, chin up, breasts thrust out on display.

My lips tilted with renewed pleasure. "Good girl."

I had one sweet moment to register her shocked expression before I closed the door behind me. Another chuckle rumbled from my chest, the sound strange from disuse.

I quickened my pace to leave my penthouse. The sooner I finished with my meeting, the sooner I could return to her. No matter what Cristian said, I was going to keep her. Samantha was mine.

CHAPTER 3

I retrieved my phone from the desk drawer where I kept it locked and powered down while I was in the private sanctuary of my penthouse. This was my space to relax and keep my own schedule. I used my laptop to do my work or to play a game of chess online, but otherwise, I mostly disconnected while I was in my haven. It also meant that I couldn't be distracted when I was focusing on my sweet new captive. She had my full attention; something that would be required to bend her to my will.

Even though my brother had summoned me to leave her side, chaining her to my bed would keep her focused on my control in my absence. She'd quickly come to learn that she was completely powerless to resist me or defy me in any way.

As I entered the elevator to exit my penthouse, I called Lauren and requested that she take care of Samantha in my absence. Unlike the woman locked in my bedroom, I wouldn't order Lauren around. She'd suffered enough powerlessness from the sick drugs my brother used against the women who served in the brothel on the third floor of my building. I hated the way the Bliss left them broken and empty inside, but that wasn't something I could force my brother to change.

He'd made it clear that I couldn't defy him when he punished me three years ago. Any thoughts of resistance had died in that basement.

I also put in a call to Ben, the young man who was tasked with keeping my home clean. This time, I did issue stern orders. He was not allowed to so much as glance at Samantha. He needed to go about his duties, but I wouldn't tolerate another man coveting what was mine.

His fear of my infamous, ruthless retribution would guarantee he obeyed.

I made my way down to the third floor, where my brother had commanded me to meet him. I knew he chose the brothel to bait me.

At least Lauren wouldn't be there for him to touch and torment while I watched. The sweet woman—little more than a girl, really—had earned my affection and my pity. She didn't flinch at the sight of my scars; she was devoted to me, despite what she suffered in my home. I treated her with a kind but firm hand. My commanding demeanor calmed and comforted her. She wasn't afraid of me like the other girls. It was why I'd trust her to take care of Samantha.

I'd never touched the beautiful, willowy blonde with the haunted green eyes. The very idea of using her sexually made my stomach twist. But I was still determined to care for her and see to her wellbeing as best I could.

By the time the elevator stopped on the third floor, I'd concluded my threatening phone call to Ben. I took a breath in the final moment of privacy, unwilling to betray even the smallest show of weakness in front to Cristian. Still, I needed to brace myself for whatever he had in store for me. Especially now that Samantha's fate hung in the balance. I believed she was a field agent—although a very inexperienced one. She'd never been tested in the field, and it was already obvious that she didn't have it in her to lie or truly harm another human being.

Not even one as terrifying as me. Her instincts for self-preservation weren't strong enough to quash her submissive nature, no matter how fierce she tried to appear.

The way she'd softened under my harsh hands and grown wet when I punished her let me know she was a perfect match for my more perverse needs. Even if she wanted to deny it, she would accept me eventually.

She didn't have a choice.

Now, I had to convince my brother to let me keep her.

I RETURNED TO MY PENTHOUSE AS QUICKLY AS I COULD. My meeting with Cristian had gone surprisingly well, but he'd still insisted on coming to speak to Samantha in person. He would arrive at my suite only minutes after me.

I wanted to check in on Samantha and ensure she was covered before my brother came barging into my private haven. I didn't want him breathing the same air as her, especially when I'd barely begun to tame her. Her fiery spirit might get her into trouble. I'd do what I could before Cristian arrived to encourage her good behavior.

A harsh male voice greeted me when the elevator doors slid open.

"Do you know what he'd do to me if I helped you? I have a future to think about. I'm not about to fuck it up by pissing off the boss. Especially not for some whore."

Rage ignited in my gut, and my steps quickened, carrying me toward my bedroom. Ben had defied my orders. He was talking to her. He was *looking* at her. Looking at what was mine.

"I can help you," Samantha said quickly. "If he's threatened you, my friends can—"

He barked out a laugh. "You think I'm being threatened into staying here? I'm paying my dues, you stupid bitch. Don't fucking talk to me ever again. And don't you dare tell him I spoke to you, or I'll—"

"You'll what?" I demanded, the deadly calm of my voice belying the fury simmering within me. I paused at the threshold to the bedroom. If I continued advancing on him, I'd rip the boy apart with my bare hands. Samantha didn't need to see that kind of gory violence. She'd proven how innocent she was—in so many ways—and I didn't want to mar that with a show of brutality.

"She was asking for help," Ben said quickly, his voice hitching. "I was just saying—"

I took a single step toward him, maintaining my icy mask. "You were threatening her. You were looking at her." It took effort to keep the growl locked in my chest. "I told you not to look at her. You're lucky she's covered. Do you know what I do to men who look at what's mine?"

The boy shook his head and tried to retreat. He made the mistake of moving closer to Samantha.

I was on him in a heartbeat, grabbing his upper arm and jerking him away from her. I stared down at him, and satisfaction threaded through my ire when he trembled in my grip. The monster inside me wanted more of his fear. He deserved to be punished for defying me. For daring to look at my pretty captive.

But I was mindful of her wide, pale blue eyes on me. I couldn't spill his blood in front of her.

I might savor her fear, her tears, but I didn't want her to shed them for him.

"Look at her again, and you'll lose an eye," I warned on little more than a whisper. "Threaten her again, and it'll be the last thing you ever do. You're relieved of your duties. Never come into my quarters again."

He nodded, but he couldn't seem to manage to speak. I finally released him, shoving him away from Samantha. Just knowing his eyes had been on her was like a taint on her lovely porcelain skin. I wanted to brush it away with my fingertips, to brand her with my touch, so her body knew I was her Master.

"Leave." I bit out the order before I lost my tenuous restraint and snapped his neck.

He hastened to comply, ducking around me and darting out of the room.

My full attention riveted on my captive. Her eyes flew wide, and her pulse jumped at her throat. The way her pretty pink lips parted on a gasp made dark lust pulse through my veins.

She really was lovely when she was frightened.

She shrank away from me, scrambling across the bed: prey attempting to flee the predator.

The collar I'd locked around her throat stopped her short, but she yanked against the chain frantically.

I took a breath and dropped the cold, threatening mask I'd worn to intimidate Ben. I might relish her fear, but I didn't want her panic. She'd hurt herself if she struggled too hard. I didn't want the collar to rub her slender neck.

She flinched when I reached for her. That didn't dissuade me. Samantha would accept my touch.

This time, my intent was to comfort with my hands rather than punish.

"Calm, *cosita*," I urged in my most soothing tone. My rage

threatened to rise again at the thought that Ben had incited this fearful state. I swallowed my anger and focused on her, stroking my fingers through her silken hair. "You're safe. He won't hurt you."

"I'm not worried about *him*," she said shrilly. "You're the one who just calmly threatened to cut out someone's eye. And I'm chained to your bed. Naked. I'm freaking afraid of *you*."

I knew I'd been right to avoid mutilating Ben in front of her. She was shaken by simply the threats I'd made. Samantha was far more delicate than she'd like to think, I was certain.

She tried to push me away, but I easily captured her wrists and secured them at the small of her back with one hand. With her hands trapped, she no longer held up the bedsheet, and the fabric dipped slightly to reveal the upper swell of her small breasts.

After the few seconds it took to subdue her, I resumed stroking her hair as though there had been no interruption. I would touch her how I wanted, when I wanted. She needed to learn.

"He's lucky I didn't kill him for threatening you," I responded, a calm statement of fact. "I ordered him not to speak to you or look at you. He did both. I can't have a man in my organization who thinks he can disobey me."

"So, you murder anyone who defies you?" Her melodic voice shook slightly. I could feel her pulse jump where I held her delicate wrists.

She didn't understand yet that I wouldn't harm her. Now that she was mine, no harm would come to her ever again.

No one would ever cause her pain.

Except me.

"I will never harm you, Samantha," I promised, careful with my words. She didn't need me to reveal my darkest plans for her yet. She wasn't ready to truly understand what I wanted from her.

"No matter how defiant you may be," I added, my scar tugging with another strange smile.

"But you spanked me. You said you want to punish me." Even in her fearful state, she remained argumentative. Her innocent, submissive nature didn't diminish her fire.

"Only to correct your misbehavior," I reminded her. "I'd never do anything that would damage you. But yes, I won't hesitate to punish you when you deserve it."

"I don't *deserve* any of this," she countered hotly, tugging uselessly against my grip on her wrists. It only took a fraction of my strength to keep her locked in place.

She was fragile, yet strong.

Fascinating. Bending her to my will would take time.

That thought cooled some of my mounting desire. I wasn't certain how much time I had. I wanted to savor the process of taming my pretty captive. I wanted to train her, so she lived to please me.

She would be mine completely, but Cristian had his own timeframe in mind to coerce her compliance with his plans for her.

She'd claimed she didn't deserve this, but that didn't matter.

"Maybe not," I allowed. "But you're mine now, and there's no going back. I'm keeping you, and you're my responsibility."

"I'm not yours," she insisted, her eyes sparking. "And you're not *keeping* me. You said that's your brother's decision. Did you tell him you believe I'm FBI? Have you both seen reason and decided to let me go before the Bureau comes for you?"

Just having her mention Cristian cooled all that remained of my lust. I didn't want her to talk about him. I didn't want her to think about him.

But even now, I could hear the soft slide of my elevator doors opening in the next room, granting my brother access to my home.

"I'll let him discuss this with you," I replied, pulling up my carefully blank mask.

I finally released her wrists and wrapped my hand around her nape, guiding her up onto her feet so she stood beside me. She clutched the sheets, covering her body.

Good.

I didn't want Cristian to see her naked. I might have shamefully coveted the first glimpse of her when he sliced her clothes away with his wicked knife, but he would never lay eyes on her bare flesh again.

"Behave," I commanded, a low warning in my tone accompanied by a soft squeeze on her neck to reinforce my control.

I called out in Spanish, inviting my brother and his two bodyguards into my room. My permission wasn't necessary, but I preferred to keep the illusion that it was.

As soon as Cristian entered the bedroom, Samantha shrank into herself, her fire dimming. She took a small step back, moving closer to me.

Was she looking to me for protection? Or was she simply trying to put distance between her fragile body and my sadistic brother?

She'd have my protection, whether she sought it or not.

I eased my grip on her neck, my fingers threading through her hair to massage her scalp in soothing circles. I anticipated tears, possibly begging for her life. Instead, she drew in a soft breath and straightened her spine.

She didn't shut down or panic. She stood by my side and faced Cristian.

Perhaps she was even stronger than I thought.

She started to ease away from me, but I fisted my fingers in her hair before she could shift more than an inch. She responded to my silent directive, stilling her efforts to get away from me before she'd fully committed to them.

I'd keep her at my side by force, if necessary, but it seemed a firm grip was enough to warn her to behave.

Pleased with her responsiveness, I resumed massaging her. Running my fingers through her copper hair probably soothed me more than it did her, but I indulged myself nonetheless. Touching her grounded me, as did focusing on monitoring her responses and controlling her. Around Cristian, control was something I lacked, and it felt good to have this lovely creature under my power and my protection. To have her on display for him, wearing my collar.

Mine.

"You are Samantha Browning," Cristian announced. "Andrés is convinced, and I had my people look into your story. You're a fed." He sneered the last.

To my surprise, she didn't shrink away when his lip curled. She lifted her delicate chin, defiant. "So, you'll let me go?"

"No." Cristian said the same word aloud that roared through my mind.

"But you have to," she insisted in a rush. "If you keep me here, my friends—"

"They won't find you here," he cut her off, informing her of the cold facts. "One of my shell corporations owns this building. They won't trace it back to me."

"They know I was investigating your organization before you took me," she said. "They'll suspect you're behind my disappearance. They'll follow you until you lead them to me."

"Then it's a good thing I don't come here often. This is my little brother's home. Besides," he continued. "It's not like I'm stupid enough to get out of my car out on the street. And your people don't have surveillance cameras in our private garage for this building. Which, I'll remind you, they have no idea I own. So, Samantha Browning, no one is going to find you."

Her shoulders slumped. I considered pulling her closer to me to comfort her, but my brother wasn't lying or issuing idle threats; he simply told her the truth.

Her next words surprised me. "You're going to kill me." The words were soft, but heavy with defeat.

I firmed my fingers against her scalp, reminding her of my protective presence.

She didn't seem to notice, or maybe she didn't care for my protection or my presence at her side.

"No," Cristian said before I could untangle my thoughts. "You're going to work for me from now on."

"What?" she asked on a little puff of air.

"You're going to erase all the evidence the FBI has on me. You will protect me and my business from them. If you do, I'll let you live."

She hesitated for a heartbeat before her eyes flashed. "Okay," she agreed quickly. "I'll need a computer."

I swallowed a chuckle. She really was terrible at deception. My little captive had no intention of helping us if I let her anywhere near a computer.

Cristian didn't bother to smother his cold laughter. There was no amusement in the sound, only mockery.

"Do you think I'm a fool? You'll contact the feds as soon as you get online. Now, I could just threaten to kill you if you try, but then you'd be useless to me if you're dead. So, I'm going to leave you with my brother for a while longer. I'm sure he'll break you in for me. He's so good at that."

I growled at his words. I didn't intend to break her *for him*. I'd train her to obey my will. He wouldn't touch her. Not once I was finished with her training. Not ever.

"She's mine," I snarled, the words ripping from my throat

in my Spanish before I could think. She wouldn't be able to understand me, but Cristian would. My fingers tightened in her hair, tugging at the fiery strands so I could yank her closer to my body. "I'm keeping her. I'll make sure she's compliant, but she's *mine*."

Cristian smirked, clearly pleased by my agitated state. "All right, *hermanito*," he drawled. "You can keep this one. Just make sure she's useful to me, and we won't have any problems."

I didn't allow myself to take a breath to collect my roiling emotions. In the space of a second, I schooled my features back to a blank mask. I was becoming dangerously attached to Samantha already, and my brother wouldn't hesitate to use her against me if I continued to sink into this obsession. I wouldn't put her at risk by making her a target for his cruel games.

I was behaving like a boy with a new favorite toy. Samantha might be the first woman I'd had in my care since I'd been scarred, but that was no excuse for my childish, reckless behavior.

"Give me a month." I told Cristian coolly.

"You can have three weeks," he countered. "I don't have time for you to play with your new toy. Break her, or I'll find another way to guarantee her cooperation."

My new toy. His use of the terminology that had just run through my own mind let me know that I'd shown my hand. I'd always been possessive of my toys as a child, because Cristian reveled in stealing them and breaking them.

He'd do the same to Samantha if I gave him even a shadow of an excuse.

Keeping my expression carefully neutral, I nodded my agreement.

Samantha trembled at my side. "You can't do this to me," she whispered. Her porcelain skin was completely devoid of any trace of rosy color, her freckles standing out starkly on her slender nose.

Without thinking, I hooked my fingers through the collar at her nape, adding just enough pressure so it would pull snugly against the front of her throat. I controlled her body, her breath.

She belonged to me now.

"Quiet, *cosita*," I chided, calm settling over me when her pretty eyes flew wide and she softened in instinctive submission. "It's done."

Her sensual lower lip trembled, and her thick lashes glistened as her tears began to overwhelm her.

I was dimly aware of Cristian and his men leaving my bedroom, but I couldn't look away from the pretty tears shining on her pale skin.

A rush of jealousy soured my mounting desire. Cristian had caused these tears. I wanted her to cry for *me*.

And she would. She'd cry in pain; she'd cry for mercy; she'd cry from excruciating pleasure.

She wouldn't understand yet, but she would learn.

I wrapped my arms around her and pulled her against my chest. The warm wetness on her cheeks dampened my shirt. I wanted to strip it off and feel her tears on my skin, but that could come later. When her tears truly belonged to me, I'd allow them to soak into me and cleanse my soul.

CHAPTER 4

"You haven't eaten, *sirenita*," I eyed the untouched food on the tray beside the bed. Despite the admonition, I continued to run my hands up and down her back.

She sniffled against me, and I savored the last little sound of vulnerability before she pushed away from my chest to fix me with a glare. I firmed my arms around her lower back, pinning her against me.

Her pale gaze sparked. "I didn't want to be drugged again."

My stomach twisted at the very idea of Samantha subjected to the Bliss that my brother and his men used against the women in his brothel. She'd be mindlessly compliant and weakened by artificial lust. It would hollow her out, just like Lauren.

"I don't need to drug you to keep you compliant. I wouldn't do that," I promised.

"You drugged me last night," she shot back, reminding me of how I'd sedated her so I could tend to the cuts Cristian had sliced into her skin.

I fixed her with a frown. "You were hurting. I was sparing you more pain. Would you have preferred to suffer?"

She lifted her chin. "Yes," she declared, defiant. "Then I could have at least kept the dignity of my clothing. You stripped me as soon as I was unconscious."

If she thought she could make me feel guilty for revealing her body, she was mistaken. She was mine to admire, and I'd keep her fully bared to me at all times.

"Do you really think you'd still be wearing clothes if I didn't want you to? You can't hide from me, Samantha."

To prove my point, I fisted the sheet at her lower back. I'd allowed her to remain covered for far too long. The challenging tilt of her chin proved that much.

She twisted against me in a vain attempt to hide from me. Her squirming only made the sheet fall away that much more easily. Within seconds, her naked body was pressed to my suit-clad form. I liked her like this: wearing nothing but my collar while I kept her slim body locked in my embrace.

"You shouldn't have covered yourself," I issued a stern reprimand.

Her brows drew together, her lips thinning. "So you would have paraded me naked in front of everyone? In front of your brother? How fucked up is your family?"

My jaw tightened. She didn't have the faintest idea about my fucked-up family dynamics, but that was none of her concern. Her only concern should be pleasing me.

"I would have covered you before I invited Cristian in. I don't let other men look at what's mine."

Her small hands shoved at my chest in a fruitless attempt to push me away. "I'm not your property," she seethed.

That was exactly what I wanted her to be: my pretty captive, my possession.

I wound her silky hair around my fingers and tugged her head back, trapping her beneath my implacable stare. "You could be," I informed her, softening the hungry edge that threatened to roughen my tone. I didn't want to frighten her, but she needed to understand the extent of my control. "I could make you my plaything, my eager little fucktoy. And I think you would be eager, Samantha. Your body aches to be touched."

Her cheeks turned scarlet, and she writhed in my grip. Did she realize how she rubbed her peaked nipples against my chest?

No. I doubted my sweet little virgin was aware of how my dark desires affected her. It would make corrupting her that much more delicious.

"I don't want to be your..." She trailed off, as though she couldn't repeat my crass word. It wouldn't issue from her innocent tongue.

There were all sorts of ways I wanted to train her to use her tongue, and none of them involved her cursing.

"You do," I countered calmly. She might not want to acknowledge it, but that wouldn't save her from the truth. I smoothed my fingers over her hair to prevent her defiance from melting into panic. She teetered on a knife's edge; if I pushed too hard without gentling her, I wouldn't be able to elicit pleasure from her untried body.

"But you're still afraid," I said softly. "You're so innocent, you're scared for me to touch your little pussy. That ends now. Your innocence is mine. Your pleasure is mine. You will accept my touch."

She glowered at me. "I won't. I won't invite you to rape me."

The disgusting word barely pricked my desire. It was a natural conclusion for her, and it was time she fully understood the terms of our relationship.

"I will never rape you," I said evenly. "And I won't fuck you at your invitation. You will beg and weep for my cock before I give you what you want."

She shuddered in my arms, her body softening into mine as she trembled for me. The storm clouds of fear and desire in her expressive eyes captured my full attention. I relished her fear, because it was a manifestation of the power I held over her. But the desire she tried to deny intoxicated me. Samantha was perfect for my perversions, her psyche and body reacting to her fear with lust that matched my own.

I watched with a touch of awe as the storm clouds cleared, dissipating in a flash of flame-blue. My little captive was still deliciously defiant. The monster inside me stirred, my cock stiffening in anticipation. I'd relish taming this fierce, fragile creature.

"Go ahead and *punish* me, then," she challenged. "You can spank me all you want, but I'll never beg you to violate me."

My scar twisted on my perverse smile. "I do enjoy a challenge." I leaned down, so I could murmur the truth in her ear, allowing my lips to brush against her sensitive flesh. "You enjoyed your spanking, so it's hardly a punishment." My cock pulsed at the memory of her pert little ass turning red-hot beneath my hand.

I pushed that particular desire aside.

"But that's not what I have planned for you. You owe me an orgasm. Your first. I want it. I'm going to make you come hard, so your body has no doubt that I'm your Master. I can give you pleasure. I can give you pain. Obedience is taught through discipline: punishment and reward. It's time you learned exactly what that means."

She trembled, and I could see her pulse jumping at her throat. A frightened doe had replaced the angry kitten in my arms. I wasn't sure which I found more entrancing.

My cock throbbed, pressing into her belly. I pushed against

her, reveling in the way her breath hitched as I forced her to acknowledge the erotic tension between us.

"Do you feel what you do to me, *sirenita?*" I asked, unable to prevent lust from roughening my voice. "You are so beautiful when you're like this; your little body shuddering in my arms. Are you frightened? Or aroused?" I nipped at her ear, and she sucked in a sharp breath. "Or both?"

I knew the truth, but she wouldn't acknowledge it. Dark anticipation swirled within me as I proceeded to prove it to her. Keeping one arm locked around her waist, I trailed my free hand down her ass before dipping it between her legs to test her arousal. I'd already smelled the intoxicating, feminine scent suffusing the air around me, but I needed to show her the evidence she wanted to deny. I touched two fingers to her soft folds, swirling them in the wetness I found there.

"Both," I concluded with satisfaction, pleasure unfurling in my chest.

My lips ghosted over her neck, just below her ear. She shivered in response, and my kiss firmed on her sensitive skin without thought. I didn't usually treat women with such unwitting tenderness, but Samantha's needs were so well-suited to mine that I couldn't help myself.

I shook off the moment of weakness and issued a low command. "Stay."

She didn't so much as twitch when I released her from my hold and stepped away. Only her eyes moved as she watched me cross the short distance to my chest of drawers. I selected the items I needed, careful to block her view with my body. I didn't want her to know what was coming. If she was prepared, she might not be as fearful.

I certainly didn't want to dim her mouthwatering trepidation. Keeping her on edge gave me more of the heady sense of control I craved; her helplessness kept my cock hard and ready to ravage her tight pussy.

As badly as I wanted to fuck her, I'd told the truth when I'd said I wouldn't rape her. Taking what I wanted from her by force would be easy. Boring.

Bending her to my will and shaping her into my eager fucktoy? That took skill. I could be a very patient man, especially when it came to claiming a woman, body and soul.

I pocketed all of the perverted items I'd selected for her, except for the blindfold. I wrapped the length of silky black cloth around my fingers, holding my fist out slightly as I approached her once again. Her gaze flitted to the blindfold, and she took a step back with a slight shake of her head.

"I like watching your lovely eyes when I'm playing with you, but this will make you more aware of what I'm making you feel," I told her.

"What?" she asked faintly.

I didn't give her time to collect herself. She didn't try to flee or fight when I lifted the cloth to her face. Instead, she closed her eyes as I pressed it against them and knotted the blindfold in place at the back of her head.

Finally, her body reacted, and she reached up to pull the cloth away. I caught her wrists easily and redirected her arms to her sides.

"Settle, *cosita*. This isn't going to hurt."

Her next words went straight to my cock. "I'm scared," she admitted on a shaky whisper.

A low rumble left my chest; a sound of dark satisfaction. "If I were a good man, I'd tell you not to be frightened. But I'm not a good man." I grasped one of her delicate hands and pressed her palm against my erection. "I like having you at my mercy, Samantha. I like when you tremble and whimper for me."

"Please." Her high whine and feeble attempt to tug her hand away made my blood run hotter.

My fingers firmed around hers, forcing her to continue touching my cock through my slacks. "Just like that." My voice was a bit rougher, less controlled than I would have liked. "But soon, you'll be begging me to touch you, not to release you."

I forced myself to release her for the moment, or I might guide her hand beneath my slacks and make her touch me skin-to-skin. She wasn't ready for that. My spooked little virgin needed to be in a lust-drunk cloud before I exposed her to my cock. Not to mention, I needed to be sure that she was thoroughly docile first. I didn't want the angry kitten to surface again and try to scratch me where she might actually do some damage.

I gripped her waist and lifted her slight body, positioning her where I wanted her on the bed. She immediately flailed and tried to roll away, the blindfold making her even more adorably awkward than ever. She'd already proven that she wasn't a skilled fighter, but with her sight taken, she really was helpless.

It only took a second for me to retrieve the handcuffs from my pocket, grab her wrists, and secure the metal shackles around them. I looped the chain over one of the hooks affixed to my headboard. She wasn't going anywhere.

That didn't stop her from twisting in blind panic. I gripped her forearms, stilling her wild movements.

"Don't struggle," I ordered. "You'll only bruise yourself. I'm interested to see how easily your pretty skin marks up, but not like this."

I wanted *my* marks on her, not self-inflicted injury.

My words seemed to increase her panic, and she twisted beneath me. A small frown tugged at my scar. I needed to calm her, or she really would damage her wrists. She responded well to physical dominance, so I settled my palm over her throat, wrapping my fingers around her slim neck. I didn't apply much pressure, but she stilled instantly.

"*Cosita*," I said, dropping my voice deeper with warning. "I gave you an order. Settle down. I'm not going to hurt you."

"But you want to," she whispered tremulously. "You want to break me."

I didn't release her throat, but I stroked her hair with my free hand, gentling her. "I won't break you. But I am going to tame you."

"I don't want to be tamed. I want to go home." Her voice hitched, and I could hear the tears in her words, even if I couldn't see them sliding down her cheeks; the black cloth over her eyes caught them before they could fall.

"You're scared," I said softly, continuing to pet her. I liked the silky glide of her copper hair beneath my calloused palm. "That's natural. But it will pass. You have to trust me, Samantha."

"Trust you?" she asked on a maddened laugh.

"You will trust me." The command came out a bit more fiercely than I intended. "You will give me everything. Trust that I will take care of you. I will give you pain, but you don't yet understand the pleasure I can offer." I took a breath and softened my tone to something more cajoling. "Now, be a good girl and don't pull against the cuffs."

Her delicate features tightened as her rage surfaced once again. "Fuck you," she hissed.

I couldn't allow this small show of defiance. And I didn't like the crass words issuing from her sweet tongue. She'd have to learn better manners.

"Mind your language." I increased the pressure of my fingers around her throat, carefully restricting the blood flow to her brain. I allowed her to breathe, but this would force her to soften and clear the anger from her mind.

She tensed for a few seconds, gasping in fear. It didn't take long for her to relax beneath my hand. I released her before she passed out, tracing the line of her artery with my fingertips as she drew in a breath and let it out on a shuddering sigh. The return of oxygenated blood to her brain would flood her with euphoria, and I wanted to elicit pleasure from her, by any means necessary. She didn't control her body. She didn't control her pleasure. It was mine to give or take as I saw fit.

Now, I wanted her shuddering and sobbing for release. Her first orgasm.

Something hot and savage raced through my veins, a possessive heat I'd never experienced before. I'd never had the pleasure of claiming a woman as innocent as Samantha.

"That's better," I praised, continuing to stroke her neck as she drew in deep, even breaths.

My savage satisfaction licked at my chest like flames when she let out a soft moan. She arched slightly, turning her head and offering her vulnerable throat to my hands, inviting more.

I would give her so much more.

More than she could bear.

She'd take everything I gave her and surrender everything I demanded of her.

"Stay just like that," I murmured before pushing off the mattress and moving to the foot of the bed. I quickly secured her ankles with leather cuffs attached to my bedposts by short chains, spreading her wide for me. Her pink pussy was flushed and wet with her desire.

I retrieved the final item I'd prepared for her from my pocket: a small tube of arousal cream. I applied a generous amount to my fingers and indulged in caressing that pretty pussy.

When I stroked over her folds, she tensed and tugged against her restraints. She didn't twist as wildly as she had earlier, but it was evident that her fear was resurfacing. My innocent captive really was skittish.

I shushed her and coated her clit with the cream. It began to harden as I circled it, her desire rising despite her trepidation.

"This part will be over soon," I reassured her. I would wait until she was so lost to lust that she forgot to fear my hand on her cunt.

She gasped and shuddered as I continued circling her clit. She stopped pulling against the cuffs, but her shudder turned to a fine tremor that raced through her entire body. Her desire was souring, so I finished rubbing the cream into her tender flesh as quickly as possible and gave her a reprieve from my touch on her pussy.

I sat back for a short time, watching her tremor turn to a needy quiver. Her legs jerked, but she wasn't trying to fight her way free. She squirmed to seek stimulation against her sex as the cream began to affect her, making her flesh heat and tingle.

"What are you doing to me?" she asked breathily.

I applied more cream to my fingertips and began stroking around her nipples, rubbing the substance into the pink peaks. They tightened to hard buds beneath my touch. Her mind might not understand what she was feeling, but her body responded beautifully.

"This is arousal cream," I explained. "Not that you need it to feel pleasure. You've already soaked my hand when I spanked you. This is to help you get past the fear. Soon, you'll be desperate for me to touch your pretty pussy. You'll beg for me to grant you release. Need will outweigh fear. Then, we can move forward with your training."

"I don't want to be trained," she protested on an adorable

whine as she began to squirm. Her back arched, pressing her breasts into my hands as she mindlessly sought more stimulation.

A strange sound rolled from my chest. I wasn't accustomed to laughing so much, but Samantha really was delightful. "Most wild things don't. And you are a wild thing, aren't you? You're innocent, untouched. But your body hungers to feel pleasure. Once we get past your fears, I suspect you'll be a very greedy girl. You'll crave my touch. You've already responded so well to your spankings. You'll learn to respond to positive reinforcement, as well."

"You make it sound like I'm an animal." Her protest was ruined by her panting breaths. "I'm not."

"No, you're not," I agreed, skimming my hands down her sides so I could learn the slight flare of her hips. "You're a woman. But you're *mine*. That means you're whatever I want you to be. My plaything, my pet. Your sole purpose is to please me, to serve me. I'm your Master now, and it's time you understood what that means."

"But I—"

"Shhh." I blew a stream of cool air over her nipples, the soft sound shushing her far more effectively than any rebuke. She let out a soft cry as her back bowed, thrusting her breasts toward me in offering.

A low sound of approval rumbled in my throat, and I pressed my lips against the soft swells, teasing her with the heat of my lips. She wiggled, her small breasts bouncing slightly as she tried to stimulate her nipples against my mouth. She groaned in frustration, and my cock twitched at the sound of her desperation. I was thoroughly in control; I'd earned the full focus of her mind and body.

"Has any man ever touched your breasts?" I asked, greedy

to hear that I was the first. I wanted to be the first to claim her in every way possible.

I flicked my tongue over her tight nipples, and she let out a rough shout. I pulled back immediately, denying her further contact as I blew cool air over her heated peaks. She whimpered and writhed, slipping deeper into my control. She had none. She was helpless to resist the sensations I was inflicting upon her, the pleasure I was eliciting from her untried body.

"Answer me," I prompted, relishing toying with her. I didn't have to torture her to draw out the truth; my perverse form of torment would achieve the desired result. "Be honest, and I'll kiss your pretty pink nipples."

"No. Not really. Not like this." The confession streamed from her lips. "I went to a convention once. I dressed up like The Dark Phoenix. From *X-Men*. Cosplay, you know? So, this guy was Wolverine. I met him at an after-party. He kissed me and copped a feel. But it was over my costume. So I guess that doesn't really count. Does it? I used to think so. But I—"

I ended her rapid-fire speech by sucking her nipple into my mouth and swirling my tongue around the needy bud. I didn't want to hear about this other man. It was enough to know that I truly was the first to touch her this way, to know that she'd never experienced this with another man.

I allowed myself to be a little rougher with her, testing her pain tolerance as I pinched and tugged at her nipples. The little keening sounds that left her lips made dark pleasure suffuse my system. She was lost, completely in my power.

Her head thrashed from side to side as her sexual frustration mounted, and she began to lift her hips in wanton invitation.

I rested my palm low on her belly, my fingertips teasing the soft curls above her clit. "And your pretty little pussy," I prompted. "Has any man ever touched you here?"

"No," she admitted on a whimper.

"Poor little virgin," I murmured, half-mocking. Her innocence made her that much more susceptible to me. She didn't have the faintest idea of how to suppress her lust, how to put up mental barriers to resist the pleasure I was eliciting. "You need to be touched, don't you?"

"I... I want..." She bit her lip, her cheeks flushing beneath the blindfold.

"Tell your Master what you want," I cooed. "Tell me how you like to be touched. Do you put your fingers inside your tight pussy? Or do you rub your little clit?"

"I don't. I can't. It's..."

She tensed slightly, so I continued stroking her until the little flare of unease dissipated in the wake of need.

"You don't touch yourself?" Shock colored my satisfaction. I'd already learned that another man had never touched her this way, but I could hardly fathom that she'd never brought herself pleasure. Now that I thought about it, even the idea of her panting alone as the touched herself under the darkness of her covers made something like jealousy pierce my gut. "You've never made yourself come?"

"I... No," she whined, shifting instinctively beneath my hand.

"So, you've never had an orgasm at all?"

She shook her head and tried to lift her hips. I pressed my palm down on her belly to prevent her from rubbing her clit against my fingers where they teased just above her soaked cunt.

"Then let me show you what your body is capable of." I growled out the words, hungry for her orgasm. *My* orgasm. She'd never forget that I owned her, not after this. I'd intended to make her beg to come, but my innocent little captive wouldn't even know what she was pleading for. "In the future, you will beg me for this."

I finally slipped my hand farther down her cunt, sliding one finger between her slick folds. Her inner muscles contracted, and I bit back a curse at how tight she was. I'd have to train her to take a lot more than just my finger before she'd be prepared for my cock.

That would come another day. Hopefully, not too far into the future. I ached to drive inside this tight heat, to feel her pussy gripping my cock the way it was squeezing my finger.

I strengthened my resolve, relishing this moment instead of anticipating what was to come. This was her first orgasm, and it was all mine.

I pressed farther, easing inside her. I noted with mild surprise that her hymen didn't stall my progress, and for a moment, I doubted her. Had she been lying about her virginity?

No. Samantha wasn't capable of lying, especially not when she'd fallen completely under my thrall. Her hymen could have been broken in other ways; it wasn't uncommon.

When my palm cupped her pussy, my finger buried deep inside her, a broken sob wracked her chest.

"Too much," she gasped. "It's too much. Please—"

"Don't fight it." I wouldn't allow her to resist me. Not now. Not ever. I found the spot at the front of her inner walls that would make her come undone. I curled my finger against it and pressed my thumb down on her clit at the same time. "Come for me, *sirenita*."

She came undone on a scream, her flushed body writhing as pleasure overtook her. She shifted her hips mindlessly in a wanton, greedy display as she rode out her orgasm.

Her wild undulations eventually stilled, leaving her panting and trembling as I continued to stroke her through the final moments of her orgasm.

We might have a lot more work to do before Samantha acknowledged her place at my feet, but in this moment, I'd thoroughly conquered her.

CHAPTER 5

I watched her as I got undressed. She was still bound to my bed, her slender body stretched out before me. Her ragged breathing had finally begun to even out. I wasn't entirely certain she was conscious. The blindfold still covered her eyes. I wanted to peer into them and study her reactions to me now that I'd given her unknown pleasure.

I decided to allow her to float in her post-orgasmic haze for a while longer. When I was naked, I went about freeing her from her bonds. I unlocked the handcuffs and pressed a kiss on the pink rings around each of her wrists, my lips brushing them with reverence. The marks were so pretty on her pale skin. I couldn't wait to see what her flesh would look like when I took my whip to her ass.

That would come a little later. I couldn't wait much longer; the monster in me growled for her pain. For now, I'd take care of her immediate needs. I didn't want to break my little doll by pushing too hard, too fast. A broken toy was of no use to me, so I'd treat her with tenderness for the moment.

She remained still as I unlocked the collar from around her

throat and unbuckled the cuffs around her ankles. When I tugged the blindfold free, her eyes remained closed. Her breathing was deep and even, but I suspected she was awake. Her flushed features were smooth, relaxed as she drifted in her blissful haze.

I lifted her up and carried her toward the bathroom, holding her a bit more tightly to my chest than absolutely necessary. I liked the contrast of her creamy flesh against my tanned coloring. She was so soft against me, her perfectly smooth skin practically glowing. It made the scars that crisscrossed my chest seem darker than ever.

I swallowed a grimace and set her down on her feet. Her lashes fluttered when her soles made contact with the cool tiles, and I took a moment to steady her before I turned on the shower. Water sprayed in every direction, streaming from all six showerheads. Neither of us would get chilled while the other stood beneath the cascade. I hadn't indulged in having company in my shower in a long time, and I moved almost eagerly as I closed my hands around Samantha's waist and half-lifted her into the glass-fronted stall.

The temperature was close to scalding—just how I liked it—but her skin flamed red almost instantly. I adjusted the knob to cool the water. I didn't want her to feel any discomfort after the pleasure I'd just given her.

Now, it was her turn to please me, and I wouldn't do anything that might pull her out of her submissive state of mind.

I settled my hands on her hips and guided her to lean back against me, pulling her ass flush with my erection. A soft whimper slipped through her lips, and I stalled my plans for a moment.

"You're still afraid of my cock," I surmised gently. "But you're not afraid when I touch you anymore, are you?"

I pumped soap into my hand from the dispenser on the wall. The sea-salt scent usually clung to my skin, and the idea imprinting my scent on her made something stir in my chest. I rubbed it into her breasts, teasing her nipples under my palms. They quickly hardened beneath my touch, and I indulged in plucking at them, tugging and teasing. The torment elicited a soft moan from her, and she relaxed back into my chest. Samantha liked a little bite of pain.

My lips curved into a twisted smile. I kept one hand at her breasts while I skimmed the other down her belly. I teased my forefinger over her clit, applying pressure as I rubbed the little nub for a few seconds. She shuddered, and her head dropped back onto my shoulder as she melted.

"You are a greedy girl," I said, my voice thick with satisfaction. "I knew you'd be like this. But you don't deserve a reward. Not yet."

She let out the most adorable little whine when I withdrew my hand. Training her might be easier than I'd anticipated. I'd relished the challenge in her stormy eyes, but now that I had her soft and plaint in my hands, I found I didn't mind that our transition into Master and slave might not take as long as I'd thought.

My cock was so hard it ached. I was more than ready for her to bring me release.

I grasped her shoulders and turned her to face me. My lust soured when her gaze darted around the bathroom, flitting from one spot to another to avoid falling on me. On my scars.

When she'd been blindfolded, it had been far too easy to forget that I'd been carved up, my monstrous exterior matching the demon inside me.

"You don't like looking at me," I said, the words coming out in a careful monotone. "My scars frighten you."

"It's not that," she said quickly, still avoiding looking directly at me. "I mean, you're scary. But your scars aren't why you scare me. Well, kind of, because they mean you're violent. But this is just a tic I have. I don't really like looking at anyone. I have to for work, sometimes. It takes effort. It makes me uncomfortable. I mean..." She trailed off, swallowing hard.

Silence settled between us, tension gripping my muscles as I contemplated my next words. "Would it make you more comfortable if I told you I didn't get these scars in a fight?" I finally asked. She thought the furrows in my flesh were marks of my violent nature. I was a brutal man, but I didn't want her to think of me that way. If she feared me too much, I'd never earn her devotion. She needed to understand that I'd never cause her pain on cruel impulse. I'd always be fair and careful with her.

She blinked, her lovely blue eyes finally meeting mine. "What? Then how—"

"That's enough questions." I cut her off. "I am a violent man, but I won't harm you. I'll never let anyone harm you. You're mine, which means you'll be protected. It also means you'll accept my touch and my cock. Look at me." Her gaze hadn't left mine, but I wasn't ordering her to meet my eye. "All of me," I prompted.

She remained locked under my steady stare, and she didn't obey.

"Now, *cosita*." The edge on my words served as sufficient warning. Her eyes flicked down my body, skipping over my scarred chest to fix on my cock.

Her lips parted when her jaw dropped. Now that she'd finally looked at me, she appeared transfixed. She'd never seen a naked man before, and her fascinated reaction made me impossibly harder.

"Touch me," I ground out, losing some of my control over myself.

Her fingers didn't so much as tremble when she trailed them down my shaft, feeling me for the first time. Her sharp intake of breath as she explored my cock made me want to groan. I swallowed the sound of weakness. I wasn't an inexperienced boy who was going to come all over her belly before she even gripped my length.

Her slender fingers wrapped around me, pumping down in a tentative slide.

"Good girl." My praise was ragged with suppressed lust. The innocent little virgin I'd toyed with and taken under my power only minutes ago was threatening to unman me. It was almost shameful, but I was far too aroused by her fascination to experience any chagrin. She'd never looked at my scarred face like she was now looking at my cock; there was something greedy in the way she watched my shaft pulse beneath her tentative touch.

I reached between us with my soap-slick hand and applied a liberal amount, easing the glide of her fingers down my length. This time, I couldn't bite back my groan, but I no longer cared.

"Do you know how hot it is watching you touch me?" I rasped, possessive lust raging through my veins. "Knowing I'm the first man you've touched. The only man you will ever touch. Your first and only, my sweet virgin."

Shock lanced my desire when she used her free hand to cup my balls, feeling their weight as she explored me further.

A filthy exclamation slipped from my tongue before I could hold it back.

The corners of her lips curved in a sly smile. I'd given too much away in that moment. She knew my control was cracking beneath her inexperienced hand.

"Naughty *gatita*," I rebuked, fisting her wet hair around my hand. "Very naughty."

She squeezed my shaft, and I cursed again. My fingers tightened in her hair, but her smile ticked up in smug satisfaction.

"Make me come, *sirenita*." I issued the command in a vain attempt to cling to my power over her. The way my hips pumped toward her betrayed the true shifting power dynamic between us, but I couldn't stop myself.

I came on a rough shout, transfixed by the sight of my cum lashing at her belly, marking her before the streaming water washed it away. As I finished, I pressed my body against hers, pushing her back against the tiled wall and bracing my hands at either side of her head. My muscles felt oddly weak in the wake of my climax, and I blinked hard to clear the stars from my vision.

She continued stroking me, to the point of discomfort.

"That's enough." I should have been ashamed of the shudder that raced through my shoulders and down my arms, but I was too sated to care. I'd never experienced release that intense, and she'd only used her hands. I supposed the torment of denying myself while I played with her and made her come for the first time had pent up my lust more than I'd expected.

Whatever the reason, she looked far too pleased with herself. I wanted to fuck the sly smile right off her face, but that lesson in humility could come later.

For now, there were other ways to humiliate her and remind her of who was really in charge.

I didn't bother to hide the menace from my sharp grin. "Time for your reward, *gatita*."

"What?" she asked, her smile slipping.

"Good girls get positive reinforcement." I stroked her cheek to communicate my pleasure with her, but I didn't soften the cruel intent from my expression. "Remember, my pet?" I leaned in, so I could whisper in her ear. "Your Master is training you to please him. You did very well. You've earned a reward."

"No." Her denial shook slightly.

Satisfaction unfurled in my chest in response to the fresh fear in her eyes. She might be defiant, but it wouldn't be difficult to subdue her. My mouth watered at the prospect.

"You don't get to refuse, pet."

"I'm not your pet." An hour ago, she would have snapped the words. Now, they were a whispered, weak protest.

"Aren't you? You wanted to act like a naughty *gatita*. You will be tamed, Samantha."

"I won't." I doubted she could hear the perverted desire in her breathy refusal. She really did find arousal in her trepidation when I threatened her with erotic torment.

"Your little pussy wouldn't get so wet for me if you didn't want this," I countered smoothly. "You wouldn't have come so hard while you were bound and at my mercy."

"That's so fucked up. You're—"

I clamped my hand over her lips, smothering the dirty words before more could spill from her pure lips. This was a particular bad habit I was keen to discipline out of her.

"We're going to have to work on that tongue of yours. I have a pretty gag that I think will suit you well until you can learn to mind your language when you speak to me."

Her long, ginger lashes flew wide, and she tried to shake her head in denial. I firmed my fingers on her face to still the sign of refusal.

"Hush now, *gatita*. It's time for your reward."

Just like a naughty kitten, she clawed at my forearm, struggling to free her mouth. I barely felt the sting of her nails on my flesh, but the aggressive action elicited a growl from my chest.

I released her lips so I could grab her shoulders and spin her away from me. I pressed my weight into her back, forcing her breasts against the cool tiles. She yelped and tried to push back, her hands slipping uselessly against the slick wall.

The shocked sound stopped abruptly when I wrapped my hand around her throat, applying pressure to her windpipe. I allowed her just enough space to draw in shallow breaths, but in her panic, her throat contracted beneath my hold.

"Breathe, *cosita*," I urged, not alleviating any of the mild pressure I was exerting. She could still breathe, if she focused and stopped struggling. She would get as much oxygen as I allowed her to have. It seemed she truly did need a lesson in humility.

She stopped fighting, her body softening against mine as she drew in as much air as she could. I continued to hold her slender neck as I reached between her legs with my free hand.

She was even wetter than I'd anticipated, her labia still slick despite the water cascading over her skin. Was she aroused from stimulating my cock and drawing out my orgasm? Or was she turned on by my hand on her throat?

I allowed myself to imagine it was a little of both. Samantha was perfectly suited to my needs.

Her pulse jumped beneath my palm as I moved my touch farther back, my forefinger finding her puckered bud. She jerked in my hold and choked when she tried to suck in a gasp. I gave her a moment to remember how to breathe before applying pressure to her asshole. She clenched, denying my entrance. Although I could easily penetrate her by force, I didn't want to damage her. I intended to train her to enjoy every form of sexual stimulation. She would take me in all her holes, in every way I desired.

I nipped at her earlobe, giving her the little bite of pain that I'd already learned she enjoyed. Her lower muscles contracted, then eased. My fingertip slipped inside her, stretching her virgin asshole for the first time.

"Are you sorry for scratching me?" I asked evenly.

She managed a little whine, and she nodded as best she could with my hand around her neck.

I kissed the hollow beneath her ear. "Good girl. Don't do it again."

I reinforced my edict by pressing forward, sliding my finger deeper inside her. She squirmed slightly, but she could barely move with my body trapping hers against the wall. The little wiggle of her hips only eased my way in, her tight ring of muscles gripping me hard.

I finally released her throat, and I had to catch her around her waist as soon as she drew in a deep gasp. The rush of oxygen would make her head spin, and she sagged in my arms.

That didn't spare her from her lesson in humility. If anything, her vulnerable state only helped drive home the message: she was powerless to resist me. She would be a meek, good little fucktoy; utterly obedient and devoted to me.

I slid my middle finger into her soaked pussy, impaling both of her tight holes as I braced my palm on her ass to support her weight.

Something between a defeated sob and ecstatic shout tore from her throat, and her inner muscles convulsed around me. I pumped into her gently as she shuddered in my arms, her orgasm claiming her with shameful force. She loved everything I did to her, despite what she might want to tell herself. Her body told the truth. Her mind would come to accept the irreversible reality of our Master/slave dynamic.

When she began to tremble and went quiet, I decided to

give her a reprieve. I released her from my disciplinary hold and quickly cleaned up before shutting off the water.

I lifted her in my arms again, noting that her eyes were closed. If she thought she could hide from me by floating in darkness, she was mistaken.

For now, I'd allow her mind to drift. She wasn't fighting me or sassing me, so I'd permit her this moment of peace.

Her eyes squeezed more tightly shut when I began to run a fluffy towel over her sensitized skin, drying her with tender care. Her chin tucked closer to her chest, and her cheeks colored. She might be trying to shut me out, but she was thoroughly aware of her shameful defeat.

CHAPTER 6

When I was satisfied that the droplets of water had been dried from Samantha's skin, I laid her down on the bed so I could dry my own body. After a moment's hesitation, I slung the towel low over my hips. I'd spare her more contact with my cock until later. For now, I needed to take care of *mi sirenita*. Her brow remained furrowed, and her knees lifted close to her chest as she curled up protectively on the bed.

She didn't need protection from me. I'd prove that to her.

I sat on the edge of the mattress and lifted her back in my arms, positioning her so she was curled up in my lap instead of on the bed. She was stiff in my hold, but she remained upright when I released her, leaning into my chest slightly for support despite her rigid spine.

I picked up the hairbrush I'd brought from the bathroom and began to carefully work it through her damp hair, smoothing the tangles I'd created when I'd wrapped the fiery strands around my fist. She let out a little sigh, the fine lines easing from her brow as she softened slightly, leaning deeper into me.

"I'm not a doll," she grumbled, but there was no bite in the words. Her eyes remained closed, but she slowly melted against me as I continued to stroke the brush through her hair, allowing the bristles to stimulate her scalp.

"Hmmm," I mused, pleased with her submissive posture. Her weak attempt at defiance was cute. "You're not a pet. You're not a doll. Is there anything you do want to be, *sirenita*?"

"What does that mean?" she asked instead of answering my question.

I decided to let her evasiveness slide. She likely didn't have an answer for me, anyway. She wasn't ready to admit that she enjoyed being my pretty plaything, even if she had just shattered twice under my hands.

"A literal translation would be *little mermaid*," I replied.

Her eyes finally opened, but they were narrowed as they searched my face. "You mean, like the Disney princess?"

I chuckled. "It's an endearment. It means I find you beautiful." I traced the line of her lower lip with my thumb, and my voice dropped to a deeper register. "Sensual."

She blinked up at me, doubt darkening her pale eyes.

"You don't believe me," I surmised. "Do you think my cock would get so hard for you if I didn't want you? You are lovely, *sirenita*."

"You're trying to manipulate me," she accused. "It won't work."

"It already is working." I didn't avoid revealing the blunt truth. It didn't matter if her clever mind had identified the motivations for my actions. That wouldn't make them any less effective. "I'm not lying when I say I find you beautiful. But everything I do to you is a manipulation, and I won't pretend otherwise. You're being very sweet and well behaved right now. If I'd known how obedient you'd become when I played with your ass, I would have filled it sooner. You came so hard for me. I thought you were going to pass out. I think you enjoy being manipulated, being shaped into my good girl."

She scowled, but she didn't so much as tense in my arms. "You're a bastard."

I smothered my own frown, remembering her needs. "That might be true. But you will learn to speak to me with respect. There's a consequence coming for that, but right now, you need to eat."

She pursed her lips, clearly debating if it was worth arguing with me. "Okay," she finally agreed, hunger winning out over stubbornness.

I reached around her and tugged at the wheeled cart that Lauren must have brought while we were in the shower. I'd asked the girl to tend to my quarters. I wouldn't risk inviting another man near Samantha for any reason. Lauren had enough tact to know not to enter my bedroom while my captive was moaning in ecstasy. She'd waited until we moved into the bathroom to deliver our food.

I removed the silver dome covering the plate, and the rich scent of salty steak wafted toward us. Samantha's stomach rumbled, making her cheeks color with embarrassment.

I already knew she hadn't eaten anything today, so there was no shame in her body's natural reaction.

She grabbed the jug of water on the tray and filled a glass, quickly tipping it back and gulping down the cool liquid.

I frowned my disapproval. "You didn't drink anything today, either?"

"I thought you might drug me again."

"And you believe I won't now?"

She shrugged. "I figured that steak is huge enough for two

people. There are two glasses, one water jug. So, I'm assuming that you're not going to drug yourself too, you know?"

It seemed she was capable of exercising logic and reason when it came to my intention to care for her. Even if she hadn't trusted me before, she now compliantly sat naked in my lap as she poured another glass of water and drained half of it. When she reached for the utensils, I grasped her hand, redirecting it to her side. I also took the glass from her and set it down on the tray.

I was going to show my sweet pet that I'd always see to her needs. She didn't have to take care of herself, because that was my job. She was no longer allowed autonomy in even the simplest tasks.

"Do you really think I'm going to let you handle a fork and knife?" I asked drily.

She glowered at me, but she didn't try to grab the potential weapon. "I just want some fucking food. I'm starving."

My scar tugged down as my expression drew into harsher lines. "I will train your tongue later," I warned. "And I'm sure you're hungry, which is more pressing than your punishment. I will always see to your wellbeing, Samantha, but don't continue to test me."

"I wasn't going to use the knife on you," she said, her voice clear with honesty. "I just want to eat."

"I'm going to take care of you, *cosita*. Trust me."

She snorted. "You're not really giving me a choice. Is it trust if you don't have a choice? Probably not. No, I don't think it is. Nope. Definitely not."

I studied her for a moment, my lips curving into a smile despite my efforts to maintain a stern mask. "Do you always speak this way?"

"What way?"

"You talk very fast. Like you're speaking every thought that pops into your head as it comes to you. Are you doing it because you're nervous around me? Is this the same as why you don't like looking at people?" I needed to figure out what made her tick so I could better manipulate her, but truthfully, I found her fascinating.

"I mean, I guess," she admitted. She shifted in my lap, but she didn't drop her eyes in discomfort at my scrutiny. "But I don't talk like this because I'm nervous. Well, I guess it's worse when I'm nervous. I just have a lot of thoughts, and they kind of pop out, like you said. My brain is really busy all the time. Like, my thoughts never slow down. I can't focus on only one thing at a time, unless it's really challenging."

"You focus on me quite intently." My smugly satisfied grin held a savage edge. "Does that mean you find me *challenging*?"

"It means I find you terrifying," she retorted, but she wasn't trembling in fear anymore.

I laughed. "Such a feisty *gatita*. You're not terrified. Not like you should be. Then again, I suppose I haven't shown you what I'm fully capable of yet." My grin sharpened, and she shrank back a little. My arrogant laugh boomed through the room, filling the space in a shock of sound. The strangeness of it sobered me. "I promised to feed you, and it's getting cold."

My arms bracketed her body as I reached for the knife and fork. I cut the steak into several bite-sized pieces before shifting the utensils into one fist. I didn't think Samantha would go for the knife, but I'd err on the side of caution. She'd proven to be unpredictable, which I found delightful. Although I didn't believe she was capable of doing any real damage after the razorblade incident, it wouldn't hurt to silently communicate that she had no chance of resisting me.

With my free hand, I picked up a piece of steak and lifted it to her lips. She turned her face away, her eyes lifting to mine.

"What are you doing?"

"Feeding my pet. Aren't you hungry, *gatita?*"

She blew out an exasperated sigh. "Fine. But only because I'm hungry, not because I'm your pet."

"Can't you be both?"

"No."

I chuckled. She really was adorable, and it wasn't worth arguing with her when she'd already lost. "Eat."

She didn't defy me this time. Her lush lips parted, and I placed the steak on her tongue. Her eyes practically rolled back in her head, and her low moan went straight to my cock. Her lips closed around my fingertips, sucking them clean. I'd come less than half an hour ago, and already she stirred my lust for her.

"You like *carne asada?*" I asked, my voice rougher than I intended.

She pulled back, flicking her tongue over my fingertips before releasing them. "I like meat," she replied, seeming oblivious to the obvious innuendo. "All kinds of meat. If it used to *moo*, I'll definitely eat it. This is so good. I want more."

"Greedy and savage," I remarked with amusement. "You can have as much as you want."

"I'm not savage," she mumbled. "I couldn't even kill you properly."

"No, you couldn't." The small scratch on my chest from her pathetic attack with the razorblade was evidence of that. "I don't think you have it in you. That doesn't mean I'll give you access to a knife anytime soon, though."

"I'm a trained field agent," she said, defensive.

"Not a very good one." It was a simple observation, not an insult. I was pleased with her sweet nature, and I wouldn't mock her for her tender heart.

"I shouldn't have transferred from tech analyst," she lamented instead of taking offense.

"Probably not," I agreed. "My brother has his own tech team. They looked into you. By all accounts, they were very impressed. It's why Cristian let you live." My levity melted at the thought of my brother. I didn't like mentioning him around her. I didn't want her thinking about him at all.

"Because he wants me to protect him from the FBI," she said glumly. "He wants me to save his miserable life."

"He does," I responded in a monotone. "And you will. It's my job to make sure you do. You won't do it for Cristian, but for me. I want you to stop thinking about my brother and start thinking about pleasing me." I needed to shift her focus back to me, or my possessive ire would break through my controlled façade. She belonged to me, not Cristian.

"And you can start by finishing your meal," I directed.

"You're the one who insists on feeding me one tiny piece at a time," she complained.

"If you'd stop sassing me, this would go faster," I drawled, her fiery streak distracting me from my mounting anger.

She narrowed her eyes at me in an attempt to communicate displeasure, but the annoyance was wiped from her features as soon as I resumed feeding her. It seemed she couldn't hold on to her indignation when succumbing to the simple satisfaction of a good meal, especially when she hadn't eaten all day.

When she finally turned her face away to indicate that she was full, I tucked into what was left of the steak. She'd devoured more than half of it, but I didn't begrudge my savage little pet's appetite. I'd enjoyed feeding her from my hand as much as she'd enjoyed the meal.

I finished the steak and set down the utensils before shifting her off my lap. "Stay." I squeezed her hips to reinforce the command.

She didn't budge as I wheeled the cart out of the bedroom

and into the sitting room. No need to tempt her by leaving the knife right beside the bed.

I returned to the bedroom and shut the door behind me. She'd stretched out on the mattress, and she blinked at me slowly as I approached. She appeared relaxed. Exhaustion from her tumultuous day seemed to be dulling her desire to resist me.

As much as I liked seeing her sleepy and sated in my bed, she needed to take care of the few essential needs I'd allow her to handle on her own.

I grasped her hand and pulled her upright. "Go brush your teeth and wash your face."

She grumbled as I tugged her to her feet, but the sound quickly morphed into a yelp when I swatted her ass. "Go on."

She trudged into the bathroom, and for a few minutes, the sound of water running drifted through the closed door.

She paused when she re-entered the bedroom. "You got a new razor," she remarked, puzzled.

I fixed her with a level stare. "And you didn't break it apart and attempt to cut my throat. I don't need to worry about you trying that again, do I?"

She dropped her eyes and shifted on her feet, looking like a child caught doing something she shouldn't. "No," she replied, her voice small.

"Smart girl," I said with satisfaction. "Come over here."

I pulled back the covers, gesturing for her to get in.

She didn't move toward me.

"What are you doing?" she asked.

"Putting you to bed."

Her lips tugged down at the corners. "I'm not a little girl. I don't need you to tuck me in."

My small smile met her slight frown. "Must you be so difficult about everything? You seem to love contradicting me." I patted the mattress. "Do you want a spanking before bed, or are you going to be a good girl for me?"

She huffed out a frustrated breath and closed the distance between us. "Only because I'm tired," she said petulantly as she slipped beneath the sheets.

"If that's what you need to tell yourself," I allowed. "One way or another, you obeyed me, Samantha. That pleases me."

She rolled onto her side, facing away from me. Her knees curled up to her chest again in a protective gesture. Undeterred, I pulled the covers over her, tucking her in. I lingered for a few minutes longer so I could stroke her hair, lulling her into relaxation. She softened, and her breathing turned deep and even as she fell into sleep.

Satisfied that exhaustion would keep her under, I stepped into my sweatpants and left the bedroom. I didn't like the loss of her gentle heat, but I had work to do.

I could wait to fulfil my darker plans for her. I suspected she'd soon make a futile attempt to escape me.

I shoved aside thoughts of the punishment she had coming. Whenever she tried it, I'd paint her ass red. I'd finally get to see the marks of my whip on her pale flesh. Then, she'd learn what I was really capable of.

I almost regretted the prospect of taming the defiant streak out of her.

Almost.

The image of her kneeling at my feet and obeying my every command was far more enticing than her little shows of fire. Soon, her pretty eyes would glow with devotion, not defiance.

CHAPTER 7

Hours later, I returned to the bedroom. I'd indulged in a few games of online chess after finishing my work for the day, but I'd actually lost twice. It was a rare occurrence, but I'd been distracted by thoughts of my lovely captive sleeping in the next room.

I stripped and got into bed with her. She let out a little disgruntled groan when the mattress dipped. My first instinct was to pull her against my chest and pet her until she fell back into a deep sleep.

After holding her for a short while, I smiled into the darkness. If I woke her, she might try to sneak out while she thought I was sleeping. I wasn't tired at all, despite the late hour. The prospect of taking her in hand kept my blood pumping hot and fast in my veins.

I closed my eyes and rolled away from her, jostling the mattress a little. She made another sound of sleepy irritation, so I pretended to snore softly to rouse her further.

I heard her breath catch, and I smothered another smile. My little pet was awake. Would she do something naughty?

It only took a minute for her to climb out of bed. I continued snoring, feigning sleep as I listened to her soft footfalls padding against the carpet. The soft *snick* of the latch disengaging when she opened the door should have been almost imperceptible, but my senses were heightened; a predator lying in wait for his prey.

I opened my eyes in time to see her crack the door behind her, allowing a sliver of light to spill into the bedroom. The city lights from the floor-to-ceiling windows in the sitting room would illuminate her pale skin. My mouth watered in anticipation of the sight.

Not denying myself a moment longer, I slipped out of bed and went to the bedroom door so I could watch her. Her skin was as pretty as I'd imagined, the soft blue glow that filled the room reflecting off her flesh with a pearlescent shine.

Her head swung from side to side as she searched for an exit. She took a few steps toward the playroom, where I would train her.

My lips curved in a cruel smile.

Not that way, gatita. *Not yet.*

I knew the instant she spotted the elevator, because she quickly changed course, racing toward what she thought was the path to freedom.

Her entire body jerked when she pressed the call button, making a loud buzz echo through the room. She punched the button again, hoping for a different outcome. The buzzer sounded in angry denial.

I opened the bedroom door all the way and leaned against the doorframe. "It won't open for you," I drawled.

She yelped and spun to face me. The city lights caught in her wide eyes, making them flash through the darkness as she scrambled back. Her butt hit the elevator, and she jolted at the contact with the cold metal. Desperate, she pressed the call button a third time.

Buzz.

I grinned my savage amusement. "That elevator is accessed through thumbprint recognition. The only people who can come and go from this suite are those who have my permission. You don't have permission, my curious *gatita*." I finally began prowling toward her. She shrank back, but there was nowhere for her to go.

"Did you want to explore my home?" I asked, my tone silky smooth. "Were you so eager to see the rest of it? I'm more than happy to show you."

She shook her head wildly. "I didn't... I don't... I just want to go home."

"This is your home now."

My cock was rock hard by the time I reached her, and I didn't waste another second before pressing it into her soft belly, letting her feel my arousal. I slid my fingers through her hair at her nape, pulling her flush with my body so she was undeniably aware of the dark desire coursing through me.

She trembled, but her next words were sharp with accusation. "You weren't really asleep."

"Clever and curious," I remarked with satisfaction. "No, I wasn't asleep." I leaned in, my cheek whispering against hers as I spoke low in her ear, letting her feel the insidious weight of my words. "You can't escape me, Samantha. There's only one way out of this penthouse, and it's barred to you. I don't have to keep you collared and chained to trap you here. I just like it. I like knowing you're naked in my bed, waiting for me."

"You're sick," she said shakily.

A soft, cruel laugh rolled from my chest. "You've called me worse already. Do you really think your little insults wound me? I'm going to tame your barbed tongue because I enjoy training you, not because it's capable of hurting me. If you continue to defy me in this, the only time you'll be allowed to use your tongue is when you're worshipping my cock."

I'd finally get to punish her in the way I'd craved ever since I'd seen her bound to that chair in my basement. Her sexy little sounds of distress had called to my more sinister nature. I'd never punish her without cause, but she'd more than earned her discipline with her futile escape attempt. Now, I could indulge in all the perverted things I wanted to do to her.

"But you wanted to see the rest of my home," I continued smoothly. "Let me show you."

"I don't want to," she squeaked out. She squirmed against me, accomplishing nothing but stimulating my cock. It jerked against her belly, demonstrating my sadistic anticipation.

"Please," she begged. "I'll go back to bed."

I clicked my tongue at her. "The time for being a good girl has passed. You've been a curious *gatita*. You know what happens to curious kittens, don't you?"

She shuddered in my arms. "You said you wouldn't kill me. Your brother wants me alive."

My hand tightened around her nape, my fingers digging into her neck. "This is about what *I* want," I snarled. How dare she mention him when I held her trapped against me? She was mine to torment, not his. "I don't want you dead. I want you crying out and begging for mercy. *My* mercy. Don't talk about my brother. Don't think about him. He's not your concern. I am."

I'd show her who she needed to fear. She'd tremble and weep for me. My brother would never touch her. She belonged to me. Her tears were mine. Her fear was mine. Her body, her soul, were mine.

She'd never forget it after tonight.

Keeping my grip on her neck, I forced her to walk toward

my playroom. She stumbled, her feet dragging on the carpet. Her small show of resistance was nothing against my superior strength. She couldn't fight. She couldn't run. She couldn't avoid her fate.

She stalled when we reached the door. "Please. I don't want to go in there."

"You don't even know what you're scared of." Mild amusement rose, and some of my possessive rage ebbed.

"Whatever it is, I do"t want it. You wouldn't want to take me in there if it were anything good. You're scaring me."

"You should be scared. You've been very naughty, trying to escape from me."

"But you just said I can't escape. I can't use the elevator. You don't have to hurt me to keep me from using it," she babbled.

Spurred on by her desperate pleas, I reached for the knob and pushed. The door swung open into darkness.

"Don't," she gasped out as I propelled her forward.

I flipped the light switch, and crimson lighting flooded the room, revealing all my kinky toys and furniture. I'd introduce her to each piece, each whip. I'd strap her down and lash her until she cried for me. Until she surrendered to me.

She gasped and tensed at my side, and I stalled, allowing her to take in this part of her new home. She'd be spending a lot of time in here.

"This isn't like Dusk," she whispered. "It's not. Dusk is Safe, Sane, Consensual. This isn't. I don't want this. Not like this."

My rage resurfaced, surging back to burn through my body. I was familiar with Dusk, although I'd never been there myself. My brother planned to deal Bliss at the club. He'd gotten the idea from the Russians, who'd done the same with fetish clubs in New York. A sex club was a prime location to move the sickening product. What better place to distribute a drug that induced uncontrollable lust?

I might be very aware of Dusk and the perverted activities that took place there. But Samantha shouldn't know about it.

Not unless she'd lied to me from the very beginning. My ire flamed in my chest at the thought of her deception, at the loss of the idea of her innocence.

"You've been to a BDSM club?" I didn't release my harsh hold on her neck, but I stepped in front of her, so my full wrath could bear down on her. "I thought you were my innocent little virgin. Did you lie to me, Samantha? I wondered when I didn't feel your hymen intact. But those can be broken in other ways, and I thought your surrender was genuine." My scar drew tight as my jaw ticked. "I wasn't the first man to touch you. If you think you've suffered under my hand before, that's nothing compared to what's about to happen to you."

"No!" she sobbed. "I wasn't lying. I am a virgin, I swear."

"Then how do you know about Dusk?" I demanded, not yet willing to believe her, despite her wide-eyed panic.

"I went there one time," she gasped out. "I was looking for Dex. I followed him there. I wanted to see him. I wanted him to see *me*. But he didn't. He never does. I got drunk and left. I didn't do anything but drink at the bar. I promise, I didn't do anything. I didn't lie to you. Please, don't hurt me."

I didn't know who this *Dex* was, but he obviously wasn't a threat if he'd been so stupid to ignore the allure of the pure woman I held so cruelly.

I eased my hold on her nape, massaging away the bite of my grip in gentle, circular motions.

"All right, *sirenita*. I believe you. I don't think you could lie convincingly if you tried. You will explain more about this later. For now, you have a lesson to learn."

"I just want to go back to bed." The first tear slid down her cheek. I wiped it away, relishing the warm wetness on my thumb. She'd give me far more tears tonight.

"I'll put you to bed when we're finished in here. You must be punished for trying to escape. You need to understand that your behavior has consequences."

A harsh sob tore from her chest, then another. Her delicate body convulsed.

I frowned. This wasn't what I wanted. I might enjoy her trepidation, but I didn't want this terror. She couldn't focus on me if she was mindless with panic.

This was my fault. I shouldn't have gotten angry. It wasn't like me to lose control of my emotions, especially not when training a woman.

I took a breath and exhaled the last of my ire.

"Come here." I pulled her into a firm embrace, tethering her to me as I continued to massage her nape. "It won't be so bad. I'm not angry with you."

"It will be," she insisted, her voice hitching. "Just because it would be worse if you were angry doesn't mean it won't be bad. This place is... It's not right. I don't want to be in here."

She shuddered against me, so I stroked my hand up and down her back in a reassuring motion.

"You'll get used to it," I told her calmly. "We are going to spend a lot of time in here. I think you might even enjoy it, in a way."

She'd responded so well when I'd spanked her. I wondered if her pussy would get wet when I whipped her, too.

Even if she didn't become aroused, she'd attain a different kind of release in surrendering to me. There was peace in submission.

"Take a deep breath," I ordered softly. She complied. "Good girl. Another."

I waited until her even breaths matched mine. She stopped shaking, and I decided she was ready.

"Come with me." I finally released her neck and stepped away, taking her hand in mine so I could lead her across the dungeon.

She appeared dazed, her eyes slightly glassy and her features slack. I was relieved that I'd managed to calm her, but I didn't like her unfocused gaze. I'd call her attention back to me soon enough.

She stopped dead in her tracks when her eyes finally landed on our destination: the spanking bench. Her mouth gaped in horror, and I knew she must recognize its function.

Fascinating.

I had so many questions for her. How did my innocent little virgin know about such things?

"No." She distracted me with her staunch refusal.

"You don't get to say no. This is your punishment."

"You said you wouldn't hurt me." She tried in vain to jerk her hand out of my vise-like grip.

"I said I wouldn't harm you," I corrected her. "This won't leave any permanent marks. Although, I'm interested to see how easily your pretty skin bruises. I do like seeing my marks on my pet."

She shook her head in wild denial. "Stop it! Stop. I'm not your pet. I don't want be marked or bruised."

"How else will you learn?"

"I don't need to learn anything. I just need you to let me go."

"You don't know what you need. I know what's best for you."

"You don't know shit," she spat. "You're fucked up. You're so fucking messed up. Fuck you."

She continued to curse at me as I pulled her inexorably

forward. She wouldn't get any tender treatment from me until I tamed that filthy mouth.

My silence seemed to make the expletives come faster. While the disrespect rankled, the insults didn't raise my wrath. She'd practically been begging for a punishment every time she'd used foul language with me. It was past time to discipline her.

I was careful not to bruise her as I maneuvered her body, bending her at the waist so her torso pressed against the bench. I buckled her wrists in place at either side of her head. I didn't grant her any lingering touches as I worked on her restraints. I wouldn't use violence against her to make her comply; my movements were firm but methodical. The pain I planned to administer would be controlled, deliberate. I was more than capable of securing her without resorting to brutal force.

Despite her cuffed hands, she tried to push up off the padded bench. I drew a thick leather strap around her waist and buckled it in place, pinning her down. All she could do now was shift on her feet, and I quickly stilled even those efforts by spreading her legs and cuffing her ankles wide apart.

She was completely exposed and vulnerable to me, her pink pussy and tight asshole on display. She continued to jerk and writhe against her restraints, her curses becoming more high-pitched as she realized her helpless predicament.

She didn't seem to notice my brief withdrawal as I went to the far wall, where all my implements for torment hung in neat rows. I selected what I needed and returned to her.

On her final curse, I took advantage of her open mouth, slipping the ball gag between her lips. Her teeth offered some resistance, but shock made her pliant. I buckled the leather straps at the back of her head, forcing the gag deep. She'd barely be able to move her tongue, much less cuss at me.

She thrashed, trying to shake the gag free. It wasn't going anywhere until I decided to remove it.

That wouldn't happen for quite some time.

I gripped her hair, tugging her head back to still her shaking head. She cried out at the little bite of pain as I forced her to become aware of my presence where I loomed over her. Her shocked cry was muffled by the gag, the smothered sound making my cock jerk back to attention.

I stared down at her, watching as she struggled for breath. After a few seconds, she learned how to breathe through her nose, but my harsh hold on her hair kept her head tipped back, further restricting her airflow.

She finally quieted, her gaze focusing on my face as I took full command of her attention for the first time since she'd slipped into her little tirade.

"That's better," I praised, tracing the line of her lips around the red rubber ball. "Very pretty."

A fine tremor raced through her, and my cock stiffened further. There were other ways I wanted to train her tongue, but now was the time for punishment. I had enough self-control that I could suppress my own base desires.

She relaxed against the bench, tears glittering in her aquamarine eyes as she surrendered fully.

"You're so beautiful when you cry," I murmured, stroking the wetness on her cheeks with reverence. "Don't you feel better now? You don't have to yell. You don't have to fight. Your Master is in control, and you don't have to pretend otherwise. Not when you're strapped down and spread wide for me to play with. All you have to do is submit. All you *can* do is submit."

She couldn't even nod in response with her head tipped back, her hair wrapped around my fist.

I didn't require a response. If she didn't understand now, she would soon enough.

I pressed a kiss to her forehead. Confusion threaded through my mounting high. When I'd trained women in the past, I'd used my mouth to tease and torment, but not to show tenderness.

I shook off my worry and centered my attention on her, my lips lingering against her soft skin. "Time for your punishment, *gatita*. You've more than earned it."

I held her there for a few seconds longer before finally straightening to my full height and releasing her hair. Her head dropped forward, and she meekly rested her cheek on the red leather beneath her.

I settled my palm on her lower back, letting the heat of my hand sink into her. "Good girl. I'll be right back."

I forced myself to break contact and retrieve what I needed from my wall of toys. I didn't have to keep touching her. I had to discipline her. I needed her cries of pain and supplication, perhaps even more than she needed her naughty behavior corrected.

What I had in mind for her would achieve both ends.

I selected one of my heavier floggers, with two dozen thin leather falls. The swinging weight would thud deep into her flesh, while the smooth leather would leave a fierce sting on her skin. This wasn't the time for a soft, lightweight deerskin flogger. She might enjoy that too much.

This was punishment, and I wouldn't show any leniency.

When I approached her, I noted that her eyes were closed, her breathing regulated. I hadn't expected the gag to be quite so effective at calming her, but it seemed to have silenced her racing thoughts as well as her crass words.

I simply watched her for a while, waiting for her to start

squirming as the tension built. It didn't take long for her brow to crease with worry.

Satisfied that she was hovering on the edge of fear once again, I touched the falls of the flogger between her shoulder blades, allowing the cool leather to tickle her skin.

Her eyes flew open on a shocked yelp. Her gaze focused on the flogger, and recognition flashed in her eyes as a shiver raced through her body.

"You know what this is?" I asked, fascinated.

I trailed the leather falls down the length of her spine. She whimpered and nodded, with no thought of refusing to respond. I enjoyed watching her slip into submission despite her efforts to deny me. She couldn't resist her nature. She couldn't resist *me*.

"But no one has ever flogged you before." It wasn't really a question; I already knew her answer. But I wanted her to admit it. I craved confirmation that I'd be the first to torment her this way.

She shook her head.

My lips curved in a satisfied smile. "Kinky virgin. When I decide to allow you to speak again, you'll tell me every depraved thought you've ever had. I knew we'd get along."

Her needs suited mine perfectly. She obviously had some interest in domination and submission. And while she probably had a pretty fantasy of BDSM in her head, she didn't yet understand the pleasure she'd find in a true, complete power exchange. She didn't get to hide behind safe words, and her distress wouldn't save her from my dark desires. Nothing would prevent me from bending Samantha to my will. I would master her and turn her into my sweet, compliant slave. She'd live to please me.

The prospect of earning her unconditional devotion stoked my lust, making me ache to claim her.

If I couldn't claim her tight pussy tonight, I'd take control of her mind instead. I wouldn't relent until she was completely lost, completely under my power. Samantha might be clever, but my will was stronger than her formidable intellect. She'd shatter under my whip, and I'd put her back together again, shaping her into the pretty plaything I desired.

My thoughts were becoming more sadistic as I fell into the intoxicating headspace I could only achieve through asserting dominance. I'd been deprived of this for so long. It had been years since I'd toyed with a submissive woman. And none who had come before had been as enticing as Samantha. She was mine to keep, to covet. To pleasure and punish. I was greedy for the sound of her pained cries, the sight of her reddened flesh.

I took a step back, so I was positioned behind her. I swung the flogger down in a slow arc, allowing the falls to slap lightly against her ass. They slid over her round cheeks, black tendrils standing out in stark contrast to her porcelain skin.

"This is going to hurt," I warned. "It's supposed to hurt. One day, I'll show you how good it can feel. But not tonight."

I delivered the first real blow, landing the whip hard on her ass. I hadn't warmed her up, and she shrieked into the gag. I paused, watching as she struggled against her restraints in a fruitless effort to escape the pain that bloomed beneath her skin; the deeper burn that followed the initial sting.

She craned her head back, her watering eyes pleading for mercy as her high whimper caught behind the gag.

"Your eyes are so lovely," I murmured, barely aware that I spoke the words aloud.

I wanted those shining tears to spill down her cheeks.

I lashed at her again, twice in rapid succession. Her chest heaved on a sob.

I had no intention of granting her a reprieve from the

whip, but I wanted to take a minute to admire her. My fingers trailed over her heated, reddened flesh. She whined at the sting of my gentle touch, but she would take so much more.

"So pretty and red," I remarked.

I gripped her ass hard, digging my fingertips into her soft cheek. "I want to see my fingerprints on your ass tomorrow. The bruises from the flogger will remind you of your punishment, but this marks you as mine."

I increased the pressure of my cruel hold, and tears finally streamed down her cheeks. Calm settled over me, and I drew in a deep, cleansing breath.

Releasing her, I stepped back and swung the flogger down again, not giving her a moment to collect herself. She threw her head back and screamed into the gag. The sound only stoked my savage satisfaction. Her tears, her screams, were for me. I possessed her body, controlling her pain.

I spread out the burn, lashing at her upper thighs as well as her bottom. After a while, her screams turned to ragged shouts, before subsiding to soft whimpers. She quivered, her tense muscles reaching the point of exhaustion from jerking against her bonds. Finally, she went limp against the bench, her tears falling onto the leather as she cried silently.

"Good girl." My voice came out deep and smooth. She was slipping into full submission. I just had to push a little more. "Accept your punishment. You know you've earned it."

She wouldn't try to escape me again. Not after this. Her behavior would be modified, her misguided thoughts of freedom eradicated.

Her breathing began to even out, her features going slack as her eyes turned glassy. She'd hit the quiet, peaceful headspace that could only be obtained through complete surrender. In the future, she would come to crave this release. I'd train her to love it.

I stopped whipping her, allowing the flogger to drop to the tiled floor. I began to unbuckle the straps that held her down, my fingers lingering on the pink marks they'd left on her creamy skin. Hardly aware of what I was doing, I murmured soothing words in my native tongue, telling her how pleased I was with her, how well she'd taken her punishment.

She was a ragdoll in my arms as I lifted her up, cuddling her close. Her tears wet my skin, and I relished their warmth as they slid down my chest.

By the time I carried her into the bedroom, she'd fallen into sleep. I tucked her under the covers and got into bed beside her, pulling her back flush with my chest as I shaped my body around hers. My cock was still semi-hard, but my lust was subsiding. I'd achieved a deeper satisfaction than any orgasm could give me. I possessed the beautiful creature in my arms.

With that knowledge, I followed her down into peaceful, contented sleep within minutes.

CHAPTER 8

I shifted on my feet as the elevator ascended to my penthouse, anxious to get back to Samantha. I'd avoided my brother today, but I'd still had to "oversee" a transaction with the Latin Kings to push Bliss into the Chicago clubs. My presence was meant to intimidate, my scarred face a warning to those who might cross Cristian Moreno. I much preferred the days when my work consisted of keeping the books and coordinating meets between key players in our organization. I craved solitude and quiet, not issuing threats when reckless fools reached for their weapons.

Tensions ran high between our men and the Latin Kings. We were only connected by a loose alliance, in which we both profited from trafficking Bliss and cocaine. Our people brought the products into the country from Colombia, and the Kings distributed it on the streets, putting themselves in the authorities' crosshairs while we remained mostly under the radar.

The revelation that Samantha had been watching our

people was troubling. If the FBI was investigating my brother, our position here might be in jeopardy.

It was essential that I secure Samantha's compliance. We needed her to work against the Bureau to protect us.

My hand twitched at the memory of the whip in my fist as I swung it down on her tender flesh. I couldn't wait to inspect the marks I'd left on her skin. I'd seen some of the bruises when I slipped out of bed this morning, but they would've darkened further by now. The brand might only be temporary, but this first time, I'd savor the evidence of our power exchange.

I stepped out of the elevator and paused in the sitting room. Feminine voices drifted through the open doorway to the bedroom. I'd given Lauren very specific instructions about how to care for Samantha today in my absence, but I'd expected her to be gone by now.

It sounded as though she'd been held up by a heated conversation.

"I'm not going to roll over and give up just because you told me to," Samantha's words became clearer as I took another step toward the bedroom. "I'm not going to behave for my sadistic captor who gets off on torturing women, no matter what you say."

My stomach twisted at her description of me. Perhaps I had been a touch sadistic with her last night, but my measured punishment had been far from torture.

I realized my captive didn't have the faintest idea what torture truly was. Maybe I should be gentler with her.

I resolved to keep her out of the playroom until she was ready to face it again. Unless she really did something to deserve it. Now that I'd set a precedent for discipline, I couldn't alter the dynamic between us.

"You don't understand him." I recognized Lauren's girlish voice. "You don't know him."

"And you do? Just how well do you know *Master* Andrés? What did he do to you, exactly?"

Something dark stirred within me when she said *Master*, but her disgusted tone soured my desire.

"He's nice," Lauren insisted.

My heart softened as the abused girl came to my defense. Truthfully, I'd done little to deserve her loyalty. She'd latched on to the smallest kindnesses, finding stability in my stern orders.

I finally reached the bedroom. "Thank you, Lauren," I said softly, expressing my gratitude for more than her obedience in taking care of Samantha. "You can go now."

My pretty captive jolted at the sound of my voice, and she jerked the bedsheet up to her chin.

I stepped across the threshold, prowling toward her. "You know you're not allowed to cover yourself, *cosita*," I chided. "Show me your pretty pussy. I want to see it."

Lauren scurried past me, quickly leaving the penthouse to give me privacy with my pet.

Samantha stared at me, her lips parted slightly as she drew in short, shallow breaths. For a moment, she tensed with indecision. Her eyes tightened, and I assumed she was recalling the punishment she'd faced the last time she defied me. It should still be very fresh in her mind.

Slowly, her fingers fisted in the sheet, and she pulled it down her body.

It seemed she could be taught to obey.

My gaze dropped to her bare cunt. The ginger curls that had protected her from my full scrutiny were gone, thanks to Lauren's neat work with wax. I would have done it myself, but the blonde girl's hands were more practiced at this particular skill.

It was enough that she was completely exposed to me.

"Very pretty," I approved. But there was something else I craved. I twirled my finger as I ordered, "Turn over. I want to see my marks on you."

She glared at me, but I simply waited, fixing her with an implacable stare. I could forcibly turn her, but this was a test in obedience.

She huffed out an angry breath and rolled onto her front. My scar tugged on a crooked smile as I took in the purple marks I'd left on her skin. She must have felt the lingering discomfort of my discipline all day.

I'd push her a little further.

"On your hands and knees," I commanded. "Spread your thighs. I want to see my marks and my pussy."

Her eyes narrowed, her delicate jaw setting into a harsh line. It seemed I hadn't worked all the defiance out of her.

Truthfully, I hadn't expected to tame her with one training session. I found myself smiling at the resurgence of her fire. My kitten was adorable when she wanted to scratch.

I didn't give her the opportunity. I snaked my arm beneath her waist and pulled her up onto her knees.

"Hey!" she cried out, sounding almost surprised.

I smacked her thigh, careful not to strike her bruised flesh too hard. Even though I'd been relatively gentle, she shrieked. I had a feeling that had more to do with indignation than pain.

"You will learn to obey me," I informed her smoothly. "Spread your legs. Now," I bit out when she didn't immediately comply.

She scrambled up onto her hands to support her weight as she reluctantly shifted her knees apart. I kept my arm braced under her stomach, just in case she got any ideas about scrambling away from me.

"Beautiful," I rumbled, admiring her exposed sex. I wanted to see it glistening with her arousal.

I touched my fingers to her labia, stroking the soft folds. When my thumb brushed her clit, she sucked in a small gasp. Her skin pebbled, and the first signs of her desire wet my fingers.

I let out a dark chuckle. "I think my kitten likes when I pet her pretty pink pussy."

"Stop," she begged on a groan. Her hips shifted back toward my hand, and she didn't bother lying and telling me she didn't like it.

"But I like petting your pussy, *gatita*." She grew slick beneath my fingers, flowering open for me. "You were very well behaved for Lauren, weren't you? I think you've earned another reward."

I intended to give her an orgasm, but her venomous words forestalled me.

"Is this what you did to her?" she hurled at me. "Beat her and manipulated her until her mind warped? Did she used to hate you before she started worshipping the ground you walk on? Did you—?"

That was enough. She didn't have the faintest clue what she was talking about, and I couldn't stand to hear any more. Yes, Lauren was broken, but it hadn't been by my hand. Even if I hadn't done anything to save her.

Guilt tinged my anger as I abruptly flipped Samantha onto her back and settled my hand over her throat. I stopped myself from applying pressure, but the warning was clear.

"I've never harmed Lauren," I ground out.

A maddened laugh bubbled from her throat. "You've never *harmed* her? Just like you didn't harm me when you strapped me down and whipped me after mindfucking me into thinking I had a chance to escape? How crazy are you?"

Cold settled over me, my face shifting to a forbidding mask as I stared down at her. "I never claimed to be sane," I said, my soft tone more chilling than if I'd shouted. I could hear the menace in it, could feel her trembling beneath me. Samantha obviously didn't understand what she was dealing with. She thought I was a rational man who possessed the ability to empathize with her plight.

She was mistaken. I felt nothing for her but possessive hunger. I didn't pity her, and I certainly didn't entertain any ideas about releasing her when she so desperately wanted her freedom.

"Do you think a normal man wants to take an innocent woman and turn her into his plaything?" I continued. "Do you think a good man wants to bend her will and shape her into his obedient little fucktoy?"

"So you..." She choked on her words. "You did do this to Lauren."

"No," I declared, still frigid. "The Bliss broke Lauren, not me."

Her eyes sparkled. "So, you do want to break me," she whispered in horror.

A frown curved my lips. She didn't understand what I was saying. Just because I was a monster didn't mean I wanted to destroy her. I just wanted to mold her into a different version of herself. A version whose sole desire in life was to meet my every perverted need.

"I told you, I'm going to tame you. I'm going to make you mine and teach you to obey. I don't want to see you broken."

"You told your brother you'd break me for him," she countered, starting to shake in earnest.

My scowl did nothing to ease her mounting fear. I hated

when she mentioned Cristian. That was another tendency I'd have to tame out of her.

"My brother likes to break things. He likes to take things that aren't his and shatter them. If I left you with him, he'd torture you until he discovered what you love most in the world. Then he'd make you watch while he destroyed it. Is that what you'd prefer? That I hand you back over to him?"

Terror clouded her eyes, and tears slipped down her cheeks. "No," she breathed.

I wiped at the wetness on her face and reined in my anger. My ire was making me lose control, and I was frightening her unintentionally.

"I'm not going to let him break you," I promised. "He'll never touch you again. You're mine now. I will be harsh with you. I will hurt you sometimes. And I will enjoy your pain. But I will never cause you harm, not to your body and not to your heart. Do you understand?"

She closed her eyes and turned her face away from my touch, hiding from me.

I sighed, realizing I really had lost all semblance of control. I couldn't be around her when I was like this. I might do something I'd regret.

"I can see that you don't understand," I said. "But you will. It won't be so bad, *cosita*. I'm not so bad." I murmured the last, the words barely registering in my brain as they dropped from my lips.

I pushed up off the bed, and she shivered on top of the sheets. I didn't like leaving her alone when she looked so fragile, but I might do something to shatter her if I didn't take time to collect myself.

I strode out of the bedroom, hardening my resolve. I allowed my emotions to get the better of me when I was around Samantha, especially when she mentioned Cristian.

Training a woman was supposed to give me a sense of control, not lose it entirely.

I recalled the heady sensation of power that had overtaken me when I'd flogged her.

Yes, she needed more of that treatment. I could be gentle with her when necessary, but I had to assert my dominance at all times. She needed to learn who was Master and who was slave.

She would accept her place, even if that meant I had to be more ruthless with her.

I'd never been a warm man. I'd been cold, isolated ever since I was a boy. Samantha's charms and endearing sass were messing with my usual process. I'd become too attached because she was mine to keep. I'd gotten possessive to the point of obsession, and I'd only had her for a few days.

She existed to give me pleasure. I would teach her where she belonged: worshipping me on her knees.

CHAPTER 9

"You're sad," I observed, studying her drawn features and too-pale cheeks. I tucked her hair behind her ear. I'd almost forgotten how silky it felt beneath my fingertips in the hours I'd been away from her.

I'd thrown myself into work, leaving her all afternoon and well into the evening. I'd needed the time to collect myself, and leaving her chained to my bed was good for her, too. She would have had plenty of time to think about her new role in my home, her new life with me. I'd hoped to find a sweeter, more submissive Samantha waiting for me. I'd anticipated that she'd be eager for my company after thinking about me all day. She wouldn't have had any other option; the collar around her neck served as a constant reminder of my control over her.

Instead, I found her wan and defeated.

"I'm not sad," she lied. "I'm pissed." There was no true spite in the words.

"You're not angry." I cupped her cheek so I could study her expression more carefully. Her usually sparkling eyes were dulled, her lips a few shades lighter than the lush pink I'd become accustomed to. "My angry *gatita* is cute and fierce. You're sad."

She blew out a long breath. "I'm bored," she admitted. Finally, a small blue spark illuminated her eyes. "You keep me chained up. I can't even use the freaking bathroom. Do you know how fu—" She caught herself before the curse word left her lips "—messed up that is?"

She obviously remembered her lesson about cussing at me. That pleased me, as did the renewed flush in her cheeks. "There's my angry *gatita*," I said with satisfaction, ignoring her accusations. "I was worried about you."

She crossed her arms over her chest, pushing her small breasts together. "If you were worried about me, you wouldn't leave me alone for hours with nothing to do. I'm going crazy here. Solitary confinement drives people crazy, you know that, right? Especially people like me."

Some of my levity dropped. I hadn't intended to make her crazed or sad. "What do you mean, *people like you*? The purpose of leaving you like this is so you'll wait for me. You'll depend on me for everything. It helps you feel my control, even when I can't be here with you."

She shoved at my chest in a token show of annoyance, but I didn't bother restraining her. She wasn't really trying to fight me, and she clearly needed to bleed out some of her frustration.

"Do you know how many thoughts I have? Like, all at one time? If I don't have something to focus on, they overwhelm me. I can't live like this."

"It's only been two days," I pointed out. "You'll adjust."

"I won't. You don't know me at all. I'll go nuts if you keep leaving me like this."

I considered her for a moment, my face drawing tight with disapproval. "If you're trying to manipulate me into letting you walk freely around the suite, it's not going to work. That's a privilege you have to earn."

"I'm not trying to manipulate you," she burst out, exasperated. "That's what you do, right? Manipulate people. Mindfuck them. Well, I'm not like you. I'm telling you the truth. I can't handle this." She tugged at the collar for emphasis. She was no longer chained to the bed, but I'd left the collar locked around her throat. I liked the way the dark leather looked against her fair skin.

Now, she had me questioning that decision. She had me questioning every decision I'd made about her today. Was I really mishandling her so badly? I'd never had so much trouble reading a woman. Samantha was unpredictable, a puzzle I hadn't quite solved.

"No. You're not like me," I finally allowed. "I'll take this into consideration." I brushed a soft kiss over her forehead; a small, involuntary show of contrition.

A devious idea came to me. I didn't like that I'd upset her, and if her mind was whirring that fast, I would provide her with release. "I think I have a way to calm that busy brain of yours. You were so good accepting your punishment last night and behaving for Lauren today. I never did give you your reward."

"I don't want it. Having you touch me is not a reward."

"You're still upset," I noted, unruffled now that I'd decided on my course of action. "This will help you calm down. And before you keep arguing with me, I'll promise that I won't make you come, unless you ask me to. Does that make you feel better?"

She eyed me warily, distrustful. "What are you going to do to me? I don't want to go back into that torture room."

"It's not a torture room," I countered calmly. "But no, we won't go in there. I want you to relax, not get more worked up.

No more questions," I dictated when she opened her mouth to speak. "Come with me."

I assumed she might give me trouble, so I simply picked her up and carried her to our destination.

She crossed her arms over her chest, petulant.

I laughed, succumbing to her charms once again. As much as I wanted to treat her as nothing more than my plaything, Samantha kept amusing me. It would be a shame to alter this aspect of her personality. She really was adorable when she was feeling feisty. As long as she learned not to lash out at me and to speak to me with respect, I might allow some of this behavior in the future.

"You really are cute when you're angry."

"You think I'm cute when I'm angry. You think I'm pretty when I cry. You're messed up, you know that, right?"

"Yes, so you've told me," I said drily, unaffected by the barbed comment. She couldn't seem to help herself; she'd been riled by the solitude of her day. I'd resolve that for her. After all, it was my job to take care of my pet. "I'd like to see you smile, too, but I don't think that will happen for a while yet."

Her jaw dropped. "You think I'm going to *smile* for you?"

"I think you'll settle down and find a way to be happy with me. Once you adjust and accept your place here."

"*Accept my place?*" She slapped my chest in a burst of anger.

I clicked my tongue at her, remaining calm rather than falling prey to the anger that had gripped me that morning. Now, I understood that this little fit she was having wasn't much more than a tantrum, and a mild one at that. This was completely different from her accusations about Lauren that had cut me so deeply.

"That wasn't very nice," I rebuked. "But you're not trying very hard, either. You're upset, and I'm going to make you feel better."

"Short of releasing me, that's not going to happen," she said flatly. "Do you really think I'm going to *feel better* about being trapped with a sadistic psycho?"

"Mind your tongue." This order was sharper. I wouldn't allow her to pull me into the same turmoil she'd created with her comparisons to my brother. I wouldn't lose control again. "I've indulged you too much. You will speak to me with respect."

"Right." Sarcasm dripped from the word. "You've been so indulgent with me. Beating me, violating me, chaining me up. You're so *nice*," she finished with spite.

I set her on her feet and studied her, curious rather than incited to anger. "You really can't stop yourself, can you? You're not capable of holding in your thoughts, even knowing they could get you into trouble. I think a little discipline will be good for you. You can learn some self-control over these tics of yours."

She instantly clapped her hands over her bottom. "I don't want you to punish me again."

I trailed my fingers over her hair to soothe her. "Discipline doesn't necessarily mean punishment. Now, try your best to be quiet and stay right here."

I left her, walking the few steps it took to reach my desk. She remained rooted in place, but her eyes swept the room. I noticed her shoulders slump in relief when she realized we were positioned several yards away from the closed door to the playroom. I really had frightened her more than I'd intended. That was something I could work on another time.

I drummed my fingers against the desk, calling her attention to me. A wicked grin split my lips when she gasped and lunged for my laptop. I'd suspected she'd try to reach it.

As though I'd give her a chance to touch any technology.

It was fun toying with her, though.

I grabbed her waist and wrestled her to the floor with little effort, pinning her on her front with one hand between her shoulder blades. Her fingers scrabbled against the carpet, her feet kicking out wildly.

Keeping her pinned, I reached into one of my desk drawers and retrieved a pair of handcuffs, wasting no time before securing her wrists together at the small of her back.

She thrashed uselessly. "Do you just have kinky shit stashed everywhere?" she demanded on a growl.

"Of course." My penthouse had been designed with my perversions in mind, and I'd made sure to stock restraints in various locations since I'd captured Samantha. "Settle down. This won't hurt."

"You think I'm going to *settle down* when you basically just taunted me with a laptop? Do you know how starved I am for the internet? For technology? You don't even have a real clock, for god's sake, and you've been hiding a *laptop* from me?"

I curled my fingers around her nape, pressing her cheek against the carpet to still her shaking head.

"I need my laptop for work," I replied calmly. "I'm going to take care of some business, and you're going to be quiet and look pretty for me while I do."

"Work," she spat, scathing. "You mean drug trafficking and selling women."

My fingers tightened around her neck. "Be very careful what you say next, Samantha. I know you struggle to control your tongue, but I'm warning you to try very hard. I don't want to punish you now, but I will."

I'd made allowances for her sass about being left alone all day, but we were skirting dangerously close to topics that would rile my anger. I didn't like being angry around her. It made me erratic. Dangerous.

I didn't want to harm her by accident. She was so fragile in my grip. I could damage her by exerting a fraction of my strength.

"But it's what you do." Her mouth was running away with her again, the words streaming from her lips. "You and your brother. That's your *business*."

"I take care of a lot of things for my brother." My voice was rough, but I managed to prevent my fingers from tightening around her delicate neck. "I do all the things he'd rather not bother with; I deal with the boring details. I keep things running. And yes, what you've accused me of is part of it."

"But you don't like the Bliss."

I stilled, wondering how she could possibly know that. Had she talked to Lauren? Would the devoted blonde girl have spilled any of my secrets to Samantha?

I decided Lauren wouldn't have done that. However Samantha had come to the conclusion, her quick mind had put together some pieces of information she'd gathered.

"What I like or don't like about my business isn't your concern," I finally said. "I need to work, and you need to be quiet. Your runaway mouth is very distracting."

I'd already retrieved the gag from my desk before she began to issue her rebuttal.

"But—" I smothered her question when I slipped the rubber ball into her open mouth. She tried to twist her face away, but that only allowed me to pull the gag deeper, buckling it tightly in place.

Before she could panic, I rested my hand on the side of her head, holding her cheek against the plush carpet. I lightly massaged her head, soothing her.

"This isn't to punish you," I said gently. "You can't control your tongue, so I'll control it for you. You'll be much calmer now."

She responded with a fierce little growl.

"There's no need to keep arguing with me," I reassured her, running my fingers over her hair. "There's no point trying to fight. Surrender. You'll feel much better. We'll calm that busy brain of yours."

She started wiggling again, but she couldn't gain purchase with her arms cuffed behind her back. Satisfied that she wasn't going anywhere, I grasped the rope that lay coiled in my desk drawer.

"I think you'll like this, my kinky virgin."

My plans for her involved more than quieting her mind. Once she reached her submissive headspace, I intended to question her. All day, my thoughts had wandered back to our time in the playroom. She knew about BDSM. She'd expressed interest in being dominated, even if she didn't yet care for my harsher methods of asserting control.

Tonight, I would learn her darkest secrets. I just had to take her to a mindless, lust-addled state, in which she'd answer all my questions just to attain release. Although I had never bound her in rope, I suspected she'd enjoy it. Rope could be sensual or punitive, depending on the tie. One day, I'd put her in predicament bondage and show her what true helplessness was. But I'd promised this wouldn't hurt, and I didn't intend to inflict any pain this time.

I grasped her right thigh and lifted it off the floor, wrapping the rope around it. She tried to kick out at me, but I grabbed her flailing ankle and forced her to bend her knee. I wound more rope around her calf and connected it to the bindings around her thigh, pulling tight so her heel touched her bottom.

When one leg was fully restrained, I grasped her shoulders and pulled her into a kneeling position.

She wobbled slightly, and I knew she was trying to wriggle free. She didn't stand a chance.

I wasn't nearly finished with her.

I continued to bind her, drawing the rope around her waist and looping it between her thighs, framing her swollen pussy. The first signs of desire shone between her legs, so I tugged the binding a little tighter. The slightly rough fibers grazed her labia, making them puffy and flushed.

I tied off my work and moved up her body. I began to wind a second length of rope around her, passing it beneath her breasts, wrapping behind her back, and coming back over her chest. I looped it over her neck and through the lengths that framed her breasts.

When I pulled the bindings tight, her lashes fluttered, and a soft gasp left her lips. The rope hugged her chest, accentuating her breasts so they were on display for me. They rose and fell quickly as her breathing turned more ragged.

I trailed my fingers beneath the soft swells, knowing they'd be growing achy and sensitive.

Her head dropped back on a groan, and she arched into my touch, seeking more decadent stimulation. She stared up into my eyes, her own cloudy with lust and a touch of confusion. She didn't understand what I was doing to her, how I was subtly restricting her blood flow to heighten her awareness of her most vulnerable areas.

"You like being bound, don't you, kinky virgin? Has anyone ever tied you up before? Of course not." She didn't have to respond for me to know the truth. I traced the line of her lower lip with my thumb, making her shiver as I stimulated more of her sensitive nerve endings. "So innocent," I rumbled. "And so beautiful in my ropes."

She blinked several times, shaking her head slightly as though to rid herself of my influence.

I wouldn't allow her to evade me. Her clever brain needed

to be shut off, lulled into silence as she became fully focused on the pleasure of my touch.

I fully cupped her breasts and pinched her nipples with just enough pressure to call her attention back to her body. She moaned, her lids lowering as lust rolled through her.

"That's better," I praised. "You don't have to fight me. You don't have to worry or think."

She tried to shake her head again, but the effort was weaker this time. It took a handful of seconds for her to still and soften in my hands as she succumbed to my control.

She didn't seem aware of what was happening when I briefly stopped toying with her breasts so I could unlock her handcuffs. She remained pliant and supple as I directed her to grasp her elbows behind her back. I bound them in place with the length of rope that remained from her chest harness. She hissed in a breath when the harness tightened farther as I finished securing her arms.

Her breathing stuttered, and she began to sway. She was falling deep into her submissive headspace, her mind finally accepting that she was powerless against me. All she could do was surrender.

Judging by the desire dripping down her thighs, she reveled in the release.

I placed one hand on top of her head, lightly gripping her hair to steady her. With my other, I pressed the button beneath my desk that would lower my suspension point. The metal ring glinted under the lights as the thick cable unwound, bringing it to the desired level.

Samantha's eyes fixed on the ring, and a high giggle slipped past the gag. The sound made warmth unfurl in my chest, a deeper burn than the heat of my lust for her.

I rubbed my fingertips over her plump lips. "That's a lovely sound. I'm almost sorry I gagged you so I can't see that pretty smile." A slightly cruel grin twisted my scar. "Almost. You're very sweet when you can't do more than moan and whimper." I loved having her like this: completely vulnerable to anything I wanted to do to her.

My pretty fucktoy.

The word stuck in my mind. It didn't elicit the same sense of excitement as it had when I'd first captured her. I might still want to tame her, but I wanted her to be more than my sex object. Now that I'd heard her laugh, I craved to savor the sound again.

I'd thought of her as mine from the very beginning, but now, my plans for her shifted slightly. I'd still train her to please me, but I'd be more careful with her. I'd keep most of her personality intact. The prospect posed a fresh challenge for me, but I looked forward to facing it. Dark anticipation raced through me as I imagined this clever, quick-witted woman choosing to place her trust in me and submit to me.

Yes, that was much better than shaping her into something solely meant for my twisted pleasures. She would give me everything, and she would cede all herself willingly.

Eventually.

Her brow wrinkled, her formidable mind threatening to start firing in every direction again. I wouldn't allow her to escape this submissive state.

I tapped her nose in light reprimand. "Stay just like you are. Focus on me."

Her eyes glazed over slightly as she sank back down into submission, but they remained fixed on my face. She'd succumbed to the first part of my plan: quieting her mind and bringing her to a state of calm.

It was time to prepare her for my interrogation. She'd be mindless by the time I questioned her. I wouldn't have to intimidate her to get the answers I desired. She'd give them eagerly in exchange for her reward.

The metal ring dangled a few feet above her head. I retrieved one last coil of rope and began looping it through the metal, weaving it between the knots on her body at strategic points. I focused on her right side, intent on suspending her horizontally. She could maintain the position for much longer than an inverted suspension, and I'd be able to keep a closer eye on her expression, assessing her mood and wellbeing.

I fed the ends of the rope through the ring and pulled. She let out a strangled cry as her bonds shifted around her, wrapping her in a tight embrace and stimulating her in new ways.

I lifted her, not stopping until she hung in midair, a meter off the ground. I tied off my work, leaving her with nothing by the artfully-arranged ropes holding her aloft. Her body was parallel to the floor, turned on its side so she was facing my desk.

Her left ankle still dangled, so I secured it with the remaining rope, forcing her knee to bend. The tighter harness around her right thigh worked against the gravity that dragged her left leg down, leaving her spread wide for me. Her pink cunt wept for attention, open and inviting.

I'd leave her wanting for a while longer, allowing her need to build.

She stared at me in rapt fascination, as though I was the center of her world. Her head began to droop toward the floor, her long copper hair cascading down in a shining wave. I cupped her cheek in my hand, craving more eye contact before her lids inevitably closed. The way she focused on me so intently made me feel worshipped, adored. In this moment, I was her god: all-powerful.

That power flooded my system, making my muscles flex as I

seemed to expand in stature. My size was already intimidating to most men, but she made me feel invincible, super-human. I held her delicate face, my big hands curving around her skull. She was so physically fragile, but she'd surrendered her fierce, fiery will to me. The knowledge made something swell in my chest.

Disconcerted by the foreign sensation, I braced myself to back away. "I'm going to take care of a few things now," I murmured. "You look very pretty, *sirenita*. I think I'll keep you like this more often."

I finally released her and settled down in my desk chair. I flipped open my laptop, and a high whine eased around the gag that filled her mouth.

"Hush now," I commanded, not looking in her direction. If I did, I wouldn't be able to resist touching her, and she needed time to simmer in her mounting desire. "The sooner I finish, the sooner I can play with your wet little pussy."

She whined again in response, a needy, keening noise. Now that I'd planted the promise in her head, she'd be consumed by erotic anticipation. Once I was satisfied that she was fully malleable to my questioning, I'd begin the interrogation.

The wait was almost as difficult for me as it must be for her. I couldn't help glancing at her every minute or so, watching her slip deeper into her helplessness. Slick arousal dripped down her thigh, but she couldn't stimulate herself. She could only wait for my merciful touch.

Her face went slack, her head lolling forward as she floated. It didn't take long for her eyelids to droop, blinking slowly a few times before lowering her lashes to her cheeks.

I couldn't focus on my work, not with this gorgeous distraction. Instead, I decided to devise a means of entertainment to keep her mind occupied while I was away during the day. I wasn't sure of her interests, but she'd said something about *X-Men* and cosplay. I searched my memories of her desperate confession of her innocence when I'd tormented her with the arousal cream.

Yes, she'd definitely mentioned that she'd chosen to dress up as The Dark Phoenix.

I wasn't familiar with comic books, but I'd provide them for her amusement. After some searching online, I managed to find first editions of the story she wanted at a store in New York. I fired off an email to one of my men, a low-level underling who'd do any grunt work I gave him without question. I arranged his overnight flight to New York and a morning return to Chicago, giving him just enough time to get to the store and purchase the items I'd selected for Samantha.

By the time I finished, she was completely limp in her bonds, the ropes caressing her body as they held her aloft.

I put my laptop away and closed the distance between us, kneeling beside her and leaning in so she could feel the heat of my words on her neck. "Is my pet sleepy? Or horny?"

A pitiful, needy whimper teased around the gag, providing me with the response I desired.

"I have a few questions for you, kinky virgin," I murmured, keeping my voice low and even. "If you're honest with me, I'll let you come."

I finally unbuckled the leather straps that kept the rubber ball between her teeth, tugging it free so she could speak. She swallowed several times, regaining the use of her tongue.

"I'm the first man to touch you, is that true?" I asked.

"Yes," she answered softly.

"But you know about BDSM. You've been to a club. You knew what the flogger was when I used it on you, even though no one has disciplined you before, correct?"

"Yes," she confirmed again.

"I want you to tell me how you know these things."

"Porn," she responded. "I watched Dex's porn."

Something ugly stirred in my gut at another man's name issuing from her lips, but I kept my tone even and calm. "And who is Dex? You've mentioned him a few times."

"He's my...my best friend."

Some of the tension inside me eased, but that didn't clear away my confusion. "Why did you watch your friend's porn?"

"I wanted to know what he liked. So, I hacked into his browser history."

"Why would you care what kind of porn your friend watches?"

"I love him." Her slurred words made rage ignite within me, my possessive fury swelling to fill my entire being.

I gripped her jaw hard, my harsh touch on the edge of violence. "Look at me," I snarled.

Her eyes snapped open, her pupils immediately dilating with fear when she met my furious glare. She tried to scramble away, but the ropes held her fast, twisting and tightening around her. The fresh sensations elicited a moan, and her lashes fluttered as bliss began to fog her mind again.

My fingers firmed around her jaw, forcing her face up to mine. "No," I commanded roughly. "Look at me."

Her eyes opened once again, her full attention riveted on me. Her intense focus eased some of my ire, but not the possessive heat that burned in my chest.

"You're *mine*," I growled. "From now on, you don't think about other men. You exist to please *me*." I reached between her legs, driving two fingers into her wet heat. My palm curved against her clit, locking her cunt in a proprietary hold. She cried out at the sudden intrusion, the sound holding an edge of pain. I curled my fingers against her g-spot, intent on drowning her in pleasure so intense that I obliterated all thoughts of other men from her psyche.

"You're mine," I declared, savage. "Your body, your mind.

All of you. Your pain, your pleasure, they belong to me." I released her jaw so I could twist her nipple. She shrieked at the shock of pain, even as her core contracted around my fingers.

"Come for me. Come for your Master."

I continued to pinch and pull at her nipples as I ruthlessly pumped my fingers in and out of her pussy, rotating my palm against her clit. Tears spilled down her cheeks, and she screamed as her orgasm claimed her.

Driven by mad possessiveness, I crushed my lips to hers, tasting the flavor of her scream, her surrender to my declaration of ownership. I devoured her, my teeth sinking into her lower lip as I continued to assail her with pain, using it to tether her to me. And to punish her for uttering another man's name.

I subjugated her mouth with mine; an act of force and dominance.

She continued to come, her pussy fluttering around my relentless fingers as she moaned against my lips. I didn't show any mercy until she shuddered and whined, her sex growing sore and sensitive from my rough treatment.

I didn't feel a shred of remorse at how I'd ravaged her untried body. She'd feel the effects of my cruel fingers tomorrow; she'd remember who owned her.

Even though I withdrew my hands from her pussy and nipples, I couldn't release her mouth. My kiss slowed, my lips caressing hers with more finesse. She opened for me on a sigh, and I slid my tongue inside to claim her mouth.

I didn't free her lips until she was desperate for oxygen. She drew in deep breaths as her head lolled toward the floor, all the strength leaving her sated, conquered body.

I left her just long enough to get the blunt-tipped shears from my desk, and I quickly cut through the knots that held her aloft. I braced her limp form, easing her into my arms as I lowered her from suspension.

I pulled her close to my chest, craving her soft heat. The last of my lingering fury faded when she snuggled into me, seeking comfort under the cruel hands that had just tormented her minutes earlier. I stroked her back, murmuring to her in Spanish.

Then, she tucked her face against me and pressed a kiss to my neck.

Despite the disgusting words that had spilled from her lips and incited my ire, hope unfurled in my chest. I'd resolved to treat her more gently to earn her devotion, but it seemed my show of savagery had affected her deeply. Samantha would surrender herself to me willingly. It was just a matter of time.

CHAPTER 10

I allowed her to sleep in the next day, waiting with her until her present arrived. I wanted to watch her open the gift box, so I could study her reaction when she discovered the comic books. Would she smile for me?

That could wait until after breakfast. Right now, she didn't seem pleased with me.

"Do you have to do that?" she complained as I locked the collar around her throat.

I chuckled, my good mood immune to her grumbling. "The fact that you still take that tone with me means yes, I definitely have to." I grasped her hand and pulled her upright. "Go brush your teeth and come back here."

"And then you won't chain me to the bed?" she asked with asperity.

"With that attitude, of course I will." I laughed, delighted with her. I remembered the feel of her lips beneath mine, the way she'd kissed my neck when I freed her from my ropes.

Did she remember what she'd done? Or had she been too drunk on lust to register her actions?

I decided it didn't really matter. She'd kissed me as she cried into my chest, and that small show of affection was enough for now.

She mumbled under her breath as she trudged toward the bathroom, but I couldn't discern what she was saying. Her obedience was all that mattered, and she complied with my command. Already, she was becoming amenable, despite her flashes of defiance. She hardly noticed her nakedness around me, not bothering to cover herself when I studied her body with open hunger.

She'd adjust to so much more. She'd be happy here with me, just like I'd promised.

Then again, her progress might not be as advanced as I thought. The docile woman who'd disappeared into the bathroom suddenly rushed toward me, launching herself at me with a fierce growl.

Moving on instinct, I dodged her punch and pushed her away with shove to her sternum. She fell back on the bed, cushioned from harm by the mattress. I'd knocked the air from her chest, and I took advantage of the moment it took her to gasp for air. I settled my body over hers, pinning her down with my weight as I grabbed her wrists. I secured them above her head with one hand and grabbed the length of chain attached to the bedpost with the other, locking it to the front of her collar so she was effectively leashed.

Still, I didn't release her wrists. When she began to thrash wildly beneath me, I gripped her jaw to still her shaking head.

"What's this about?" I demanded.

"You leave Dex alone," she shouted, jerking desperately against my hold. "I'll kill you if you do anything to him. I swear, I'll kill you."

My hand tightened around her jaw, my muscles rippling as wrath gripped me. I thought I'd wiped all other men from her mind when I'd ravaged her last night. Apparently, the lesson hadn't been effective.

"I have no interest in this man," I snarled down at her. "And from now on, neither do you."

"But you said Cristian would kill him if he found out," she squeaked, on the edge of panic.

I recalled telling her that Cristian would take away everything and everyone she loved in order to break her, making her watch as he destroyed them.

I love him, she'd slurred about her friend as she dangled in my ropes.

She'd confessed her feelings for this *Dex*, and now, she believed I'd hurt him to hurt her. She still thought of me as her sadistic captor, not her Master. She still loved *him* and feared me.

"I am *not* my brother," I growled, the words so roughened by possessive fury that they were barely discernable. "I won't torture you or threaten the people you care about to get what I want out of you." I leaned in closer, so the weight of my glare would bear down on her. I would remind her of her powerlessness against me, that she already belonged to me, whether she wanted to or not. "I don't need to torture you to get what I want."

"And what do you call tying me down and whipping me until I scream?" she shot back. "Is that not torture?"

My stomach twisted, her words making phantom knives slice through my flesh. "If you knew what torture really was, you wouldn't have to ask."

"And how would you know?" she challenged. "It's not like you'd ever let anyone whip you until you cried."

My hand squeezed her wrists, tethering her to me as horrific memories threatened to spill from the dark corner of my mind where I'd locked them away.

"You think I don't cry when I'm hurt? You think I don't bleed when I'm cut? You think I don't scream just like any other man in pain? I might not be sane, but I'm still human, Samantha. Don't talk about things you don't understand."

Her breath caught. "Is that how your face…"

A feral snarl ripped from my chest, the ferocious sound making her query die in her throat.

"Don't talk about things you don't understand," I repeated, enunciating every word. "And don't say your friend's name ever again. I don't want you to even think about him. I'm the only man you should be concerned with, the only one you should think about. Your purpose is to serve me, to please me. No one else."

"Please." She winced, her eyes watering "You're hurting me."

I realized my fingers were digging into her cheeks, gripping her with brutal force. I'd lost all semblance of control, and I was on the edge of violence, on the verge of damaging her.

I released her and pushed to my feet with a curse. I strode to my wardrobe and began to pull on my clothes in jerky movements, rage simmering just under the surface of my skin.

When I was dressed, I walked toward the bedroom door, not glancing in her direction. I had to get away from her, or I might do something I'd regret. My emotions were roiling, the memories I'd so carefully suppressed rising to the surface. I needed to regain control, and the only way I could think to do that would be to drag her into my training room and whip her until she screamed for mercy.

That would destroy any chance at establishing trust between us. And in my unstable state, I might accidentally cause her real harm.

I didn't want to break my toy.

That's all she was to me. She thought of me as her

monstrous captor, so that's what I would be. She didn't have to willingly surrender to be utterly devoted to me. I could still tame all the fire out of her and turn her into my docile, obedient plaything.

Contemplating any other course of action had been misguided. Kissing her had been foolish, irrational.

"Andrés." The soft, tentative way she said my name almost made my final thread of control snap.

My thoughts instantly shifted from plans to make her scream in pain. I wanted her to scream my name as I pinned her to the bed and fucked her ruthlessly.

I stiffened, but I forced myself to keep moving away from her.

"I'm sorry," she whispered.

I froze in my tracks. She might have driven me close to madness with her defiance, but her sweet contrition threatened to shatter me. My life had been devoid of tenderness for almost as long as I could remember. When was the last time someone had said "I'm sorry" to me without pissing themselves in fear?

Samantha wasn't frightened. I wasn't threatening her. She offered her apology out of kindness.

"I got something for you," I forced out after a few tense seconds. I didn't look at her. I wasn't sure what I'd do to her if I looked into her lovely eyes. "It's on the tray next to your breakfast."

"What—?"

"I'll see you tonight." I strode away from her, sparing her from my mercurial mood. If I stayed, I'd consume her. I'd hurt her and fuck her and claim her in every way possible. She would scream and weep, bleeding out more pretty tears for me.

She would never forgive me, would never trust me.

I won't break her. I won't.

CHAPTER 11

By the time I finished my work for the day, I'd managed to bury the turmoil Samantha had incited within me that morning. My mood was still dark, but at least I was stable. I'd regained control by planning every detail of her training tonight. It had been too long since I'd had release. Having her melt in my ropes and come on my hand had left me aching for her, but she hadn't been ready to serve me in the way I wanted.

That would change tonight. I'd given Samantha pleasure, but she had to learn that her main purpose was to bring *me* pleasure.

My plans were cold, calculated.

But the ice inside me melted as soon as I stepped into the bedroom. She beamed at me, and the brightness of her joy hit me square in the chest. She held one of the comic books I'd left for her, her fingers barely gripping the edge of the pages, as though it was something precious she didn't want to damage.

"Thanks," she said, the word warm with gratitude.

I blinked, feeling as though I'd been blinded by the sun. My lips spread wide in a grin of my own. "You are even more beautiful when you smile than I imagined."

Her smile faltered. "You're manipulating me again."

The accusation didn't puncture my satisfaction. "So, you don't want the comic books?" I teased.

"No," she exclaimed, clutching the book closer to her chest like a child clinging to her favorite teddy bear. "I mean, I want them. I um, actually already read all of them. But I'll read them again," she added quickly.

"You read all of them today?"

"I tried to go slow, but they're so good." Her eyes practically rolled back in her head when she said *so good*, as though she experienced transcendent pleasure while reading. "And I process things really fast. I usually do more than one thing at a time to stay occupied. But this was good," she hurried on. "Way better than staring at the ceiling."

"I'll have to get you more, then."

"You don't have to get first editions," she replied, still speaking rapidly. I'd thought it was a nervous tic, but it seemed words tumbled out of her when she was excited, too. I rarely saw anyone express this level of passion about any subject, but she practically bubbled with enthusiasm. She really was adorable.

"I like newer stuff, too," she babbled on. "Graphic novels are awesome. Works by Frank Miller and Alan Moore are great."

"I'll get those for you, then," I told her, my smile remaining fixed in place. It felt strange to hold it for so long without my lips curving in cruel amusement or twisting in an arrogant smirk. Samantha's levity was infectious. "And more first editions."

I'd give her anything she wanted if it made her this happy. The innocence about her I'd found so enchanting went beyond her sexual inexperience. There was something sweet and pure in her, and I craved more of it.

"But I just said you don't have to," she protested, but her eyes still shone with excitement. "I've read most of them online, anyway."

"But they made you smile. So, you're getting more. Don't argue with me, Samantha," I added sternly before she could protest further. "I'll put in an order tonight, and they'll be here in the morning."

"How did you get them so fast? These had to be really hard to find."

"There was a store in New York that had them in stock. I sent someone to go get them."

"But I just told you I was bored last night."

I shrugged. "It's not a long flight."

I gaped at him. "You flew someone from Chicago to New York and back again overnight to get me some comic books?"

"Yes, and it made you smile. So, the fifteen minutes it took me to set it all up was more than worth it."

Her joy deflated, her smile melting as her eyes tightened.

"What's wrong?" Had I said something to destroy her happiness? Now that I'd experienced her levity, its sudden absence made my stomach drop.

"I don't want anything you bought with your Bliss money," she said quietly.

My jaw tightened, my pleasure effectively doused. "You'll get the books anyway," I declared. I'd promised I'd get them for her, so I would follow through. She'd smile for me again, regardless of her wishes at the moment. She would learn to be happy around me.

"I won't read them." Her stubborn streak resurfaced.

"That's your choice. You'll still have them."

I could wait her out. If I left the comic books by the bed

and kept her isolated with them, she'd eventually turn to them for entertainment. She'd expressed her misery at being chained up with nothing to occupy her busy mind.

She glared at me, her clever brain immediately processing my ruthless plan. "You're trying to manipulate me again. You know I'll go out of my mind and end up reading them if they're in here."

A ghost of my smile returned. "If you already know this, then why bother fighting me on it?"

"Because you're a smug bastard, that's why."

I shook my head at her, but my smile didn't waver. She'd just given me the excuse to implement the training I'd been plotting for her all day. "I'm going to find a better use for that dirty mouth."

I finally closed the distance between us and unlocked the length of chain from the bedpost, but I kept the other end attached to her collar. I gave a gentle tug, urging her to her feet.

"Come." She didn't move immediately, so I applied a little more pressure.

She eyed me warily, but she had no choice. She got to her feet and began to follow me out of the bedroom. "Where are we going?"

"What was it you so charmingly called it?" I mused. "Oh, yes." I shot a wicked smirk at her. "My *torture room*."

She didn't seem to find the words remotely funny. She stopped in her tracks, refusing to take another step. I kept walking and pulled harder on the chain. She stumbled, fighting me. Her hands fisted around the chain, and she tried to yank it out of my grip.

My arm barely twitched toward her, despite the fact that she was pulling with all her strength. Her panic made me pause and turn to face her.

Her chest rose and fell rapidly, as though she'd been wrestling against me for long minutes rather than a few seconds. "I don't want to go in there," she said, her voice higher than usual. "I won't cuss at you again. I won't."

I shook my head, my smirk a touch indulgent. "You will. You can't seem to help yourself."

"I'll try really hard," she promised. "Just don't take me in there. Please."

I took a step toward her, intending to soothe her. She flinched away.

I frowned and pulled on the chain, forcing her body to tumble against mine. She clutched at my shoulders for balance, and I grasped her waist to steady her.

"This is part of your training," I told her, keeping my tone even and smooth to calm her. "It will feel good. Not everything in that room is meant to cause you pain."

"It scares me," she admitted on a shaky whisper.

All my resolutions from the morning to treat her as nothing more than my sex object crumbled away. After witnessing her joy, her terror made something tighten in my gut. I wanted her to trust me implicitly. I wanted her to willingly follow me into my playroom and submit to her training.

I leaned into her and softly pressed my lips against hers. I intended to be gentle with her this time, since she was spooked.

But then, she tried to pull away. I curved my hand around the back of her head and locked her in place, slanting my mouth over hers so she had no choice but to shape her lips to mine.

Unlike the savage way I'd claimed her mouth while she'd been suspended, this kiss was deliberate: a slow, thorough seduction.

Her body softened, and her fingernails dug into my shoulders, clinging to me. I growled my approval and nipped at her lower lip, demanding that she open for me. Her lips parted, and her tongue tangled with mine. I kissed her, long and deep, until her knees sagged and she meekly accepted my claim, giving me full control of her mouth.

I finally pulled away, satisfied that she was ready to accept more of me in that pretty mouth. My cock was rock hard against her hip, straining toward her in anticipation of those soft lips wrapping around my shaft, her tongue caressing my length.

She gasped for air, her body melded to mine. I supported her with my arm around her lower back, so she was sure to feel my desire for her pressing into her soft flesh.

"Are you still scared?" I asked, running my fingers through her hair.

Warmth flooded my chest when she leaned into my touch. "No."

"I promise this isn't going to hurt," I reassured her. "Only pleasure today."

A little wrinkle creased her brow. "But I cussed at you. I called you a bastard."

"I heard you the first time," I said drily. "We're going to train your mouth. From now on, every time you curse at me, you're going to make it up to me by using your tongue another way."

She trembled in my arms, fear stirring in her pale eyes. "I don't... I haven't ever..."

I continued to stroke her hair, quieting her. "I know you haven't. I'm going to teach you. And I'll make it feel good for you, so you associate my cock in your mouth with pleasure."

"You're trying to condition me again." I wasn't sure if her voice shook from trepidation or tentative anticipation. "I don't like when you do that."

"You'll like this." I skimmed my hand over her bottom before dipping between her legs. My fingers played through her soft folds, stimulating her until she began to grow slick in response.

"Did you know your body is capable of having multiple orgasms?" I asked as I played with her. "I wonder how many you'll have before you can't take any more."

"Please..."

"Please make you come?" The question lilted with arrogant mockery. "Not yet, *sirenita*. You have to come into my playroom first."

"It's a torture room," she countered, but the contradiction came out huskily.

"It's where I play with my fucktoy. That makes it my playroom." That had been true with the other women I'd trained. With Samantha, I wasn't so sure. I wanted her to please me sexually and serve me eagerly, but that didn't feel like enough from her. I craved more.

Then, her wetness coated my hand in response to the crass word. It seemed a dark, secret part of her enjoyed the idea of servicing me.

"I'm not your fucktoy," she tried to deny me.

"It's not an insult, so there's no need to look so spiteful." My tone deepened, so the words would reach inside her and touch the devious little part of her soul that had her soaking wet. "You're my toy, my plaything, my pet. And you love when I play with you and pet you. See? You're creaming all over my hand."

Her breathing stuttered. "Just because my body feels one way about it doesn't mean I like it."

"Don't lie, *cosita*." I understood her a little better now. "You wouldn't have watched all that kinky porn if you didn't like it. If you didn't long for it."

"I longed for...I don't want this with you."

More lies.

"Then why am I the only man who's ever touched you? You were so skittish at first. Do you really think you would have found pleasure with someone else? They wouldn't have understood how to handle you. Not like I do. You need a firm hand."

"I don't," she protested weakly.

I brushed a kiss over her lips. Her head tipped back in response, accepting me.

"No more lies," I murmured, my lips brushing hers

Her pride was telling her to argue, so I'd relieve her of that impulse. "You don't have permission to speak. I'm not going to gag you, but know that there will be other consequences if you defy me. The next time you use your mouth, it will be to suck my cock. Once I come down your throat, you'll be allowed to talk again."

She gaped at me, and I traced her parted lips with my fingertips.

"Just like that," I said with satisfaction. "I'm not going to force your mouth, but you will accept me before we leave the playroom."

She shook her head in denial, but she didn't utter a word. My satisfaction with her easy compliance faded when her eyes began to slide out of focus. I recognized the signs that she was about to shut down on me, the way she had when I'd touched her pussy for the first time.

I threaded my fingers through her hair, tugging slightly. "*Cosita*," I called her back to me. "Don't be afraid." I spoke sternly, commanding her attention. "This is new for you, but I'll guide you through it. You're safe with me."

Her full attention focused on me, the same way she'd looked at me when I bound her in rope: like I was the only thing in her world.

Something expanded in my chest as she nodded her agreement, obeying my order for silence. Taking away her ability to speak seemed to calm her in a way any demonstration of force couldn't. I could spank her ass red until she stopped arguing with me, but that left her humiliated and chastised, even if it did arouse her.

When I gagged her, she was able to let go of her panic and her pride. She couldn't argue, because she didn't have the option. Now, a simple order for her silence effectively muzzled her. It could be the result of successful training, but I suspected it also brought her peace from her runaway mouth. Samantha found secret release in this aspect of submitting to my control.

When I finally released her and began to lead her toward the playroom, she followed meekly in my wake, all earlier terror melted away.

I opened the door and flipped on the lights. She shuddered and took a step back, her eyes fixing on the spanking bench. Maybe I'd made a mistake in pushing her so hard for her first punishment. It was time to teach her to crave being brought into my playroom.

"No, *cosita*," I chided her for her hesitance and wrapped my arm around my waist, guiding her forward. "We're not using the bench today," I promised, leading her farther into the room. I pointed at the black, curved device that was built for her to straddle while on her knees. "Do you know what this is? You have my permission to speak."

"A Sybian," she answered immediately.

Satisfaction curved my lips. "Such a clever, kinky virgin."

"But I can't..." Her cheeks flushed crimson. "There's not a dildo attached."

My little virgin had certainly done her research. How

depraved was the pornography that she preferred? Probably not half as perverted as the things I planned to do to her.

"My fingers and my cock will stretch your tight little pussy before I put anything else inside you. The vibrations will be strong enough that you'll feel it everywhere. Your clit, your pussy, your ass. I don't need to fill you with a fake cock to make you scream in pleasure."

She swallowed, her cheeks glowing brighter. "That... That sounds...intense."

Her gaze fell to my erection, which was clearly visible through my slacks. Our kiss had aroused me, and anticipation of her hot, untried mouth around my cock kept me hard.

"I won't be able to fit... It won't fit," she mumbled, staring at the bulge.

I smothered my amusement. I didn't want her to think I was laughing at her inexperience, but I did find her embarrassment adorable. Such a kinky girl to be so shy about saying the word *cock*.

"We'll go slow," I told her. "You can take me. You will learn."

Her chin lifted slightly. "And if I say no?"

I met her challenge with a level stare. "Are you saying no?"

"I... I'm nervous. I mean, you're so big. And I've never... I don't know..."

I captured her lips with mine before her nerves could overwhelm her. The kiss lasted for several minutes, until I was certain her mind had quieted. The anxious tension eased from her slender frame, and I allowed her space to breathe.

"You don't have to talk anymore," I murmured, my lips brushing her cheek in a feather-light kiss. "It's okay to be nervous. I'll be right here to tell you what to do."

She nodded, her crystalline eyes shining with relief.

I grasped her upper arms, guiding her down so she straddled the Sybian. "On your knees."

She moved with uncharacteristic grace, her body supple as I positioned her where I wanted her.

"So beautiful," I praised as she settled down onto the machine. The sight of her on her knees before me made my cock throb. She'd never been more alluring, not even suspended in my ropes. Her eyes were clear of fear or worry; she simply looked up at me, waiting for what I would tell her to do next. Her serene expression could almost be mistaken for one of absolute trust.

She didn't trust me. Not fully. Not yet.

I didn't think she'd try to rise up off the Sybian once I turned it on, but after her first orgasm, she might try to squirm away for relief from the relentless sensations. Flooding her system with ecstasy was a key component in my plan. After this session, her pussy would grow wet at just the thought of my cock in her mouth.

I strapped her down on the machine, so she couldn't escape the stimulation. When her ankles were cuffed and locked in place, I secured her arms above her head. Another pair of cuffs dangled from a chain bolted into the ceiling. It only took a few seconds to buckle them around her wrists, effectively shackling her in place for erotic torment.

She didn't struggle or protest. If anything, she seemed curious, her sky-blue eyes watching me as I locked her where I wanted her.

Was she interested in the effects of the Sybian after watching her porn? Or was she secretly curious about what it would be like to taste my cock?

The idea didn't seem to disgust her. If anything, her nervousness about taking me in her mouth had pertained to her physical ability to accept all of me. She'd been embarrassed about her inexperience.

I would thoroughly enjoy teaching her how to bring me pleasure.

Keeping her locked in my gaze, I reached into my pocket and pressed the button on the small remote that controlled the Sybian.

"Oh!" She let out the cutest little cry when the machine began to rumble beneath her. Her shocked expression quickly turned to one of bliss.

I smirked and pulled the remote from my pocket, so she could see that I controlled her stimulation. "You like your new toy, *gatita*?"

She moaned and nodded, remaining nonverbal. She didn't have to use words to communicate, not when she was in my power. Her only concern was to submit to whatever I wanted to do to her. She made the sexiest little sounds when she couldn't speak.

I stroked her cheek, communicating my pleasure with her. "Greedy girl. I want you to keep count of how many orgasms you have. Can you do that for me?"

She swallowed and nodded again. Moving almost tentatively, she rocked forward slightly so she could press her clit against the vibrating machine. Her lashes fluttered, and she rolled her hips, obviously enjoying the sensations against her pussy and ass. Once she started, she couldn't seem to help herself. I watched her grind against the Sybian, my own unfulfilled lust tormenting me.

"You're going to be so beautiful when you're riding my cock like that," I said, my voice rough with need. I traced the line of her parted lips with my thumb. She didn't turn her face away, so I applied pressure, slipping inside her mouth.

I rubbed my thumb against the tip of her tongue, stimulating her nerve endings. Her body was primed for sexual pleasure, so I stopped rubbing to test her. She groaned and immediately licked my thumb, seeking more sensation. I started to gently pump in and out of her mouth, pushing a little farther each time. When I neared the back of her tongue, I applied pressure. Her throat contracted, but I didn't let up. She adjusted quickly, learning to breathe through her nose and suppress her gag reflex.

"Good girl," I ground out, desire consuming me. She'd worried that she wouldn't be able to accept my full length, but I'd been right in saying she'd be able to take me.

I kept my thumb deep in her mouth, and she continued licking me. She rocked against the Sybian, her tongue moving against my finger almost frantically as she neared completion. Her gaze dropped to my erection, and she let out a needy little whine.

Rewarding her, I reached down with my free hand and pinched her nipples. "Come for me."

She didn't take her eyes off my cock as she screamed out her orgasm. I resumed stroking in and out of her mouth. Her lips clamped down on my thumb, as though desperate to keep me inside. She licked it like her favorite candy, her ecstatic moan vibrating on her tongue.

I pulled my thumb away, and she whimpered her disappointment.

"Don't forget to count for me," I reminded her as I turned off the machine.

She remained silent, her eyes lifting to mine. She stared up at me, appearing almost entranced. Her lovely eyes were dark with lust, her mouth open and waiting for more.

A low laugh rumbled from my chest as arrogant pleasure rolled through me. She didn't find the sight of my face horrifying, as she had in the beginning. Instead, she regarded me with open fascination. I was the first to introduce her to this bliss, the first to show her what her body was capable of.

I would give her pleasure, but I also intended to take, to claim.

"You were supposed to count your orgasms," I prompted.

She blinked, dazed. "What? Oh. One."

"That's not nearly enough for my greedy *gatita*, is it? I want more, too."

I turned the machine on again. As soon as the vibrations started, her gaze riveted on my erection again. Her body was already responding to my conditioning: focusing on my cock earned her an orgasm.

She licked her lips, seeking more stimulation against her tongue.

"You want to see me?" I asked roughly.

She nodded and rolled her hips, resuming her grinding motion at the thought of looking at my dick.

A feral sound slipped through my teeth, and I unbuckled my belt, almost fumbling in my hurry to free myself from my slacks.

Her eyes widened, and her jaw dropped. She scooted back a little, as though startled. This wasn't the first time she'd seen me, but the view from her kneeling position would be different for her. More overwhelming.

The fact that she found my size intimidating, despite her obvious hunger, took me to the edge. I fisted the base of my shaft and squeezed, staving off my need to come on her face.

"You're going to make me lose control," I growled. "Do you have any idea how delicious you are? So innocent and nervous about pleasing me." I touched two fingers beneath her chin, lifting her face. "You do please me, Samantha. Very much."

Her lips curved up at the corners, her spine straightening as she basked in my praise. I trailed my fingers over her soft cheek. "You're perfect. So pretty with your body bound and shaking for me. Do you want to come again?"

"Yes," she gasped, rolling her hips against the machine.

"You can come when you kiss my cock. Show me how much you want to come. Show me how much you want me." I ground out the command. I needed her to want me, to crave me.

She pressed her lips to my cockhead in a kiss that would have been chaste if it weren't for the lewdness of the act. A little needy sound slipped from her when my pre-cum painted her mouth.

"Come," I commanded, triggering her orgasm in time with her lips touching my cock. I pinched her nipples in the way I was learning she liked, giving her just the right amount of pain to push her over the edge.

She shrieked out her ecstasy, and I rubbed my cock over her parted lips, stimulating her mouth as the Sybian stimulated her cunt.

She started to come down from her orgasm, panting against my shaft as she became overly sensitive. I didn't turn off the machine this time. She didn't get another reprieve. She'd come over and over again, until I decided I was satisfied and came down her throat.

"Please," she begged for mercy, her legs trembling. "It's too much."

"Count," I demanded.

"Two," she whined, squirming on the machine. My restraints kept her locked in place, helpless to escape the sensations I inflicted upon her.

I released her nipples and twined her flame-red hair around my fist. "You're going to have another one. You're going to cry out in pleasure while your mouth is full of my cock. I want to feel you scream."

She shuddered, and her squirming regulated to a steady rocking motion as she rolled her hips against the Sybian.

My filthy words had eased her discomfort, reigniting her lust.

"Taste me," I ordered. "You can come as many times as you want."

She flicked her tongue against my cockhead, making teasing contact. I hissed in sharp breath through gritted teeth. "More."

She obeyed, exploring me with her tongue. There was nothing tentative or shy about the way she tasted me, learning the feel and flavor of my cock.

"Very good. Just like that." I dimly noted that my accented words were barely discernable, but she seemed to understand the encouragement.

She pressed her tongue flat beneath my shaft, and another orgasm rolled through her body, incited by my rough praise. Samantha was enjoying pleasing me. Training her to love sucking my cock was even easier than I'd thought it would be.

And more erotic than I could have imagined.

She started licking my length as she quivered from bliss. I bit out a curse as my own pleasure crested in response. I ruthlessly suppressed it.

"How many?" I demanded as she came down from her peak.

"Hmmm?" she hummed, her lips vibrating against me.

My fingers tightened in her hair, as though that would help me cling on to my control. She was getting saucy with me. My kinky virgin was beginning to understand the unique power a woman on her knees could possess: the power to make a man come undone.

I'd train that idea out of her before it could take root.

"You know, *gatita*. Don't toy with me," I rebuked. "How many?"

"Three," she sighed, rubbing her cheek against me apologetically.

"That's it," I encouraged. "Worship my cock. Just like that."

She rubbed her lips down my shaft, but the light contact wasn't enough for me anymore. I needed to feel the wet heat of her mouth around my dick.

"Suck me."

She opened her mouth on my command, stroking my length with her tongue as I slid inside. My eager girl tried to lean forward to take me deeper, but I stopped her with my grip on her hair.

"Slowly, *sirenita*," I corrected her.

I held her in place and eased back, until only my cockhead remained between her lips. She swirled her tongue around it, her eyes lifting to mine. The sight of my innocent captive staring up at me with my cock in her mouth filled me with savage satisfaction. An almost vicious sound tore from my chest, and her lithe body shuddered as she came again. She screamed against me, the vibrations around my cock driving me to madness.

I thrust forward, hitting the back of her throat. She gagged, and I pulled back so she could breathe. Her reaction wasn't going to stop me. I wasn't going to go easy on her this first time. I couldn't. Not with her wide doe eyes locked under my hungry gaze, her innocence tempting and tormenting me. I wanted to ruin her, defile her. Mark her with my cum.

"Relax," I growled. "I'm going to come down your throat."

She moaned, the only sound she was capable of with my shaft filling her mouth. I slid into her again, and she suppressed her gag reflex.

"Good girl." I eased my hold on her hair and massaged her scalp as I pushed into her throat.

My orgasm slammed into me, and I released my pleasure

on a feral roar. I held myself deep inside her mouth for a moment before pulling back, coating her tongue with my cum.

"Swallow," I snarled. "Take everything I give you."

I wasn't sure if it was the sight of my completion, the taste of my cum, or my crass orders that made her come apart again. As she swallowed my seed, she shuddered and tensed, moaning against my cock. I pulled free from her lips, but her hungry tongue followed, licking me clean as the last of my high faded.

I ran my fingers through her hair, murmuring words of praise. I slipped into Spanish, but she seemed too lost to care what I was saying, anyway.

Finally, I pulled away from her and turned off the Sybian. She collapsed in exhaustion, and I had to support her as I freed her wrists from the cuffs. I dropped down on one knee and claimed her mouth. The salty tang of my own release mingled with her unique flavor, an intoxicating cocktail. I didn't mind tasting myself on her. It felt right to mark her this way, to spill my seed between her lips as she eagerly accepted everything I gave her.

After a while, I freed her from my kiss and uncuffed her ankles. When she was no longer bound, I lifted her in my arms, holding her close. I loved the feel of her pressed up against my chest, her cheek resting against me as though she felt perfectly safe and content there.

"How many times did you come?" I asked as I carried her out of the playroom.

"Oh. Um...like, five? Maybe?"

I chuckled. My kitten was very cute when she was sleepy, especially after an orgasm. I didn't even think about punishing her for forgetting to count them.

She let out a happy sigh and snuggled into my chest. Our training session had been far more successful than I could have hoped for.

CHAPTER 12

Over the last week, Samantha had been very well behaved. She hadn't begged me to fuck her yet, but I was content to wait for that a while longer. She was becoming highly skilled at sucking my cock, and I kept her drunk on pleasure, as well. It hadn't taken me long to learn exactly how she liked to be stroked and pinched.

When she got too sassy, a sound spanking was enough to correct her. I hadn't taken her back into the playroom, even though the idea of whipping her appealed to me.

But she'd become so terrified after our first punishment session that I couldn't bring myself to push her that hard again. I'd resolved to earn her willing submission, and she wouldn't surrender herself to me if I hurt her without cause. If she earned another whipping, she'd get one. Otherwise, I was content with her progress.

She allowed me to feed her and bathe her without complaint, and she snuggled close to me in the night. She hardly even complained about being kept chained to my bed anymore. She was settling into acceptance of our routine, and

I always made sure to leave her with new reading material. I didn't want my clever Samantha to get bored in my absence. I liked her smile too much to make her sad. Besides, she was much more cooperative when she was in a good mood.

Things had been going so smoothly, I hadn't realized we were halfway to Cristian's deadline until he summoned me to a meeting. I tried to ignore the nauseating churning in my gut as I rode my elevator down to the basement. Cristian only ever wanted to meet me here if he had gruesome plans or he wanted to bait me. Or both.

He didn't order me to bring Samantha, I reassured myself for the dozenth time. If he intended to torture someone, at least it wouldn't be her.

I'd sworn I wouldn't allow him to touch her ever again, but my brother was as smart as he was sadistic. And he controlled a small army of men. If he really wanted to take my pretty captive from me, he'd find a way to do it. I'd fight for her, I'd bleed for her, but I knew the reality of the situation.

"*Hermanito*," he greeted me when the elevator doors opened, his voice devoid of any brotherly warmth. "It's good to see you."

The only seating in the concrete room was a rigid metal chair, where Cristian liked to restrain his victims. That, or he chained their wrists and hung them from the ceiling, so his knife had better access to all parts of the body.

I barely looked at the chair. Sitting on it was out of the question.

I strode into the room, as though the pervasive smell of damp, blood, and piss didn't make my stomach turn. I stopped several feet away from my brother, keeping a careful distance between us. I could feel his bodyguards flanking me. Their nearness at my back set my teeth on edge.

"What do you want?" I demanded. I wouldn't play into his

sick game. He could say whatever he needed to say, and then I'd leave. Maybe I'd go back to Samantha for a little while, even though it wasn't even midday yet. Burying my cock in her hot mouth would clear the chill from my bones.

"I want to check in on Samantha Browning's progress. How is your new toy? Have you broken her in yet?"

"You said three weeks," I reminded him, keeping my voice as even as I could manage.

He stroked his chin, pretending to consider something. I knew from years of experience that this was something he feigned when he'd already specifically devised how to provoke me.

"Hmmm. I did say that, didn't I? It just that I've been thinking. If you're not making progress with her, I have a strategy of my own to make her cooperate."

I tamped down my possessive rage, bit back the furious declaration that she belonged to me, not him.

That was exactly what he wanted from me. I wouldn't give him the satisfaction.

His brows rose. "Aren't you interested in my idea? If you're not making headway, I'm happy to work on her myself."

"I won't let you mutilate her," I snapped before I could stop myself.

A slow, icy grin spread over his face. "I have no intention of cutting her up," he said in a soothing tone, as though trying to placate me. "I'm going to dose her with Bliss."

"You won't touch her," I growled and took a step toward him. I felt the guards shadow my movement, and I forced myself to freeze before I did something stupid. If Cristian managed to neutralize me, I couldn't protect Samantha.

His smile curved with malice. "You misunderstand me. I have no intention of touching her. The opposite, in fact. I'll chain her down, dose her with Bliss, and watch her scream and beg for me to fuck her. Have you ever seen what the drug does when the user doesn't get release? I've broken in a few of my more reluctant whores with one dose. They'll do anything to avoid experiencing that pain again. And I don't even have to bring out my knife. Not a drop of blood spilled or a single scar left behind."

Nausea curled up my throat as he spoke. I swallowed it down and clenched my jaw to hold in my tirade. Cristian was toying with me. He didn't intend to follow through.

"I'm sure it wouldn't take three weeks for Samantha to break under that kind of pressure. The only complication is that might shatter her mind completely, and then, she wouldn't be useful to me. So, little brother. I'll leave her with you for a while longer, until she's ready to work for me. I need her brain intact when you give her back to me."

"Samantha belongs to me," I snarled, my fingers curling to fists at my sides. "I'm keeping her."

Cristian held up his hands in a false show of contrition. "Fine. Keep her. She's not much to look at, so if you want to fuck her, that's fine with me. I know you don't have many other options, and it's not like she can say no." He smirked as his gaze lingered on my ruined face.

I had to leave before I tried to tear him apart. I knew I was physically capable of it. My brother wasn't a small man, but I was much bigger.

But I knew better than to challenge him. If I did, he'd find a way to punish me, and I'd already shown my hand when it came to my obsession with Samantha. If Cristian wanted to hurt me, he'd use her to do it.

"Message received," I ground out. "You said three weeks. She'll be ready."

His smirk remained fixed in place, his black eyes glittering under the spare yellow lightbulb. "I think you understand what will happen to her if she's not. You can go."

I turned and walked stiffly back to the elevator, trying not to breathe in the stench that surrounded me. My senses were on high alert, and everything about this room made me want to vomit. Images of my sweet Samantha strung up for my brother's sadistic torment flickered at the edges of my mind. I tried to shove them away, but they began to blend with my own memories of blood and screams and shame.

As soon as I stepped into the elevator and the doors closed, I sucked in a deep breath. I tasted a coppery tang on my tongue, and I realized I'd bitten the inside of my cheek.

I shook my head to clear away the memories and focused on thoughts of Samantha.

Yes, she was what I needed right now. I wanted to make her scream for *me*. Not my brother.

She would tremble and cry. Her pale skin would turn red under my whip.

The elevator finally stopped, granting me entry to my penthouse. I stormed into the bedroom, but she didn't so much as glance up from her graphic novel.

I didn't hesitate to harness her full attention.

I hooked my fingers through the back of her collar, drawing it tight against her throat as I gripped it at her nape.

"Andrés," she gasped, jerking in surprise. "What are you doing here?"

I didn't respond. I didn't have to explain myself to my fucktoy. Instead, I focused on unlocking the chain at the front of her collar. When she was free, I tossed her over my shoulder.

"Put me down!" The fact that she thought she could still make demands just proved how poorly I'd been handling her. I'd indulged in a fantasy where I could have all of her, not just a devoted slave. It was past time that she learned her role in this relationship. Her obedience to my will was all that would save her from my brother.

I slapped her thigh with more force than usual, ignoring her indignant squeal as I carried her into the playroom.

She squirmed in my hold. "I didn't do anything wrong," she protested, her voice high with mounting fear.

Good. I wanted her fear. I wanted her tears.

I wanted her completely under my control.

She beat her fists against my lower back, but her blows felt like little more than a massage. When that accomplished nothing, she thrashed, desperate to fight her way free. "No! Please."

She'd beg a lot more before I was finished with her. She'd scream for mercy until she couldn't form the words to plead with me.

I'd show her who was Master and who was slave. I'd treated her with too much affection, and she'd become spoiled.

I manhandled her down onto the spanking bench, positioning her with ruthless force. I teetered on the edge of violence, and only the knowledge that I was about to extract her pain with my whip kept me from bruising her with my hands as I strapped her in place.

"What did I do wrong?" she sobbed. "I didn't do anything. I didn't. Please."

Once she was fully bound beneath me, I paused to stare down at my captive, my possession. She really was lovely. Her eyes were sparkling with fear, her trapped body trembling. All for me.

I drew in a deep, shuddering breath, and the jagged edges of my dark thoughts smoothed slightly. Touching the leather restraints that pinned her in place grounded me. She was in my power.

I brushed my fingertips over the warm wetness spilling

down her cheek. She tried to turn her face away, but there was nowhere for her to go. She couldn't escape me.

"Please," she whispered. "I promise I didn't do anything wrong. Don't hurt me."

"I'm not going to hurt you." The promise tumbled out before I really thought about it, my desire to soothe her automatic. "Much," I amended.

Her tears fell in thick streams, running over the backs of my fingers.

"Hush now," I cajoled, stroking her shaking body. "This isn't a punishment."

"But you're angry," she said tremulously. "You're going to hurt me."

"I'm not angry with you. My brother..."

She winced, and I realized my fingers had firmed on her skin, pressing too hard.

I didn't want to talk about Cristian. I wouldn't tell her the horrific torture he had planned for her if I didn't succeed in bending her to my will.

I drew in another breath and resumed petting her, treating her gently now that I had her bound and at my mercy. "I need to accelerate your training. My brother is not a patient man."

She tensed, so I shifted my attention to her silky hair, running my fingers through it in the way she liked. When I did this in our bed, she practically purred. It would work to calm her now. She didn't need to fear Cristian when I was here to keep her safe.

"I'll protect you," I promised. "But I've been too indulgent with you. You must learn your place."

"So, you're going to beat me," she said in soft accusation.

"I'm going to train you," I countered. "You will experience a little pain, but you will enjoy it. I know you will. You like your spankings. You'll like this, too."

She might not have recognized the peace in her surrender after the first time I'd whipped her, but she understood submission a little better now. She'd come to learn that there was release in pain.

"I don't want you to flog me again," she whispered.

That was exactly what I intended to do. I just needed her to settle first. "I don't want you to be scared of me, *cosita*."

"I thought you like it when I'm frightened," she said bitterly.

The moment soured slightly, and for some reason, I found it difficult to meet her eye. "That doesn't mean I want you to fear *me*. But yes, a part of me likes your fear."

"Please, let me up," she begged. "You don't have to do this."

I focused on her again, imposing my will on her. "Yes, I do. It's for your own good."

I cupped her nape, squeezing her neck slightly to ground her in my control. She didn't need to worry about what was going to happen, because she was powerless to stop me. All she could do was submit.

"You'll like this." There was a ring of command in the words. She *would* enjoy it. I would train her to love my whip. "You'll see. You have to trust me."

She'd looked at me with something close to trust before; when I'd suspended her the first time, and when I taught her how to suck my cock.

This time, her eyes didn't focus on me as though I was the center of her world. They clouded over, as though she wasn't seeing me at all. Her skin pebbled, and she shuddered violently as her teeth began to chatter.

I dropped to my knees beside her, peering into her face. She was staring straight ahead, but she wasn't looking at me. My stomach twisted, the nausea that had gripped me in the basement returning. Something deep in my chest squeezed to the point of pain.

"Samantha," I rasped. "You're okay. You're safe with me."

"I'm not," she said, her voice hitching. "I'm scared. You're scaring me. And you like it."

"I don't." My own voice wavered as my gut churned. "Not like this. Please. Don't be afraid."

"I don't want to be in here," she whispered.

"All right, *cosita*. It's all right. You're safe."

I started murmuring to her in Spanish, not really paying attention to what I was saying. All I wanted was to soothe her. I wanted her to look at me again. I wanted her to smile.

Her skin was too cold beneath my hands as I unbuckled the straps that held her down. When she was free, I cuddled her close, trying to lend her some of my body heat.

The squeezing sensation in my chest eased slightly when she tucked her face against me and curled her fingers into my shirt, clinging to me as she sobbed in relief.

I carried her back into the bedroom and settled down on the edge of the bed, holding her in my lap. She remained chilled, so I rubbed my hands all over her body, until her goose bumps began to subside.

I was still talking to her in my native tongue, a few unbidden apologies slipping in between the words meant to comfort.

Finally, she blinked and looked up at me.

The last of the tension left my chest on a heavy exhale. I pressed my lips against her forehead in a tender kiss. "I was worried about you." My arms tightened around her, holding her closer. "I didn't mean to upset you."

"You did," she countered quietly. "You wanted to see me cry. You wanted to hear me scream."

My eyes dropped from hers again. Something burned in my

stomach. It felt a little like shame. "I do want those things from you, Samantha," I admitted. "But not like this. I won't break you. I won't." I was barely aware that I spoke the last aloud.

"I don't want this," she said, her voice small. "I don't want to be here. I don't want to be tamed. I don't want to work for your brother."

My gaze snapped back to her face. She would stay here with me. She would be tamed.

And she would work for my brother.

"You don't have a choice in that," I said, still unwilling to tell her Cristian's terrible plans for her if I failed. "Neither of us do," I added bitterly, more words dropping from my lips without thought.

Her brows drew together. "What do you mean?"

Instead of answering her, I crushed my lips to hers. She parted for me on a surprised gasp, and my tongue surged inside her mouth, desperate to taste her. My kiss was hard, demanding. I didn't relent until she finally softened against me, her creamy skin flushing with warmth.

Samantha was safe in my arms. Safe from my brother, and safe from my darker urges.

CHAPTER 13

I resolved to stay with Samantha for the rest of the day. After her panic, I needed to know that she was content and calm.

She seemed much happier now, snuggled up against my side as I read her graphic novel along with her. I had to admit that *Watchmen* was intriguing, but it mostly captivated my attention because she was enamored with the story. I wanted to understand her better, to ease her transition into her new life with me.

I never wanted to see her mindless with terror again, especially not at my hands.

I realized I'd been turning the pages, reading at my own pace instead of accommodating her. I glanced down at her to assess her mood, hoping she wasn't falling into listlessness after the intense scene in the playroom.

She was staring up at me, her eyes scanning my face.

"Am I more interesting than your superheroes?" I asked, ruffling her hair.

"Anti-heroes," she corrected me. "Well, some of them, anyway. That's what makes them interesting."

"Then why are you looking at me?"

She shrugged. "I already read it. I know the story."

I set the book aside. "Then I'll get you a different one. I don't want you to be bored."

"I'm not. You can keep reading it."

My smile twisted. "I don't want to read right now. Not when you're watching me like that, my curious *gatita*." I took her hand and pressed it against my growing erection.

Her pupils dilated, and her cheeks flushed pink as her own arousal rose in response. I'd conditioned her well, and she reacted to my needs beautifully.

I gripped her waist and shifted her body off mine. "On your hands and knees."

She didn't hesitate to comply. There was something different about her now; something had shifted between us in the last few hours. She was softer, sweeter. Almost needy in the way she stared at me, waiting for my next command.

I traced the line of her spine, communicating my pleasure with her. "You are so beautiful," I murmured. "Stay."

She let out a little sigh as I stepped away, but she didn't move from her position. If anything, she seemed to relax into her submissive pose, her head dropping forward as her ass lifted in offering to me.

It only took me a minute to go to the chest of drawers and retrieve the items I wanted, but that short time of separation seemed to trouble her. By the time I returned, fresh tension had gripped her body, even though she remained still and compliant.

"Settle, *cosita*." I smoothed my hand down her back, and she relaxed instantly. "I'm not going to restrain you, so you're going to have to be very good for me." Her head dipped forward again, exposing her nape to me, making her fully vulnerable. "Just like that," I approved.

"I want you to trust me," I confessed. After her bout of horror, I never wanted her to look at me like that again: like I was the villain, the monster.

"So, I'm going to trust you, too," I continued. "I'm going to trust you to stay in position for me. I wanted to tie you down so you wouldn't be able to move away from me. It's safer for you if you stay still. That way, I won't inflict pain unintentionally."

I anticipated her renewed tension at the mention of pain, and I shushed her before anxiety could grip her. "You'll like this. I'll make sure you do, I promise. But you have to trust me. Can you do that for me?" The question was edged with strain. Her response was everything to me. I craved her affirmation.

She remained silent for agonizing seconds. I could simply restrain her and whip her, regardless of her wishes. But that would be a hollow victory. My control wouldn't be real if I used force against her. Her submission wouldn't be real.

Finally, she spoke. "Yes. I can trust you."

Warmth expanded in my chest, and my lips split in a wide grin. My pleasure was more than twisted satisfaction at her capitulation; this was unadulterated joy. It felt strange and hot and bright, and I quickly became intoxicated by the foreign emotion. No one had ever made me feel like this. It made me crave her all the more. This was what I wanted from her: this sweet perfection.

My touch eased down her back, over the curve of her bottom, before tracing the line of her soft folds. She moaned and pushed back, welcoming me to press inside. I slowly penetrated her tight channel with my fingers. Her body began to rock slightly, so I pumped in and out of her to stimulate her in the way she liked.

While she fell into lust, I picked up the lubed anal plug that I'd prepared and placed on the nightstand. She didn't seem to have noticed it, but it certainly got her attention when I pressed it against her virgin asshole.

She stilled and stared back at me, her pretty features slack with surprise.

"Trust me," I urged. "This will feel good."

I withdrew my fingers from her sheath so I could play with her clit, distracting her from the discomfort of the unyielding red plug pressing against her puckered bud. As I traced teasing circles around her hard clit, her tight ring of muscles eased. The plug slipped inside, barely penetrating her. I worked it in slowly, careful not to damage her as I stretched her tight hole. I wanted her to associate this with pleasure, not pain.

She surrendered her most vulnerable area to me, flowering open and accepting the intrusion of the plug. Little moans and panting noises filled the bedroom, soft sounds of perverted desire and sweet submission.

When the plug entered her at its widest point, she whined in discomfort. I rubbed her clit more firmly, not easing the pressure. She'd learn to take much larger plugs than this during the course of her training.

"Almost there," I assured her. "You're doing so well. You're going to love taking my cock in your ass, once you're properly prepared."

The plug sank all the way inside her, stretching her in a way she'd never experienced. She continued to draw in panting breaths as she struggled to adjust to the intrusion.

Keeping my thumb on her clit, I dipped my forefinger back into her wet cunt. She groaned as I slid into her sheath, filling her up in both virgin holes. Her muscles contracted around my finger, and I knew she was about to orgasm.

"Come for me." I increased the pressure of my thumb on her clit as I found the sweet spot at the front of her inner walls. She shattered on a shriek, her body clamping down on my finger. I bit back a groan as my own desire crested. I could hardly imagine the ecstasy I'd experience if her hot little pussy squeezed my dick so tightly.

I didn't relent until she gasped against the sheets, struggling to find air after screaming out her completion.

"Stay just like that," I ordered, my voice thick with my own desire. "Don't move."

I picked up the crop where I'd laid it on the bed behind her. She was too drunk on lust to notice my actions, and she cried out in shock when I delivered the first smack against her ass. She jerked to attention, her eyes jumping to mine.

Her cry melted into the sexiest moan, her gaze locking on my face. The way she stared at me was intoxicating; her sky-blue eyes fixated on me with something like awe. A rush of pleasure and lust flooded my being. There was nothing twisted about my satisfaction, no dark taint of cruel triumph. She'd incited a matching sense of wonder in me. In this moment, she'd placed herself completely in my power, trusting me and ceding to me willingly.

I touched the leather tongue of the crop beneath her chin, lifting her face. "I like when you look at me like this. My kinky virgin."

I slid the crop up to her lips to let her taste the leather, intending to overwhelm all her senses. Desire tore through me when she tenderly kissed the implement I would use to paint her ass red. She wanted the pain, the pleasure. She wanted everything I had to give her, would accept anything I chose to do to her.

I wouldn't violate her trust. I wouldn't risk shattering it by using her cruelly.

"You please me, Samantha. Very much."

She let out a little happy humming noise and licked the length of the crop, worshipping it the same way she showed reverence to my cock. My arousal sharpened to something almost painful, but my pleasure with her overshadowed any discomfort.

"You like the crop? You're not scared of it? You're not scared of me?"

"No," she moaned, lifting her ass in wanton invitation. "Please."

I laughed, the sound of my delight rolling from my chest. "All right, greedy *gatita*. Don't move."

I tapped her ass with the crop, letting her get a feel for the light sting. She let out a long sigh, and her head dropped forward as she surrendered fully. I struck her again, harder. She didn't cry out or shift away, so I increased the intensity, giving her a harsher bite with each lash.

Her entire body relaxed, and her eyes slid closed. She didn't so much as flinch or grunt in pain. Her breathing turned deep and even, and I knew she was beginning to find her blissful, quiet headspace, freed from her frenetic thoughts.

"Andrés." She'd never moaned my name like that, her voice husky with need.

I dropped the crop and leaned over her, so I could murmur in her ear. In her current state, she'd give me anything I demanded of her. "I could fuck you right now, couldn't I, kinky virgin? Your tight little pussy would welcome my cock."

"Andrés, please..."

"You shouldn't say my name like that, *sirenita*," I warned. The way she was moaning and begging took me to the edge of my control. "You really shouldn't." I cursed and unbuckled my belt, aching for relief. "Open your mouth."

Her lips parted, her eyes fluttering open as I surged inside. I slid all the way to the back of her throat, unable to rein myself in. Taking her mouth was the only way I'd be able to restrain myself from claiming her cunt.

She accepted all of me, her body well-trained to handle my size, my demands. My fingers tightened in her hair, and I held myself deep for a few seconds before sliding back, allowing her to breathe.

"I'm going to fuck your mouth," I told her roughly, surging forward again. "The way I want to fuck your little pussy. But not today. Not when you're like this." She was barely lucid right now, her mind lost to my will. I wouldn't take her virginity when she wouldn't really be aware of what she was offering to me. I couldn't bear to lose this trust she was placing in me.

I held her face in both hands, my fingers threaded into her hair as I used her mouth the way I wanted. She encouraged my rough treatment, swirling her tongue around my cock and sucking me.

I wanted to feel her scream. I picked up the crop and began tapping it against the base of the plug, stimulating her ass. She shrieked around me, the sound of her ecstasy vibrating against my dick. I released into her mouth on a feral roar, pumping in mercilessly as I spilled my cum all over her tongue. She swallowed everything I gave her, just like I'd taught her.

I withdrew from her and scooped her up as I laid down beside her, spent and sated. I pulled her tightly against me, running my hands over her soft skin as I kissed the top of her head. She snuggled in, as though she couldn't get close enough.

My pretty little captive no longer feared me.

CHAPTER 14

I couldn't linger in my penthouse much longer. I'd stayed with Samantha well into the morning, but after our intense scene yesterday, I wasn't yet ready to part from her. If I didn't have obligations, I wasn't certain I'd choose to leave her side at all.

I didn't like the distance between us now, the barrier of the bathroom door. She was taking longer than usual with her morning routine, and even the few extra minutes of separation set my teeth on edge. Her nearness soothed something inside me. So, I ordered her to return to me.

"*Sirenita*," I called out. "Your breakfast is getting cold. Come."

The door opened seconds later, and she obediently walked across the bedroom to join me where I sat on the edge of the mattress. Despite her easy compliance, tension stiffened her shoulders.

"What's wrong?" I asked, concerned.

She made a little dismissive wave. "Nothing."

Something sharp pierced my gut. "Don't lie to me." I

grasped her wrist and tugged her toward me, settling her in my lap where she belonged.

Her eyes dropped, avoiding my gaze. She didn't respond.

"*Cosita?*" I prompted, demanding her honest response.

Her gaze lifted to mine, no longer shutting me out. "I am a little upset this morning," she admitted. "But I don't want to talk about it."

The pang in my gut intensified. I cupped her cheek in my hand and stared into her eyes, as though I could peer inside her mind and read her thoughts. "You don't have any secrets from me." I tried to command her, but I realized that I couldn't force her to confide in me. It was up to her to choose whether or not she wanted to share with me, regardless of my wishes. I wouldn't use cruel methods to extract her secrets as I might have done when I'd first captured her. I valued her trust too much to risk losing it.

Her brow wrinkled. "Please," she whispered. "I don't want to think about it right now."

I frowned, considering her. I decided that as long as she wasn't attempting to deceive me, I'd allow her a reprieve from questioning.

"You do have a very busy brain," I acknowledged, pressing a kiss against her forehead to soothe her. "If your thoughts bother you, let me put them at ease."

I could stay with her a little while longer to ensure she was content again before I left her alone for the day. If she needed a spanking and an orgasm to relax, I'd provide them for her.

I leaned in to capture her lips with mine.

She turned her face away. "Wait."

I gripped her jaw, locking her in place for my kiss. "No. I know what's best for you. You're upset. I'm going to make you feel better."

Her head tipped back slightly. "You can't just kiss me and

make everything okay," she defied me, despite the way her body reacted.

Something hardened in my chest. "I can. But I don't have to. I can distract you from your thoughts in other ways, if you don't want me to kiss you."

I shifted her on my lap, turning her away from me so her back pressed against my chest. I hooked her ankles around my calves and eased my legs apart, spreading her wide. She was naked against my suit-clad form, her creamy bare skin standing in stark contrast to the black material. This was exactly how I wanted her: stripped and on display for me, vulnerable to my desires.

My fingers tangled in her hair, and I tilted her head to the side so I could sink my teeth into her neck. My free hand explored her breasts, my palm rubbing her hard nipples.

Her harsh cry made my cock stiffen, and I growled against her flesh. When I released her from my bite, I ran my tongue over the little indentations I'd left in her skin. She'd have a mark there, and the idea of seeing the bruise when I returned to her in the evening made my arousal spike.

She moaned and tipped her head to the side, offering her throat to be ravaged. Instead of biting again, I trailed feather-light kisses along her neck, and her skin pebbled beneath my lips.

I released my hold on her hair so I could skim my hand down her waist and over her belly, making my way to her pussy as I continued to play with her breasts. Biting down on her neck again, I slapped her cunt.

She shrieked and writhed on my lap, but I held her fast with my teeth. Her squirming stimulated my hard cock, so I bit down harder and spanked her sex again. She whimpered and stilled, surrendering.

I resumed kissing her neck, the tender touch of my lips

contrasting with the sharpness of my bite. I smacked her again, and this time, a wet sound accompanied the slap of my hand against her labia. She groaned, and her head dropped back on my shoulder as she melted.

"Are you still upset?" I murmured, my lips brushing the shell of her ear.

"What?" she asked faintly. "No. I'm not upset. I'm..." She trailed off when I traced a little teasing circle around her clit.

"Horny?" I finished for her. "Does your wet little pussy want to be filled after being spanked?"

"Yes," she begged on a ragged whisper. "Please."

Please. She was begging. I'd make her plead more specifically for what she wanted; what we hadn't shared last night, even though we'd both wanted it.

I maneuvered her body into place, stretching her out on the mattress. I towered over her, and she stared up at me, wide-eyed and waiting. Trusting. Wanting.

A grin lit my features. "I do like when you look at me like that, *sirenita*." I reached for my zipper and freed myself from my slacks. She licked her lips, and I growled in satisfaction. "Are you as hungry for my cock as you were last night?"

She nodded, her pulse jumping at her throat.

"But what about your pussy?" I asked, my voice dropping deeper, rougher. "I could have fucked you last night. But you weren't aware enough to know what you would be agreeing to. You weren't capable of knowing what you were begging for." I began to stroke my shaft. "*This* is what you're begging for. I'm going to fuck you, Samantha."

She didn't say anything, so I continued. "You have to beg me." I fixed her in my steady stare, imposing my will on her. "Beg me to fuck you."

"Andrés..."

Confusion clouded the lust in her eyes, and her delicate

features tightened with unease. I watched as her desire melted away, my stomach souring.

"I can't," she said, her voice small. "I don't want to. Not like this."

My teeth clenched, my jaw working as I suppressed the brutal instinct to possess her, to force her to accept me. That cruel impulse felt better than the rejection that gnawed at my gut.

I clung onto control by a thread, managing to tuck my raging hard-on back into my slacks.

She'd beg me to fuck her, or she'd get nothing at all.

Yes, punishing her through erotic denial eased some of the burning in my chest. Knowing that I was managing to hurt her in this way felt better, even if my stomach was twisting.

I turned sharply and started walking away from her.

"Wait," she called out. "I didn't mean... I'm sorry."

I paused on her apology, the pain in her whisper calming me just enough that some of my wits returned. I'd almost forgotten something important.

I rounded on her, striding back toward the bed. Her eyes sparked with something I couldn't quite identify, so I chose to ignore it. Instead, I picked up the collar that was already chained to the bedpost and locked it around her neck.

I turned to leave, but she caught my wrist. I could have easily jerked my arm away, but I stilled.

"Wait," she beseeched. "Don't leave like this. I didn't want to upset you. I just... I can't give you what you want."

I mastered my black emotions, summoning up my usual cool composure. "I won't force myself on you." I wouldn't lose control like that. I'd sworn to her that she'd beg me to fuck her before I'd give her the satisfaction of my cock stretching her tight pussy, and I wouldn't settle for anything less.

"Thank you," she whispered. She lifted my hand to her lips and kissed it, the brush of her lips contrite.

The last of my anger deflated as I realized the truth: I wouldn't force her because I wouldn't betray her like that. I wouldn't spoil my claim over her by taking her virginity without her consent. Not when I craved for her to surrender it to me freely, eagerly.

I blew out a shuddering breath, and most of the furious tension eased from my muscles. I leaned down and pressed my lips to hers in an apologetic kiss of my own. "I'll see you tonight," I promised. I needed to leave, needed some space to finish cooling off and to get the last of my possessive lust under control.

The knowledge that she was chained to my bed helped calm me. She'd still be here when I returned. She didn't have a choice.

***

"A BOARD GAME?" SHE ASKED, NONPLUSSED. "YOU WANT TO play a game that involves an actual board?"

My brows rose as I set the chess board, placing the white pieces in front of her. "Is there some other kind?"

"You're kidding, right? How about *World of Warcraft*? You know, something with multi-layered storytelling, cool effects, and kick-ass heroes?" She gestured at the board. "Who's the hero in this game? What's the story? There isn't one. It's just us, staring at some funny pieces that don't have any special abilities at all."

"Chess is a battle of wits. It's just you, against me. But you can be the hero in this scenario, if you want." My smile was a touch indulgent. All my consternation had melted when I'd returned to find her sprawled out naked on my bed, right where she belonged.

Her nose wrinkled, her lips thinning with distaste.

"You don't have to look so disdainful," I said, my smile tugging up at one corner. "I'll teach you how to play. If you really hate it after a few games, we can stop. I'll warn you now, I will win. So don't let that deter you from enjoying the game."

"You're a little cocky," she remarked drily, reaching for her queen to examine the exquisitely carved piece. It was worn from age and use, but the quality of craftsmanship was still discernable.

I pushed aside memories of the days when the set had been brand new. Those were too bittersweet, and I preferred to stay in this moment with Samantha.

"I've been playing for years, and it's an impossibility for a new player to beat someone with my kind of experience."

"Who says I don't know how to play?" she challenged. "They do have online chess, you know. I've dabbled. I know the rules, even if I do find it boring."

I grinned, perhaps a bit sharply. "Knowing the rules won't prepare you for playing against me, but it will certainly make these first few games more interesting. How advanced are you? Who taught you how to play?"

"An online tutorial taught me how to play. I get the rules and know some trickier strategies. I pick things up quickly."

I shook my head. "A tutorial isn't going to prepare you for playing against me, but show me what you know, and we'll go from there."

Her full lips twisted in a frown. "Why bother playing chess with someone when you think they won't be able to beat you?"

"Because I believe you will be able to challenge me, just not in the first few games. Or even the first dozen."

Her eyes narrowed, considering me with irritation. After a

moment, her attention returned to the chess pieces, examining them. "How long have you been playing?"

Any tension I might have felt over her exasperation with me melted back into amusement. My clever captive wanted to size me up as her opponent.

I picked up one of my knights, not realizing that I was tracing the contours of the well-worn piece. As a child, my sister had loved the design of the black knights in this set. She'd preferred to take the slight disadvantage of playing black for that very reason. She'd also claimed she was a better player, and I could use all the help I could get. Valentina always had been a clever girl, and she'd loved to tease me.

"This was my first chess set. I got it for my tenth birthday," I told Samantha. "That's when *Abuela* taught me how to play."

"*Abuela?*"

The fond memories of my childhood turned bitter as I returned to the present. That life had belonged to a different person, a naïve boy who'd thought he could hide from his responsibilities.

"My grandmother," I explained shortly, not offering any further information. I never talked about my family. Cristian was my only family now, and I definitely didn't want to talk about him with Samantha.

"Oh." She shifted, her fingers knotting at her lap as her anxiety rose.

I placed my knight back on the board and focused on her again. "White goes first," I prompted.

She flipped her fiery hair over her shoulder. "I know."

She immediately moved her pawn from E2 to E4. The way her eyes sparked and her decisive movements let me know she already had a plan in mind. She'd claimed she'd learned to play chess online, and it seemed my smart Samantha had done her research. This wasn't the hesitant, random opening move of a complete newbie.

I narrowed down her possible strategies and made my countermove.

Then, my naughty *gatita* decided to try to deceive me. She cocked her head to the side, biting her lip in an uncharacteristic show of confusion. I noted that her fingertips tapped against her thigh, betraying her excited anticipation.

I smothered my amusement, deciding I'd prefer to watch her play her little game. She really was adorable in her innocent attempt at misdirection. She couldn't lie convincingly, no matter how hard she tried.

She moved slowly as she placed her bishop on C4, obviously trying to make it look like she was uncertain.

Her choice revealed her full strategy, and I knew exactly how to block her.

Instead, I let her stew in silence, pretending to study the board for a full two minutes before making my move. The longer I waited, the more palpable her excitement became. She practically vibrated with it by the time I completed my turn. Pleasure unfurled in my chest. There was something almost childlike about her, despite her sensual appeal. That sense of innocence called to me. I wanted it for myself. I wanted to cage it and keep it for my own.

She didn't bother to hold back when she moved to attack my pawn. A triumphant grin illuminated her pale features as she clicked her queen down on the board.

I no longer bothered to hold back my grin. Observing her attempt to deceive me had been amusing, but taking her by surprise after my own ruse was even more gratifying. I might covet her innocence, but I reveled in conquering her.

"Scholar's Mate," I observed. "I'm impressed. You did study properly, *cosita*."

I moved my knight to F6, blocking her.

"Now, we can play," I declared.

"When did you realize my strategy?" she asked, a small pout plumping her lips.

"I suspected on your first move. I knew by the second."

"But you didn't try to stop me."

"You were so cute, trying to fool me. I thought I'd let it play out for a few moves. You're not capable of lying to me, Samantha. You can't play dumb with me, either. I know you better than that."

Her cheeks colored, and her pout curved into a small smile. "Who do you play with?"

"Believe it or not, I do play online mostly. There's not anyone here I'm interested in playing against. It doesn't compare to sitting across from your opponent, though. Studying you is part of the game." I could sit and study her all day, and I was sure she'd still find new ways to surprise me.

"You play online? I thought you only got on your laptop to work. There's like, no technology in this penthouse. I never even see you with a phone."

"I don't like to be easily reached once I come home," I replied honestly. "This is my space. And if you're worrying that I'm wasting my time playing chess while you're tied up, don't." I recalled all the nights I'd suspended her in my ropes, so I could idly admire her while I worked at my desk. She really was a terrible distraction, moaning and sighing while I tried to focus on my laptop.

My voice dropped deeper. "I'd much rather play games with you. I really am taking care of my business in the evenings. This is the first time I've played a game in weeks. Don't be too disappointed when I win this game," I added. "I really am impressed with your knowledge of chess. But I've known

Scholar's Mate for years. Valentina beat me with it half a dozen times before I caught on."

"Who's Valentina?" Her lips twisted around the feminine name.

I didn't have a chance to parse out the meaning of her expression. My dark emotions shut down my curiosity. "My sister," I replied tersely.

Her shoulders slumped. "I'm sorry." She hesitated for a moment, then spoke tentatively. "You lost her?"

"Yes," I bit out. "I lost her."

"How—"

"It's your move."

I hadn't spoken Valentina's name aloud in years. Why had I mentioned her to Samantha? And *Abuela*? They were my past, and I kept them buried there.

Samantha didn't pry any more. Instead, she returned most of her focus to the game. But she wasn't really paying attention, because I managed to beat her in a few coldly calculated moves.

"Can we play again?" she asked timidly.

I blinked, my full attention returning to her rather than remaining caught up in my memories. "You want to?" I'd beaten her with cruel indifference, all earlier joy in the game forgotten. Her request to try again surprised me.

"Yes. I'll do better next time." She straightened her spine, seeming to shake off the influence of my dark mood. "I know I can beat you."

A half-smile tilted my lips. "Tomorrow," I promised. "I have another game I want to play with my clever *gatita*."

There was a way she could help me alleviate the darkness that had claimed my thoughts.

I stood from where we'd been seated at my desk and held out my hand. "Come."

She took it without question and followed me docilely into the playroom. When I continued our progress toward the spanking bench, her steps faltered.

"Andrés..."

I paused and turned to her so I could cup her cheeks in my hands. I stared down into her eyes, attempting to impose my will on her. Instead, something like desperation gripped my chest.

"I need you to cry for me." The rough words tumbled from my lips, almost beseeching. I wanted her consent. I wanted her to cede this to me willingly.

A fine tremor raced across her body, but she swallowed and nodded. "Okay," she agreed quietly.

I blew out the breath I hadn't realized I was holding. I stroked her cheekbones with my thumbs. "I know it scares you, but you'll enjoy this, kinky virgin," I promised. "You will come to crave it."

She nodded again, her eyes cautious. She was choosing to place her trust in me, choosing to give me what I needed. After thoughts of my lost loved ones had flooded my mind for the first time in years, I needed to harness control over the images in my head. I needed her to siphon off some of the pain inside my soul through releasing her tears for me.

I resumed our progress toward the spanking bench, and she didn't hesitate this time. She compliantly draped her body over the furniture designed for her torment, and she didn't struggle as I strapped her into place. I ran my fingers over the leather than held her trapped and helpless beneath me, already soothed somewhat by the sight of her at my mercy.

I left her briefly to retrieve the first implement for her torment from the ebony chest of drawers set against the wall where my whips hung, waiting to wring more exquisite screams from her throat.

I lubed up the plug and returned to her. This one was larger than the one I'd used when I'd cropped her. It would test her limits, but I intended to push her to the edge of what she could handle.

She jerked in her bonds when I touched the tip of the black toy to her asshole, and she remained stiff, even as I began to circle her clit with my forefinger.

"Relax," I rebuked, spanking her pussy lightly.

She drew in a shuddering breath, and her tight ring of muscles eased just enough for me to penetrate her with the tip of the plug. I pressed it forward slowly but firmly, rubbing her little bud at the same time. Despite the fact that it began to harden beneath my fingers, she whimpered at the ruthless intrusion.

"Please," she panted. "It's too big."

"Does it hurt, *cosita*?" I murmured, a hungry edge to the words.

"Yes," she whined. "It burns."

"Good. I like making you hurt. You like it, too. Your cunt is soaking my hand."

A soft sob left her chest, and my tumultuous emotions began to subside. "Take it for me. You want to please me, don't you?"

"Yes," she said, her voice high and thin. She began to squirm on the bench, grinding her clit against my fingers. She got off on pleasing me, despite the discomfort I was inflicting. Or perhaps because of it.

"Good girl," I praised, pushing the plug all the way in, so it was seated deep inside her.

She gasped, and her muscles tensed. I stroked my hand down her spine. "You'll adjust soon. I'm going to train your tight little ass to accept me."

As I continued to pet her, she began to relax. Her head

dropped forward, her cheek resting meekly on the padded leather surface of the bench.

"Very good," I rumbled. "I need more. You'll take whatever I give you."

She nodded, her silence communicating that she was falling into her quiet headspace. She'd find peace in surrendering to me, just as I'd find peace in her screams. She'd cry out the pain I couldn't release from my own soul.

I flipped the small switch at the base of the plug, and it buzzed to life. She shouted her surprise, and her back arched as much as possible in her restraints. After a moment, she moaned and shuddered, finding dark pleasure in the sensation as her ass fully accepted being stretched and filled.

Satisfied that she was thoroughly in my thrall, I selected the whip I wanted. It was softer than the flogger I'd chosen for her when she'd tried to escape from me. This one wouldn't elicit the same cruel sting, but it was heavy enough that she'd feel the impact thrumming through her. I didn't intend to punish this time, but I would extract my pleasure from her.

Her eyes widened when they fell on the whip, but I shushed her before panic gripped her, placing a steadying hand on her lower back. The heat of my palm sank into her, and she shivered and quieted.

"This is going to hurt," I told her smoothly, falling into my own intoxicating headspace. Desire for her flooded me, but I'd attain satisfaction from her tears rather than burning with the need to claim her pussy. I was thoroughly in control, power humming in my veins.

I threaded my fingers in her hair, tugging her head back as I leaned in to murmur in her ear. "Will you cry for me, *sirenita*?"

A small whimper teased through her lips, but she nodded as best she could with my grip on her hair. I eased my harsh hold and stroked the silken strands. She sighed, and her eyes drifted closed as she settled into submission.

I stepped behind her and swung the flogger. The first blow made harsh impact, and she jolted forward as she cried out. I didn't pause to give her a reprieve. Instead, I worked her harder, until beautiful tears spilled down her face, glistening on her flushed cheeks. Her shrieks melted into tormented groans as the vibrating plug continued to stimulate her ass, her pleasure cresting despite the pain I inflicted. I drove her higher, until she relinquished all control on a sob. She shuddered, ceding everything to me as she released the sounds of my inner agony.

I stopped whipping her as my muscles finally relaxed, calm settling over my shoulders. I resumed rubbing her clit, finding her wet and needy beneath my hand. At the same time, I gripped her flame-red ass, reveling in the heat against my palm as I dug my fingers deep to mark her.

She shattered on a scream, her lithe body tensing and thrashing on the bench. Ecstatic sensation overwhelmed her, bliss claiming her senses. Just as I'd demanded, she gave me everything: her pain, her pleasure, her absolute submission to my will. She soothed the dark need in my soul, allowing the blackness to bleed out of me.

I leaned into her and kissed the delicious tears on her cheeks, reveling in the salty flavor of her complete surrender.

CHAPTER 15

Somehow, I'd lost track of time. Or maybe I'd been willfully ignoring it. I'd found too much pleasure in spending time with Samantha, either reading her comic books with her cuddled in my arms or indulging in increasingly challenging games of chess. My clever captive was a quick study, and she was becoming a formidable opponent.

I hadn't felt the need to hurt her since I'd last taken her into the playroom, but that hadn't stopped me from extracting pleasure from her body. With each passing day, I ached more to claim her fully, but I would wait until she was ready to give herself to me. The budding affection she displayed toward me and the trust she'd placed in me gave me hope that I wouldn't have to wait much longer.

While she was growing closer to ceding her virginity, she was still a long way from complying with my brother's demands that she work for him. She maintained her stubborn streak, but I couldn't bring myself to tame it out of her. I wanted *her*, not an altered version. Samantha's willing, genuine devotion meant everything.

Now, the lightness in my soul darkened once again. Cristian had called me to a meeting, and I realized I was running out of time to win Samantha's cooperation. Mere days remained before his deadline, and this meeting couldn't mean anything good.

He'd summoned me to the brothel on the third floor of my building. It was almost as bad as the basement. The women held here against their will were drugged and empty inside, hollowed out by Bliss like Lauren.

When I entered the opulent room, the scent of sex and an aura of misery hit me hard. The decadent red velvet drapes and gold gilding on the walls didn't mask the palpable despair that filled the space.

Cristian sat in a wing-backed chair, occupying it like a throne. Two bodyguards stood at his sides, and he held a naked woman draped on his lap. She trembled with fear, but I could scent her forced arousal. She must have been given a small dose to still be lucid enough to feel any emotion other than lust. Cristian did like to torment his victims. And he liked to torment me with such disgusting displays.

I schooled my features to a blank mask, resolving not to rise to his bait. It was imperative that I maintain control if I was going to defend Samantha.

"Is she ready?" he drawled when I stopped a few yards away from him, keeping careful distance between us.

My stomach knotted. "She will be soon. I need a little more time." I tasted the lie on my tongue, but I kept my tone even to prevent Cristian from detecting it.

He cocked his head at me and twisted the woman's nipples, pinching cruelly. She let out a tortured whimper, torn between pain and unwilling arousal.

My muscles tensed, and I found that I couldn't ease the

pent-up aggression from my shoulders. I barely prevented my fists from curling at my sides.

Cristian smirked. "Maybe I should find another use for our FBI agent until she's ready," he mused softly. "I think some time in the brothel might do her good. If you're not making progress with her, maybe my other men can."

I couldn't bite back my snarl. "No one else touches her. I'll kill anyone who tries. Samantha is mine."

His dark brows lifted. "Anyone, little brother? Are you threatening me? You know that isn't wise." The warning was edged with malice, but his black eyes sparked with anticipation.

He wouldn't hurt me this time. He'd punish me by harming *her*. He'd jump on any excuse to take Samantha from me, rescinding the gift he'd given me. Depriving me of my toy.

She was so much more than that. She wasn't my little doll, my fucktoy to use for my own empty pleasures.

If Cristian had any idea what she really meant to me, he'd snatch her away in a heartbeat, just to find sick satisfaction in torturing me. Unlike my rules with Samantha, my brother wasn't a fair man. He punished with impunity, just to fulfil his own sadistic desires.

"I'll make sure she's compliant," I resolved, trying to convince myself as much as him. "I just need a little more time. The Bureau doesn't know we have her. They aren't closing in on us, so it can't hurt to wait a little while longer." I desperately clung to reason.

Cristian considered me silently for a moment, drawing out my agony. His lips curved upward. "All right, *hermanito*. Keep your toy. Just make sure she's broken in soon, or I'll see to it myself. I don't think you want that."

"No," I growled out the staunch refusal.

He waved me away with an imperious flick of his fingers.

"You can go. Get back to work on her."

I managed to conceal my rage and panic until I reached the privacy of the elevator. Then, I punched the metal wall hard enough to leave a dent. My uncertainty threatened to drive me to madness. I had to protect Samantha, but that meant turning her into someone different. She wanted to be the hero; she was inherently good. She'd fight me if I tried to change the nature of her soul. I wasn't even sure it was possible.

Gritting my teeth, I strengthened my resolve. Even an altered Samantha was better than seeing my sweet pet tortured by my brother. If he broke her, he'd break me.

I stormed into the bedroom, the door slamming against the wall as I flung it open with the force of my pent-up rage. I didn't want this for her, for me. Cristian hadn't left me with any other choice.

Her eyes widened with fear, and she scooted back on the mattress as much as her tether to the bedpost would allow. She wouldn't be able to escape me.

The idea soured my stomach, stoking my frustrated fury.

"Wait!" she gasped out. "Andrés, wait. Please."

The tremor in her voice stopped me in my tracks. I could grab her in a few long strides, but her fear froze me in place.

"You're upset," she said quickly. "I don't like it when you're like this. You scare me. Please, don't...don't hurt me." Her crestfallen, betrayed expression made my soul ache.

A low, feral sound rumbled from my chest, and my fists clenched at my sides.

"Please. Talk to me. Tell me what's wrong. What happened? Is it your brother? What did he—?"

"Of course it's my brother!" I shouted. She cringed, but that didn't stop me from closing the distance between us and grabbing her upper arms. I pulled her body against mine, snarling down at her when she tried to twist out of my grip.

"He wants to see you. He expects you to be ready by now. But you're not. I've been too soft with you."

"You haven't," she squeaked, desperate. "You don't have to hurt me."

"I don't want to hurt you," I bellowed. "He does. Why can't you understand that? I'm not the one who wants to break you. I want to save you. I want to protect you. I can't do that if you continue to defy me."

"I haven't defied you," she gasped, shuddering in my grip. "I've done everything you've asked."

"No," I railed, shaking her hard. "I've given you everything *you've* asked. I've tried to make you happy here with me. I've indulged you and played with you when I was supposed to be training you. And now he wants to see you, and you're not ready."

"I am," she insisted, her voice shaking with terror.

"Don't lie to me, Samantha," I warned on a growl. "You think you can manipulate me with your pretty tears? You think I'll do anything you ask if you smile for me? I won't allow you to play games with me. I'm in control. You belong to *me*."

"You're not in control." Her pretty eyes began to shine. "You're scaring me. You're hurting me."

I realized my fingers were digging into her upper arms with bruising force, but I couldn't release her.

My heart stuttered when her expression softened, and she reached out to cup my scarred cheek. She'd never touched my face with tenderness. No one had. I flinched as keen, unbearable emotion assailed me.

She didn't relent; she pressed her palm against my scar. The sensation of her tangible touch around the damaged tissue was exquisite torment.

"Talk to me," she begged. "Tell me what happened."

"What happened is my brother takes everything from me,"

I said on a harsh whisper. "*Abuela*, Valentina. Now, he wants to take you." I pulled her closer, until my face was an inch from hers. She filled my entire vision, my entire world. "He can't have you. You're mine."

"Yes," she agreed softly. "I'm yours. I'm not going anywhere. You won't let Cristian take me away. I...I trust you."

She traced the line of my scar with her fingertips, there was little physical sensation in my damaged nerve endings, but I felt the light touch deep in my soul. I shuddered and leaned into her hand.

My hold on her arms eased, and I embraced her, cradling her body carefully against mine.

"*Sirenita*," I rasped, strained. "*Lo siento*." I turned my face into her palm, kissing it in contrition.

"What happened to them?" she whispered. "The people your brother took from you. Your grandmother and sister."

My lips thinned in a grimace, but I didn't tighten my arms around her. My Samantha was precious and fragile, and I'd handled her too roughly. I'd scared her. I kissed her palm again, placing my trust in her.

I braced myself for pain, and my confession tumbled from my lips. "Valentina..." My voice hitched on her name. "My sister. Half-sister. Cristian and I share the same father as Valentina. Our father kept her mother as his mistress after our mother passed away, but she died giving birth to Valentina. Father let Valentina's grandmother live on our estate, so she could care for her. Valentina was my best friend. Her grandmother became *mi abuela*. I spent more time in their home than my own. Cristian was always jealous of our friendship, our little family. As the oldest, father was harder on him. He had more responsibilities, a legacy resting on his shoulders."

I understood why my brother possessed such sadistic tendencies. He'd learned them from my father at a young age.

That knowledge didn't erase the years of torment I'd suffered at his cruel hands.

"Your father dealt in cocaine," Samantha prompted gently, pressing me to continue. "He wanted Cristian to take over the business?"

"Yes. But then father died when I was sixteen. Heart attack."

"I'm sorry."

My jaw firmed. "He was not a nice man. But I had a home with *Abuela* and Valentina. Until Cristian took over father's organization. He resented us, our family. Maybe if I hadn't left him alone with father, things would have been different. But he always had a sadistic streak, even as a child. I wanted nothing to do with him. He scared me, so I stayed away."

"What did he do?"

"He sold Valentina." The dark memory left me on a strained whisper. I remembered the night the men had come to take her from our home, remembered the agony of Cristian's beating when I tried to fight to keep my sister. "She was fourteen. He traded her for money, for bribes to secure his place as father's successor. Well, he said it was for money. He did it to punish me. To punish both of us for our happy childhood. One that had been denied him."

Her features drew tight with horror, but I couldn't stop myself from finishing my confession. "*Abuela* died nine months later," I said bitterly. "Breast cancer. She didn't even try to fight to survive it. Not after losing Valentina. She left me alone. With Cristian."

Cupping my scarred cheek in her hand, Samantha leaned up into me and lightly pressed her lips to mine. For a moment, my mouth was tense beneath hers; a hard, anguished slash. Then I released my pain on a long groan, and I opened for her. She'd never initiated a kiss like this. I was always the one to claim her. Her tender treatment made my chest tighten. My fingers threaded in her hair, pulling her closer. My tongue swept into her mouth, and I devoured her like a starving man.

Her hands went to my shirt, tearing at the buttons as though she was desperate to touch my bare, scarred body. She didn't find the marks disgusting. She caressed them, tracing them. Her gentleness incited a rougher hunger within me, and my cock stiffened for her. I finished stripping out of my clothes and settled my body over hers on the bed, loving the feel of her delicate frame trapped beneath mine, nothing separating us.

"I want you, Andrés," she gasped when I broke our kiss so we could both draw in much-needed air. "Don't make me beg. I want to give this to you. I want to give myself to you."

I pressed my forehead to hers, so we exchanged each ragged breath. "You don't have to beg, *sirenita*. You just have to say *yes*. I need to know that you want me. Let me in."

Tears spilled down her cheeks, but she wasn't crying from fear or pain. "Yes," she whispered. "Please, Andrés."

Her soft plea made something expand in my chest, and my cock jerked against her hip. "Samantha," I rasped her name and lined my aching shaft up with her slick entrance. "Do you feel what you do to me? You are so perfect."

I pressed my cockhead into her wet opening. Stars burst across my vision as her tight sheath gripped me, and she whimpered in discomfort. I couldn't stop myself or slow my progress. I had to claim her, to mark her with my seed.

I stroked her cheek with one hand and reached between us with the other, playing with her nipples to give her the little bites of pain that always drove her wild. Her whimper turned to a high whine, and her inner muscles relaxed as her arousal grew, easing my progress as I penetrated her in a steady slide.

Once I was fully seated inside her, I paused to allow her to adjust to my size. Her core contracted, struggling between pushing me out and welcoming me in. She touched the mark that had ruined my face again, tracing the furrow with her fingertips. I closed my eyes as bliss rolled over me. A shiver ran through my entire body, and my cock jerked inside her.

I withdrew slowly, using aching care with her untried body. I knew the moment my cockhead dragged across her g-spot. Her tight pussy relaxed, opening for me. Emboldened, she wrapped her legs around my hips and dug her heels into my ass, pulling me back inside her.

A rumbling shout left my lips at her shocking movement. I grasped her wrists, pinning them over her head with one hand while my other played with her breasts more harshly.

I pumped my hips faster and harder, clinging to my control by a thread. I struggled to hold back, not wanting to damage her perfect body.

"More," she begged, rocking her hips up to meet my thrusts. "Please, Andrés..."

Her pleading triggered me. With a snarl, my control snapped. I started fucking her in harsh, possessive strokes. My hand tightened around her wrists, pinning her beneath me so she couldn't escape.

She cried out, welcoming more. Her entire body tensed, her legs shaking around me.

"Come for me, *sirenita*," I ground out, the order barely intelligible.

She let go, her cunt squeezing my cock as she reached completion. Her scream mingled with my wild roar, and I spilled my seed deep inside her, branding her.

I held myself inside her as I emptied my cum into her. Our shaking and spent bodies remained locked together as my lips crashed down on hers. The kiss seared my soul, marking her as mine, even as I realized she'd claimed me, as well.

CHAPTER 16

I didn't lock Samantha to the bed the next morning, deciding to let her sleep late without disturbing her. I no longer feared that she would try to leave me. Besides, the elevator was still barred to her, so I didn't really have to worry about her escaping. Soon, Lauren would bring her the morning after pill and birth control shot. She'd make sure Samantha was fed and cared for.

Something clenched inside me at the idea of giving her the pill, but my rational mind told me that taking risks was beyond foolish.

I buried the discomfort as my driver pulled my car up to Cristian's building. I intended to find a way to convince him that Samantha was on the verge of cooperating, and I just needed a little more time. He'd granted me a reprieve yesterday, but I didn't expect it to hold long enough for me to convince Samantha that she had to comply with his demands. I wouldn't force her, but I had to make her cooperate, for her own good. I wouldn't allow any harm to come to her, no matter how stubborn she could be.

Unfortunately, Cristian wasn't home. Or if he was, he lied and refused to see me. I wouldn't put it past him to make me stew in my fear for Samantha for a few more days, at least.

Frustrated, I left to return to my penthouse. I didn't have much choice in the matter, and I wanted to see Samantha. I'd only left her an hour ago, but I needed to hold her to ease my worry. I needed to feel her soft body against mine and know she was safe from my brother.

As soon as I entered my building, the familiar sound of her scream chilled my bones. I didn't have time to wonder what she was doing on the ground floor. Blind panic flooded my mind, and I raced toward the sound of her terror.

A man was on top of her, pinning her slight body against the marble. She wore only one of my shirts, and he groped beneath it. His dick was exposed, pressing against her ass as he sought to violate her thrashing form.

Rage more visceral than I'd ever known surged through me, searing my veins. An inhuman sound reverberated through the hallway, and my hands closed around his shoulders before I realized I'd moved. I ripped him off her, flinging him against the wall. The back of his head cracked against the plaster, leaving a crimson smear as he slid to the ground.

Drawing his blood didn't remotely calm me. He'd touched her. He'd looked at her.

He would die in agony.

My fingers curved into claws, and I gouged his eyes out, his blood painting my hands as he screamed. I wrapped my hands around his neck, squeezing until his face darkened to purple, the empty sockets where his eyes had been staring up at me.

It wasn't nearly enough, but Samantha's keening cries cut through my blind fury. I grasped the man's skull and twisted. Bone crunched as his neck snapped. I hadn't exacted my full retribution, but the threat to her was eliminated.

I turned back to Samantha. She lay curled up on her side, her wide, pale eyes staring in horror as she gasped for breath. At first, I thought she was looking at the dead man's ruined face, but her gaze was focused on something far away. She wasn't present in the gory scene I'd created.

My rage evaporated into concern. How badly had he hurt her?

I reached for her with bloody hands, and she flinched away.

I hesitated, wary of spooking her. "*Cosita*, it's okay. You're safe now."

"Andrés?" Her voice was soft and strangely high, like a child. "I don't want him to touch my... I don't want this. I don't... I don't..."

She began to hyperventilate. I wrapped my arms around her, pulling her close to my chest. The vise around my heart eased slightly when she turned her face into me, her fingers curling into my shirt.

She sobbed, finally heaving in a breath. A stream of soothing Spanish dropped from my lips. I was barely aware of what I was saying, but I had to comfort her. All I could do was hold her until her terror passed.

Her eyes squeezed tightly shut, and she shook violently in my arms as I rushed her to the elevator and took her back into the safety of my penthouse. I carried her into the bedroom and sat on the edge of the bed, cuddling her close as I ran my hands over her chilled skin.

I stopped talking when she began whispering in a panicked litany, her voice still oddly soft. "Don't. I don't want you to touch my secret place. I don't want this, Uncle Robert. Please..." She shuddered, clinging to me more tightly.

My arms tensed around her, crushing her to my chest as my rage resurfaced, painting the back of my tongue with acid. Understanding sliced into my brain, the pain of my revelation making my gut twist. She wasn't thinking about the guard who'd assaulted her; she was lost in dark memories, ones she must have buried deep. They'd been triggered by the attack.

She hadn't been frightened of my touch in our first days together because she was an innocent virgin. Her nervous tics and anxiety weren't natural parts of her personality. Her uncle had hurt her when she was young. The fear in her high-pitched voice and her horrified words revealed her trauma.

"Where is your uncle now?" I couldn't keep the growl from my words, even though I knew I should be gentle with her. The way I'd mutilated the guard downstairs was nothing compared to the torture I'd inflict on the twisted man who'd violated her as a child.

"What?" She blinked, her eyes finally focusing on me as she surfaced from her foul memories.

"You said..." My voice garbled on a snarl. "You mentioned *Uncle Robert*. Where can I find him?"

She shuddered at his name. "Why?"

"I'm going to kill him for you, Samantha," I swore. Maybe I'd let her watch as I tore him apart. His screams for mercy might bring her some peace.

My body vibrated with barely-restrained violence, and my hand firmed on her head where I'd been stroking her hair.

"He's dead," she replied hollowly as her eyes slid out of focus again. "I cried at his funeral. I didn't know why I was so upset. I fucking cried over him."

"How old were you? How old were you when he—?" My teeth snapped closed. I swallowed against the metallic tang that filled my mouth.

"Nine," she said softly. "But I forgot. How could I forget?"

She trembled, and her gaze found mine, wide and imploring. "I'm sorry," she choked out. "I'm sorry I tried to leave. I thought you didn't care about me. I thought—"

"You thought I didn't care?" I demanded, my muscles tensing and rippling around her. "Do you know what it did to me, seeing another man hurting you, touching you? Seeing you broken and crying when you remembered what—?" I cut myself off again, tasting a fresh wash of blood on my tongue as I bit the inside of my cheek.

Something horrible occurred to me. I'd thought she'd enjoyed my claim over her when she'd finally given herself to me last night. Had I only seen what I wanted to see? "Did I hurt you?" I asked, my voice strangely thick. "Last night. Did I hurt you?"

"No." She touched her fingertips to my cheek, tracing the line of my scar just as she'd done when I'd been buried deep inside her.

"Then why? Why would you leave me?"

"I woke up, and you were gone." Her cheeks colored with something like shame. "I didn't have my collar. Then Lauren brought me the pill and the birth control shot, and I thought I must have imagined... I thought you didn't care."

Something vicious and hungry threatened to rise up and claim my emotions, but I shoved it down. I didn't want to scare her with the ferocity of the strange feelings that surged within me. "Do you want to get pregnant?" I asked, my tone carefully steady and even.

"I... No. Not...not right now."

Not right now.

Samantha wanted a child. An image of her bearing *my* child, her belly round from my seed, softened the last of my tumultuous emotions. It was an insane vision, one that could never be. That didn't stop me from coveting it.

"That's for the best." I tried to convince myself by speaking aloud. "You need to take the pill."

"I... Okay," she agreed.

I cuddled her closer, my heart softening. "You were upset because I was gone? Then I'll stay. Do you want your collar back on? I thought you resented it."

"I, um, I got used to it. I like it," she amended, her confession holding the ring of truth. "It makes me feel safe. Like you're with me, even when you're not here. But I'd rather not be chained to the bed."

I traced the line of her jaw with reverence. I wanted to see my collar back around her throat, too. "You can have your collar, but I'm not going anywhere. I left this morning to see my brother. I was convincing him to give me more time with you."

"Oh." She seemed surprised, as though that possibility hadn't occurred to her. "Thank you." She looked into my eyes, beseeching. "I still don't want to work for him. It goes against everything I believe in."

"I know. I've read enough about your superheroes to see that."

"Then what are we going to do?"

I sighed, uncharacteristic anxiety gripping me. "I don't know yet. I'll figure something out."

"*We'll* figure something out," she declared.

My Samantha might be fragile, but she was clever and brave and fierce. My uncertainty melted away, my worries dissipating into awe. I cupped her cheeks, holding her carefully as I pressed my lips to hers.

Despite the horror she'd just faced, she softened, opening for me and inviting me in. She felt safe in my arms, and my own sense of safety settled over me as I fell into her, allowing her to claim all my senses and quiet my feral instincts.

CHAPTER 17

I held Samantha through two nightmares, stroking her sweat-slicked skin as she cried. I hated the fact that her uncle was already dead, that I couldn't mutilate him with my bare hands for what he'd done to her.

But she seemed content enough this morning, curled up in her usual place in my lap as I fed her breakfast. She playfully nipped at my fingers on the final bite of bacon, but the saucy action didn't incite my need to dominate and punish as it would have in the beginning. Instead, an indulgent smile curved my lips.

Mí sirenita was herself again, and I was far too pleased with the sight of her soft smile to even consider causing her pain.

Despite her improving mood, I had no intention of leaving her side anytime soon. I had to stay to ensure she was comforted and cared for, but holding her soothed me, too. I still didn't know how I was going to get us out of this mess with my brother. Feeling her soft skin against mine eased my worry, reminding me that she was safe and under my protection.

I trailed my fingers along her bare throat. "Yesterday, you said you wanted your collar. Do you still want it?"

"Yes," she said immediately, leaning into my touch.

I beamed at her. "Then you'll have it."

I lifted her off my lap and went to the chest of drawers where I kept her kinky toys. I held the slim strip of black leather in my hands, rubbing my thumbs across it with reverence. The collar belonged to her, and she belonged to me.

"Kneel for me." It was an order, but it came out in an almost plaintive tone. I'd never demanded this of her before, and I wanted her to choose to take the supplicant pose. I wanted her to choose *me*.

She sank to her knees before me. Surprise and pleasure raced through my system when she spread her thighs wide and placed her arms behind her back, holding her elbows in opposite hands. The position thrust out her breasts and exposed her glistening pussy, offering me everything. She bowed her head in submission, baring the back of her neck so I could buckle the collar in place.

I remained silent for a long minute, robbed of words, of breath. Finally, I brushed my fingers over the top of her head, petting her to communicate my pride and pleasure.

My fingers trailed down her hair to explore the line of her jaw. I curled two fingers beneath her chin, so I could look down into her lovely eyes. They glowed flame-blue as she stared up at me. Her devotion was even more breathtaking than I ever could have imagined.

"You are so beautiful," I said hoarsely. "So perfect. *Mi sirenita.*"

She flushed, a small smile playing around her lush lips. "So are you."

I regarded her with awe. "You're not scared of me? I don't frighten you?"

"No," she promised. "I'm not scared of you, Andrés."

I drew in a shuddering breath. She didn't find me repulsive. It wasn't just my scars that had disgusted her in the beginning; she'd been horrified by my touch, by my claims of ownership. Now, she gave herself to me willingly. I'd fantasized about having her in this position for long weeks, but I couldn't have imagined the heat that flooded my chest in response to her show of affection.

I brought the strip of leather up to her throat and secured the collar around her neck. She blew out a long, relieved sigh as peace settled over her.

"Mine," I declared, tracing the line of the collar.

"Yours," she replied with fervor.

I bent and grasped her waist, lifting her to her feet and guiding her back toward the bed. "Are you ready for me?" My voice was strained with need. I craved to drive into her wet heat and seal our connection, but I was wary of the trauma she'd faced yesterday.

Her eyes were clear of fear or doubt. "Always," she promised. "I want you."

I groaned my desire, and I grasped her ankles to tug her ass to the edge of the mattress. Resting her calves on my shoulders, I remained standing as I gripped her hips and drove into her in one ruthless thrust. She cried out as her tight sheath gripped me with exquisite pressure.

I paused, concerned that I'd hurt her by being too rough.

She placed her hands atop mine, curling my fingers deeper into her hips. "Please, Andrés…"

A low sound of longing left my chest, and I withdrew from her before slowly pushing all the way back in. I claimed her in long, careful strokes, playing with her clit until she eased around me. Her body adjusted to accept my size and ruthless thrusts, flowering open for me.

This wasn't fucking. This was pure, perfect possession. Samantha owned me, body and soul.

※

I DOZED OFF AFTER WE BOTH REACHED COMPLETION, SATED and spent, but I roused when she tensed in my arms.

"What are you thinking about?" I brushed away the furrow in her brow.

She propped up from where she'd been resting on my chest.

"I thought you were asleep," she said instead of answering.

"I was, but I could hear you thinking." I gave her a languorous smile and brushed her hair back from her cheek. "You do have a very busy mind."

"Let me guess. You're going to help me make it go all quiet and blissful?" She might have spoken with asperity, but the words were tinged with longing.

"I can, if that's what you need," I said. "But I like your clever brain."

She blinked. "You do?"

"Of course. You challenge me. I find you fascinating. Did you not know?"

"I..." She swallowed, but her voice still came out a touch hoarse. "No. I guess I didn't know that. Not for sure."

I traced the line of her cheekbone. "I should tell you more often, then."

Samantha had to know how much I treasured her, especially her quick mind. She always managed to surprise me, and I delighted in her company. She was so much more than simply my sex object, a toy for my own perverse pleasures.

Her eyes began to shine, and I frowned. "Did I make you sad?"

"No," she said, her voice catching. "That...means a lot to me."

"Then why are you crying?"

"Because I don't want to leave," she whispered. "I don't want to leave you, but I should."

My jaw firmed as possessive anger flared, tinged with hurt and fear. "You're still thinking about how to escape?"

"No," she said quickly. "I mean, yes. I mean, I want to get out of working for Cristian. I don't want to spend my days locked in this penthouse, fearing the day your brother comes for me. And if you really value my mind like you say you do, you won't want that for me, either."

I scowled. "This is the safest place for you. You should fear Cristian. This is the only way I know how to protect you."

"This isn't the life I want," she said, desperate. "I can't stay trapped in a cage forever. I need to do something meaningful. I need to help people."

"You've been reading too many comic books. You can't be a superhero, Samantha. You're far too breakable, and I won't put you at risk."

"I can be a hero," she asserted, her eyes sparking as her anger rose. "I used to do it every day, before you took me. I had a life. I had purpose."

I wrapped my arms around her and rolled, settling my weight on her. She couldn't escape me. She couldn't leave me. "Your life is with me now. And my purpose is to protect you."

"You won't be able to keep me from Cristian forever," she reasoned. "Let me call my friends at the Bureau. If you go into hiding before they come for Cristian, I can cover your tracks. They won't find you. You'll be safe."

She wanted to send me away. That wasn't going to happen. I'd never allow her to be parted from me.

"And what about you?" I demanded, my jealous anger

rising. "Where will you be while I'm in hiding? Will you go back to your friends? To your Dex?" I spat the man's name.

"I...I don't know," she whispered.

"You're *mine*," I snarled. My cock stiffened against her, pressing at the entrance to her cunt. "And you're not going anywhere. Not back to your Dex. And not to my brother. You belong to me."

"I'm yours," she agreed. "But I can't—"

I cut her off with a merciless kiss as I drove inside her, reminding her of my claim, our connection. I fucked her hard, possessing her with deep, merciless strokes. She rocked her body against mine, meeting me with her own fierce need. Samantha didn't want to leave me. She was just confused, still caught up in the fantasy that she could save the day. Regardless of her wishes, I'd never put her at risk. And I'd certainly never agree to a plan that separated us.

I joined our bodies with ruthless thrusts. I'd drown her in brutal ecstasy until she realized she couldn't live without me.

CHAPTER 18

I woke her early the next morning with a soft kiss against her neck. She turned her head, offering me better access. I rumbled my approval, nipping at her. She pressed her ass back against my erection in wanton invitation. We were both naked, nestled under the sheets together. I'd allowed her to rest, studying her peaceful features for a long while. Now, I was too hungry for her to allow her to continue sleeping.

"It's time for your punishment," I murmured in her ear.

"Punishment?" she asked, her tone slurred and sleepy rather than sharp with alarm. "Why?"

"You tried to escape," I reminded her, more aroused than upset. "That was very naughty, *gatita*. I've owed you a punishment for days."

"Oh. Okay," she agreed easily.

I kissed the tender spot I'd bitten. "Good girl."

I gave her a few minutes to stir and go through her morning routine. When she emerged from the bathroom, her cheeks were pink and her eyes were sparkling.

I beckoned to her from where I stood in the threshold to the sitting room. "Come."

She came to me without hesitation, her expression serene rather than fearful. She knew pain was coming, but she wasn't terrified, as she'd once been. I'd trained her to enjoy erotic pain. Or perhaps she'd always been this way. Perhaps she'd been built just for me, my perfect Samantha.

She placed her hand in mine and walked with me into our playroom, utterly docile and willing to accept whatever punishment I chose to dole out. Her contrition for trying to leave me was genuine, and she accepted that she deserved discipline for her rash actions. We'd both feel better when she released her tears.

She followed where I led, trusting me implicitly even as we entered the room that had once terrified her. I stopped when we reached the far wall, next to my suspension frame. She enjoyed being bound, and I needed to see her trapped and helpless to resist me.

I selected a coil of crimson rope that hung on the wall by the wooden frame, and she shivered in anticipation. We'd both derive pleasure from this punishment. I'd make sure of it. I'd never hurt her with impunity again, would never whip her for my own selfish desires if she was unwilling. Her trust was my most precious possession, and I wouldn't risk losing it.

She took a deep breath and released it on a long, shuddering sigh as I began to wind the rope around her, forming a harness that framed her chest. I took extra time and care to create a lattice pattern above her breasts, adorning my pretty pet with the red rope. Her pale skin took on a pearlescent sheen beneath it, contrasting with the vibrant color.

When I finished tightening the rope around her chest, I drew her arms behind her, binding them together from shoulder to wrist. Her back arched, making her breasts stand out proudly. Her pink nipples peaked for my attention.

I didn't stimulate them. Not yet. I'd leave her aching for my sensual touch, until her body thrummed with such need that she couldn't discern pain from pleasure.

I took another length of rope and threaded it through the bindings around her arms before feeding it through the large metal ring embedded in the wooden beam above her. I pulled, forcing her arms up behind her, so she had no choice but to bend at the waist to alleviate the pressure. She spread her legs in wanton invitation, her back arched as she offered her pussy to me.

My cock stiffened, aching to get inside her. I mastered the animal urge to drive into her wet heat. She needed more pain before I could sate myself. And I needed to hear her scream her apology, her promise to never try to escape me again.

I stepped back, simply admiring her without touching, until she whined for my attention. Satisfied that she was needy and desperate, I went back to the wall, where implements for her torment were arranged in neat rows.

I held up the rubber-tipped nipple clamps so she could see them clearly. The light caught on the metal, making the chain that connected them shine silver. Little red gemstones dangled from the chain. They'd look so pretty adorning my sweet Samantha's tormented breasts.

Her eyes tightened with her own hunger as she studied the clamps. I'd gotten her worked up enough that she'd welcome any sexual stimulation, pleasure or pain.

Her lashes fluttered as I cupped her breasts, feeling her nipples harden to tight buds beneath my palms. She tried to lean into me, seeking more contact. The ropes held her immobile, the bonds I'd created denying her any control over her body.

Instead of struggling for freedom, she relaxed, falling into my thrall. Rewarding her submission, I began to roll her nipples between my fingers, tugging and pinching to get her accustomed to the discomfort that would be inflicted by the clamps.

When she whimpered and wiggled, torn between wanting relief and craving more, I caught her tight peaks in the clamps. She cried out as I turned the screws on the sides, slowly increasing the pressure to guarantee they'd stay firmly in place. I tugged on the chain, and she hissed out a breath, struggling to adjust to the pinch.

I watched her pinched expression soften as she settled into acceptance. I flicked the gems that dangled from the chain, making them glitter under the crimson lights. She moaned, and her eyes slid closed as her head dropped forward in surrender.

Her short, panting breaths followed me as I retrieved the crop from where it hung on the wall. When I stepped behind her, I was met with a delicious view of her soaked and swollen cunt. Her body practically vibrated with need, but I wouldn't provide her with ecstatic release just yet. She had to release her guilt first, had to swear that she would never again try to leave me.

When I snapped the crop against her ass, she blew out a long sigh and relaxed, accepting her punishment. I started flicking it against her skin, painting her flesh pink as I spread out the heat.

Even as lust raged through my body, something darker pulsed through my veins. Memories of the guard on top of her, violating her, flooded my mind. Fury burned through me at the thought of another man's hands on her. The sound of her horrified sobs as she remembered her childhood trauma at the hands of her uncle echoed through my mind, driving me near madness. No one would touch her ever again. I'd kill anyone who tried. I'd do anything to protect my Samantha, including hurting her. I'd eradicate her foolish plans to separate us in order to evade my brother. I had to keep her close to know she was safe from him.

I cracked the crop against her upper thigh, causing her to cry out.

"Never leave me again," I commanded, my tone fierce and desperate. I delivered another cruel blow to brand her with a burning sting. "You don't get to leave me. Never leave me."

"I won't." Her voice hitched on a sob. "I won't leave you. I love you."

My heart stopped in my chest, squeezing too hard to continue beating. The crop slipped from my hand, clattering to the ground. My pulse thundered back to life, pounding in my head as something hot and bright seared away some of the darkness that blackened my soul.

My hands curved into her ass, spreading her wide. She was soaked for me, her body ready to yield to me. Just as she was yielding her heart.

"Say it again," I ground out.

"I love you," she sobbed. "Please, Andrés."

I snarled and slammed into her, thrusting deep into her wet channel. "Tell me," I demanded, driving into her with ruthless abandon. "Tell me again. Don't stop."

"I love you!" she cried out. "I love you, I love you…" The words left her in a litany, over and over again as I fucked her hard. I became drunk on the foreign sentiment. It filled me up, sending me soaring higher than I'd ever attained through inflicting pain.

I was close to coming undone. I needed her to shatter with me. I reached beneath her and pinched her clit.

"Andrés!" she screamed out my name as her orgasm claimed

her. My raw shout echoed around us, and I filled her with my cum. I kept pounding into her, riding out the last of our pleasure with brutal force.

Finally, I stopped, completely spent. I withdrew from her and carefully removed the clamps from her nipples. She whimpered as blood rushed back to the abused buds, but I shushed her and soothed away the sting with my fingers. Her whimper dropped to a moan, and I continued caressing her until I was certain her discomfort had passed.

I couldn't bring myself to take the time to untie her, so I grabbed my blunt-tipped shears and cut her down. She sagged against me, and I held her carefully as I lowered us both onto the cool tiled floor.

"Mine," I murmured, tracing the contours of her soft body. "All mine."

She rubbed her face against the crook of my neck, her hot tears branding me. She licked at them, tasting the salt of her love on my skin. A low sound of animal satisfaction left my chest. It seemed to incite her need, even though she'd attained orgasm only minutes ago.

She shifted on my lap, turning to face me so she straddled my hips. Despite my recent release, I began to stiffen for her once again. Her bold touch made my mouth water with hunger. She no longer reluctantly submitted to my physical manipulation of her body; she initiated contact because she craved me, as well.

She lowered herself onto my hard cock and captured my lips with hers, demanding my kiss. I surrendered to pleasure as she began to ride me. My hands closed around her hips, guiding her to fuck me at the pace I desired, even though she was on top.

She screamed out my name, her fingernails scoring my back as she came. She marked me, owned me. Loved me.

CHAPTER 19

Only a few hours had passed since Samantha had declared her love for me, and I couldn't stop playing the words through my mind, remembering them in her breathy voice. I'd never heard the words from a woman I'd trained. I hadn't heard them at all since I'd lost my sister and grandmother. The emotions expanding in my chest threatened to cut off my breath and stall my heart. The sensation was so keen, it was almost painful.

I hadn't wanted to stop touching Samantha, but I knew I needed to see my brother. I'd convince him to give me more time with her, even if I had to beg on my knees. I'd do anything to keep her safe with me. We didn't have a plan yet, so all I could do was make Cristian believe that Samantha was close to cooperating with his demands.

I'd called my brother to set up a meeting, and he'd accepted. Now, I braced myself to face him as my driver pulled the car into the parking garage. I'd gotten caught in traffic, and it had taken me nearly half an hour to get here. Cristian wouldn't appreciate my tardiness. If I was going to beg for him to spare Samantha, I might as well beg for forgiveness as well. What had been left of my pride didn't exist anymore. Not when it came to protecting Samantha. Nothing was more important than her safety and happiness.

"You're late," Cristian commented when I was admitted to his office. His guards flanked me, too close. The back of my neck prickled with awareness, and my muscles rippled with the barely suppressed urge to defend myself.

I summoned up a calm demeanor, but I couldn't quite clear the tension from my body. "I apologize. Traffic," I offered in explanation.

Cristian's malicious smile set my teeth on edge. "Don't worry about it. The longer you're separated from your little whore, the longer she has to learn that there are consequences for resisting me."

My blood ran cold. "What?"

I took a breath, reminding myself that none of my men had permission to access my penthouse anymore.

Cristian's smile curved with cruelty. "I ordered Lauren to give her a taste of Bliss. Samantha is probably already in my brothel, being a good little whore. You didn't really think I'd let you keep her all to yourself, did you? Especially when you can't seem to break her properly."

I snarled and surged forward, all fear of my brother forgotten as rage washed my vision red. The guards at my back were ready. They grabbed my arms, wrenching me back. My fury gave me strength to shake them off, but the barrel of the gun that pressed against the back of my head made me freeze.

I couldn't let them kill me. If they did, I couldn't rescue Samantha.

"I wonder how many men will fuck her before she agrees to

cooperate," Cristian mused. "Or maybe that won't be enough to break her. Maybe she likes being used like a slut. Maybe that's why you're so attached to her, and why you haven't been able to break her. Tell me, little brother, have you made sure she's good at sucking cock? She's not much to look at, but she'd probably be prettier with my cum on her face."

A feral roar ripped from my chest, and I tried to twist away from the hands that held me. The gun pressed harder against my skull, reminding me that I couldn't risk my life. I had to get back to Samantha.

Cristian made a dismissive wave, as though he hadn't heard my anguished outburst. "If she enjoys my brothel too much, I'll just make sure she doesn't get relief next time I dose her. She'll break, one way or another." He tilted his chin, considering me. "Are you really going to attack me, *hermanito?*" he asked with soft amusement.

"Let me go," I growled, trembling as adrenaline coursed through my system without an outlet.

"Fine." Cristian grinned with sadistic pleasure. "You can go check on her progress. Let me know if she's ready to work for me when she's finished servicing my men. Bring her to me when she's sobered up."

The gun left my head, and the guards released me. Only the urgent need to get back to Samantha kept me from tearing my brother apart. I couldn't let another minute pass before racing back to her. Cristian's laughter followed me out of the room and down the hall.

I ran through my brother's building and out into the parking garage, flinging myself into my black Jaguar and ordering my driver to speed back to my home. My body vibrated with violent tension as I rode in the backseat, impotent and powerless to defend her immediately. If I could have gotten to her faster by running across the city, I would have. As it was, all I could do was wait and try not to punch through the car window to siphon off some of my rage.

When I reached my building, I took the stairs two at a time to get to the third floor, unable to wait for the elevator. I had to stay in motion, had to get to her.

I burst into the brothel, kicking the door off its hinges. Samantha was naked, surrounded by men. Ben—the boy who'd threatened her in my suite when I'd first captured her—fondled her breasts. His eyes barely moved from her body to my face by the time I closed the distance between us. I bracketed his skull with my hands and snapped his neck with one jerk of my arms.

I dropped his lifeless body and rounded on the other men. They all backed away. I positioned myself in front of her, blocking her nakedness from their lascivious stares.

"Who else touched her?" I roared, preparing to tear my way through all of them. "Who?"

"N-no one." Lauren's voice was a high squeak. "I'm sorry, Master Andrés. I'm so sorry."

"Do not speak to me." I bit out each word. The girl had betrayed me. She'd let them look at Samantha. She'd let the boy touch what was mine. "You're lucky I don't snap your neck, too."

Lauren heaved out a despairing sob and wisely fled the room.

"*Master* Andrés," Samantha said with distaste. "I don't like that she calls you *Master*."

The sound of my name on her tongue called my full attention to her. My fury didn't dissipate, but the need to shield her from their eyes overcame my need to destroy every man in the room. My muscles were still tense with the imperative to punish, but I handled her carefully as I picked her up and carried her out of the brothel. The smell of sex followed us, and I knew Samantha was experiencing artificial lust as a result of the Bliss. She'd have no control over her body right now. She'd obey any order, do any depraved act that was asked of her.

"You're not hers," she murmured as I stepped into the elevator. She snuggled into my chest, rubbing against me like a needy kitten. "You're mine. My Master." She giggled. "Isn't that funny? I always wanted a Master. And you're mine."

My stomach twisted.

Master.

I'd craved to hear that title fall from her lips. Now, it made nausea curl up my throat. Once, I'd desired her mindless devotion, her absolute, unquestioning obedience. The little sex doll in my arms would comply with my every deviant order.

But it wouldn't be real. She wouldn't be willing. She wouldn't be *Samantha.*

And she'd hate me for using her when she had no control.

I'd hate myself.

We arrived at my penthouse, and I carried her to the bed. I tried to set her down. Her nearness and the scent of her arousal stoked the madness that threatened to overtake my thoughts. My body was conditioned to want her, to respond to her carnal desire. My cock stirred, even as acid coated my tongue.

She locked her arms around my neck before I could pull away. "Touch me, Master," she breathed. "Please. I need you."

Master. She was behaving like something out of my darkest wet dream. Anguish churned in my gut, and I pried her arms away from me, pinning her wrists to the pillow so she couldn't grab at me.

She whimpered her desire and arched her back, seeking stimulation.

"I can't," I rasped. "I can't be with you like this."

Holding her wrists in place with one hand, I smoothed her hair back from her sweat-dampened cheek with the other in an attempt to soothe her.

She nuzzled her face into my palm with a sigh. "My Master. Mine."

"You don't know what you're saying," I said tightly. "I'm sorry. I'm so sorry. I wasn't here. I didn't know. When Cristian told me..." My jaw clenched as I recalled my brother's disgusting words, his laughter as I ran away. "I should have killed him. I should have fucking killed him."

"You're upset," she observed. "Don't be upset. Make love to me, Master."

"Don't call me that," I growled, the breathy honorific tearing me up inside.

"But you are," she declared. "I love you, my Master. My Andrés."

I cupped her cheek in my hand. "Please, don't say that. Don't." Something hot and sharp pricked at the corners of my eyes.

"Don't be sad." My sweet Samantha tried to ease my anguish.

I blinked hard, and something wet spilled down my face. It dropped on her cheek, glistening against her porcelain skin.

"Make love to me," she urged again, arching her back and lifting her breasts in wanton invitation. "I need you." There was a thread of desperation in the words. I remembered how Cristian had threatened to torture her by dosing her with Bliss and leaving her without release. I wouldn't let her suffer.

But I couldn't fuck her, either. I couldn't.

I pressed a tender kiss against her forehead. "All right, *cosita*," I murmured. "I'll help you. I know you must be aching."

"I am. My pussy hurts."

"I'll kiss it better," I promised.

"Thank you," she sighed in relief. She lifted her face to mine, seeking my lips.

I turned my face away. "Not your lips," I forced out. "I can't when you're like this."

"But you said you'd kiss me," she whined. "You said— Oh!"

Her complaints ended on a sharp cry when I drew her tight nipple into my mouth. I was careful not to use my teeth, treating her gently. Her body would be hypersensitive, and all I wanted was to ease her pain, not inflict more.

"Please," she begged raggedly, lifting her hips to seek stimulation.

Resolving to do what was best for her, I released her wrists and pressed my hand down on her belly, pinning her in place so she couldn't continue to tempt me with her helpless writhing. I hated my arousal, my weakness. I couldn't help wanting her when she was hot and needy and calling me *Master*.

But this was about helping her, not fulfilling my own sick desires.

I joined her on the bed, settling my shoulders between her thighs. I'd never kissed her pussy before. I'd told myself she existed for my pleasure, and I'd always felt there was something subservient about worshipping a woman's cunt.

When I'd gone to face Cristian, I'd realized I had no pride when it came to Samantha's wellbeing. There was nothing I wouldn't do for her.

Her pale blue eyes watched me with rapt fascination as I lowered my head between her legs. I touched my tongue to her wet folds, and a low groan left my chest. I never could have imagined how decadent she'd taste, how soft she'd feel under my mouth.

Her fingers speared into my hair, and she pulled my face closer to her sex. "So good," she panted. "More."

I didn't need the command to continue exploring her sweet perfection. I traced the line of her slit, licking up to her sensitive clit. She thrashed against my mouth, and my hands closed around her thighs on a growl, my fingers digging into her flesh as primal desire overtook my mind. Why had I denied myself this mouthwatering pleasure for so long? I should have known my Samantha was perfect for me in every way.

My tongue circled her clit, applying firm pressure against the needy bud. Her thighs quivered in my hold, but I kept her pinned in place so I could devour her in the way I wanted. My cock ached with the need to part her soaked folds, to stretch and fill her until her tight muscles contracted around me. Kissing her like this was exquisite torment, tearing me between the desire to continue pleasuring her and the need to fuck her hard and deep.

"Please," she choked on a sob. "I need you inside me. It hurts. Please, Master..."

I couldn't let her suffer.

And I couldn't hold myself back. Not now that I had her taste on my tongue. Not now that I knew what it meant to give myself to her in every way, just as she'd given herself to me.

Master. The title burned into my brain, searing away rational thought.

I pressed one final kiss against her clit before I settled my body atop hers. I freed my cock from my slacks, but I managed to pause at her hot entrance, the last shred of decency in my mind whispering to me that what I was about to do was wrong.

"You shouldn't call me that," I ground out. "You really shouldn't."

She wrapped her legs around me, her heels pressing against my ass as she drew me inside. "My Master," she moaned.

A deep, pained sound tore from my chest. I craved this. I'd craved it ever since I'd first captured her. She wasn't in her right mind, but I was going to fuck her anyway, because the woman beneath me fulfilled all my darkest fantasies.

She needs me, I reasoned. *She's hurting.*

But I knew the truth: I was selfish and possessive to the point of crazed obsession, and I couldn't stop myself now.

I braced my arms on either side of her head and began to thrust deep inside her, claiming her with almost vicious force. My forehead dropped to touch hers, and I stared down into her lust-clouded eyes.

"Forgive me," I whispered, even as I slammed my cock back inside her with enough force to rock her entire body. "Forgive me, *sirenita*."

She didn't seem aware of my words as she came undone on a scream. Her fingers tangled in my hair, and she pulled my face down to hers so she could capture my lips. The intimate contact and feel of her inner walls squeezing my dick sent me over the edge, and I shouted my release against her mouth. Wet heat leaked from my eyes even as my seed branded her insides.

She shuddered and groaned beneath me. Then, her taut muscles relaxed, her tongue stilling against mine.

I pulled out of her body as her eyes fluttered closed. My stomach lurched as she slipped into unconsciousness, the full weight of my disgusting actions slamming into me.

"Forgive me," I begged on a rasp. She didn't respond.

I pushed off her and quickly stripped out of my clothes. After ensuring that her breaths were deep and even, I rushed into the bathroom and turned on the shower. The water was close to boiling hot when I stepped under it, but I welcomed the discomfort. I deserved to feel pain after finding pleasure with Samantha when she was drugged and mindless.

I stayed under the burning spray for a long time, until I finally accepted the obvious course of action open to me. There was only one way to protect Samantha from my brother. And from myself.

CHAPTER 20

A few hours after slipping into unconsciousness, she finally stirred. I hadn't been able to stop staring at her, desperate to memorize every curve and slope of her lovely face. She was still naked, but I'd put on my suit; armor between us.

She sat up and reached for me. "Thank you."

I flinched away, my gut churning. "Don't thank me. I fucked you while you were high out of your mind. I violated you."

"No," she said fiercely, grabbing my hand when I tried to retreat farther. I didn't pull away this time. The warmth of her slender fingers around mine felt too good. "I begged you to. I needed you to. I was hurting. You helped me."

I turned my face away, unable to look at her. Shame licked at my insides, but I still held her hand fast. "You shouldn't have called me Master," I said hollowly. "You shouldn't have done that. I couldn't—" I put an end to my pathetic excuses. "I'm not blaming you. You didn't know what you were saying. It's not your fault. None of this is your fault. You didn't ask to be trapped with me. You didn't ask to be beaten and raped."

Her fingers firmed around mine. "You didn't rape me," she declared hotly. "Don't you dare call it that. Don't you dare." She swiped frustrated tears from her cheeks. "You were helping me. I trusted you to help me. I love you, Andrés. And I meant what I said. You're my Master."

"Don't call me that," I barked.

She didn't shrink away from the ire incited by my self-loathing. Instead, she scooted across the bed so she could get in my face. "You did nothing wrong," she swore. "You saved me. You've been saving me this whole time. You've been protecting me from Cristian. He would have—"

"He would have what?" I shouted over her. "Ordered Lauren to slip you Bliss and whore you out? That's what he wanted, Samantha. He wanted you to scream in pleasure while they violated you. He wanted them to send you back to me, broken and used. He wanted to punish me for my failure. I should have killed him." My brother's cruel, mocking laughter rolled through my mind. "But I didn't. I ran back to you as soon as he told me. He fucking laughed while I ran away from him."

"You got back to me in time." She cupped my face in her hands, trying to capture my attention. "You saved me. You protected me."

I grabbed her wrists. I squeezed hard enough to bruise, but I couldn't bring myself to force her hands away from my face.

"I can't protect you," I rasped. "I'm a coward. You deserve better than me."

"I don't, and you're not," she asserted. "I want to be with you, Andrés. You're not a coward."

"I'm afraid of him," I admitted on a bitter whisper.

"I know," she said softly. "And I understand."

"You don't. My face..." I shuddered and cut my eyes away from hers.

She touched my scar, applying enough pressure to guide my gaze back to hers. "Tell me what he did to you." It was a steady command, compelling me to confess my darkest secrets. I owed her this. I owed her everything, after what I'd done to her.

"It was three years ago," I began, the words bleeding out of me. "Cristian made a deal with some Russians. He started dealing in Bliss. I'd never dared to challenge him, but I hated it. It was too far, too much. He was selling women, just like he sold my sister. So, I decided to stage a coup and take over the organization myself. I'd always been the one to keep the business running. I could do it without him. My life would be better without him."

I paused, the phantom ice of Cristian's knife slicing across my chest as memories threatened to suck me under. I'd never talked to anyone about this. I'd barely spoken to anyone at all since he'd disfigured me. Now, my words were no longer required at meetings with allies and enemies; my ruined face was threat enough of Cristian's retribution against those who crossed him.

"He found out," she surmised, quietly urging me to continue.

My jaw clenched. "One of my men betrayed me. Cristian came for me before I made a move against him. He strung me up in front of all of our people—the ones he hadn't killed for following me. He cut me. He made me scream. He humiliated me. Then, he stitched me up himself to make sure the marks lasted." An acidic tang washed over my tongue, and I swallowed back my nausea.

Samantha's face was pale, devoid of the pretty flush I loved so much. "Andrés..." She said my name shakily before leaning in and brushing her lips over the deep furrow in my cheek. "I love you," she said with the weight of an oath. "We're going to get away from your brother. Together."

Anguish twined around my heart. Yes, I'd get her away from Cristian. "I have something for you," I said instead of responding to her fervent declaration.

I pulled her into my lap, holding her close with one arm around her shoulders. She sighed and pressed her cheek into my neck, trusting me completely.

I reached around her with my free hand and picked up the syringe from the cart beside the bed. Her brow furrowed with confusion as I uncapped it, but she didn't cringe away or struggle.

"Lauren already gave me the birth control shot," she said.

I tightened my hold around her, trapping her in place as I slid the needle into her arm. "It's not birth control. I should have sent you away hours ago, but I had to see your lovely eyes one last time."

"What are you...?" Her question trailed off as her eyes drooped closed, the sedative taking effect.

"I can't protect you." I pressed one last kiss against her motionless lips. "Goodbye, *sirenita. Te amo.*"

I loved her. I loved her, so I had to let her go. I'd face Cristian's retribution later, but I had to get her to safety before he came for her.

I dressed her in one of my shirts. It swallowed her slim frame, covering her well enough. Still, I slipped her into a pair of slacks I'd gotten from Lauren. I couldn't bear the thought of anyone's eyes on her. Not even my own. If I allowed myself to continue holding her and caressing her bare skin, I'd never be able to release her.

When she was dressed, I removed the collar from her throat. I tucked it into my pocket, unwilling to shut it away in the drawer where it used to belong. It belonged to her now.

I'd thought it marked her as mine, but I couldn't keep her. That had been a fantasy from the very beginning. Cristian had never intended to allow me to keep her forever, and now, I had to let her go if I was going to save her from him.

I picked her up and carried her out of our bedroom, past our playroom, and into the elevator. We rode down to the garage, and I couldn't help staring down at her, drinking her in. I longed to look into her lovely eyes, but that wasn't an option. Soon, I wouldn't be able to look at her at all. Wouldn't be able to hold her. Wouldn't be able to hurt her.

This was what was best for her, in every way. She deserved to be free of me, safe from my darker impulses.

The elevator stopped at the parking garage, and I carried her to my black BMW, choosing the least flashy car I owned. I didn't want to draw attention to myself. I'd already had my people disable the security cameras at the motel where I intended to drop her, and my tinted windows would prevent traffic cams from catching her where I set her in the passenger seat.

I got in the car and started it up, driving slowly to the outskirts of the city. The motel I'd selected was nondescript, the randomness of the location ensuring she'd be safe here for a short time.

I'd instructed one of my men to check into the room, so I wouldn't be seen by the staff. He was waiting for me, opening the door when I knocked. I ordered him to leave as I carried Samantha inside and laid her down on the bed. I tucked her under the covers, just as I'd done every night since I'd forcibly brought her into my life.

I ran my fingers through her silken hair one last time. She didn't stir.

My hand clenched to a fist, and I forced myself to pull away. I didn't allow myself to linger any longer. It wouldn't be long before Cristian figured out what I'd done, and I needed her to be safely back with her fellow FBI agents by the time that happened.

I left the motel room, feeling the sound of the door locking behind me deep in my chest. I walked stiffly back to my car where I'd left it across the parking lot. When I slid back into the driver's seat, I took a deep breath and shoved down the anguish that threatened to choke me.

Clearing my throat, I put in the call to the cops, leaving the anonymous tip telling them where they could find Samantha Browning. I ended the call and waited. It only took fifteen minutes before police cars arrived, along with a black sedan. Two men got out of the sedan, weapons drawn.

I put my BMW in drive and pulled out of the parking lot. She was safe.

Now, I had to face whatever punishment my brother chose to dole out.

CHAPTER 21

I reached into my pocket and fisted Samantha's collar in my trembling fingers as I rode the elevator down to the basement. It had taken less than twenty-four hours for Cristian to summon me to the dank space where he'd savor my screams.

Sweat beaded on my brow, but I didn't even consider running. Samantha was safe now, surrounded by FBI agents. But Cristian would need to discipline me for defying him. If Samantha were still within his grasp, he'd hurt her to torment me. Now, his only option was to cause me physical pain to exact his retribution. I'd take the agony willingly. Anything to satisfy his sadistic need to punish. Anything to guarantee he didn't go after Samantha, despite the security around her.

The elevator doors slid open, revealing my nightmare.

Samantha was stripped and strung up for my brother's torture, her pale skin glowing under the spare lightbulb that lit the basement. Her wrists were cuffed above her, forcing her onto her toes in a stress position. A bruise darkened her jaw, and blood dripped from one corner of her lips.

"Samantha," I snarled her name, launching myself toward her. I didn't know how Cristian had gotten to her, but the logistics didn't matter. All that mattered was getting her away from him.

"Stay right there." My brother's voice cracked against the concrete walls. His knife was at her throat. He applied pressure, and a crimson line appeared beneath the blade.

I froze in my tracks, still several yards away from where Cristian stood behind her, holding his knife against her vulnerable artery. My entire body shook with impotent rage and horror.

I'd done everything in my power to protect her. How had he gotten to her?

"Be a good boy and have a seat, or I'll cut her open right now. Do you want your pet returned to you scarred or dead?"

"Let her go," I ground out, my muscles flexing with the need to unleash the violence pent up inside me. "I know I'm the one you want to punish. Just let her go."

"And send her back to the feds, like you did? I don't think so. Samantha has agreed to work for me, once we're finished here. Sit down, *hermanito*. Or I'll slit her open and let you watch her pretty insides spill all over the floor."

The gory image made my stomach turn. I couldn't risk Samantha. Helpless to do anything else, I obeyed. A growl slipped through my teeth as I moved stiffly to the metal chair. Sitting in it willingly made my skin crawl. This was where Cristian had started working on me the last time, when his knife had sliced so much deeper than my flesh.

The two guards who always watched Cristian's back were at my sides, shoving my shoulders so I dropped down onto the metal seat. I didn't resist as they tied my arms behind me and trained their guns on the back of my skull. I'd do anything my brother asked of me, if only he'd spare Samantha. With his knife at her throat, I had no choice but to comply with his demands.

"That's better," Cristian said with satisfaction.

He withdrew his blade, and she heaved in a gasping breath.

"How should we punish my little brother for his transgressions?" he mused. He cupped her breast, squeezing hard. Samantha winced, but she didn't cry out. Undeterred, Cristian twisted her nipple cruelly, until her pain left her lips on a rough shout. Tears slipped down her cheeks as he took his satisfaction in the sound of her agony.

Driven by blind rage, I tried to push to my feet. The guards behind me applied pressure to my shoulders, forcing me down.

"He doesn't like that," Cristian observed. "I thought you enjoyed when she cried, Andrés. Or are you the only one who's allowed to enjoy her tears?" He leaned forward, so his face was close to hers. His tongue snaked out to lick at the wetness on her cheeks. She shuddered and flinched away.

"I should fuck her raw while you watch," he continued, his tone conversational.

"You said..." She gasped for breath. "You said this was for show. You promised I could hurt him if I worked for you."

Confusion fogged my mind, even as my gut tightened. Samantha wanted to hurt me? Cristian was the one torturing me by making me watch while he touched her. I didn't understand her words.

Cristian laughed, running his hand along the curve of her hip.

"She's a vicious little thing," he said. "No wonder you couldn't manage to break her. Is that why you're so obsessed with her? All of your other pets were very obedient by the time you handed them over to me."

She paled, her eyes going wide as they fixed on me. I'd never told her about the women I'd trained in the past. I'd never told her about how I'd taken my pleasure from them before my brother inevitably stole them away. The horror in her taut features told me she found me repulsive. I'd kept those women because I'd been starved of devotion, affection. I'd known Cristian would take each of them away, but that hadn't stopped me from hoping he wouldn't. It hadn't stopped me from indulging in my dark needs.

Samantha had been meant to be mine to keep, but Cristian had taken her, too. Or maybe she'd never been mine.

She'd just said she wanted to hurt me.

I had hurt *her*. This was only what I deserved after what I'd put her through.

"Let me down," she insisted with vindictive fervor. "Give me what I want, and I'll give you what you want."

"Savage," Cristian remarked with approval. "Your little pet is going to cut you up for me," he told me. "You risked your life to set her free, and she came back here to kill you. But don't worry. I won't let her take things that far. You'll survive this, and I'll patch you up again after. I'll always take care of my baby brother."

She'd said she loved me. Had it all been a carefully crafted deception? Or had she come to her senses when I'd released her, realizing that I'd used and violated her? I didn't blame her for hating me. Not after I'd fucked her while she was high on Bliss and helpless to resist me.

I met her pale gaze and nodded my silent agreement. I didn't begrudge her the retribution she deserved. If she needed to hurt me, I'd take it. Especially if it saved her from Cristian's knife. It seemed she'd made a deal with him: she'd work for him in exchange for the opportunity to punish me for my sins.

Cristian unbuckled the cuffs around her wrists, and she dropped to the concrete floor. I jerked with the impulse to catch her, despite everything she'd just said about wanting to harm me. I didn't care how she felt about me or what she might do to me. I would always protect her, regardless of the circumstances.

"Get up," Cristian said coldly. "You have work to do."

She pushed to her feet, turning to take the knife he offered her.

She moved with more brutal coordination than I'd ever seen, punching my brother in the throat at the same time as she grabbed the hilt of the knife. I bellowed out my fear for her as the guards' guns left my skull to turn on her. Shots blasted through the room, and her body jerked slightly. She moved quickly, darting behind Cristian for cover as he choked and clutched at his throat. He dropped to his knees, and she followed him down, crouching at his back. Her fingers fisted in his hair, and she pressed the blade against his artery.

The guards stopped firing at her.

"Drop your weapons," she ordered. "Do it, or I'll kill your boss."

They slowly lowered their guns to the ground, keeping their eyes fixed on the knife at Cristian's throat. He was still choking, unable to draw in air. Samantha had gotten in a solid punch. Pride heated my chest as my fierce *gatita* took full command of the situation. She hadn't intended to hurt me and work for my brother. She'd been playing him. The relief that washed through me made my head spin.

She loves me. Everything we'd shared was real. The few minutes I'd thought she hated me had been far more agonizing than any torture Cristian could have devised.

"Untie Andrés," she barked.

The guards complied, sealing their fates. The need to protect Samantha gave me almost inhuman speed and strength. I moved with vicious precision, snapping both the men's necks in a matter of seconds.

I prowled toward my brother, closing the distance between us. When I reached him, I dropped down onto one knee, so I could look into Samantha's eyes. They were sharp with adrenaline, but her fingers were loose around the knife. Despite her violent precision in taking down Cristian, she still didn't have it in her to kill a man. My sweet, innocent Samantha.

I'd do it for her.

"Hand me the knife, *cosita*," I ordered, my voice smooth and calm as I settled into my decision.

She allowed me to pluck it from her fingers, but her other hand remained fisted in his hair, holding his head in place. My gaze slid from her to my brother. He was still struggling to draw in air, incapable of crafting any cruel words. He'd taken everything from me: Valentina, *Abuela*. He'd tried to take my Samantha.

I'd never allow that to happen.

A feral snarl rumbled from my chest, and I slashed at his face. He screamed as the blade grated against bone and teeth, revealing a flash of white through the crimson gore. I closed my eyes and took a deep breath, savoring the sound of his suffering. Then, I looked my brother in the eye for the last time. I drew the knife back and slammed it into the center of his chest, twisting it to shred his black heart. Cristian's entire body shuddered before going still. His lifeless form sagged against Samantha, and they both fell back.

Something was wrong. She didn't try to push him off her. Blood pooled on the concrete beneath both their bodies.

I heaved his dead weight off her, and panic sharper than Cristian's knife pierced my heart. A dark hole had been torn through her right hip, and blood seeped from the open wound where one of the guard's bullets had caught her.

"*Sirenita*," I said, strained. "Stay with me."

"I came back for you. I'll never leave you," she promised, her voice faint. "I love you."

I scooped her up, and a strangled cry ripped from her throat. I rushed toward the elevator and started speaking to her in Spanish, promising her that she was going to be okay, that I'd keep her safe. She pressed her cheek against my chest, and her eyes fluttered closed.

Her blood soaked my crisp white shirt, but there was nothing I could do to stem the flow.

As soon as I got back to my penthouse, I grabbed up my phone from where I kept it in my desk drawer. My private physician answered on the second ring, and I ordered him to come to me, explaining Samantha's injury.

I laid her out on the bed and waited for the doctor to arrive with his team. A hospital would be more sterile, but I didn't have time to take her. My physician lived in the next building over, and he'd get to her much faster than an ambulance. Still, the few minutes it took for him to arrive seemed to take an eternity.

I didn't want to let go of her hand, but I stepped back, allowing him to work. He managed to stop the blood loss and patched her up enough so I could move her. We couldn't linger here, or the feds might close in on us. They'd separate us, and I wouldn't allow that to happen.

Satisfied that she wasn't going to bleed out on my bed, I decided it was time to get out of Chicago. I put in a call to ready my private jet. We'd leave the city before the FBI could locate my home. Then, I'd get her more medical attention, and we could figure out where to go from there. I was sure my clever Samantha would have a plan for our future. As long as I kept her by my side, we'd both be safe.

Samantha's eyes finally cleared, focusing on me when she woke from a natural sleep. I'd made sure the doctors kept feeding her painkillers over the last several days. I couldn't bear the thought of her hurting, so I'd mostly kept her under. I'd made a large donation to the hospital in Cancún, and they didn't ask questions when I made demands to ensure her comfort.

"Andrés?" Her voice rasped from disuse.

I picked up a cup of water from the tray next to her bed and helped her drink. After a few sips, she cleared her throat and tried again.

"Where's Cristian?" Her eyes widened as her memory resurfaced. "Oh."

I squeezed her hand. "He's gone," I confirmed. "He'll never hurt you again."

"I'm glad," she said with sudden fervor. "If he's dead, he can't hurt you, either."

"How did he get you away from the FBI?" I asked the question that had been burning in my mind ever since I'd entered that basement to find her strung up for torment. I didn't understand how Cristian had managed to capture her, and I hadn't stayed in town long enough to figure it out. I'd abandoned all my people, my drug empire. I didn't want it. I never had; I'd simply been born into it.

Running away with Samantha, knowing we were free from Cristian, was the sweetest relief. And now that she was awake and alert, peace settled over me.

"He didn't get me away from the FBI," she responded. "I left them. I came back to save you."

My hand tightened around hers. "You what?" I demanded.

She speared me with a level stare. "Did you really think I was going to leave you alone with Cristian? Knowing he'd hurt you for letting me go? Do you think I'd ever leave you for any reason? I love you, Andrés. I won't let anything keep us apart. Not Cristian, and not you."

I stroked her palm with my thumb. "I didn't want to let you go. It was the only way I knew to protect you."

She blew out a sigh. "I understand. Just don't try to do it again, okay? I'm safest with you."

"You are," I agreed.

She shifted toward me, then stopped on a wince. "I got shot, huh? So, what's the damage?"

"They had to remove one of your ovaries, but you'll make a full recovery."

"Oh." Her face fell. "Does that mean I can't... Can I still get pregnant?"

I smoothed her hair back from her forehead. "Yes, *cosita*. You'll be able to have children."

Her features softened with relief before her quick mind moved on. "Where are we, anyway? Please don't say a hospital in Chicago, because it's going to be really hard to get away from my friends a second time if they find me."

"We're in Cancún. I took you out of the country."

She nodded. "Smart. Where are we going next?"

A small smile curved my lips. "I thought we could figure that out together."

She beamed at me. "Cool. Well, I was thinking like, a private island or something would be good. As long as I have an internet connection, I don't mind being isolated. I mean, I'm not exactly a people person, and neither are you. I can move some of your money to an offshore account, so we have enough to live. And I'll move my money, too, but I'll be honest, that's not going to buy the private island. I figured we can donate the rest, you know? Do some good with it." She barely drew breath as she laid out her plan, her clever brain working in overtime. By the time she finished, a wide grin split my face. Samantha really was adorable.

"A private island sounds perfect. I'll have you all to myself."

She poked my chest playfully. "And I'll have *you* all to myself. This goes both ways. You're mine, Andrés."

I took her hand and placed it on my heart. "Yours," I promised.

EPILOGUE
TWO MONTHS LATER

"I have something for you, *gatita*." I leaned over Samantha from behind, wrapping my arms around her. She jolted, shocked out of her focused state. Then, she shivered and sighed as I kissed her neck.

"Put your work away," I commanded.

"But I'm super busy," she protested.

We might have made our home on our little slice of paradise over the last two months, but my clever Samantha hadn't been wasting her time lounging on the beach. She'd insisted on shifting back into hero mode, taking down bad guys from the safety of her ergonomic chair.

After sending all the information on my laptop to the FBI, she'd ensured that her friends at the Bureau cleaned up what was left of my former criminal organization.

That hadn't been enough for her. She attained a sense of purpose and satisfaction out of helping others, and she insisted on continuing to fight crime. I allowed it, as long as she did it under my watchful eye.

Her hacking skills really had been wasted in her brief time

serving as a field agent. My Samantha was brilliant and as fierce as ever. She could do far more damage from behind her screen than she could with her fists.

I also allowed her to keep in touch with her former coworkers, even though I didn't care for her continued interaction with her male friends. Knowing that she'd safeguarded our location and it was untraceable eased some of my worry. And knowing that an ocean separated the men from my pretty pet helped suppress my violent impulses when it came to asserting my ownership.

I nipped at the shell of her ear. "You can go back to your work tomorrow. I have plans for you tonight."

She drew in a shuddering breath, but she didn't put her laptop away. "I thought you were working on a project today."

"I was," I allowed.

She thought I'd been working on our new home. I derived calm satisfaction from making custom additions to the house that had already existed on our private island. I was crafting kinky furniture for one particular room in our own personal, depraved haven. I'd never had the opportunity to build something with my own hands. Although my efforts were slow as I learned, it felt good to create rather than destroy.

"Close the laptop," I ordered, dropping my tone with warning. "Now, *cosita*."

She huffed out an exasperated breath, but her little tremor let me know she was as responsive to my dominance as ever. She saved her work and closed the laptop.

"Good girl." I kissed the top of her head. "Come. I got you a present."

I took her hand, and she followed me into our bedroom without question. The large windows were open, gauzy white curtains swaying in the warm breeze. Brilliant pink and orange painted the sky, giving us a picturesque view of the sunset over the water.

It was beautiful, but not nearly as breathtaking as the perfect woman by my side. She wore a silky black robe—one of the only items of clothing I allowed her. She preferred to be covered while she was in "work mode," so I'd bought her some pretty lingerie. Otherwise, I kept her stripped, so I could admire her at my leisure.

Tonight, I did have something for her to wear. I released her hand and gestured to the large white box on our bed. It was wrapped in a pale blue ribbon, which I'd thought was appropriate for the occasion.

"Open it," I ordered.

She hastened to comply, a delighted grin illuminating her delicate features. Samantha loved presents, and I relished showering her with gifts. I'd give her anything she desired, just to see her heart-stopping smile.

"What's this?" she asked as she pulled the white dress from the box. It was long enough to cover her entire body down to her toes, and the high neck and long sleeves appeared demure. When she held it up in both hands, her eyes widened. The garment was crafted of delicate lace, without any lining beneath. It wouldn't hide her from my covetous eyes.

"It's your wedding dress," I told her, my voice rough with something more than carnal hunger.

Her pale eyes lit up, but her jaw was slack when she turned to face me. "What?" she asked faintly.

I traced the curve of her cheek and rubbed my thumb over her parted lips. "We can't make it official legally, but we're going to have a ceremony."

"Andrés, I..." She swallowed and trailed off.

I couldn't read her reaction, so I issued a command. "You're going to be my wife."

She placed her hand over mine where it rested against her cheek, leaning into my touch. "Yes," she answered, even though I hadn't asked a question.

Samantha was mine, and I'd tie her to me in every way possible.

I brushed a kiss over her lips. "Good girl. Get dressed and meet me outside."

I already wore my slacks and crisp white shirt. In the last two months, I'd become accustomed to more casual clothes—it was far too hot on the island to wear my customary suits. Besides, there was no one here I needed to intimidate by enhancing my aura of power. The only person I craved to control was Samantha, and she ceded to my power willingly, giving herself to me completely.

In a few short minutes, I'd possess her in a new way. I didn't need a legal document to tell me that Samantha belonged to me, but I wanted to vow to her that I'd always keep and protect her.

I stepped onto our porch, which extended out to the edge of the beach. I'd lit torches and driven them into the sand, adding soft illumination in the waning light of the setting sun. Flowers were scattered along the wooden floorboards, waiting to cushion Samantha's bare feet as she processed the short distance toward me.

There would be no witnesses to our union, but we didn't need any. I wouldn't allow anyone to look at Samantha in her pretty wedding dress. This moment was just for me. For us.

When she stepped into the open doorway, my breath stuck in my lungs. The white lace hugged her body, covering her completely while revealing everything to my hungry gaze. I could clearly see the curve of her breasts, her tight pink nipples peeking through the sheer fabric. Her pussy was a little more concealed, but the teasing glimpses of her pale flesh made my mouth water.

Her copper hair shined as it caught the light from the torches, reflecting their fiery glow. The pretty flush on her freckled cheeks reminded me of her innocence. Somehow, she'd managed to maintain it despite the perverted things I did to her body.

I held out my hand, beckoning. She closed the distance between us, moving gracefully as she glided toward me. Her glowing aquamarine eyes filled my world when she stood before me and took both my hands in hers.

"I love you, Andrés," she murmured, going up onto her toes to press a sweet kiss against my scarred cheek. "This is perfect."

"You're perfect. *Te amo, mí sirenita*," I swore.

A melodic giggle bubbled from her throat. "So, what are we going to do?" she asked, curious rather than teasing. "Is there a cake to cut or something?"

"What we're going to do is say our vows," I told her. "Then, I'm going to rip this dress off you and fuck you senseless, until you scream for mercy."

She shivered, but her delighted smile didn't falter. She didn't fear me in the slightest. I still gave her pain with her pleasure, still demanded her tears when I needed to soothe the darkness inside me. But she wasn't afraid of me. By some miracle, this perfect creature desired me, almost as desperately as I needed her.

"I guess I'll go first," she offered.

I nodded, giving her permission to continue. My heart squeezed, then beat faster in anticipation of her declaration of devotion.

She stared up at me, her eyes shining. "I need you, Andrés. I mean, I know we had a weird start and all, but that doesn't change how I feel. I didn't know what it meant to really be happy before you. I was always anxious and—let's be honest—pretty awkward. I guess I'm still kind of awkward. But you make me better. I'm not anxious when I'm around you. I'm not scared. You make me feel safe. You make me feel loved and cherished. I love you, and I'm never going to leave you. I won't let anything separate us. I'm yours."

By the time the rapid-fire words stopped spilling from her lips, a wide grin twisted my scar deep into my face. She wasn't repulsed at the sight of me. She looked at me like I was her world.

I cupped her cheek in my hand, threading my fingers through her silky hair. "Samantha," her name came out on a rasp. I took a breath and tried again, getting my surge of emotion under control. "I don't know how to exist without you. I'm going to keep you with me always, no matter what. You're mine, but I belong to you, too. Body, heart, and soul. I'm yours."

My vows were more concise than hers, but I mirrored her final words, promising her a lifetime of love and protection.

She beamed up at me. "Are we married now?"

"Now and forever, my sweet Samantha."

My fingers tightened in her hair, trapping her in place so I could claim her lips with mine. She opened for me, her low moan rolling into my mouth. The needy sound made my own arousal stir, and my cock stiffened against her hip.

Wasting no time on following through with my wicked promise, I fisted her lace dress in both hands and ripped it apart. The delicate material shredded, fully exposing her breasts and pussy. I palmed her cunt, running my fingers through the wetness that soaked her labia.

She gasped and shuddered, and I growled against her lips.

Unwilling to wait a second longer, I tossed her over my

shoulder and carried her into the bedroom. A giggle burst from her chest as her body draped docilely against my much larger frame. She didn't fight or shriek for me to release her.

But she would be screaming my name in a few minutes.

I dropped her on the bed, the soft mattress cushioning her fall. She laughed, thrilled at my harsh treatment. The tattered remnants of her dress pooled on the sheets at her sides, framing her lithe body like an offering. My pretty, perverted, perfect bride.

I quickly stripped off my clothes and settled my weight over her, lining my cock up with her slick opening.

"My birth control shot might not be effective anymore, you know." Her voice was breathy, and I wasn't certain if she was warning me not to come inside her.

"I know," I replied evenly.

She blinked. "You haven't given me another one."

"I haven't."

Her eyes widened, and she sucked in a small gasp. "You're not going to, are you?"

"No," I growled, thrusting into her.

She cried out and wrapped her legs around my waist, digging her heels into my ass to pull me deeper. "Good," she panted. "I don't want you to."

I pulled back and slammed into her again, taking her with brutal force. She wanted me. She wanted to have a child with me.

Possessive hunger surged through me, and I fucked her with primal, ruthless strokes. She rocked her hips against me, welcoming my claim.

"Andrés!" she screamed my name, her inner muscles contracting around me as she came undone. I followed her on a rough shout, my heat lashing into her.

I spilled my seed deep inside her, sealing our fate, our future.

My Samantha.

My baby.

My family.

All mine.

CAPTIVE EVER AFTER

CHAPTER 1

SAMANTHA

This wasn't the first time I'd paced back and forth across my opulent bathroom for five agonizingly long minutes, but that didn't mean the waiting became any easier with experience. Guilt nipped at me, adding to my anxiety. I really shouldn't be sneaking around Andrés like this, but I had to know. And I didn't want to get his hopes up again just to disappoint him.

We'd been trying to get pregnant for almost a year now, but my tests kept coming up negative. My periods had always been irregular, so Andrés wouldn't necessarily suspect that I might be pregnant this time. I'd asked our housekeeper to buy extra tests for me, and she'd promised not to tell my husband. It wasn't exactly as though I could make a covert trip to the drug store and buy some for myself. Our private island didn't have a Walgreens.

I wanted a baby with Andrés more than anything, but right now would be really bad timing. Like, the worst.

No matter what the result, I wouldn't tell him I'd taken another test. If it was negative, he didn't need that disappointment on his emotional plate at the moment. And if it was positive...

I couldn't stand the tension any longer. I'd been pacing along the far side of the massive bathroom, tracking an invisible path from the jacuzzi tub to the huge shower stall. Now, I rushed across the tiled floor to the double sinks, my gaze fixing on the little white stick.

All the air whooshed out of my chest. Two pink lines. Not one.

I'm pregnant.

I braced my hands on the marble-topped counter to support my trembling frame. Joy rushed through me, fizzing along the pathways of my veins to flood my system. A giddy, delighted laugh bubbled up from my chest before I could hold in the ecstatic sound.

A sharp knock on the door made me jolt with a yelp. My guilt rose in a wave, diminishing my happiness.

Shit.

How the hell was I going to keep this secret from Andrés?

"Are you okay, *sirenita?*" His deep, rumbling voice drifted through the closed door.

"I'm fine," I promised, my voice catching. I cleared my throat and tried again. "Just about to take a quick shower."

"Do you want some company?"

"No!" I took a breath. "No," I said, more calmly. "I'll be right out. Ten minutes."

I stifled a groan. Why hadn't I said I was taking an hour-long bubble bath? Now, I only had ten minutes to get my shit together and pretend like my world hadn't just changed forever.

I couldn't hear his footsteps retreating, and I suspected he was still outside the bathroom door. Knowing my husband, he'd just break the lock and come barging in if he thought I was distressed for some reason. I loved his fierce protective streak, but that could prove problematic today. It was going to be hard enough arguing my case without him knowing I was carrying his child.

I pressed my palm against my belly, but I didn't dare linger by the sink. I rushed to the shower and turned on the water. Andrés must have decided to leave me to it, because he didn't smash down the door to check on me.

I stepped under the hot spray and drew in several deep breaths, willing my fingers to stop shaking. Moving on autopilot, I washed my hair and quickly shaved my legs. I needed to feel and smell normal to Andrés, or I might rouse his suspicions. He was almost unnervingly perceptive. Probably because he focused on me so obsessively. He would keep track of my heartbeat at all times, if he were able to.

Usually, I didn't mind his obsession. I was equally enamored with him, even if my devotion didn't manifest itself in the same way as his controlling behavior. But that was why we worked as a couple. He needed to dominate me to express the depth of his love, and I needed to submit to him. In my absolute surrender, I proved that I loved him enough to give him anything he asked of me. He might have the upper hand in our power exchange, but our relationship was symbiotic. We were partners in life.

I would definitely need to leverage all my willpower to remind him of that today.

I straightened my shoulders and turned off the shower, bracing myself for the argument we were about to have. It took less than two minutes to dry off and run a brush through my wet hair. At the last second, I hid the evidence that could ruin all my plans; I stuffed the pregnancy test into an empty tampon box and secured the lid closed before tossing it into the trash. There wouldn't be any reason for Andrés to go snooping through the garbage.

Satisfied that I'd successfully covered my tracks, I slipped into one of my silky black robes and stepped out of the bathroom. I padded through the house on bare feet, looking for my husband.

I found him in the bedroom, his massive body taking up nearly half of our king size bed. Every mouthwatering inch of him was on display. His thick cock jerked in response to my sudden presence, and his tanned skin practically glowed in the tropical sunlight that streamed through the huge windows. They provided a stunning view of the pristine beach, but I wasn't at all distracted by the picturesque scene outside.

He stretched, his corded muscles rippling and flexing. My lips parted, my full attention fixating on his powerful physique. I didn't notice the scars that marred his chest and abdomen, or the wicked furrow that had been carved into his cheek. He was utterly perfect, and he was all mine.

A low sound of approval rumbled from his chest. "You look hungry, *gatita*." His voice dripped with arrogant amusement, and his scar twisted around a smirk.

Damn it. Busted.

I licked my lips and forced myself to maintain eye contact.

Don't look at his cock. Don't look at his cock.

His dark gaze swept down my body, admiring me at his leisure. "Take off the robe," he commanded.

My fingers fisted in the silky material, and I instinctively drew it closer around my body, willing it to protect me like armor.

His smirk dropped to a frown. That fearsome expression had brought many men to their knees, and my own threatened to buckle in supplication.

I locked up my joints, standing straight and holding my ground. "I need to talk to you."

His eyes narrowed, and he slowly got to his feet, moving with the controlled grace of a predator. He stalked toward me. "That was an order, *cosita*," he said, an edge of warning in his soft tone.

I swallowed hard and took a step back. "This is important," I insisted breathlessly. Even as trepidation made my heart flutter in my chest, my sex pulsed in response to his erotic threat. I had to stay focused, or Andrés would obliterate all of my rational thoughts with carnal lust.

It was more imperative than ever that I keep my wits about me.

He didn't stop advancing on me until a mere inch separated us. I could feel his body heat pulsing against me, his aura of power teasing across my pebbled flesh. For a few seconds, he simply stared down at me, pinning me in place with his sharp black gaze. When he finally lifted his hand and trailed his calloused fingertips down the line of my vulnerable artery, I was practically quivering with need, desperate for his demanding, punitive touch. My pulse jumped beneath his fingers, and he cocked his head at me, studying me with open curiosity.

"My little pet is nervous," he drawled. "Did you do something naughty, *gatita*?"

"I think I found Valentina." The words tumbled from my lips. I hadn't wanted to tell him so abruptly, but this truth was better than revealing the results of my secret pregnancy test.

The incisive spark vanished from his eyes, and the harsh lines of his face went slack. His hand stilled on my throat, his thumb resting on my artery while his fingers curved around my nape. His entire body tensed, his hand flexing against my neck.

I'd seen Andrés driven to the edge of madness with rage before, but I'd never seen this... I wasn't sure how to put his expression into words. His mind seemed to have shut down, his shock as visceral as though I'd stabbed him through the heart.

Fear fluttered in my belly. My anxious explanation began to spill out of me in a frenetic stream.

"I mean, I'm almost positive it's your sister. A 'Valentina Moreno' appeared online this morning. I've had a search constantly running to ping me if her name comes up. So, it did. She just appeared out of nowhere. It was on an order placed with a florist in California. The payment wasn't in her name, but they noted Valentina Moreno in their system for pickup. So obviously, I checked who paid for it. The card they ran belongs to Adrián Rodríguez. And I remembered you told me that your brother, Cristian, sold Valentina to Vicente Rodríguez when she was fourteen. There wasn't any online trace of Valentina Moreno after that."

I gasped in a breath and continued babbling, very aware of Andrés' hand on my throat. "I did more digging on Vicente and his associates. I couldn't find anything on your sister, but starting a few months ago, there are traces of a 'Valentina Sanchez.' I hacked some email accounts and found out that her husband, Hugo Sanchez, was looking for her because she'd been, um, taken by Adrián Rodríguez." I didn't want to say *abducted*. The implications of Valentina's story were already horrific enough without painting an ugly verbal picture for Andrés.

"So anyway, it looks like the order placed with the florist in Los Angeles is for a wedding. It looks like Hugo Sanchez disappeared, and now she's, um, well... Valentina is marrying Adrián Rodríguez. Vicente's son. And, yeah. That's it. I have some footage of her that I grabbed from some traffic cams around the florist shop. I thought maybe you could take a look and make sure it's her? I mean, I'm pretty sure it is, but you should probably check. Before you do anything, um, drastic. Like, we should be sure. You know? I mean—"

My unrelenting stream of words abruptly ended when Andrés' big hand shifted from my throat to cover my mouth. Something finally flickered in his eyes, and his gaze focused on my face.

"Breathe," he ordered.

I drew in air through my nose, and oxygen rushed to my head. I realized I'd barely paused to breathe in my anxious babbling. The resultant rush made my brain buzz, and I grasped at Andrés' strong shoulders for balance. His arm closed around my lower back, the iron band supporting me and drawing me closer to his body. He released my mouth and eased his long fingers into my hair, petting me in the way that always calmed both of us.

I let out a shuddering sigh and pressed my cheek against his hard chest. His hand curved around the back of my head to trap me there. I didn't want any space between us, and he clearly didn't, either. I could feel his heart thundering against his ribcage, and he drew in a deep breath to center himself.

After several seconds, he seemed to master his emotions. His heartbeat slowed to its normal, reassuring rhythm, and his grip on my body eased to a gentler hold. His warm breath ruffled my hair as he pressed a tender kiss on the top of my head.

"Show me," he murmured. "I need to see the footage."

"Okay," I agreed. "It's on my laptop."

He allowed me to extricate myself from his embrace, and I noted that he slipped on a pair of boxers while I walked across our bedroom to retrieve my laptop. When I returned to him, he'd settled his bulky frame on the edge of the bed. He patted the mattress, indicating that I should sit next to him. I complied, pressing my body so close to his side that I might has well have been molded to him. He needed my support right now, and I craved his nearness. What I was about to show him could lead us down a dangerous path.

I swallowed my worry for his safety and opened my laptop, clicking on the file I'd saved for his inspection. The video filled my screen. Since I'd pulled it from a traffic cam, it had been recorded at a distance from the woman. I'd zoomed and enhanced her image as much as I was able.

I already knew the woman was Andrés' sister; all the information I'd uncovered pointed to that fact. If I hadn't been basically ninety-nine percent certain, I wouldn't have presented him with the possibility that I'd found his beloved Valentina. Beyond her bronze skin and thick, wavy black hair, there weren't many physical similarities between the half-siblings. Her face was drawn in fragile lines, whereas Andrés looked as though he was carved out of granite. There was a hint of commonality in their high, defined cheekbones, but her eyes were obscured by stylish sunglasses.

Andrés stared at the video in silence for a moment. Then, he reached out and trailed his fingertips along my screen, as though he could reach through it and touch his long-lost sister for the first time in over fifteen years. I looked up to study his features. His jaw ticked, and he swallowed hard. His dark eyes were over-bright, and he blinked quickly to suppress tears.

I pressed my palm against his scarred face, directing his gaze to me. "It's okay to be emotional," I said gently. "It's her, isn't it?"

"Yes," he replied thickly. "It's Valentina." His hand left the screen, and he buried his fingers in my hair. "You found her," he rasped. A single tear spilled down his cheek. I brushed it away with my thumb.

"What are we going to do?" I urged softly, knowing he'd want to act immediately. We had to formulate a plan to rescue his sister. If I didn't start discussing it calmly and rationally now, he might descend into a mindless, vengeful rage and rush headlong into a dangerous situation. I'd done my research on Adrián Rodríguez, and the powerful drug lord was notoriously sadistic and lethal.

I suppressed a shudder at the idea of Andrés' sister being trapped with a man like that. Andrés didn't need me to show any hint of weakness or worry at the moment. Now, my job as his partner was to get him through this without it blowing up in our faces. I wanted my husband to get his sister back, but not at the cost of his safety.

"So," I began when he didn't respond immediately. "I already found a suitable mercenary group we could contact for tactical support."

When Andrés and I had retired to our private island to live our lives in peace, he'd abandoned his criminal empire, and I'd ensured that my friends at the FBI could locate and arrest all of his former associates. Andrés no longer commanded a small army of ruthless killers, but that wasn't what we needed right now, anyway.

Well, we needed men, but not an army and definitely not killers. I wanted to rescue Valentina, but I wouldn't allow Andrés to blacken his soul with more blood on his hands.

"We can do a simple extraction," I continued. "We just need a handful of men to back us up when we go in to get Valentina."

Andrés' dark brows immediately drew together, casting forbidding shadows over his onyx eyes. "*We?*" he repeated, clearly ready to quash the idea of me accompanying him to LA.

I lifted my chin and summoned up my bravado. "Yes, *we*. You need me on the ground with you. We're doing this the smart, safe way. There won't be a firefight, and you won't be storming Rodríguez's complex. That would be stupid, and we're not stupid. Besides, do you want to risk Valentina getting caught in the crossfire?"

His lips thinned, his scar drawing deep on a scowl. "You can work remotely from here."

"You know I'll be more effective if I'm close by. It'll be faster and easier to adapt to changing circumstances. If there's a freaking ocean between us, I can't back you up."

His fingers tightened in my hair, lighting up my scalp with a little twinge of warning pain. "I don't want you anywhere near Rodríguez."

I stared directly into his eyes, my will clashing with his. "Well, I don't want *you* anywhere near him, either. But I know you won't agree to send in the mercenary team without taking part in the op yourself. If you're going, I'm going."

"This isn't up for discussion, *cosita*," he growled.

I poked him hard in the chest. "You're right. It's not up for discussion, because I'm going with you and that's that. End of discussion."

He tugged my head back sharply, exposing my throat. "I could just chain you to our bed and leave you here."

"But you won't." My defiant declaration came out a bit more tremulously than I would have liked, but I doubled down. "You respect me too much to do that to me."

His jaw worked as he ground his teeth in frustration. He knew I'd effectively ended the argument.

"You're too clever for me, Samantha," he said tightly.

I offered him a lopsided smile. "Checkmate."

"I never should have taught you how to play chess," he muttered.

"Probably not," I agreed. "Oh, and one more thing. Promise me you won't kill anyone, okay?"

His face hardened to stone. "When it comes to Adrián Rodríguez, I'm not making any promises."

CHAPTER 2
ANDRÉS

Thank god Samantha's not pregnant, I thought for the dozenth time since we'd left the little safe haven on our private island. A week ago, I couldn't have imagined the thought crossing my mind. I wanted a child with the woman I loved more than anything, but ever since Samantha had told me she'd found Valentina—and backed me into a corner about taking her on the op with me—I'd become relieved that my wife wasn't pregnant.

As it was, my possessive instincts when it came to Samantha were an itch beneath my skin, a burning sensation in my gut. It took all my willpower to honor my promise and not chain her to our bed to keep her well away from danger. If anyone dared to threaten her during our mission, I wouldn't be able to suppress my violent urges. She'd managed to tame the monster in me, but I was almost frightened to contemplate what I would become if any harm came to her.

I'd agreed to her stipulation that I arm the mercenaries we'd hired with tranquilizer guns rather than carrying the real firepower I'd prefer. Samantha thought I was a good man at my core, and I tried to be better for her, to be worthy of her. But she would never truly understand the sadistic impulses that had been etched into my soul. Knowing that I was going to extract Valentina without mutilating anyone set my teeth on edge. The urge to punish every man who kept her in captivity was nearly overwhelming. If it weren't for Samantha's fierce insistence that I rein myself in, I would have cut a bloody path through my sister's captors.

That course of action might assuage a fraction of the guilt that plagued me. The loathing that I directed at myself for failing to protect Valentina could be unleashed on the men who'd hurt her. I wouldn't be fully cleansed by washing my hands in their blood, but it would feel good for a few fleeting minutes as they suffered and died.

Other than myself, there was one man who ultimately deserved to be punished for Valentina's grim fate: my brother, Cristian. I wished I could kill him again. More slowly this time.

My hands curled to fists at my sides as I fantasized about crushing his windpipe and watching him gasp for mercy as the light left his eyes.

"Andrés?" Samantha's gentle, soothing voice called me back to reality. Her slender fingers stroked my forearm, easing the violent tension in my muscles. I turned my full attention on her and found myself captured by her steady aquamarine stare. "Everything's going to be okay," she told me with the weight of an oath. "We're going to get your sister back. She'll be safe, and you'll protect her."

"What if I can't?" I asked on a quiet rasp before I could bite back my anxious words. I'd failed to protect Valentina all those years ago. I'd let Vicente Rodríguez carry her out of our home. I'd been too weak, too soft to fight Cristian. I'd watched them take my sister as I laid in agony on the hardwood floor of our living room, curling up in a cowardly attempt to protect myself from Cristian's beating.

Samantha cupped my cheek in her hand, threading her fingers through my hair to call me back to her. I might own her, but she possessed power over me that I'd never granted to another person. Only she could master the beast inside me.

"You can," she swore. "I know you'd do anything it takes to protect Valentina. We're not going to leave her with Adrián Rodríguez one more day. We're going to get her out, take her home with us, and no one will ever find her. I'll make sure of that. You know I can cover our tracks better than anyone. No one will hurt her ever again."

A shudder ran through my body as unbidden thoughts of what had probably been done to my little sister raced through my mind. I knew what men like Rodríguez were capable of. I knew what *I* was capable of, and I didn't delude myself that Valentina's captors possessed the shadow of a moral code I'd lived by before I met Samantha. I'd been perfectly content to train women to please me sexually, but I'd never taken a woman who didn't beg me to fuck her. Somehow, I'd convinced myself that rape was the line in the sand I wouldn't cross.

"Everything's going to be okay," Samantha promised again, commanding my attention. "We're almost in position. Then, I can scramble cell reception around campus and loop the security cams in the area. Rodríguez will never be able to track us. He won't even know who took her."

My clever pet had quickly formulated our plan to extract Valentina. Once Samantha discovered that my sister had been going by the surname Sanchez, it had taken mere minutes for her to discover that Valentina had recently enrolled at UCLA. My wife had wasted no time hacking into school records to get Valentina's class schedule, and we'd mapped out exactly where and when she'd be coming out of her lecture today.

Samantha would wait in the safety of our armored SUV at the edge of campus while I went in to retrieve my sister. The mercenaries we'd hired should already be in position, taking out the half-dozen men that Rodríguez had assigned to the area in order to ensure Valentina had eyes on her at all times. With Samantha scrambling cell service and blocking Wi-Fi for the few minutes it would take me to get to Valentina, no one would be able to call Rodríguez for backup, even if any of my sister's captors managed to evade the surprise assault of our mercenary crew.

Samantha had taken the extra precaution of assigning us false documents to get our small team into the US without arousing suspicion. We'd taken our private jet from our island to LA, but all connections to my name had to be thoroughly scrubbed from our flight pattern. My pet might still be in contact with her friends at the FBI, but we both knew they'd try to rescue her from me if they flagged me entering the country.

No one would take Samantha from me. I'd kill anyone who tried.

The SUV came to a stop. "We're here," Samantha said, still maintaining a gentle tone. Her softness helped calm me and prevented me from succumbing to the rage that simmered just beneath my skin. "Let's do this. Let's get your sister back."

My fingers sank into her copper hair, and I twisted the fiery strands around my fist to forcibly tip her head back. Her pupils dilated, the incandescent blue of her irises narrowing. Her pretty pink lips parted on a soft gasp, her body reacting to my control instantly. I kept her locked in place, imposing my will on her.

"Do not leave the car under any circumstances," I commanded. "Davis is armed with real bullets." I tipped my head at the mercenary I'd hired to man the vehicle and keep

Samantha safe while I went in to rescue Valentina. "If anyone comes near you, he will kill them."

"Andrés—"

I placed my hand over her mouth, smothering her protest. "I swore to you that I won't kill anyone unnecessarily, and I will honor that promise. But I won't risk you. Stay in the car. No matter what. Do you understand?"

She nodded as much as she was able with my grip on her hair. Satisfied that she would comply, I eased my hold and trailed my fingers through her silken locks. The feel of her softness beneath my harsh hands kept me grounded. She trusted me completely. I had to trust in her, as well. Samantha wasn't stupid, and she wouldn't put herself at risk.

Suddenly, she pressed her palm against the back of my neck, dragging me toward her so she could crush her lips to mine. She poured her strength into the kiss; my kitten was fierce despite her physical frailty. I returned her aggression with ferocity of my own, taking her lower lip between my teeth in a sharp warning. She would obey me and stay in the safety of the SUV with Davis armed and guarding her, while she protected all of us. I might be rescuing Valentina and ensuring Samantha's safety with the threat of violence, but her formidable mind would allow us to get through our op without being detected, and she'd help us vanish without a trace. In a matter of a few minutes, I'd have my sister in this car, and we'd all be on our way back to the airport.

Samantha pushed at my chest, and I allowed her to break the kiss. "You have to go," she urged, slightly breathless. "I'll be right here when you get back."

I nodded my agreement and released her. She immediately grabbed her laptop and opened it, resting it on her thighs. Her fingers began to fly over the keyboard, and I trusted that she had the situation well in hand.

"Okay, we're good," she announced. "Security cams on campus are set up on a loop. I'll handle the traffic cams as we drive to the airport. Cell reception and Wi-Fi are out now, too. We have eight minutes. Go get your sister."

I wanted to linger, to tell her how she awed me with her bravery and intelligence. But there would be time for that later. The clock was officially counting down, and I had to get to Valentina.

I got out of the car, making sure I heard the click of the locks before I strode away. The vehicle was secure.

I hurried away from the SUV, my movements slightly jerky. It felt unnatural to put distance between Samantha and myself when we were surrounded by potential enemies.

I pulled the baseball cap I was wearing farther down to obscure my features, tipping my chin toward the ground. The security cameras might not be recording any footage of me, but my scarred face was difficult to hide. If anyone stopped to look at me, they'd remember the monster they saw prowling across their campus. I didn't want any reports getting back to Rodríguez that might suggest I was the one who'd rescued Valentina. We were going to disappear, and he wouldn't have a hope of stealing her back from me.

I tried to keep my stride purposeful but not noticeably rushed. The three minutes it took to reach the lecture hall seemed to drag on for hours, and by the time I stopped outside the building's entrance, my heart pounded against my ribcage as though I'd sprinted from the car.

Right on time, the doors opened, and coeds began streaming out of the building, transitioning between classes. My heart leapt up into my throat as my eyes searched the crowd.

The sunlight caught on her shiny black hair, and her skin glowed bronze beneath its summer glare. The face I remembered from my childhood, that had haunted my nightmares for over a decade, was different now. Her cheeks were hollower, her delicate features defined more sharply than when she'd been a round-faced young girl.

My feet closed the distance between us before I could formulate any thought about approaching her.

"Valentina." Her name left my lips on a hoarse rasp. Something burned deep in my chest, and my heart expanded in my throat, cutting off my ability to speak.

She blinked away the sunlight in her eyes and focused on me. Her thick, dark lashes flew wide, her jaw dropping on a gasp. She recoiled from me.

Pain knifed through my gut, and my hand shot out to grab her upper arm, preventing her from putting distance between us. I'd longed for this reunion half my life. I couldn't bear to lose her for even a moment more.

She jerked against my hold, her dark chocolate eyes wide. I recognized the frenzied light in them. I'd seen it all too often in my lifetime.

Valentina was terrified. Her gaze fixed on my scarred cheek. She didn't recognize me as her brother; she only saw the mangled beast Cristian had made me.

My muscles flexed, my fingers digging deeper into her arm. She winced and stilled. My stomach twisted as I recognized the quick capitulation of a woman who fears violence from men.

"Let me go," she demanded, her voice low but holding an edge of steel I hadn't expected.

"I can't." My grip tightened, as though I could bring my sister back to me by force. "You have to come with me."

"I'm not going anywhere with you." She tried to twist away.

I yanked her closer.

Fuck. My emotions surged, wreaking havoc on rational

thought processes. I knew I was scaring her, but I couldn't find the words to explain myself. I'd recognized her instantly, but she didn't know me. The years hadn't been kind to me, and my horrific appearance went deeper than the furrow carved into my face. I was crueler than the teenage brother who'd been her best friend. I hardly saw anything of that boy in myself anymore. Valentina was looking at the monster I'd become, not her beloved big brother.

I deserved her revulsion. I'd failed her. I hadn't protected her when she needed me most.

I shook my head sharply, as though I could physically rid myself of the roiling emotions that fogged my mind. We didn't have time for me to succumb to my self-loathing. The seconds were ticking down, and we had to get back to the SUV before cell service was restored. Samantha could only scramble the signal for so long before we attracted too much attention due to the anomaly.

I forced myself to ease my hold on Valentina's arm, but my fingers remained iron bands, shackling her to me as I began to walk toward our getaway car.

She walked along with me, matching my pace so I didn't increase the strength of my grip. Still, her words dripped with venomous warning. "You're making a big mistake. Leave me alone, or you're going to die."

"I'm not leaving you," I vowed through gritted teeth. "Never again."

She remained silent for the space of three paces. I could feel the sharpness of her incisive gaze slicing at my skin like Cristian's knife. She was staring at my scarred cheek, my ruined face. Of course she wouldn't recognize me. I had to get her back to the car, back to Samantha. My clever pet was smarter than me. She was better than me; the superhero I could never be. She'd be able to explain everything to

Valentina. I couldn't seem to string two thoughts together, much less coherent sentences.

"Andrés," Valentina's soft voice whispered over my scarred flesh, and a shudder ran through my body.

I didn't pause to look down at her, even though I craved to see the recognition in her eyes. All I could do was keep walking. We were running out of time, and if I faced her now, I wasn't certain how I'd react. All I was certain of was that hesitating now would put all of us in danger. I wouldn't allow Rodríguez time to realize something was wrong. I had to get Valentina out of LA.

"Andrés, wait," Valentina implored. "You have to let me go. Just stop and listen to me. Adrián will kill you if—"

My muscles seized as rage slammed into me. I froze in my tracks and rounded on my sister. "He will never hurt you again," I swore on a snarl. "I'm taking you somewhere safe."

She clutched at my shoulders, holding on to me with desperate strength. "I am safe. Adrián loves me. He would never hurt me. But he'll kill you if he thinks you're trying to take me away from him. Please, listen to me. If his men see you touching me, they'll shoot you before I can explain."

"There's nothing to explain," I growled. "I'm your brother, and I'm going to protect you. I know I failed you, but I won't now. Never again. Rodríguez's men won't shoot me. I've taken care of them. But we only have a couple more minutes. Samantha is covering our tracks, but we have to go."

"Who's Samantha? And what did you do to Adrián's men? He won't like it if you've killed them, Andrés. You have to let me call him and explain before this gets out of control."

"Samantha is my wife." My entire body practically vibrated with the need to get back to her. I'd left her alone for too long, and if Rodríguez realized I was trying to take Valentina, Samantha would be in danger. "We have to get to the car."

I started walking again, and Valentina stumbled along beside me. "I can't leave with you," she said, anxiety straining her tone. "Please, let me call Adrián. We can sort this all out."

"I won't negotiate with the man who's holding you hostage," I snapped.

"He's not holding me hostage. I love him, Andrés. I want to be with him."

"No." I dismissed the idea immediately. "You don't."

She dug in her heels, refusing to budge another step. She straightened her spine and lifted her chin. I caught a flash of the headstrong girl who had been my best friend when I was a boy.

"Yes, I do," she replied bluntly. "Adrián saved me. I'm with him willingly. I love him, and I'm marrying him tomorrow. Now, please. Let me call him and explain what's going on before he tries to kill you."

I stared down at her, my brain struggling to comprehend what she was saying. For so many years, I'd loathed Vicente Rodríguez. Ever since Samantha had told me Valentina was marrying his son, Adrián, I'd focused that hatred on him. He was my enemy, a threat to my little sister that should be eliminated.

"Andrés," she said my name again, speaking in a low, rational tone I often heard from Samantha when I was being particularly mercurial. "I want you to meet the man I love. I won't lose you again. You're my family, but Adrián is my family, too. I'm not going to allow you to kill one another over a misunderstanding."

I bit out a curse. "We have to get back to the car."

Her dark eyes narrowed. "Did you not hear anything I just said? I can't leave with you, big brother."

"I heard you," I replied grimly. "But you're not going to be able to call Rodríguez until we get to Samantha. She's made sure that cell service is down in the area while I came in to get you."

Valentina started walking more briskly. "We'd better get to her before Adrián's men realize I'm with you, then. They will shoot you if they see us together."

"They won't be a problem. I already had my team handle it."

She sighed. "Adrián's going to be really pissed at you for killing his men. I've dreamed about finding you and us all being together as a family, but this isn't how I imagined things would go."

"You've been looking for me, too?"

"Adrián's been helping me. He told me Cristian is dead that that you disappeared about a year ago. I didn't know if you were even alive, but I hoped..." She trailed off and swallowed hard. "I don't have time to get emotional right now. Let's just get to Samantha, and we can work everything out back at the house."

"Agreed. I don't think Rodríguez will be too mad, though. Samantha insisted I arm my team with tranq guns. She wouldn't let me kill anyone."

"Good. That's good. He's going to start freaking out if I don't call him in the next few minutes. He usually gets updates as soon as I leave campus. He can get very... Well, he worries about me."

My gut reaction to the implication that Rodríguez was a controlling, possessive bastard was to grab Valentina and put an ocean between them. But my sister claimed to love him, despite what Samantha had discovered about the man's ruthless reputation.

I supposed my own reputation for brutality wasn't all that different from Adrián's. And I most certainly would slaughter anyone who tried to take Samantha away from me. If it weren't for the fact that we were completely isolated and safe on our private island, I probably would have her watched at all times, too. In fact, I probably wouldn't let her out of my sight at all.

I released some of my violent tension on a resigned sigh. "I understand," I conceded.

I understood all too well. That didn't mean I was happy about the situation. I didn't want my little sister to marry a man like me. She deserved better.

CHAPTER 3
SAMANTHA

Jamming cell reception and disabling Wi-Fi in a ten-block radius was super easy. Like, so easy it was almost kind of boring and a little anticlimactic. Even though I was no longer an active FBI agent, I still spent my days digging through the deep web, following leads, and connecting dots. That was a process, a pursuit; a puzzle to solve. This was just...a party trick. Literally, I scrambled the frequencies in a matter of seconds with a few keystrokes. Looping the security cameras on campus was also ridiculously simple.

Now that Andrés had gone to get Valentina, there wasn't much for me to do other than try not to become consumed by my anxiety for his safety. I knew the mercenary team we hired had already done their job quickly and cleanly. Davis—the man who was currently sitting the front seat, waiting to drive us back to the airport once we extracted Valentina—was connected to the rest of his team via wireless comm units. They'd all confirmed that Rodríguez's guards around the lecture hall had been neutralized.

I stared at the data on my screen, as though obsessively monitoring it would somehow get Andrés back to me unharmed. I'd done everything I could to ensure the path to rescue his sister was safe. All I could do now was wait at my laptop to reassure myself that everything was going smoothly.

Cell service frequencies: jammed.

Wi-Fi: blocked.

Wireless comm unit frequency for the mercenary team to communicate: clear.

I watched the data report and repeated the three confirmations in my mind with each second that passed.

Jammed.
Blocked.
Clear.
Jammed.
Blocked.
Clear.
Jammed.
Blocked.
What the fuck?

Another device was interfering with the frequency of the comm units. It only took a few heartbeats for me to lock in on the rogue device's GPS signal.

Well, shit. I'd pinpointed my exact location. And the signal wasn't coming from any of my equipment. Which meant it was one of Davis' devices. One he hadn't disclosed to me before the op.

Fucking satellite phone.

A few more heartbeats, and I decrypted the phone.

Davis had just sent a text. The message popped up on my screen: *I've been hired to kidnap your fiancée, Valentina Sanchez. Will return her to you for $50 mil. You have 6 minutes to decide.*

My stomach dropped.

A reply text came through almost instantaneously: *How do I know this is real?*

Davis: *Try to contact the men you assigned to guard her. My team has handled them. I want $50 mil. 5 minutes.*

Holy shit, Davis was betraying us to Adrián Rodríguez. I had to warn Andrés. Davis was armed with real firepower, and he could kill us all in a matter of seconds.

Damn it, I shouldn't have paid mercenaries to do this job. Obviously, Davis' services were for sale to the highest bidder. I'd thought this team was our best option, since I couldn't exactly ask my friends at the FBI to help us out.

Rodríguez texted back: *Deal. $50 mil. Where are you?*

Davis: *Not a chance. I'll deliver her to you. After you give me the down payment.*

Davis included instructions to wire half the funds to an offshore account. Rodríguez replied with an address where Davis was to bring Valentina.

I glanced at the clock on my laptop. Only four minutes until Andrés returned with his sister. I had to tell him what was going on, but I couldn't stop jamming cell reception or Davis might get tipped off.

Fuck. If Davis realized what I was doing, he would probably shoot me on the spot. I pressed a hand to my belly, thinking about my child.

But I couldn't let Andrés walk into an ambush. I'd be dead as soon as he returned to the SUV, anyway. Davis would kill both of us and take Valentina back to Rodríguez.

I had to chance it. Moving as surreptitiously as possible, I picked up my phone from where I'd left it resting on the seat beside me. I didn't have to look at the screen as I typed out my message; my thumb slid across the electronic keyboard with practiced ease.

Don't bring Valentina to SUV. Davis is dirty.

Using my free hand to operate my laptop, I restored cell service in the area and pressed the *send* button on my phone. Five seconds later, I jammed the frequency again.

I didn't have a moment to take a small breath of relief before a soft buzz sounded from the front seat. My heart sank. In the brief window I'd restored cell service so I could get my message to Andrés, a waiting text had come through to Davis' phone.

He immediately spun to face me, shoving his gun in my face.

"Close the laptop and drop your phone," he ground out.

Shit. I complied immediately, even though I was tempted to delay a few seconds to try to send another message to Andrés. But I couldn't gamble with my safety, not when it wasn't only my life at stake. I was in a pretty bleak situation, but I'd do everything in my power to protect my baby.

My laptop snapped closed, and my phone dropped down onto the floorboard. I'd been disarmed more effectively than if Davis had forced me to hand over a semi-automatic rifle. I'd just surrendered my most valuable weapons.

"What did you do?" Davis demanded, his thin lips peeled back from his teeth in a furious snarl. His ice blue eyes held no compassion, and I knew he wouldn't hesitate to pull the trigger if I so much as breathed in a way he didn't like.

"You won't be taking Valentina anywhere," I informed him in as calm a tone as I could manage. "I sent a message to Andrés. He won't bring her to you. You should let me out of the car and drive away. If anything happens to me, Andrés will kill you, and it won't be quick."

Davis cursed and ran his free hand over his buzzed blond hair. "Nosy fucking bitch. Rodríguez will kill me if I don't deliver."

"I guess you'd better let me go and start running," I

reasoned. "Take the SUV. Get as much of a head start as you can. If you let me go now, I swear Andrés won't come after you."

He jerked his head to the side in a sharp refusal. "I'm not taking a vehicle you can track so easily. I have my own car waiting." The taut lines of rage eased from his harsh features, smoothing into calm resolution. "You're coming with me," he announced.

"What? Why?"

Davis raised his gun slightly, aiming dead between my eyes. "Shut the fuck up and do as I say. Hand me that laptop."

I picked it up and passed it to him. He tossed it into the passenger seat without taking his icy gaze from my face.

"Don't move an inch. If you go for your phone, you're dead. I'm getting out of the car now. Then, I'm going to open your door, and you'll follow me to my sedan. Don't even think about running or screaming for help. This whole op is already fucked, so I don't care about leaving your body behind for the cops to find. Got it?"

"Yeah." I barely breathed the word.

I couldn't afford to linger if Davis was determined to take me with him. Now that I'd sent my warning message to Andrés, there was no guarantee that he wouldn't come tearing across campus to get back to me, even if he knew that might be a suicide mission. He wasn't armed, and no matter how strong my husband might be, a bullet to the head would put him down.

All I could do was comply with Davis' demands and hope that Andrés could regroup, get the necessary weapons, and come after me. For now, I needed both of us alive, and I needed him to get Valentina somewhere safe.

When Davis got out of the driver's seat and quickly opened my door, I didn't hesitate to follow his orders. The possibility of catching him by surprise and attempting to disarm him flitted across my mind. He'd been forced to holster his weapon at his side to conceal it as we moved to his waiting black sedan, which was parked three spaces up from our SUV.

I dismissed that plan before it could fully form. I might have trained as a field agent, but I'd never excelled at hand-to-hand combat, and I was over a year out of practice, anyway. Even more importantly, I couldn't risk getting injured and losing my baby.

I allowed Davis to grip my elbow and steer me where he wanted me to go. When I slid into the passenger seat of his car, he snapped the door shut and settled into his own seat in a matter of seconds.

"I don't understand why you're taking me with you." I made a final attempt at reasoning with him as he turned the key in the ignition.

He didn't glance at me as he put the car in drive and pulled out into traffic. "I'm not going to Rodríguez emptyhanded."

My heart fluttered in my chest. "I don't mean anything to him."

"You can tell him where Moreno is taking Valentina."

"I could, but I won't." My voice remained steady, but my fingers trembled. I fisted my hands in my lap.

Davis didn't so much as glance at me as he spoke. I recognized the cold focus of a man on a mission. "I know Moreno is more than your employer. You were eye fucking each other the whole drive from the airport to UCLA, and judging by the way he kissed you, he's not going to let you go so easily. You're leverage."

Acid coated my tongue, but I swallowed it down. "Andrés won't trade Valentina for me, if that's what you're thinking."

Davis shrugged. "If he doesn't want to do that, then I'm sure you'll tell Rodríguez where he can find his fiancée. I heard he really took his time carving up the last person who tried to take Valentina from him. You'll talk eventually."

A metallic tang washed through my mouth, and I realized I'd bitten the inside of my cheek. I took a deep breath and tried to calm my racing heart. I might lose a lot more blood today if Adrián Rodríguez proved to be as sadistic as his reputation proclaimed.

CHAPTER 4
ANDRÉS

I hadn't taken two steps to close the remaining distance between me and Samantha when my phone buzzed in my pocket.

My stomach dropped. My phone shouldn't be receiving any messages. Not until we got back to the SUV and Samantha restored cell service.

Had I lingered too long talking to Valentina and run out of time?

I grabbed the device from my pocket and unlocked it to check the notification.

A text from Samantha: *Don't bring Valentina to SUV. Davis is dirty.*

A snarl slipped between my bared teeth.

"Andrés? What's going on?"

Valentina gripped my arm, but I was barely aware of her presence at my side. The entire world blurred around me, my vision washing red.

I wrenched free from my sister's hold. "Stay right here," I barked at her, already sprinting toward the SUV.

My heart pounded against my ribcage, sending fury and fear coursing through my system. I had to get to Samantha. Valentina would be exposed, but the men who'd been guarding her had been neutralized, and Rodríguez was no longer a threat.

Now, Davis was the threat. I'd left my Samantha with a calculated killer, and he was armed with a lethal weapon.

I didn't have a weapon of my own, but that didn't register as a problem in my mind. My bare hands were violent enough to rip apart anyone who threatened my wife.

I could see the black SUV parked where we'd left it at the curb, but my feet couldn't move fast enough to reach it. The windows were tinted so dark that I couldn't see the inside of the vehicle.

Dread twisted my gut, and I sprinted impossibly faster to get to her. I launched myself at the back door on the passenger side, grabbing the handle and wrenching it open.

An inhuman sound tore from my chest, something between a snarl and an agonized howl. Samantha was gone. The car was empty.

No blood. I assessed the scene in the space of a heartbeat. *He didn't shoot her. She's not dead. She's not dead.*

Her phone was on the floor, her laptop abandoned on the front seat. She wouldn't have left them behind if she hadn't been forced to leave them.

Davis had taken Samantha.

But why? For ransom?

Fucking mercenaries.

I hastily checked my phone to see if I'd received any sort of message from Davis that might give me a clue about where or why he'd taken her.

No signal. Samantha had managed to get a message to me to warn me about Davis, but cell service was still down. He'd taken her laptop from her, and she hadn't been able to stop jamming the frequency.

"Andrés, what's going on?" Valentina approached, despite my command for her to stay away.

I slammed my fist into the side of the SUV, impotent rage washing through my system. "He took Samantha." My words were so harsh that they were barely discernable, but Valentina seemed to understand.

She cursed under her breath. "I'll call Adrián. He can help us find her."

I rounded on my sister. "How do you know Davis didn't take her on Rodríguez's orders?" I bellowed, unable to rein myself in.

Valentina paled. "If Adrián has anything to do with this, it's only because he thinks I'm in danger. I'll just call him and explain. Everything will be fine."

"Your fucking phone won't work. Fuck!"

"Okay," she replied, her voice hitching slightly despite her calm tone. "Let's get in the car and drive to my house. Adrián will help us. I promise. If he has anything to do with this, he won't hurt your wife. It's just a misunderstanding. And if Davis acted on his own, Adrián will be able to track him down."

Her reasonable plan calmed my roiling emotions for the space of a few heartbeats. Then, I registered that the keys were no longer in the ignition. Davis must have taken them with him. And I didn't know how to hotwire a car.

With every second that passed, Samantha was taken farther away from me. I felt the pull toward her like a tug on my soul.

"Let's get going," Valentina prompted, her words strained.

"I don't have the fucking keys."

"Shit." She drew in a sharp breath and grabbed my hand. "Come with me."

I remained rooted to the spot, barely registering that she was yanking on my arm. It felt wrong to move away from the place where I'd left Samantha, as though I'd be abandoning the only connection I had to her if I left the SUV.

"Come on," Valentina urged, pulling at me with all her strength. "I know someone who can help us. He's on campus. If we get to him, he'll be able to take us to Adrián."

I jerked my body away from the car and started moving. Valentina picked up the pace, running faster than I would have expected. I could surpass her with my longer strides, but I needed her to guide me. As it was, I was grateful for her speed.

We were probably attracting notice, sprinting across campus. I no longer cared about that. If Rodríguez truly wasn't my enemy, then it wouldn't matter if anyone saw my disfigurement and rumors of a monster with Valentina got back to him.

We arrived at the lecture hall where I'd first spotted Valentina, and she led me across the threshold. Our pace slowed as we moved through the building, but she strode with brisk purpose toward our destination.

We rounded a corner, and my focus instantly caught on the massive man who was leaning casually against the wall. He was a big fucker, jacked muscles straining against his black t-shirt. As soon as his dark eyes landed on my scarred face, he pushed away from the wall and assumed an aggressive stance. Monsters tended to recognize one another on a primal level.

Valentina stepped in front of me, coming to an abrupt stop. My first instinct was to shove past her and put myself between her and danger.

"Andrés, wait," she ordered sharply. "Mateo," she addressed the big motherfucker. "This is my brother, Andrés. He's not a threat. We need your help."

Mateo's head cocked to the side, his square jaw working as

he ground his teeth. His eyes narrowed on my face, assessing me.

"Stop it," Valentina insisted, cutting through the mounting tension between us. "Mateo, we need a ride back to the house. I can't get in touch with Adrián."

The animosity left his gaze as his attention turned back on her. "What's wrong with your phone?"

"Cell service is down," she explained quickly. "You won't be able to call him, either. Please, Mateo. I'll explain in the car. We have to get going."

The man hesitated, his lips pressing together in indecision. "I don't want to leave Sofia."

I didn't know who the fuck Sofia was, and I didn't care. Before I lost my tenuous hold on my rage, Valentina spoke up.

"Sofia will be fine. Class just started, and you know she won't be out of her lecture for an hour and a half. You can drive us to the house and get back here in time."

"I don't know—"

"Come with us right now, or I'll tell Adrián you chose to stand outside Sofia's completely safe classroom while I begged you for help." The threat was clear in Valentina's scathing tone. Maybe Rodríguez really did love her, if he allowed her the power to threaten his men.

Mateo spat out a curse. "If anything happens to Sofia while I'm gone—"

"Nothing's going to happen to her. Do you think I'd take you away from her if I thought she was in danger? You might be guarding her, but let's not pretend you're her bodyguard. Now, get moving."

I had no idea what was going on between Mateo, Sofia, and Valentina, but I barely wasted any of what was left of my rational thought processes puzzling it out. The imperative to find Samantha pounded through my brain, the thunderous sound of my racing heartbeat echoing in my ears.

Mateo dropped his aggressive stance and closed the distance between us. Valentina took my hand again and started pulling me along.

"Hurry," she urged Mateo, breaking into a jog. "We have to get back to Adrián." She squeezed my hand as we picked up the pace. "Everything's going to be fine, big brother. No one's going to hurt Samantha."

The worry that roughened her tone betrayed her lie. If Rodríguez had Samantha, my little pet wasn't safe from harm.

CHAPTER 5
SAMANTHA

"There's still time to turn around and take me back to Andrés," I said, fighting to keep the tremor from my voice. Davis had driven us into a neighborhood that was obviously inhabited by the ultra-rich. Greenery surrounded the winding road, and homes were hidden down long driveways. There was some serious real estate tucked away behind those trees, and the privacy factor made my gut clench.

Once the wrought iron gates before us opened up, there wouldn't be any going back. I'd be locked away on Adrián Rodríguez's estate, isolated and alone.

Davis was on his phone, likely typing out another text to Rodríguez to tell him we'd arrived. When he finished sending his message, he glanced over at me.

"Not happening," he replied curtly. "As it is, I won't get the rest of my payout from Rodríguez. If I don't show at all, he'll hunt me down and kill me. He has far more resources at his disposal than Moreno. The fact that you hired me proves that you don't have any loyal people of your own. I'm going to deliver you to Rodríguez and get the hell out of town with twenty-five million in my account. It's half of what I wanted, but it's better than nothing."

The gates eased open, and Davis drove in.

Okay, I reasoned, struggling to remain calm. *I'll be okay. Andrés will figure out where I am, and he'll come get me. I just need to stay alive until he arrives.*

I realized I was pressing my palm against my belly, and I forced my hand back to my knee. I'd do whatever it took to protect my baby. I just had to trust in Andrés. And hope that Rodríguez wouldn't start carving me up immediately.

My stomach turned, and I swallowed back bile.

Davis drove for a couple minutes before the house came into view. The sprawling Spanish-style mansion probably had plenty of rooms to imprison me. Or torture me. Or...

I took a breath, cutting off my erratic thoughts before my wits became scrambled by fear. There was no way I'd be able to fight my way out of this, but violence had never been my strong suit. I needed my mind clear if I was going to survive long enough for Andrés to get here.

If he makes it here alive. I couldn't stop that particular unbidden thought when Rodríguez stepped out onto the porch, flanked by two burly men. I recognized him from the research I'd done on Valentina's captors. He had a cruel sort of beauty about him, with his sculpted face and tailored suit. Even from this distance, I could discern his glittering, pale green eyes. I recognized a predator when I saw one, no matter how alluring he might appear.

All three men were armed. The guards trained their weapons on Davis, marking him through the windshield. Rodríguez held his piece casually at his side, as though it were an extension of his arm.

Davis put the sedan in park and held up his hands in a

show of goodwill. Rodríguez gave him silent permission to get out of the car with a single nod.

"Stay put," Davis ordered as he opened the door and stood to face Rodríguez.

"Tell your partner to get out, too," Rodríguez commanded, tipping his head in my direction without taking his eyes off Davis' face.

Davis kept his hands up as he spoke. "She's not my partner. She's working with the man who took your fiancée."

Rodríguez's brows drew together, shadowing his remarkable eyes. "Where is Valentina?" he demanded on a snarl.

Davis gestured at me. "Ask her. The bitch intercepted our messages and warned him not to bring Valentina to me. I brought her here so you could—"

Rodríguez raised his weapon and fired three rounds directly into Davis' chest without another word. The man was dead before he hit the ground.

Then, glowing green eyes focused on me.

Oh, fuck.

He prowled to the car and opened my door. His weapon was back at his side rather than aimed at me, but I knew that didn't mean shit. He'd just proven how quickly he could end someone's life without batting an eye.

"Where is Valentina?" he growled, his predator's eyes burning into me from above.

I lifted my chin and met his intense stare. "I don't know."

That was true enough. I had no idea where Andrés might take his sister to ensure her safety while he gathered the resources he'd need to come after me. It was possible he'd take her to the airport and put her on the jet back to our island, but I didn't know that for sure.

Rodríguez raised his weapon again, moving with smooth

grace as he pressed the barrel of the gun to my forehead. "You have three seconds to tell me where she is."

"You can't kill me. If you kill me, you won't have any way to find her. You won't have any leads or leverage. So, that's a really bad idea. You definitely shouldn't do that."

I swallowed the stream of anxious words that threatened to spill from my lips. Babbling wouldn't help my case.

Rodríguez's nostrils flared, his crystalline eyes glittering with rage. "Get out of the car."

He withdrew his gun, allowing me space to unbuckle my seatbelt and clumsily get to my feet. I wasn't graceful at the best of times, and fear made my knees weak.

Rodríguez's iron fingers closed around my upper arm. He didn't squeeze hard enough to bruise, but he could shatter my bones with very little effort.

"Don't disturb me for any reason," he ordered his guards. His voice was icy, his cold control far more terrifying than if he'd been shouting threats at me.

He started walking, pulling me along beside him. I stumbled but managed to remain upright. I had a feeling he would have continued dragging me where he wanted to take me, even if I'd fallen. He probably wouldn't care if I dislocated my shoulder.

He wasn't taking me into the house. Instead, he directed us over a spacious back patio that provided a stunning view of the city. We didn't pause to take in the vista. He led me onto a gently sloping, lush green lawn, which was sheltered by trees. There wasn't a neighboring home in sight. Or earshot, most likely. I could scream myself hoarse, and no one would hear me.

My skin pebbled, a block of ice forming in the pit of my stomach. We were walking toward a shed. Nothing good happened in a place like that. I'd been concerned about being imprisoned in his fancy mansion, but this basic structure was designed to get messy. Rodríguez wouldn't worry about bloodstains on the concrete floor.

Fuck, fuck, fuck...

My feet stalled, my body instinctively recoiling. He didn't seem to notice my small act of resistance; he kept walking with brisk purpose, and I had no choice but to follow.

By the time we reached the shed, my heart had pounded up into my throat, threatening to choke off my air supply. Rodríguez hadn't so much as looked at me as he'd dragged me across his property, and he didn't spare me a glance as he turned the knob and pushed open the shed's metal door. His silence and cold disregard for me as a human being were terrifying enough, but then I noticed his jaw tick as he ground his teeth. I recognized rage in the taut lines of his defined features. He appeared aloof and collected, but Rodríguez was a man on the edge of control. If he snapped, he'd kill me instantly and brutally. The prospect of interrogation made nausea roll through my stomach, but I couldn't save my baby if I didn't survive long enough for Andrés to rescue me.

A single metal chair waited in the center of the cramped space. It gleamed dully under the spare lightbulb overhead. The unyielding metal was spotless, but I knew it had likely been painted red with gore many times. It would be easy to hose down after...

I drew in a shaky breath, struggling to keep my mind clear.

Rodríguez shoved me down into the chair and grabbed a small coil of rope from a table set beside it. I kept my eyes trained forward as he wrenched my arms behind my back and secured them with a tight knot. I didn't want to look at what else lay on that table. As it was, my wild imagination was almost as horrifying as facing the torture implements.

He stood back, towering over me. My gaze was drawn to his, and I found myself locked beneath his glowing green glare.

"Who are you working for?" His controlled tone held a steely edge.

My fingers shook, and I jerked against the rope that bound me to the chair. "I'm not working for anyone," I insisted tremulously.

If I stuck to the truth, maybe I could buy myself some time. Outright lies would lead to harsher methods of extracting answers.

Rodríguez leaned into me, bracing his big hands on the arms of the chair. His cruel, beautiful face filled my vision. He was close enough that I could smell his expensive cologne. Perfect white teeth flashed as he growled at me.

"I don't usually hurt women, but I will tear you apart piece by piece until you tell me where I can find your employer. If he doesn't surrender her to me, I'll tear him apart, too. Valentina is mine, and I will get her back, no matter what it takes."

Defiance surged through my terror. I wouldn't betray Andrés, even if it did cost my life. "I'm not telling you shit. You'll never see Valentina again."

His muscles rippled and flexed, and he bared his teeth like a wild animal. The man was insane with possessive rage.

Suddenly, he gripped my jaw, forcing me to face the objects on the table beside me. The wicked instruments for my torture glinted under the dim light. For a moment, I saw Cristian smirking down at me, scraping his hunting knife across my skin. My stomach rolled, my entire body convulsing in horror.

"No one will keep Valentina from me," Rodríguez snarled. "You will tell me where I can find her. How quickly the pain ends is up to you."

"Please," I whispered, the truth slipping from me before I could think. "I'm pregnant."

Rodríguez recoiled from me, a frustrated roar echoing through the shed. He retreated a few steps, until his back hit the door. He braced his hands on the metal behind him, as though anchoring himself there.

"Tell me where I can find her." His pale eyes were wild, his words rough with something like panic. The man staring at me with a mix of horror and desperation was closer to the brink of madness than the cruel killer who'd tied me to this chair.

Confusion threaded through my terror. This wasn't the reaction of a sadistic captor who wanted his possession returned to him.

I wasn't the only one in this shed who was afraid.

My mind raced, reevaluating the situation in light of this new information. Valentina was marrying Rodríguez tomorrow. She's been allowed to enroll in college and given the freedom to move around the city, even if she had been guarded at all times. She'd been the one to put in the order with the florist. She'd chosen the flowers for her wedding.

Because she wanted to marry Adrián Rodríguez.

"You love her." The words popped out of my mouth.

His entire body jerked, dark shadows pooling over his eyes beneath his drawn brows. He pressed his lips together, as though holding back the admission. He didn't want me to know that he loved her, because he thought his vulnerability would give me power over him.

I took a breath, trying to sort through the best way to reason with him. "Listen, Adrián. There's been a mistake. We didn't know—"

A deafening *bang* shattered the tension between us like a bullet through glass, and I shrieked in shock. Bright sunlight seared my vision, momentarily blinding me after the dimness of the shed. I registered rough, animal sounds, and for a moment, I thought a rabid dog had burst into the shed.

I blinked the sunlight from my eyes. The dull thud of flesh hitting flesh accompanied the scene that coalesced around me.

Andrés was on top of Adrián, pinning his body against the concrete floor as he brought his fist down on my captor's jaw. My husband's face twisted with feral rage, his scar drawn deep into his cheek. I'd only seen him wear this terrifying, furious mask once before: when Cristian had threatened my life.

He'd killed his brother that night. He'd kill Adrián if I didn't stop him.

"Andrés!" I screamed his name to call him back to me before he did something he might regret.

His big body jerked, as though I'd slammed the full force of my weight into him. My desperate cry caught his attention, distracting him from his murderous intent.

Adrián took advantage of his moment of hesitation, using the opening to get the upper hand. He shoved Andrés away, grabbing his shirt and wrenching him upright. Adrián slammed my husband back against the wall, and his head cracked against the heavy metal beam behind him.

"Stop! Adrián, stop!" Valentina appeared in the ruined doorway, her delicate features twisted in horror.

Just as my scream had distracted Andrés, Valentina's distress seemed to pierce Adrián's body like a knife.

Andrés' lips peeled back from his teeth, and I knew he was about to punch Adrián again.

"Andrés, don't!" I twisted against the rope that kept me trapped. I had to get to him and end this before someone died. Because it was clear that neither of them would stop until the other was eliminated.

"He's my brother," Valentina yelled, darting toward the enraged men. She grabbed Adrián's arm, as though she could physically restrain him. "Adrián, please. Just stop and listen to me. I'm right here. Andrés brought me back to you."

"Andrés, look at me," I demanded as soon as Valentina reached her fiancé. My husband's black eyes fixed on me immediately. His body swelled with rage at the sight of me bound, so I quickly continued reasoning with him. "I'm okay," I promised. "I'm not hurt. This is a misunderstanding. Valentina wants to be with Adrián. He loves her. He won't hurt her, and he didn't hurt me."

Valentina tried to reason with the man she loved, too. "My brother wanted to save me. He didn't know I'm with you willingly. This is his wife, Samantha. He's worried for her safety. What would you do to someone who threatened me?"

Adrián abruptly shoved away from Andrés, placing his body in front of Valentina.

"Andrés." I kept his attention on me to prevent him from attacking Adrián again. "Can you help me up? I'm not hurt, but I need your help, okay?"

His nostrils flared, his dark eyes sharp on my face. He pushed away from the wall and closed the distance between us, not sparing his enemy another glance. His entire focus was centered on me.

"Everything's okay," I swore, soothing the beast that lived inside the man I loved. "I just need you to untie me. Adrián didn't do anything. He didn't hurt me," I reiterated. If Andrés thought I'd been harmed in any way, he would turn on Valentina's fiancé again, no matter what I said.

He dropped to one knee before me, his big hand cupping my cheek. He turned my face gently, studying me for any sign of injury. I met his keen gaze with a steady stare, taking deep, calming breaths. After a few heartbeats, he mirrored me, and the violent tension eased from his massive frame.

His arms closed around me, his fingers finding the knot at my wrists and freeing me with expert ease. As soon as he untied me, he pulled me into a fierce embrace.

"Samantha," he rasped my name, his body shuddering with relief as he breathed in my scent.

"I'm right here," I promised, tucking my face closer against his chest. "I'm safe."

I heard Valentina murmuring to Adrián in a similar low, reassuring tone. After a few minutes, their footsteps sounded on the concrete. Andrés didn't release me or glance in their direction.

I couldn't see anything other than his massive chest, but Valentina's request reached me as they moved away.

"Just wait outside the house, big brother. I'm going to talk to Adrián, and we can all meet each other properly when everyone's cooled off."

Andrés didn't respond, and I wasn't certain if he was really capable of comprehending his sister's words.

I pressed my palm over his heart, tethering him to me. "Hey," I said gently. "Can you take me out of here? There's a nice patio behind the house. Let's go wait there."

His grip shifted on my body, and he lifted me with ease. I was happy for him to carry me away from the shed. I'd put on a brave front for him, but I'd been really fucking scared just a few minutes ago.

The warm sunlight hit my skin as we stepped out onto the lawn. I drew in a shaky breath and turned my face into my husband's chest, seeking his strength. I marveled that we were okay. I'd thought our lives were on the line.

We were all safe now: Andrés, me, and our baby.

CHAPTER 6
ANDRÉS

It took concerted effort to restrain myself from crushing Samantha's slight body as I held her close to my chest. I matched her deep, calming breaths, easing most of the violent tension from my muscles. My instincts told me to hold her with all my strength, as though she was my prized possession that Rodríguez might try to take away from me again.

I pressed my face closer to hers, nuzzling her silky hair so I could feel her softness against my scarred cheek. Her slender fingers closed around my nape, locking me in place. My little pet was just as desperate for my nearness as I was for hers.

A low stream of words in my native tongue dropped from my lips, the reassuring cadence meant to ground me as well as comfort her.

Lo siento.

I hadn't realized I'd said the apology aloud until she pulled back from me, capturing my face in her delicate hand.

"Hey," she said softly, piercing my soul with her aquamarine gaze. "There's nothing to be sorry for."

"He took you," I growled, my arms tightening around her before I could hold back the impulse.

She didn't seem to mind my harsh hold; she remained relaxed and supple in my iron grip.

"*Davis* took me," she countered firmly. "Adrián didn't hurt me. He didn't want to. He was just trying to frighten me into telling him where he could find Valentina. He really loves her, Andrés. He was scared for her safety when he thought she'd been taken. Just like you were scared for me."

"Where is Davis now?" I demanded. If I couldn't punish Rodríguez for taking my Samantha from me, then I'd rip apart the mercenary instead.

"He's dead." She trailed her fingertips over my cheek, soothing me. "Adrián killed him as soon as we got here."

I pulled her closer to my chest. "I don't want my little sister with that drug lord," I ground out. "He's dangerous."

She fixed me with a steady stare. "And what would you have done to Davis if you'd gotten to him first?"

I gnashed my teeth. My pet was too clever sometimes. It would be much easier to settle into my rage than look at the situation objectively.

"Andrés?" she prompted, refusing to allow me to evade the question.

A series of bloody images flashed across my mind as I envisioned all the ways I would have mutilated Davis before finally letting him die.

"You don't want to know," I admitted. I'd promised my wife I wouldn't kill anyone while we went in to rescue Valentina, and she wouldn't approve of the vicious things I would have done to the mercenary if I'd gotten my hands on him.

"That's what I thought," Samantha said smoothly. "I can't say that Adrián Rodríguez is a good man. He's a ruthless criminal, but he loves your sister. She wants to marry him, doesn't she?"

My scar drew tight on a frown. "She says she does. But how can she know what she wants? She's been imprisoned by the Rodríguez family since she was fourteen. It would be better for her to marry someone else."

"But she doesn't love someone else," Samantha reasoned. "She loves Adrián."

I jerked my head sharply to the side. "That's probably because she doesn't know how to love anyone else. She was trapped with that family for years. She didn't have a choice."

Samantha's copper brows rose, and she fixed me with a challenging stare. "And what do you think my friends at the FBI say about my relationship with you? They don't approve. They don't think I have a choice. But I do, and I choose you. It doesn't matter what circumstances brought us together. I love you, Andrés. I always will. No one would be able to take me from you and convince me otherwise."

I blew out a long sigh, defeated. "I love you, too. I wouldn't let anyone take you from me." I'd almost lost my mind just a few hours ago when Davis had tried to steal her. I would have done anything necessary to get her back.

A pinging sound distracted me momentarily, but I realized it was just Mateo's phone receiving a text. The massive man had been keeping an eye on us while we sat on the patio. He hadn't threatened me in any way, and he kept a careful, respectful distance. But he'd been watching me, nonetheless.

I supposed I would have done the same, in Rodríguez's position. I wouldn't have allowed a man who'd just attacked me to lounge outside my home without a guard.

"Adrián says you can come inside," Mateo announced. "He wants to talk to you."

I pushed up off the cushioned chair I'd been sitting on for the last hour while I'd kept Samantha in my arms.

"You can put me down now," she urged.

I glowered at her, my first instinct telling me to keep her tucked as close to me as possible.

She stared right back at me, implacably calm and reasonable. "We're safe here. Valentina wants you to meet her fiancé. You don't have to carry me around like a caveman. That would be weird. Okay?"

I didn't care about adhering to social norms. I just cared about Samantha's safety.

"The boss says you're welcome guests here," Mateo interjected. "No one's going to hurt your wife. Valentina won't allow it."

I would have been skeptical of his assertion, but the declaration that Valentina wouldn't allow it swayed me. I realized that she truly did wield power in this house. Possibly more than Rodríguez himself. If such a notoriously ruthless man allowed my sister to influence his decisions, he really must love her.

I carefully set Samantha down on her feet, my touch lingering around her waist. She firmly caught my hand in hers and started walking across the patio, urging me to accompany her. My fierce pet was too brave for her own good sometimes, but I allowed her to march toward the man who'd been holding her hostage and terrorizing her only an hour ago.

The memory of her tied to the chair in that shed made my muscles tense with rage, and she squeezed my hand in silent comfort, reassuring me.

I took a breath. I should be the one reassuring *her*.

As always, Samantha's strength and goodness reminded me that I needed to be better if I ever had a hope of deserving her. I would face Adrián Rodríguez, and I wouldn't try to kill him this time. If Samantha could forgive him so easily, I'd try to emulate her.

Mateo walked ahead of us, ushering us around the massive mansion until we reached the front door. Valentina waited at the threshold, the soft lines of her heart-shaped face drawn sharp with anxiety. As soon as she caught sight of me, she shifted to close the distance that separated us. Rodríguez placed a restraining hand on her hip, pulling her back against his body and tucking her close to his side. His strange, luminous green eyes fixed on me, glinting with warning.

Without thinking, I mirrored his movement, tugging Samantha closer to me so I could wrap my arm around her and shield her fragile body. I heard her huff out an exasperated breath, but she knew better than to try to pull away. My control over my roiling emotions was tenuous, at best, and if she tried to extricate herself from my protective hold, that control would snap. I needed to feel her safe beside me.

We came to a stop at the edge of the front porch, several feet separating Samantha from Rodríguez. I wanted to go to Valentina, but I wouldn't put my wife at risk.

"Can I go now, boss?" Mateo asked. I'd only been peripherally aware of the hulking man as a secondary potential threat. He might be huge, but he was silent as a shadow.

Rodríguez's jaw ticked, but he didn't take his eyes off me or give his guard permission to leave.

"Adrián," Valentina said, all softness and persuasion. "Mateo wants to get back to Sofia. I promised him he could. She should be out of class by now. She really shouldn't be left alone. I already told you that Andrés won't try to take me away from you. He came to find me. Everything else has been a misunderstanding." She turned a pointed stare on me. "Isn't that right, big brother?"

"Of course it is," Samantha said immediately. "I misread

the situation. The extraction plan was my idea. So really, this is on me. Sorry if I—"

She stopped her apology on a little gasp when my fingers curved into her hip, squeezing hard in rebuke. She was trying to put herself in Rodríguez's crosshairs and take the heat off me.

Not fucking happening. My pet was in so much trouble when I got her somewhere private. She should know better.

Rodríguez's glowing stare shifted to her. "You're the one who found Valentina?"

"Samantha was looking for my sister as a favor to me," I snapped. "She's not responsible for anything that happened today."

She stiffened in my hold. "Andrés," she hissed my name indignantly. "I've been trying to help you find Valentina for over a year. I came up with the plan. I covered our tracks and had your backs. Don't you dare say I had nothing to do with reuniting you with your sister. This whole op was my idea."

"Thank you," Rodríguez said before I could throw my wife over my shoulder and haul her away for punishment.

I blinked and focused on him, but his full attention was fixed on Samantha. His pale eyes were intense but strangely earnest. "Valentina has missed her brother. I wasn't able to find Andrés for her. I'm glad you brought them together. I'm sorry if I scared you earlier."

Samantha waved away his apology, as though his attempted torture was of no consequence. "That's okay. Andrés would have done the same thing in your situation, I'm sure. We're all good now. I know you wouldn't have hurt me anyway, would you?"

He cut his gaze away, as though he was ashamed of his weakness. "No," he muttered. "I wouldn't have."

Mateo cleared his throat pointedly, interrupting the emotional moment.

"Oh, just go on, Mateo," Valentina sighed. "We're fine."

Rodríguez spared a brief nod to his man, dismissing him. Valentina really did call the shots around here. The small display of the true power dynamic in this house helped ease the last of my fury with Rodríguez. I believed his admission that he wouldn't have actually hurt Samantha.

"I'm so glad you're here, big brother," Valentina said, her dark eyes shining. "I've missed you so much." Her voice hitched, but she continued on. "I'm marrying Adrián tomorrow. I know today has been...tense. But I want you to be with us at the wedding. More than anything. Will you stay?"

I hesitated. Lingering in America hadn't been part of the plan. If Samantha's friends at the FBI caught wind of the fact that I was in the States, they'd come after me. They'd try to take my wife away.

She placed her hand on my forearm, silently lending her support and approval. "It's okay," she said softly. "No one knows we're in LA. We're safe here."

"Yes, you are," Rodríguez swore. "My people will protect you."

"Adrián..." Valentina said her fiancé's name in a cajoling tone, prompting him to say something more. He stared down at her. She stared right back, a challenge in the strong lines of her smaller frame.

He pressed a tender kiss to her forehead. The sweet show of affection from the sadistic drug lord was completely at odds with his reputation for abject cruelty.

His attention turned back on me, all animosity gone from his pale eyes. "I'm sorry I scared your wife. You are both more than welcome at our wedding. I would be honored if you'd give us your blessing. Valentina would like you to walk her down the aisle."

A refusal teased at the tip of my tongue. I didn't want to give my little sister away to a criminal.

"Please, Andrés," Valentina beseeched my approval. "You're my family, but Adrián's my family, too. I've always loved him, ever since we were kids. I want to marry him, and I want you to be there with me."

"It's true," Adrián interjected. "I've loved Valentina since I was sixteen years old. I let her go once, but never again. I'll never allow anyone separate us or cause her pain."

"See?" Samantha urged quietly. "It's okay, Andrés. This is a good thing. They're happy together. Just like we are."

The reminder that my relationship with Samantha seemed unconventional to outside observers helped sway me. I might be a monster, but I would lay down my life a thousand times over to protect Samantha. If Rodríguez would do the same for my sister, then I could overlook his criminal lifestyle.

"Yes," I agreed, my throat tight. "I'll walk you down the aisle, Valentina."

She beamed at me, and I caught a flash of the carefree girl she'd once been right before she launched herself at me. Samantha stepped away, giving me space to embrace my sister. Her small body shuddered, and I realized I was shaking, too.

"I didn't think I'd ever see you again. I was so worried that you were dead." Her warm tears wet my shirt.

A matching heat trailed down my cheeks, as well, but I didn't feel any shame at the display of raw emotion. After more than fifteen years of separation, my family was finally whole again. I had my sister back, and my wife stood at my side. I'd never felt so complete. Before I'd met Samantha, I'd spent years in isolation, growing cold and cruel. Now, I was with the only two people who had ever mattered to me. The gratitude and relief that surged through me was almost overwhelming.

Valentina pulled away slightly, so she could look up at me. I hungrily drank in her features, memorizing the more mature shape of her face. We'd been robbed of our childhood together, but I'd never stopped being her big brother. I never would.

Her dark eyes landed on my scarred cheek, reminding me that my face had changed far more than hers.

"What happened to you?" she asked softly.

"Cristian," I bit out his loathsome name. Samantha had helped me let go of the humiliation that haunted me over the memory of my torture at my brother's hands, but now, guilt swelled. "I'm sorry I didn't protect you from him. He sold you, and I didn't do anything to stop him. I let him—"

Valentina shushed me, placing her hand over the furrow in my cheek, as though she could heal the mark with her gentle touch. "You did everything you could," she reassured me. "That's all in the past now. He can't hurt us anymore. Adrián says Cristian is dead. Isn't that right?"

"Yes," I confirmed with savage satisfaction. "I killed him."

"I'm glad," Valentina replied with savagery of her own. Neither of us would shed a tear over the loss of our older brother. I should have done the job years earlier. Fear had held me back, but I didn't have to be afraid anymore. Samantha had liberated me from that life of cowardice and shame.

"I can't believe you're really here," Valentina said thickly. "Everything is perfect now. Will you stay? After the wedding, I mean."

I hesitated. I didn't want to leave my sister so soon, but it would be unwise to stay Stateside for longer than necessary. Samantha's little blackout that she'd coordinated around UCLA this afternoon wouldn't have gone unnoticed, especially considering that she hadn't been able to undo her work before

Davis had taken her. By now, law enforcement had likely located our getaway vehicle and her abandoned laptop.

"We have some time," Samantha supplied, as though reading my thoughts. "I scrubbed my biometric data from the FBI database, so if anyone pulls prints off that laptop, I won't pop up in the system. I can always run interference on security cams around the wedding venue tomorrow. We won't get flagged by any facial recognition systems. I can't hold off my friends at the Bureau forever, but they did lose their best asset when I left, so I can definitely buy us more time."

"You're an FBI agent?" Valentina asked, her attention turning on Samantha.

"Well, sort of. I used to be. I'm kind of a rogue agent now. Like, I still fight crime and whatnot, it's just on my own terms. You don't have to worry about me ratting you out to my friends at the Bureau. This is none of their business. I mean, if I were still an agent and had never met Andrés, I'd totally be investigating the shit out of Adrián. But I won't," she added quickly. "I did a ton of research, and I'm not a huge fan of the drug trafficking or, you know, the murdering people stuff, but you seem to stick to your own turf wars. You don't kill innocent people, and you're not involved in human trafficking. So, I'll let it slide. There are worse bad guys in the world who could use a good ass-kicking. I'll focus on them, instead."

"That's very generous of you," Rodríguez said drily.

"No problem," Samantha replied, as though it was no big deal and she was doing him a favor. "We're family now, and I won't turn on my family. Just try not to do anything too shady, or my friends will totally come after you. I'd rather not get into that situation, so be cool, okay?"

Rodríguez chuckled, and I breathed a small sigh of relief. Samantha could have gotten herself into trouble with all her warnings, but he seemed to find her rambling charming.

"I'll try," he allowed.

"Thank you, Samantha," Valentina said with genuine gratitude. "Anything you need to make sure you can both safely attend the wedding, just let me know. You can fix the security footage around the venue?"

"Oh yeah." Samantha waved her hand as though it was already taken care of. "Super simple. I'll just need a laptop for five minutes at some point before the ceremony tomorrow. Andrés and I can go back home after the reception. Buy you'll have to come visit us. We have this awesome island and a guest room in our house that we've never had a reason to use. I mean, we're the only people who live on the island, so I don't even know why we have a guest room. Well, I guess this is why. Now, you can come stay with us whenever."

Valentina grinned. "I'll come as soon as I can. The next break from classes, for sure. We could go on vacation. Right, Adrián?"

"Whatever you want, *conejita*."

Rodríguez's bemused expression matched my own feelings. Somehow, I'd gone from wanting to kill him this morning to accepting him as my brother-in-law. While the women we loved made vacation plans.

I shrugged. If Rodríguez could get over this afternoon's unpleasant events and get on board with playing family, I could, too.

CHAPTER 7
ANDRÉS

"You can stay here, big brother," Valentina said, gesturing for me to take Samantha into one of the guest rooms in her sprawling home. "I'll send someone out to get fresh clothes for both of you. Will you join us for dinner tonight?"

"Aren't you hosting a rehearsal dinner?" Samantha interjected, pausing at my side.

Valentina's glossy black hair swayed around her face as she shook her head. "I'm canceling it. I'd rather have dinner with my family. Adrián and I don't need to rehearse our wedding. It's not my first time getting married, and I'm sure he can figure out what to do."

A shadow passed over her eyes at the mention of her first marriage, but her flippant tone indicated that she'd prefer to joke about the situation than dwell on her true feelings. I wanted to know what had happened to my little sister, but I didn't feel like pressing for details, either. Valentina might have been in love with Adrián Rodríguez since she was a teenager, but she'd been forced to marry another man. I was all too familiar with the ugliest parts of our criminal underworld, and I could easily guess what had happened to Valentina.

For the first time, I registered gratitude that she was with Adrián. He claimed he'd always loved her and that he would protect her. Whatever she'd been through in the past, it was clear now that Adrián would slaughter anyone who tried to harm her. I might not like that she was marrying a drug lord, but there were advantages to the absolute devotion of a sadistic madman. No one would ever hurt my sister again.

"So, you'll come to dinner?" Valentina prompted. "Our chef can put something together in a couple hours. It'll just be the four of us in the dining room, so we don't need to worry about leaving the grounds. I know Samantha can cover your tracks, but I'd rather not go out in public more than absolutely necessary."

"Good call," Samantha approved. "We'd love to have dinner with you and Adrián. Wouldn't we, Andrés?" She poked her elbow into my side, urging me to agree.

"Yes," I replied. "But if you wouldn't mind, I need to talk to my wife about everything that's happened today. Privately."

Samantha instantly caught the low threat in my tone. She'd let her mouth run away with her when she'd spoken to Rodríguez. Just because everything had worked out peacefully didn't mean she wasn't going to be punished for putting herself at risk. I needed to feel her flesh heat beneath my harsh hands, needed to brand every inch of her body with my touch. After almost losing her today, my gut burned with the impulse to dominate her until she softened and submitted. I needed to hear her call me *Master* and promise that she belonged to me, now and forever.

"Um, that's okay," Samantha said, her voice higher than usual. "We should all keep hanging out before dinner. I mean, I don't need to change clothes or anything, if we're just eating at the house."

She tried to edge away from me. I wrapped my hand around her nape and anchored her in place at my side.

Valentina glanced from my face to Samantha's pink cheeks. "I think I'll give you two some privacy," she said after a moment. She fixed me with one final, significant stare. "I know you're a good man, Andrés. I'm sure you just want to spend some time with your wife after worrying about her this afternoon. You should make sure she's okay."

"I'm fine," Samantha insisted.

Valentina offered her a sympathetic smile. "You're definitely safe in our home. I'll see you both at dinner."

As soon as my sister retreated down the long hallway, my full focus centered on Samantha. Keeping my hold on her neck, I firmly guided her into the bedroom and shut the door behind us. The room was spacious and luxurious in an understated way; shades of tan and cream emphasized the enormity of Rodríguez's home, and a huge sliding glass door revealed the lush green grounds behind the house, which rolled out to a distant view of the city.

I only spared the space a cursory glance to ensure we were completely alone. No one was guarding us. And we were far enough away from the common spaces of the house that I was fairly confident no one would hear my naughty pet cry out and beg for mercy. I doubted anyone in Rodríguez's employ would interfere, anyway.

Samantha tried to edge away from me again, her slight body radiating nervous tension as she sought to put distance between us.

A warning growl slipped through my teeth, and I jerked her against me, hooking my free arm around her lower back to trap her in place. Her chest pressed tight to mine, and I could feel the rise and fall of her panting breaths, the rapid beat of her heart. Her nearness calmed my heart to its normal rhythm for the first time since I'd realized Davis had taken her.

Her shining eyes were wide, her pupils dilated. She licked her lush lips, a nervous tic she displayed when she was both anxious and aroused.

"Listen, Andrés. I—"

My fingers sank into her hair, tangling the copper strands around my fist as I forced her head back. Her pulse jumped at her throat.

"Quiet, *cosita*." My roiling emotions finally began to calm as I settled into my control over her. "I don't have one of your pretty gags, but I will find something to tame your tongue if necessary. No more arguing or talking out of turn. You put yourself at risk today. You shouldn't have spoken to Rodríguez like that."

"But I just explained what was going on," she protested, the defensive words popping out before she could hold herself back. "I talked us out of trouble, not into it. Davis would have killed both of us hours ago if I hadn't bought us time. I tried to convince him not to take me with him, but he did, and I couldn't stop that. He would have shot me on the spot if I'd challenged him. So, I let him take me to Adrián. And everything worked out, right? We're—"

I pulled sharply on her hair, and she stopped babbling on a gasp.

"Tell me exactly what Rodríguez did," I commanded.

"That doesn't matter now. Really, I—"

"Do not test me," I warned. "You have a punishment coming already. Answer my questions, or the consequences will only get worse."

She trembled against me, and more of my lingering tension eased. I'd stopped fighting my twisted nature a long time ago.

Samantha responded to my darker needs; she accepted all of me. She even loved the monster in me, even though she feared it.

I drank in her fear like a man dying of thirst. If she was shaking in my harsh hold, she was real and safe. My pet had returned to the cage of my arms, and she wasn't going anywhere.

"Adrián was just asking me questions," she said on a tremulous whisper. "He just wanted to know where Valentina was so he could get her back. He thought you were my employer, and he wanted to know how to find you. But I didn't tell him anything," she added quickly.

My gut tightened, a shadow of my anger returning. "He would have tortured you for answers eventually," I ground out. "You should have told him where to find me. I would have handled him."

Her eyes flashed, defiance slicing through her fear. "I would never betray you."

I crushed her body closer to mine. "You should have trusted me to keep you safe. You should have told him everything he wanted to know, so he would leave you alone and come after me."

Her delicate jaw set in a hard line. "I did trust you. I trusted that you'd figure out where I was and come for me. But I wasn't going to give Adrián information that would allow him to ambush you. Besides, none of this matters now. Everything worked out fine."

"It matters to me," I growled. "Never do something like that again."

The anger cleared from her eyes, her features softening. "I won't, because I'll never be in a situation like that again. We're safe now. And we always will be, because we have each other's backs. We'll go home after the wedding tomorrow, and no one will be able to find us. No one will be able to hurt me. Or you. I won't let them."

I eased my harsh hold around her waist and trailed my fingers down her throat. Samantha's bravery awed me. I'd descended into madness when Davis took her from me. My clever pet might tend to ramble when she was nervous, but her formidable mind was a more powerful weapon than my brute strength.

I pressed a reverent kiss to her forehead, holding her in place with my grip on her hair. She blew out a shuddering sigh, her warm breath fanning my neck.

"*Te amo, mí sirenita*," I murmured, rubbing my scarred cheek against her soft, flawless skin.

Her slender fingers slid up into my hair, urging me closer. "I love you too," she promised.

I closed the hairsbreadth of distance between us and caressed her lips with mine. I kept my commanding grip on her hair, but I explored her mouth slowly, savoring her. I still intended to reprimand her, but there were other ways to reinforce the lesson than handling her body harshly. I wanted her to feel my control, my ownership of every inch of her flesh. I could do whatever I wanted to her, manipulate her pleasure and wield it as a tool for her punishment just as effectively as I could lash her with my whip.

My hands finally left her hair and throat, trailing down her sides to trace the curve of her hips. I fisted the material of her thin cotton t-shirt and eased it up her torso, stripping her at the pace I desired while I held her lips captive in mine.

Her hands were more frenzied as she tore at my clothes, her fingers shaking with residual fear and anticipation. I allowed her to fumble at my belt, enjoying her desperation for me.

When we were both naked, I scooped her up in my arms

and carried her the short distance to the bed. In the few seconds I held her, she pressed sweet kisses against my neck, worshipping my scarred body just as I revered her alabaster perfection.

I laid her beneath me, settling my weight over her to keep her pinned. She didn't squirm or struggle, and that suited my mood. I wanted to take my time with her, not manhandle her.

I skimmed my palms up her arms, guiding them over her head. I cradled her hands in mine, lifting each to my mouth so I could press a tender kiss to the insides of her wrists. She shivered and sighed, softening under me.

Her eyes widened when I picked up my belt from where I'd placed it beside her on the bed. My needy pet hadn't noticed when I'd picked it up along with her.

I looped the leather over my fist and rubbed it against her cheek. She inhaled and let out a low moan as the scent permeated her senses. I'd conditioned her lustful response to the smell of leather. Her nipples pebbled against my chest, and she arched into me, seeking stimulation on her aching buds.

I allowed her to tease herself as I wound the length of my belt around her wrists, binding them together. There wasn't a means to secure her arms in place, so my will would have to be enough to fully restrain her.

I pressed her wrists into the pillows above her head. "Keep them there," I ordered. "I'm going to check you over to make sure you don't have a scratch on you."

"I don't," she protested weakly. "I'm fine."

I rested my palm on her throat, asserting my dominance. "This is for my satisfaction, not yours." My scar tugged on a twisted smile. "But you're welcome to enjoy my examination. Now, be a good girl and stay still. And no more arguing. You're already going to have to wait a long time for your orgasm. If you continue to be a naughty *gatita*, I won't allow you to come at all."

I pressed my thigh between her legs, and her silky arousal wet my skin. She whimpered and rocked against me. I let more of my weight bear down on her, denying her the stimulation she craved.

"No," I said sternly. "You've been very forgetful about who is in charge today. You're mine, Samantha. I control your pleasure. You will obey me." I rubbed my thumb over her artery.

Her lashes fluttered, and she tipped her head to the side, offering me better access to one of the most vulnerable points on her body.

I leaned in and traced the shell of her ear with my tongue. "Good girl." I allowed my praise to roll over her skin, and I felt her flesh pebble beneath my lips when I dropped a kiss on her neck. I sank my teeth into her shoulder, and she cried out. I held her more firmly, refusing to release her until she surrendered.

She stilled beneath me, and I eased my bite, tracing the little indentations I'd left in her skin with my tongue.

"The only mark you'll bear is mine," I murmured, kissing the spot I'd bitten.

A low humming sound of satisfaction slipped between her lips, and she closed her eyes on a small smile.

"You like being marked and owned, don't you, *cosita*? You love being mine. Everyone will know it when they see this." I brushed my fingertips over the reddened oval left by my teeth. "And you want them to know that you're my sweet little pet, that I'll keep and protect you at any cost. No one gets to touch you but me. You belong to me."

"Yes," she moaned. "I'm yours."

A rumble of savage approval rolled from my chest, and I

began to work my way farther down her body, so I could continue branding her with my touch.

I caressed her breasts, nipping at her skin as I rolled her tight nipples between my fingers. She gasped and thrust her chest into my hands, welcoming more sweet torment. She could have lowered her hands and pulled my face closer to her flushed body, but my obedient pet kept her arms stretched over her head, trapped by my command as effectively as iron shackles.

I flicked my tongue over one of her hard buds, teasing until her head thrashed and she whined in need. I eased one hand up her thigh, finding the wet heat between her legs. I petted her pussy, barely brushing my fingers over her swollen lips. In contrast to my gentle touch on her cunt, I bit down on her nipple. She cried out, arching toward me in a futile effort to alleviate the sting. I only allowed her a brief respite in the second it took me to switch over to her other breast, making sure she was thoroughly tortured.

Her hips undulated beneath me, and she rubbed her sex against my hand as I continued to torment her nipples.

When I was satisfied that she'd been adequately punished in that particular area, I skimmed my palm down her stomach, feeling her creamy skin for any signs of injury. I was mostly convinced that Rodríguez hadn't harmed her in any way, but checking for my own peace of mind calmed me.

I settled myself between her legs, grasping her thighs and spreading her wide. I traced the line of her slit with my thumbs, gently examining her sex.

She tried to lift her hips toward my face, and I cupped her cunt in my hand, forcing her back down.

"I have to make sure you're not hurt," I told her, not bothering to hide my cruel pleasure at her frustrating predicament.

"You know I'm not hurt there." She pouted down at me, helpless and completely adorable.

"Hmmm," I mused, nuzzling her inner thigh. "So, you're telling me that your pussy isn't aching?"

"Please." She tried to rotate her hips again, and I increased my grip on her sex, holding her in place while I delivered a punitive bite to the sensitive skin just beside her outer lips.

I waited for her to shudder and stop defying my control. She stilled, but her muscles quivered with need. My hands eased back to her thighs, gripping firmly as I lowered my face to her wet and waiting cunt.

A low groan left my chest at the first taste of her on my tongue. I explored her slowly and thoroughly, memorizing every contour of her soft body, every little place that made her whimper and jerk beneath me. I'd learned all her erotic triggers a long time ago, but after almost losing her today, I had to take my time savoring her.

I nearly lost myself in her, all rational thoughts leaving my mind as I settled into a more primal headspace. All that existed was her need and my desire to wring pleasure from her body.

I traced my tongue around her clit and rubbed my forefinger over her g-spot. She began to clench around me, on the verge of orgasm.

Suddenly remembering my plan to punish her, I quickly withdrew, denying her just as she reached the peak.

A sob caught in her throat. Before she could wriggle toward me or beg for release, I grabbed her hips and flipped her over, hooking my arm beneath her and dragging her onto her knees. She tried to push up and move with me, but I wrapped my hand around her nape and pressed her cheek back against the mattress.

"Stay," I commanded. "I'm not done checking you yet."

I stared down at her for several long seconds, imposing my will. Her lovely blue eyes began to sparkle with the first hint of her pretty tears. My pet had been a fierce lioness today, but it was time to take her in hand and tame her. I stroked the length of her spine, petting her until she softened and practically purred like my sweet kitten.

I released her nape and returned my attention to her pussy, dipping two fingers into her slick arousal before pressing them against her puckered bud.

She tensed, some of her defiance returning. After being so strong and brave in her determination to protect me this afternoon, Samantha was having a hard time fully surrendering control.

"I'm definitely not hurt *there*," she protested breathily.

My free hand cracked against her upper thigh, and I applied pressure to her asshole as she shrieked.

"You don't get to decide where I touch you or how," I reminded her. "Every part of you belongs to me. I want to make sure your body is exactly as responsive as I like it. And you always respond so sweetly when I penetrate your tight little ass." I gripped her hair, forcing her back to arch toward me as I slid my fingers deep inside her. "You know better than to defy your Master, don't you?"

Her entire body shook, and her inner muscles began to contract around the intrusion of my fingers. I wasn't touching her pussy, and she was on the edge of orgasm just from my invasion of her most intimate area.

I tugged on her hair, commanding her attention. "Answer me."

"I... What did you ask me again?"

She drew in short, panting breaths, and her flushed skin began to glisten with the heat of her arousal. I used my grip on her hair to turn her head to the side, so I could see her face.

Her aquamarine eyes slid out of focus, and I had to hold her in my gaze for several heartbeats before she managed to really look at me. When she did finally meet my eye, her lips parted in awe, and she stared at me as though I was the center of her world.

"Master." She whispered my title with reverence.

Something swelled in my chest, something so hot and bright that my body could barely contain it. I had to find release, or it would burn me up.

I gripped my cock and lined myself up with her slick opening. I entered her in one swift, brutal thrust. I'd been taking my time teasing and tormenting her, but this harsh coupling was about satiating my needs now. My desire overwhelmed me. Raw, animal craving took hold of my psyche, and I fucked her at the rough pace that pleased the monster in me.

I kept my fingers deep inside her ass while my free hand sank into her hip, locking her in place so I could claim her in the way I wanted.

She responded to my brutality, coming apart on a sharp cry. Her inner walls gripped me hard, and I hissed with something close to pain at the torturous tightness of her sheath. I gritted my teeth and held back my release. I wasn't nearly done taking my pleasure from her body.

I rode her through her second orgasm, rutting into her until she whimpered and shook beneath me. I braced my hand beneath her belly, holding her upright so I could continue fucking her.

As I began to lose my grip on my own pleasure, I rubbed her clit firmly. She came a third time on a helpless sob, her body responding to my every demand. Her pussy fluttered around me, squeezing my cock with delicious pressure that set my teeth on edge.

I finally released into her with an animal roar, burying

myself deep, so my seed would lash inside her belly. I wanted to brand her, to tie her to me in every way possible.

A rough sound of savage satisfaction rumbled from my chest as I kept her captive in my hold, emptying every last drop of my pleasure into her hot cunt.

I'd marked my pet inside and out. Samantha was all mine, and no one would ever take her from me.

CHAPTER 8
SAMANTHA

I tried not to be too conspicuous as I shifted in my seat, easing into a more comfortable position. Valentina and Adrián had a beautiful home with fabulous décor, but their dining chairs weren't nearly cushy enough. I was sore after Andrés' thorough, rough treatment of my body. Even though he'd stroked me in the shower and soothed me, I would feel the aftermath of our harsh lovemaking for a few days, at least.

Even as I tried to surreptitiously shift my weight off my butt, a small smile tugged at my lips. I liked the ache my Master had left deep inside me. I'd managed to hold myself together throughout the scary events that had unfolded earlier today, but I'd needed to feel his strength now that the danger had passed. It reassured me that we were together and safe. It was the sweetest relief to finally let go and cede control to the man I loved and trusted more than anyone else in the world. I could be completely vulnerable with him, and he would always protect me.

"So, that's how I ended up in California." Valentina

finished regaling us with the wild story about how she and Adrián had gotten together after years of separation. His hand rested on hers atop the table, and he didn't bother hiding his affection for her. While she spoke, he watched her with something between adoration and hunger.

"I'm glad you're happy." Andrés sounded like he actually meant it, and he'd stopped shooting Adrián threatening glares.

Valentina beamed at him. "I didn't know I could be this happy. I can't believe you're here for the wedding." She turned her dark eyes on me. "Thank you for bringing us back together, Samantha. I know we just met, but we're about to be sisters. I'd be honored if you'd stand with me at the altar tomorrow. Sofia is already my maid of honor, but you could be co-matron of honor."

My throat tightened, and the corners of my eyes burned at a sudden swell of emotion. Until today, Andrés had been the only family member I had left. He was more than enough, but having a sister was a major bonus.

"I'd love that." My words hitched slightly, and I cleared my throat. "But I don't have a dress or anything."

Valentina waved away my concern. "We can order one tonight, and it'll be delivered in the morning. It'll just take a few minutes to pick one out that you like. I have Sofia's dress in my closet, so you can take a look at it and figure out how you want to coordinate. She's actually about to come sleep over tonight. Will you stay with us?"

Adrián frowned and squeezed her hand. "I don't want you to sleep without me tonight."

She leaned into him and brushed a kiss against his cheek. "We talked about this. It's tradition. The next time you see me, we'll be at the altar."

Adrián's lips thinned, and for a moment, I thought he'd

insist on getting his way. I understood his desire to be close to the woman he loved after thinking he'd lost her today.

I glanced over at my own husband. He didn't look too pleased about the prospect of me leaving his bed, either.

"I'd really like to stay with Valentina," I said gently. If I made a demand, he might refuse. Not because he was cruel, but because he'd be hurt that I was rejecting him, and he'd react by shackling me to him so he wouldn't lose me. Even though I belonged to him completely, he was still terrified of being separated from me. He might seem controlling, but his possessive behavior came from a place of vulnerability. I didn't want to cause him any pain.

"Please," Valentina cajoled, appealing to both her fiancé and her brother.

The men sighed, capitulating at the same time. Neither seemed to notice that they mirrored each other; they were too focused on us.

Valentina offered me a small, secret smile. She seemed to understand the commonalities between them, even if they wouldn't admit it to themselves. On the surface, Adrián seemed like a bad guy. He was perfectly content to run his criminal empire, whereas Andrés had easily forsaken his. But in the ways that counted, both men were capable of deep love and devotion. I might not approve of Adrián's nefarious enterprise, but he obviously adored Valentina, and that was good enough for me.

Adrián fixed Andrés with a stony stare. There was no warmth in his hard features, but his pale eyes softened with resignation. "If your wife is staying with Valentina, you're welcome to join Mateo and me for whiskey and cigars this evening."

Andrés inclined his head, accepting the invitation. After a

beat of silence, he reluctantly offered an apology. "Sorry for bruising your jaw before your wedding."

Adrián shrugged. "How's your head?"

Andrés didn't have any visible marks on his face, but I remembered his skull cracking against the metal beam in the shed. He hadn't shown any signs of injury, but he probably had a headache.

"Harder than it looks," Andrés replied. "Nothing a little whiskey can't fix."

"Great." Valentina grinned. "Come on, Samantha. Let's go pick out a dress for you."

We all stood, but Adrián grabbed her before she could walk away, catching her wrist and tugging her against him. Her head tipped back, her body instantly softening in offering to him.

I caught Andrés' attention before he could get worked up about seeing their public display of affection. I went up on my toes and pressed a tender kiss to his lips. The distraction was simple and effective. He responded instantly, his hands bracketing my hips to hold me in place as he claimed my mouth. I forced myself to pull away before I became lost in him.

"I'll see you tomorrow," I promised. "I love you."

He caressed my cheek before releasing me. "I love you, too."

Adrián allowed Valentina to extricate herself from his arms, as well. "My bedroom is this way," she told me, walking out of the dining room with one last lingering look at her fiancé.

I followed where she led, making our way through the huge house until we reached the master suite. Similar to the room where Andrés and I had made love, her space was decorated in shades of tan and cream, giving the room a modern, sophisticated vibe. Her style was obviously understated luxury.

She crossed the spacious room and opened a closet door to reveal a massive space that was as big as my bedroom in my old apartment. She quickly sifted through the rows of beautiful dresses and found a pretty, periwinkle blue gown. The floor-length organza seemed to fall too long for her, but she cleared up my confusion.

"This is Sofia's dress for tomorrow," she explained. She eyed the dress, then my figure, assessing my size. "This shade will look lovely with your eyes. And I think the sweetheart neckline will work, but maybe some cap sleeves for you instead of strapless. You and Sofia can coordinate rather than matching exactly. Is that okay?"

"Um, sure," I agreed, a bit baffled by her knowledge of fashion. My style was more casual graphic tees and jeans. Well, it had been before I'd met Andrés. I was mostly naked these days. He made me feel beautiful every day, but it would be nice to wear a pretty dress for him.

"Perfect." Valentina was practically luminous when she smiled. I was very pale and skinny compared to her tanned, voluptuous perfection, but I wasn't plagued by insecurity like I used to be. Andrés loved me exactly as I was, and I didn't need to worry about what anyone else thought. I could appreciate Valentina's beauty without feeling self-conscious about my own appearance.

She led me back into the bedroom, where she retrieved a tablet from atop her vanity. With a few swipes of her well-manicured fingers, she opened a webpage with images of bridesmaids' dresses. She offered the device to me, seeking my approval of her choice.

"It's gorgeous," I agreed.

"It'll look amazing on you. I'll send an email to the boutique owner now to make sure they have it ready for you first thing in the morning. And I'll reach out to my seamstress, too, to make sure she can be on hand for any last-minute adjustments."

"Um, cool. Thanks." I couldn't imagine having a boutique owner's personal email or a seamstress, but Valentina seemed completely at ease with this lifestyle. She was definitely glamorous, and I didn't begrudge her feminine indulgence. If wearing pretty dresses made her happy, more power to her. She would be stunning in yoga pants with no makeup, but she certainly had a figure that practically begged to be adorned.

A knock on the door distracted us.

"That's all done," Valentina announced, setting her tablet aside. "You can come in, Sofia," she called out.

The door opened, and a pretty girl with a mass of glossy black curls stepped inside. She appeared younger that Valentina and me—maybe in her early twenties. Her bright, perfect smile faltered when her deep green gaze fell on me.

"Oh, hey," she said, clearly taken aback by the presence of a stranger in Valentina's bedroom.

"I'm so glad you're here," Valentina said warmly, closing the distance between them and pulling the girl into a firm embrace. When she pulled away, she introduced me. "This is Samantha. She's going to be my sister-in-law tomorrow." She practically buzzed with giddy excitement. "Samantha, this is Sofia. She helped me pick out my classes at UCLA. She was so great making me feel welcome when I moved to California, and now she's stuck with me."

Sofia elbowed her good-naturedly. "It's not exactly a chore hanging out with you, V." She turned to me, and I shifted awkwardly, not sure if I should shake her hand. That felt a little formal when we were about to have a sleepover.

She cleared away my anxiety by pulling me into a familiar hug. "If you're going to be Valentina's sister, then you're mine, too," she declared. "It's really nice to meet you, Samantha."

"You too," I offered, returning her infectious smile. "You

can both call me Sam, if you want. That's what all my friends call me."

"Awesome," Sofia approved. "Sam, it is."

Something swelled in my chest. I'd never had many friends, and definitely not female friends. Before I met Andrés, I'd pretty much just had work colleagues and Dex in my life. Sofia and Valentina were welcoming me into their lives with open arms.

I jolted as a loud *pop* pierced the sweet moment.

Valentina giggled. "Sorry. I didn't mean to startle you. We have celebratory bubbles." She hefted a bottle of Champagne that she'd pulled out of her mini-fridge. "If the men are going to have whiskey, we can indulge in a little wine."

"Oh, none for me, thanks," I said before she could pour a third glass.

She glanced up at me. "Are you sure? We're not going to get drunk or anything. Just a glass or two each. I definitely don't want to be hungover tomorrow."

"Yeah," I replied. "I shouldn't drink any alcohol."

Valentina's jaw dropped. I realized I'd placed my hand on my belly, and I quickly jerked it away.

Shit. I hadn't meant to out myself. Andrés didn't even know I was pregnant yet.

"Oh my god," she gushed. "Oh my god!" She quickly set down the bottle of Champagne and stepped toward me, taking my hands in hers. "I'm going to be an aunt?" Her dark eyes sparkled with emotion, and I realized my own eyes were burning. I blinked, and a joyful tear rolled down my cheek.

"Uh-huh," I said thickly. "But please don't tell Andrés. I'm already going to be in so much trouble with him."

Valentina's brow furrowed. "Won't he be happy that you're pregnant?"

"Oh, yeah." A shaky laugh bubbled up from my chest.

"We've been trying for a while now. He'll be ecstatic. But he's going to go all caveman crazy on me when he finds out I knew before we came to rescue you. I, um, didn't want to tell him because I knew he wouldn't let me help him with the op. He needed me to watch his back."

Valentina smiled. "Adrián worries about me, too. I don't know if he would let me help him with something like that at all if he thought he'd be putting me in a remotely dangerous situation. You're very brave."

"I mean, I was with the FBI for years." I shrugged off her praise. "I'm a kickass tech analyst, but a pretty shitty field agent. And Andrés definitely would have left me behind on the safety of our island, but I didn't let him."

Valentina appeared even more impressed. "You're being modest about your skills if you're capable of forcing my brother to do anything. I haven't seen him in a long time, but he grew up big."

"Oh, he's definitely not intimidated by my physical prowess." I laughed. "If I were capable of taking him on in hand-to-hand combat, we probably wouldn't be together right now. I'm not Black Widow or anything like that."

"Black Widow?" Sofia chimed in, her face pinched with confusion.

"You know, from *The Avengers*," I supplied. "I kind of tried to fight Andrés when he first..." I trailed off, blushing. "Well, when we first met. It was pretty embarrassing, actually. I really had no business trying to be a field agent. I'm way more badass with a laptop than my fists."

"You fought him?" Valentina asked, puzzled. "I'm guessing it's because you were working with the FBI, and Andrés wasn't exactly on the right side of the law back then. Is that right?"

"Um, well. Don't judge or anything, okay? But I figure I shouldn't lie to you, if we're family. Andrés kind of captured me while I was spying on his people. Well, Cristian did," I amended quickly. "Andrés... I mean, he was just trying to keep me safe from Cristian. Things were weird at first. I wasn't like, super happy about being held hostage and whatnot. But we worked through all that, and we really love each other. It's not like a Stockholm Syndrome thing. My friends at the Bureau don't really get it, but what we have is real. Andrés saved me. He stood up to Cristian for me and left everything behind so we could be safe together. He's the best thing that ever happened to me."

Valentina squeezed my hand. "I understand."

"Okay, good. I really don't want to mess up your relationship with Andrés by telling you this. He's been through a lot, but he's a good man. The best."

"I really do get it. Better than anyone. I feel the same way about Adrián."

I breathed a sigh of relief. I became aware of Sofia's tense presence. I glanced over at her and noticed she'd drained half her glass of Champagne.

"Oh," I said, my cheeks heating. "Sorry if I made you uncomfortable, Sofia. I know that's not um, a normal love story."

"Totally okay," she reassured me, but she tipped back her glass and swallowed the rest of her Champagne.

"You're allowed to like Mateo," Valentina encouraged the girl gently. "I know things are complicated between the two of you, but I can tell you care about him."

Sofia's curls bounced as she jerked her head to the side. She poured another glass of Champagne. "It's been a weird day," she said. "I'd rather not talk about Mateo right now."

"You know he practically worships the ground you walk on," Valentina pressed.

"Well, I wish he'd go worship the ground somewhere else,"

she snapped. "I'm sick of him watching me all the time. I'm sick of men trying to control me. This isn't how my life is supposed to go." She sucked in a deep breath and took another gulp of bubbly. "Anyway," she waved away her anger. "This is your night, Valentina. We don't need to discuss my drama. Let's talk about the wedding. Is everything running smoothly? Do you need me to go into full bitch mode on anyone? Because I totally will. You just sit back and relax, and I'll handle anyone who might annoy you."

Valentina laughed, dispelling the odd tension. I didn't know what was going on between Mateo and Sofia, but it wasn't any of my business. He'd seemed anxious to get back to her earlier this afternoon, but she made it sound like she didn't want him around her at all. If talking about the situation upset the girl, I wouldn't press. She was right; this was Valentina's night, and it wasn't the right time for drama.

"You couldn't be a bitch if you tried," she told Sofia.

"Trust me, I have a lot of bitch energy going on inside me right now. I'm more than happy to unleash it on the person of your choosing."

"Everything's going perfectly," Valentina reassured her friend. "No need to do any damage control, but thank you for offering." She let out a happy sigh and grinned at me. "I didn't know it could be this perfect, actually. You brought Andrés back to me, and I'm getting a sister, too. And a little niece or nephew," she added, practically glowing with joy. "My family is bigger than ever."

"Mine too," I said hoarsely, my eyes stinging again.

I could hardly believe how lucky I was that Andrés had come into my life. Who would have thought that being kidnapped by a drug lord could have such an awesome outcome? Our happily-ever-after might be unconventional, but that didn't make it any less perfect.

CHAPTER 9

ANDRÉS

"Are you ready?" I asked on a rasp. Valentina was radiant in her white lace wedding gown. She looked so different from the young girl I'd known, but the bright spark in her eyes and her broad smile were the same. Even though I knew she must have endured horrific treatment during the years that had separated us, she was still capable of expressing pure joy. Adrián brought her this happiness. I supposed that meant I truly couldn't hate him.

She placed her hand on my forearm, squeezing gently. "More than ready, big brother."

She took a deep breath and turned to face forward. Her full attention focused on the chapel doors, which hid the man she loved from her sight.

I nodded at the two waiting ushers, and they opened the doors to admit us. Valentina took a step forward, guiding me along in her eagerness to reach Adrián. I was symbolically giving my blessing, but she was definitely the one walking me down the aisle. I wouldn't have been able to hold her back even if I wanted to.

She might be fully focused on Adrián, but my gaze riveted on Samantha. I faltered a step, forgetting how to breathe. I was so accustomed to seeing her wearing casual clothes or nothing at all. My wife was perfect without a stitch of clothing or hint of makeup, but she was particularly stunning in her gauzy, pale blue gown. Her alabaster skin glowed, her wide, entrancing eyes sparkling. She appeared ethereal, too beautiful to be real.

She watched me with an open hunger that matched my own. She looked at me as though I was someone to be revered, not a scarred monster.

Suddenly, I was at the altar. I took a step toward Samantha, momentarily forgetting my role in my all-consuming obsession with her. She shook her head with a rueful smile, tipping her bouquet in the direction of the pew behind me. It was time for me to leave Valentina with her husband and take my place among the other seated guests.

I placed Valentina's hand in Adrián's, shooting the man one last warning glare. If he ever hurt my sister, he was a dead man.

He didn't notice my flash of animosity. His full attention was fixed on Valentina, his pale eyes sparking with awe. I didn't appreciate the way he looked as though he wanted to devour her with his possessive gaze, but her beatific expression was enough to make me step away, resigning myself to their union.

I released Valentina's hand and took my reserved seat. In my sweeping assessment of the happy scene unfolding before me, I noticed Mateo standing at Adrián's side, taking his place as best man. He wasn't watching the bride and groom. Instead, he stared at Sofia.

I glanced over at her. She resolutely kept her eyes on Valentina, the slight tension in her willowy frame indicating that she was well aware of Mateo's intense attention, and she didn't appreciate it.

I shrugged off their odd behavior. They didn't really matter to me, even though Mateo seemed nice enough after we'd shared a few drinks last night. It wasn't as though we were going to be friends, and I simply appreciated him as extra, enormous security around my little sister. What he did with Sofia was his business, not mine.

My gaze fell on Samantha again, and I didn't even try to resist staring. I was peripherally aware that Valentina and Adrián were exchanging vows, but the ceremony passed by in a blur. Samantha mostly focused on the happy couple, but she could clearly feel the sharpness of my eyes on her. Every time she looked at me, her cheeks colored with the pretty pink blush I loved so much. She shifted on her feet a few times, and I wondered if she was still aching inside from when I'd fucked her yesterday. I liked the idea of her feeling me, even though I couldn't touch her at the moment.

She tipped her head to the side, and her shining copper hair slipped behind her shoulder, revealing the mark I'd left on her with my teeth. She hadn't covered the bruise with foundation for the sake of appearances. She didn't care what the strangers around us thought; she wore my brand with pride.

My mouth watered, my gut tightening. I couldn't wait to get my wife back to the privacy of our home so I could mark her flesh in other ways. I hadn't reddened her ass with my whip in far too long. I wasn't feeling particularly sadistic, just possessive. That was as good a reason as any to torment her until she wept in desperation for me. I'd make sure to reward her with more pleasure than she could bear.

The ceremony ended with an eruption of clapping and cheers as Adrián swept Valentina up in a fierce kiss. Pretty tears glistened on Samantha's cheeks as she watched them process back down the aisle, Valentina practically bouncing with happiness as Adrián held her hand tightly in his.

Mateo took Sofia's arm and led her out of the church, and I immediately stood to go to my wife. We'd never had a public ceremony for our own wedding, and I settled into the joy of the moment. As I led Samantha down the aisle, I held her close to my side. She laughed in delight, catching onto the levity of the cheering crowd.

"Are you disappointed we didn't have a big wedding like this?" I murmured.

She looked up at me, her gorgeous eyes wide and earnest. "Of course not. Our wedding was perfect. We didn't need a bunch of people there. I don't need their validation to know you're mine."

A low chuckle rumbled from my chest. "That's my fierce *gatita*."

Her grin took on a saucy twist. "Well, you are mine, Andrés. My husband. My Master."

She was teasing and tempting me when she knew I couldn't do anything about it in public. She was fully aware of the effect her words had on me. My pet had given me all the excuse I needed to redden her ass as soon as we got home.

SAMANTHA MUST HAVE SENSED MY MOOD, BECAUSE HER tension grew the farther we got from LA and the closer we got to our island home. I allowed her to stew in it, enjoying her trepidation. I didn't take my hands off her during the whole flight. As soon as we'd left the wedding reception, I started toying with her. She'd dared to tease me, but I was much more patient than she was. She might get a little thrill out of provoking me, but I could revel in tormenting her for hours without getting bored.

By the time we stepped into the private haven of our

house, she was wound so tightly that her body was practically vibrating in my hold.

I brushed my thumb over her lush lips, drawing a soft gasp from her. "What's the matter, *cosita*?" I drawled. "Is something frustrating you?"

She swallowed. "I, um... No. I'm not frustrated. Not exactly."

"Hmmm," I mused, trailing my fingers down her throat before lightly pressing on the tender mark on her shoulder. "Tell me what's bothering you, *sirenita*," I commanded, anticipating her plea for release.

"I'm pregnant," she blurted out, like it was an admission of guilt.

Shock tore through my body, obliterating any ability to ponder over her strange tone. Several seconds of silence passed while my brain stalled out.

"Andrés?" she squeaked. "I'm sorry, okay? Don't be mad."

"Why would I be mad?" I asked, my voice rough with emotion. Unadulterated joy surged, and I barked out a laugh as I grabbed my wife and spun her around. For a few moments, I held her against me with all my strength.

I released her abruptly, setting her back down on her feet. I anxiously ran my hands over her body to soothe away any damage I might have inflicted. "Did I hurt you?" I asked. "I didn't mean to hold you so tight."

She beamed up at me, cupping my cheek in her hand to reassure me. "I'm fine. I'm not made of glass all of a sudden. You can hug me as tight as you want. I like it." She licked her lips, uncertainty flickering in her lovely eyes. "So, um, I want you to remember how happy you are right now. And, you know, I want you to hug me and all that, but maybe think about the whole taking it easy on me thing, okay?"

I gripped her chin, tilting her head back so I could study her face. "Tell me what you've done, Samantha."

"Nothing!" she said quickly. "Well, it's about what I *didn't* do. I kind of found out I was pregnant last week. I took the test before I told you that I'd found Valentina. Because, you know, you wouldn't have let me help you if you'd known about the baby. And I couldn't let you go in alone. Everything worked out fine, anyway. So, it's all good. Happy endings for everyone. Because you're happy, right? I'm happy. Don't be mad. Please?"

I kept my firm hold on her chin, but I stroked my free hand through her hair, soothing her worry. "I've never been happier in my life," I swore. "You've given me everything, Samantha. More than I ever could have dreamed of. I have my sister back. I have you. And now, we're starting our own family."

I loved her so much, I could hardly contain the heat in my chest. Samantha was my miracle, and I would never let go of something so precious. I coveted her and guarded her as closely as the most valuable treasure in the world, but I didn't feel any shame over my possessiveness. Samantha was blissfully happy in my care, and she gave herself to me willingly. I didn't have to cage her to ensure she was forever mine.

"So, we're all good?" she asked tentatively. "You're not going to punish me for keeping this from you?"

My scar drew tight on a cruel smile. "I didn't say that, *gatita*."

She trembled against me, but she didn't try to pull away. "I figured I had it coming," she admitted. "But it was worth it. I couldn't let you go to LA alone."

I wrapped my hand around her nape, applying firm pressure. "Naughty little pet," I chided. "You knew you were doing something wrong, but you chose to displease your Master anyway."

She lifted her chin. "Yep. And I'd do it again. I wouldn't ever let anyone hurt you, Andrés."

"I won't let anyone hurt you, either, *cosita*." I placed my hand on her belly. "I'll never let anyone threaten our family."

She offered a weak smile. "Then I guess it's a good thing we have a scary drug lord as a brother-in-law. It's nice to know we have backup if we ever do get in a tight situation. So, this all worked out great, right? Like, I really should be off the hook. Because we're even better off than we were before."

"Oh no, pet." I smirked. "You can't talk your way out of this one. You knew you would be punished when you made your decision. And you don't really want to go unpunished, do you?"

"No," she whispered, the truth slipping from her easily. Samantha liked when I disciplined her. And she'd more than earned the consequences for her actions this time.

I pressed a kiss to her forehead. "Good girl. Now, I think you've let your mouth run away with you far too much over the last few days. I'm sure that's been very exhausting for you. You've been practically begging me to gag you."

Her cheeks flushed scarlet, and her pupils dilated.

"That's what I thought," I said with arrogant satisfaction. I stroked my fingers through her hair, watching with fascination as she softened into her submissive headspace. "What else should I do to you, naughty pet? What punishment do you think you've earned?"

"Whatever you want, Master," she breathed.

Her response was perfect. *She* was perfect. Somehow, Samantha managed to be my sweet, obedient pet and my clever, fiercely independent wife. She might call me *Master*, but we truly were partners in life. We were family.

I'd always craved control and demanded the subservience of those around me, but I would be completely devoted to my family. I'd do anything to protect the people I loved and ensure their happiness.

And I'd start right now by seeing to Samantha's needs. My pet was going to love every second of her devious punishment. I wouldn't have it any other way.

THE END

STEALING BEAUTY EXCERPT
VALENTINA

Pale green eyes sliced into my chest, their cutting gaze keener than I remembered. They practically glowed as he glowered at me from across the church: a panther deciding whether his prey was worth bothering with the hunt. His full lips curled in a sneer, those beautiful, terrifying eyes scanning my body.

Whatever he saw in me, he decided I wasn't worth his time. He blinked and looked away, his attention turning back to the stunning blonde draped on his arm.

I sucked in a gasp, remembering how to breathe. My fingers trembled at my sides as a hit of adrenaline surged through my system.

I'd known Adrián would be here. I'd told myself I was ready to face him. I'd told myself that I'd be able to mask my ire and put on the pretty, pleasant smile that was expected of me.

But I hadn't been prepared for the hatred in his burning stare. Ten long years had passed since I'd last looked into those hypnotic green eyes. Once, they'd shined with devotion when he looked at me.

Now, it seemed he loathed me as much as I despised him.

I collected my wits, clenching my fists at my sides to still my shaking fingers. My perfectly manicured nails bit into my palms, but I welcomed the little flare of pain. It helped ground me. Pain reminded me of my role, my duties.

I'd receive a lot more of it if I didn't play my part perfectly: devoted wife to Hugo Sánchez, the second most powerful man in Bogotá.

The most powerful man, Vicente Rodríguez, was the reason I was here, participating in this farce.

A visible shiver raced through the young woman—barely more than a girl—who stood at the altar. Camila Gómez had the misfortune of catching Vicente's eye a year ago. The eighteen-year-old had gotten pregnant, giving him a son. He'd decided to force her into this marriage to ensure the boy's legitimacy. A secondary heir to his cocaine empire, in case something were to happen to Adrián.

Adrián Rodríguez. I could hardly believe the boy I'd loved all those years ago had turned into the hard, frightening man who'd taken his place in the church pew behind me. I couldn't see him, but I could feel his cruel glare on my back. It made my skin pebble with a prey's awareness, my body instinctively sensing the threat.

For the last decade, he'd been in America, consolidating the power of his father's cartel in California. I'd never expected to see him again, but Vicente's wedding to poor Camila had brought the prodigal son home to Colombia.

The girl's petite frame appeared smaller than ever as she shrank in Vicente's shadow. He'd waited long enough for her slender body to return to its youthful perfection after she'd given birth—no doubt, she was kept on a careful regimen to ensure her beauty for this day.

I was far too familiar with the practice: the restricted diet and proscribed exercise to keep my natural curves just the right size to please my husband. Mercifully, Hugo stood at Vicente's side rather than mine. As Vicente's lapdog, Hugo was a natural choice to play the part of best man at this sham wedding.

My husband's beady black eyes fixed on me, and his thin lips curved into a malicious smile. An involuntary shudder wracked my body. He'd looked at me with the exact same expression ten years ago, when I'd been the one in the pretty white dress, forced to the altar against my will. I was only sixteen at the time, but Hugo hadn't minded being wedded to a child. He'd waited too long for his turn with me to care.

And as my guardian, Vicente had given me away to his best friend, gifting me to him in exchange for his years of loyalty.

I could hardly bear to look at either of the disgusting, lecherous men. Somehow, I lifted my chin and straightened my spine. I couldn't allow anyone in the church to sense that my fear-drenched memories of my wedding night were playing through my mind.

Hugo delighted in my fear, but he also expected me to maintain the façade of perfect, loving wife when we were in public. He might be short and stocky, but his rounded belly didn't diminish his strength. His thinning black hair and ruddy cheeks were showing the signs of his age, but the years hadn't caused him to grow frail. He was as brutal as he'd been on the day I'd met him, when I was fourteen years old.

I plastered on a beatific smile, meeting my husband's gaze. To any casual observer, I'd appear to be staring at him with love and devotion, remembering the false joy of our own wedding day.

Camila's palpable terror made the dark memories I kept locked at the back of my mind push to the forefront. I shoved them away before I gagged. A metallic tang coated my tongue, and I realized I'd bitten the inside of my cheek.

The ceremony passed by in a blur. I drew in deep breaths to suppress my rising nausea. When the priest pronounced Vicente and Camila husband and wife, I managed a wide smile. My eyes watered with empathy for the girl, but I'd be able to pass it off as tears of joy.

I followed the stream of guests as we exited the white and gold opulence of the basilica, stepping out into the heavy dusk heat. Hugo waited by the black limo outside the church, gesturing that I should get in the car. Vicente and Camila were already in their vintage Rolls-Royce, which would take them to the reception space: an imposing, historic *castillo* located outside Bogotá.

I smiled at my husband and took his hand, allowing him to help me slide into the back seat. He settled in beside me, pressing his doughy body close to mine. The sickening scent of his amber cologne mingling with his sweat washed over me. I'd become accustomed to it over the years, but today, the overpowering reek made me want to retch.

Seconds later, my nausea intensified. My gut lurched as Adrián got into the limo, his stunning blonde date sliding into place at his side. Her dark eyebrows didn't match her platinum locks, but the obvious dye job didn't diminish her beauty.

I couldn't focus on her, though. My eyes locked on Adrián's burning green stare.

My breath caught, and my pretty smile melted.

Hugo's meaty hand rested on my thigh, high enough to be indecent in front of strangers.

But Adrián wasn't a stranger. He was a ghost from my past. A horrifying apparition that appeared all too corporeal. His massive body filled the space, his bulk obvious even beneath his sharply-tailored black suit.

I could feel Hugo's hot breath on my face before he

pressed a wet, stomach-turning kiss against my cheek. "Are you all right, *cariño?*"

Adrián's nostrils flared, his full lips thinning. His square jaw hardened to granite, and his high cheekbones appeared sharper than ever.

For a moment, the world spun around me, the sickly-sweet stench of my husband powerful enough to make me lightheaded.

Hugo's fingers dug into my thigh, a clear warning to behave myself.

The flare of pain helped me focus. I tore my eyes from Adrián's, staring out the window instead.

"I'm fine," I managed.

I couldn't look at my husband. I could barely draw breath when he was so close, and Adrián's hatred pressing against me like a tangible force didn't help me breathe easier.

I tried to focus on the glittering lights as the city lit up around us, the historic sites of *La Candelaria* district beginning to glow against the falling darkness. The limo's tires rumbled over cobblestones. I kept my attention on the soft, purring sound to soothe my raw nerves.

Eventually, the pavement evened out, and the city disappeared behind us. We made our way along a darker road to reach the castle where the wedding reception would be held.

The historic edifice appeared as we rounded a curve, the stone façade shining under golden lights. Vicente had spared no expense on this sham of a wedding, inviting hundreds of people to witness his defiling of a young, unwilling girl. The ostentatious display was disgusting, but everyone in attendance seemed to think it was a joyous occasion.

The limo slowed to a stop, and Hugo ushered me out of the car. We stepped onto a red carpet, which led us through the open, massive wooden doors. More golden light spilled out into the night, welcoming us with false cheer. Marble floors shined under the massive crystal chandelier that lit the foyer.

Hugo wrapped his arm around my waist, but I stepped away as my stomach lurched. Over the years, I'd become numb to his touch. Tonight, it made my skin crawl. The memories of my own wedding night threatened to bubble up, and bile rose in my throat.

"Excuse me," I murmured. I couldn't come up with a good reason to leave Hugo's side, and I knew I'd pay for abandoning him later.

But all I could think about was fleeing from his slimy touch and rank scent.

I moved too quickly as I headed for the stairs, seeking privacy on the second level of the castle. No guests lingered around the banister on the upper floor, and I darted for the solace of a quiet room, where I could break down without witnesses.

The only thing worse than leaving Hugo standing alone in the foyer would be making a public scene. He'd be able to shrug off my sudden absence as the result of illness—I was sure I'd appeared pinched and pale enough in the limo to warrant that excuse.

No matter if the guests accepted his reasoning, he wouldn't allow me to go unpunished.

I could only hope that he'd wait until we were back on our estate. It was the most likely scenario. He wouldn't want to leave marks on me at this garish event; above all, he wanted others to believe that I truly was his devoted, loving wife. Anything less would be humiliating.

The second most powerful man in Bogotá couldn't have a disobedient wife. Hugo had made sure to break me and turn me into his adoring spouse a long time ago.

That had been after Adrián left me.

The boy I loved had left Colombia, and he'd never come back. He let Hugo torment me and turn me into his perfectly polished, soulless plaything.

Now, Adrián lurked downstairs with the rest of the sharks. The man who'd glowered at me in the church might wear the boy's face, but he wasn't here to rescue me.

I'd given up on that foolish fantasy a long time ago, anyway.

I slipped into the first open room I found, closing the door behind me. Books lined the walls, gold lettering gleaming on darkly colored spines. The unique scent of leather-bound books helped calm me. The library on Hugo's estate was the place where I most often found solace from him, losing myself in fiction for hours. I took a deep breath, inhaling the familiar smell. It helped calm my nerves and my nausea.

The door clicked open behind me, and I spun with a shocked yelp.

"What the fuck do you think you're doing?" Hugo's ruddy cheeks were redder than usual, almost purple with rage.

I took a hasty step back, raising my hands to ward him off.

Surely, he wouldn't strike me. Not here. Not now.

I hadn't prepared myself for the pain of his fists yet.

He slammed the door shut behind him, advancing on me. I backed up farther, until my butt hit the desk behind me. He leaned over me, pressing his hips against mine to pin me in place.

"I'm sorry," I squeaked. "I'm not feeling well."

"I don't give a fuck how you're feeling." His spittle hit my cheek, and I cringed away. "You think you can embarrass me in front of all our guests?"

I shook my head wildly. "I didn't mean to. I'm sorry," I repeated, desperate.

He leaned closer, so I could feel his putrid breath on my face. "I should bend you over this desk and fuck you raw." His cock jerked against my thigh as his cruel arousal rose along with his violence. "But I'd rather not have anyone hear you scream. You want to show me how sorry you are?"

I nodded frantically. "Yes. I really am sorry."

He stepped back. "Get on your knees. You know what to do."

The sick feeling in my gut intensified, my stomach churning. I sank to my knees, playing the part of obedient wife.

He quickly freed his cock from his slacks. It jutted toward my face, seeking the reluctant heat of my mouth.

I swallowed against the tang of bile on my tongue.

"Suck it," he seethed. "Show me you're sorry, and I won't beat the shit out of you when we get home."

Tears stung at the corners of my eyes as humiliation washed over me. I blinked them back. I wouldn't cry for him.

"Now," he snarled, thrusting his hips toward my lips.

I turned my face in revulsion, and his pre-cum wet my cheek.

He gripped my jaw, holding my head steady. "You'll pay for that later."

The door to the library opened, and my shame spiked. I couldn't bear to have anyone witness my degradation.

A fierce growl filled the room, and Hugo was ripped away from me. I watched in dumbstruck silence as Adrián tackled him to the floor. His massive fist connected with Hugo's jaw. My husband's head snapped to the side, blood spraying from his lips. Adrián didn't stop. He pummeled Hugo's face repeatedly, until crimson coated his knuckles and Hugo went completely still.

For a few long seconds, Adrián loomed over him, breathing hard. His lips peeled back from his teeth in a silent snarl, and his dark hair fell around his angular face, no longer arranged in its meticulous style.

Finally, he pushed to his feet and turned to me. He towered over me where I remained on my knees, frozen in place by shock at the sudden, violent display. His pale green eyes burned into me, and another feral sound slipped between his clenched teeth.

He reached for me with bloody hands. I shrank back, but that didn't deter him. His long fingers sank into my upper arms, yanking me to my feet.

He glowered at me for a moment, saying nothing. I shuddered in his grip, but I didn't dare struggle against him. I'd learned a long time ago that struggling only earned me more pain.

Hugo groaned, stirring at our feet.

Adrián's jaw ticked, but his shoulders relaxed, as though a decision had settled over him.

His grip shifted to my waist, and I shrieked as he tossed me over his shoulder.

His hand firmed on my upper thigh, squeezing hard enough to leave a mark. "Don't fight me," he ground out.

"What are you doing?" I asked, my voice shaking as fear suffused my system.

"I'm taking you."

ALSO BY JULIA SYKES

The Captive Series

Sweet Captivity

Claiming My Sweet Captive

Stealing Beauty

Captive Ever After

Pretty Hostage

Wicked King

Ruthless Savior

The Impossible Series

Impossible

Savior

Rogue

Knight

Mentor

Master

King

A Decadent Christmas (An Impossible Series Christmas Special)

Czar

Crusader

Prey (An Impossible Series Short Story)

Highlander

Decadent Knights (An Impossible Series Short Story)

Centurion

Dex

Hero

Wedding Knight (An Impossible Series Short Story)

Valentines at Dusk (An Impossible Series Short Story)

Nice & Naughty (An Impossible Series Christmas Special)

Dark Lessons

RENEGADE

The Dark Grove Plantation Series

Holden

Brandon

Damien

Mafia Ménage Trilogy

Mafia Captive

The Daddy and The Dom

Theirs to Protect

Printed in Great Britain
by Amazon